PRAISE FOR CIXIN LIU

"Wildly imaginative, really interesting."

—President Barack Obama on the Three-Body Problem trilogy

"A breakthrough book . . . A unique blend of scientific and philosophical speculation, politics and history, conspiracy theory and cosmology."

—George R. R. Martin

"Extraordinary."

—*The New Yorker*

"Remarkable, revelatory, and not to be missed."

—*Kirkus Reviews* (starred review)

"A must-read in any language."

—*Booklist*

"A meditation on technology, progress, morality, extinction, and knowledge that doubles as a cosmos-in-the-balance thriller. . . . A testament to just how far [Liu's] own towering imagination has taken him: far beyond the borders of his country, and forever into the canon of science fiction."

—NPR

"The best kind of science fiction, familiar but strange all at the same time."

—Kim Stanley Robinson

"Compelling reading . . . The most mind-bending of them all . . . Liu's picture of humanity's place in the cosmos is among the biggest, boldest, and most disturbing we've seen."

—*Los Angeles Times*

"Utterly, utterly brilliant . . . Nothing short of a masterpiece."

—Lavie Tidhar, World Fantasy Award–winning author of *Osama*

"A tour-de-force walk through Chinese and world history . . . Merges virtual realities, alien invasions, and exciting science, and manages to make them all fresh."

—Aliette de Bodard, Nebula Award winner

"Cixin Liu brings to the reader a deep and insightful vision of China past and future. First-rate work by a powerful new voice."

—Ben Bova, multiple Hugo Award winner

BALL
LIGHTNING

CIXIN LIU

TRANSLATED BY JOEL MARTINSEN

A TOM DOHERTY ASSOCIATES BOOK

NEW YORK

BALL LIGHTNING

Copyright © 2005 by 刘慈欣 (Liu Cixin)
English translation copyright © 2018 by China Educational Publications
Import & Export Corp., Ltd.

Excerpt of *Supernova Era* copyright © 2004 by 刘慈欣 (Liu Cixin)
English translation copyright © 2019 by China Educational Publications
Import & Export Corp., Ltd.

Translation by Joel Martinsen

Originally published as 球状闪电 in 2005 by Sichuan Science &
Technology Press in Chengdu, China.

All rights reserved.

The first three chapters of this translation appeared in the online magazine *Words Without Borders* in a slightly different form in 2009.

A Tor Book
Published by Tom Doherty Associates
175 Fifth Avenue
New York, NY 10010

www.tor-forge.com

Tor® is a registered trademark of Macmillan Publishing Group, LLC.

The Library of Congress has cataloged the hardcover edition as follows:

Liu, Cixin, author.
    Ball lightning / Cixin Liu ; translated by Joel Martinsen.—First U.S. edition.
        p. cm.
    "A Tom Doherty Associates book."
    ISBN 978-0-7653-9407-1 (hardcover)
    ISBN 978-0-7653-9408-8 (ebook)
    1. Physicists—Fiction.   2. Ball lightning—Fiction.   3. Military weapons—
Fiction.   I. Title.
    PL2947.C59 Q25813 2018
    895.13'52—dc23

2018295778

ISBN 978-0-7653-9409-5 (trade paperback)

Our books may be purchased in bulk for promotional, educational,
or business use. Please contact your local bookseller or the Macmillan
Corporate and Premium Sales Department at 1-800-221-7945, extension
5442, or by email at MacmillanSpecialMarkets@macmillan.com.

First U.S. Edition: August 2018
First U.S. Trade Paperback Edition: June 2019

Printed in the United States of America

0   9   8

The descriptions in this book

of the characteristics

and behavior of ball lightning

are based on historical records

as of 2004.

BALL LIGHTNING

PRELUDE

I only remembered that it was my birthday because Mom and Dad lit the candles on the cake and we sat down around fourteen small tongues of flame.

The storm that night made it seem as if the whole universe held nothing but rapid flashes of lightning surrounding our small dining room. Electric blue bursts froze the rain into solid drops for an instant, forming dense strands of glittering crystal beads suspended between heaven and earth. A thought struck me: the world would be a fascinating place if that instant were sustained. You could walk through streets hung with crystal, surrounded on all sides by the sound of chimes. But in such a dazzling world, the lightning would be unbearable. . . . I had always seen a different world from the one others saw. I wanted to transform the world: that was the one thing I knew about myself at that age.

The storm had started earlier in the evening, and the thunder and lightning had quickened their pace as it progressed. At first, after each flash, my mind retained an impression of the ephemeral crystalline world outside the window as I tensed in anticipation of the peal of thunder. But the lightning had grown so thick and fast that I could no longer distinguish which thunderclap belonged to which bolt.

On a stormy night, you get a sense of how precious family really is. The warm embrace of home is intoxicating when you imagine the terrors of the outside world. You feel for those souls without a home, out there in the open, shivering through the storm and lightning. You want to open a window so they can fly in, but the outside world is so frightening that you cannot let even the tiniest breath of cold air enter the warmth inside.

"Ah, life," Dad said, and downed his drink. Then, staring intently at the cluster of candle flames, he said, "Life is so random, all probability and chance. Like a twig floating in a brook, caught on a stone or seized by an eddy—"

"He's too young. He doesn't understand this stuff," Mom said.

"He's not young!" said Dad. "He's old enough to learn the truth about life!"

"And you know all about that," Mom said, with a sarcastic laugh.

"I know. Of course I know!" Dad poured another glass and drank half, then turned to me. "Actually, son, it's not hard to live a wonderful life. Listen to me. Choose a tough, world-class problem, one that requires only a sheet of paper and a pencil, like Goldbach's Conjecture or Fermat's Last Theorem, or a question in pure natural philosophy that doesn't need pencil and paper at all, like the origin of the universe, and then throw yourself entirely into research. Think only of planting, not reaping, and as you concentrate, an entire lifetime will pass before you know it. That's what people mean by settling down. Or do the opposite, and make earning money your only goal. Spend all of your time thinking about how to make money, not about what you'll do with it when you make it, until you're on your deathbed clutching a pile of gold coins like Monsieur Grandet, saying: 'It warms me . . .' The key to a wonderful life is a fascination with something. Me, for example—" Dad pointed to the watercolors lying all over the room. They were done in a very traditional style, properly composed, but lacking all vitality. The paintings reflected the lightning outside like a set of flickering screens. "I'm fascinated with painting even though I know I can't be van Gogh."

"That's right. Idealists and cynics may pity each other, but they're really both fortunate," Mom mused.

Ordinarily all business, my mother and father had turned into philosophers, as if it were their own birthday we were celebrating.

"Mom, don't move!" I plucked a white hair out of my mother's thick, black mane. Only half of it was white. The other half was still black.

Dad held the hair up to the light and examined it. Against the lightning it shone like a lamp filament. "As far as I know, this is the first white hair your mother has had in her entire life. Or at least the first that's been discovered."

"What are you doing! Pluck one, and seven will grow back!" Mom said, giving her hair an exasperated toss.

"Really? Well, that's life," Dad said. He pointed to the candles on the cake: "Suppose you take one of these small candles and stick it into a desert dune. If there's no wind you may be able to light it. Then: leave. What would it feel like to watch the flame from a distance? My boy, this is what life is, fragile and uncertain, unable to endure a puff of wind."

The three of us sat in silence, looking at the cluster of flames as they shivered against the icy blue lightning that flashed through the window, as if they were a tiny life-form that we had painstakingly raised.

Outside, lightning flashed dramatically.

This time, though, the arc came in through the wall, emerging like a spirit from an oil painting of a carnival of the Greek gods. It was about the size of a basketball, and shone with a hazy red glow. It drifted gracefully over our heads, followed by a tail that gave off a dark red light. Its flight path was erratic, and its tail described a confusingly complicated figure above us. It whistled as it floated, a deep tone pierced with a sharp high whine, calling to mind a spirit blowing a flute in some ancient wasteland.

Mom clutched fearfully to Dad with both hands, an action I have looked back on in anguish my entire life. If she had not done that, I might have one relative left alive today.

The thing continued to drift like it was looking for something. It finally stopped and found it, hanging about half a meter over my father's head. Its whistle became deeper and intermittent, like bitter laughter.

I could see inside the translucent red blaze. It seemed infinitely deep, and a cluster of blue stars streamed out of the bottomless haze, like a star field seen by a spirit rocketing across space faster than the speed of light.

Later, I learned that the internal energy density of this mass could have reached twenty thousand to thirty thousand joules per cubic centimeter, compared to just two thousand joules per cubic centimeter for TNT. But while its internal temperature might have exceeded ten thousand degrees, its surface would be cool.

My father lifted his hand, more to protect his head than to try to touch the thing. Fully extended, his arm seemed to exert an attractive force that pulled the thing toward it like a leaf's stomata absorb a drop of dew.

With a blinding flash and a deafening boom, the world around me exploded.

What I saw after the flash blindness lifted from my eyes would stay with me for the rest of my life. It was like someone had switched the world to grayscale mode in an image editor: instantaneously, the bodies of my mom and dad had turned black and white. Or, rather, gray and white, because the black was the result of shadows cast by lamplight playing off the creases and folds of their bodies. The color of marble. Dad's hand was raised, and Mom clutched at his other arm with both hands. There still seemed to be life in the two pairs of eyes that stared petrified out of the faces of these two statues.

A strange odor was in the air, which I later learned was the smell of ozone.

"Dad!" I shouted. No answer.

"Mom!" I shouted again. No answer.

Approaching the two statues was the most frightening moment in my life. In the past, my terrors had mostly been in dreams. I had been able to avoid a mental breakdown in the world of my nightmares because my subconscious was still awake, shouting to my consciousness from a remote corner, "This is a dream!" Now, it took that voice shouting with all its might to keep me moving toward my parents. I reached out a trembling hand to touch my father's body. As I made contact with the gray-and-white surface of his shoulder, it felt like I was pushing through an extremely thin and extremely brittle shell. I heard a soft cracking, like a glass crackling when it is filled with boiling water in the winter. The two statues collapsed right before my eyes in a miniature avalanche.

Two piles of white ash settled on the carpet, and that's all that was left of them.

The wooden stools they had been sitting on were still there, covered with a layer of ash. I brushed away the ash to reveal a surface that was perfectly unharmed and icy cold to the touch.

I knew that crematorium ovens must heat bodies at nearly two thousand degrees Fahrenheit for two hours to render them to ash, so this must be a dream.

As I looked vacantly around me, I saw smoke issuing from a bookcase. Behind the glass door, the bookcase was full of white smoke. I went over and opened the bookcase door, and the smoke dissipated. About a third of the books had turned to ash, the same color as the two piles on the carpet, but the bookcase itself showed no signs of fire. This was a dream.

I saw a puff of steam escape the half-opened refrigerator. I pulled back the door to find a frozen chicken, cooked through and smelling delicious, and shrimp and fish that were cooked as well. But the refrigerator, rattling as the compressor restarted, was completely unharmed. This was a dream.

I felt a little weird myself. I opened my jacket and ashes fell off my body. The tee shirt I was wearing had been completely incinerated, but the outer jacket was perfectly fine, which was why I hadn't noticed anything until now. I checked my pockets and burned my hand on an object that turned out to be my PDA, now a hunk of melted plastic. This had to be a dream, a most peculiar dream!

Woodenly, I returned to my seat. Although I could not see the two small piles of ash on the carpet on the other side of the table, I knew they were there. Outside, the thunder had let up and the lightning had slackened. Eventually the rain stopped. Later, the moon poked through a gap in the clouds, beaming an unearthly silvery light through the window. Still I sat numbly in a fog. In my mind, the world had ceased to exist and I was floating in a vast emptiness.

How much time passed before the rising sun outside the window woke me, I do not know, but when I got up mechanically to leave for school, I had to fumble around to find my book bag and open the door because I was still staring dumbly into that boundless emptiness. . . .

A week later, when my mind had mostly returned to normal, the first thing I remembered was that it had happened on the night of my birthday. There should have been only one candle on the cake—no, no candles at all, because on that night my life started anew. I was no longer the person I once was.

Like Dad had advised in the last moments of his life, I was now fascinated with something, and I wanted to experience the wonderful life he had described.

PART ONE

COLLEGE

Major courses: Higher Mathematics, Theoretical Mechanics, Fluid Mechanics, Principles and Applications of Computers, Languages and Programming, Dynamic Meteorology, Principles of Synoptic Meteorology, Chinese Meteorology, Statistical Forecasting, Long-Term Weather Forecasting, Numerical Forecasting.

Elective courses: Atmospheric Circulation, Meteorological Diagnostic Analysis, Storms and Mid-Scale Meteorology, Thunderstorm Prediction and Prevention, Tropical Meteorology, Climate Change and Short-Term Climate Prediction, Radar and Satellite Meteorology, Air Pollution and Urban Climatology, High-Altitude Meteorology, Atmosphere-Ocean Interactions.

Just five days before, I had taken care of everything in the house and set out for a southern city a thousand kilometers away to go to college. Shutting the door to a now-empty house, I knew that I was leaving my

childhood behind forever. From now on, I would be a machine in
pursuit of a single goal.

Looking over the list of courses that would occupy me for the next
four years, I felt a little disappointed. Many of the things on it I had no
need for, and some of the things that I did need—like Electricity and
Magnetism and Plasma Physics—were not. I realized that I might have
applied to the wrong major, and perhaps should have gone into physics
instead of atmospheric science.

So I plunged into the library, spending most of my time on mathematics, E&M, and plasma physics, attending only the classes that involved those subjects and basically skipping all of the rest. Colorful
collegiate life had nothing for me, and I had no interest in it. Returning to my dorm room at one or two in the morning and hearing a
roommate mumble his girlfriend's name in his sleep was the only
reminder I had of that other mode of life.

One night, well after midnight, I lifted my head out of a thick partial differential equations text. I had assumed that at this time of night
I would be the only student left in the nighttime reading room, as usual,
but across from me I saw Dai Lin, a pretty girl from my class. She had
no books in front of her. She was simply resting her head on her hands
and looking at me. Her expression would not have been enchanting to
her scads of admirers. It was the look of someone who has discovered
a spy in camp, a look directed at something alien. I had no idea how
long she had been looking at me.

"You're a peculiar person. I can tell you're not just a nerd because
you've got a strong sense of purpose," she said.

"Oh? Doesn't everyone have goals?" I tossed off the question. I may
have been the only male student in class who had never spoken to her.

"Our goals are vague. But you, you're definitely looking for something very specific."

"You've got a good eye for people," I said blandly as I gathered my books and stood up. I was the one man who had no need to show off for her, and this gave me a sense of superiority.

When I reached the door, she called after me, "What are you looking for?"

"You wouldn't be interested." I left without looking back.

In the quiet autumn night outside, I looked up at a sky full of stars. My dad's voice seemed to carry on the air: "The key to a wonderful life is a fascination with something." Now I understood how right he was. My life was a speeding missile, and I had no other desire than to hear it explode as it hit its target. A goal with no practical purpose, but one that would make my life complete once I reached it. Why I was going to that particular place, I did not know. It was enough to simply want to go, an impulse that lay at the core of human nature. Oddly, I had never gone to look up any materials related to It. My fascination and I were two knights whose entire lives would be devoted to preparing for a single duel, and until I was ready I would neither think about it nor seek it out directly.

Three semesters passed in the blink of an eye, time that felt like one uninterrupted span, because without a home to return to, I spent all of my holidays at school. Living all by myself in a spacious dormitory, I had few feelings of loneliness. Only on the eve of the Spring Festival, when I heard the firecrackers going off outside, did I think about my life before It had appeared, but that life felt like it was a generation ago. As I spent those nights in a dorm room with the heat turned off, the cold made my dreams especially lifelike.

Although I had imagined as a child that my mom and dad would appear in my dreams, they had not. I remembered an Indian legend that told of a king who, when his beloved consort died, decided to build a luxurious tomb the likes of which had never before been seen. He spent the better part of his life working on that tomb. Finally, when construction was complete, he noticed his consort's coffin lying right at the center and said: That doesn't belong. Take it away.

My parents had long since departed, and It occupied every corner of my mind.

But what happened next complicated my simple world.

STRANGE PHENOMENA I

The summer after my sophomore year I took a trip back home to rent out the old place so I could afford my future tuition.

It was already dark when I arrived, so I had to feel around to turn the lock and make my way in. Turning on the light revealed a familiar scene. The table that had held a birthday cake during the night of the thunderstorm was still there, with three chairs still sitting around it, as if I had left just yesterday. Exhausted, I sat down on the sofa, and as I took stock of my home, I felt that something was not right. The feeling was indistinct at first, but as it gradually took shape like a submerged reef coming into view during a foggy cruise, I could not avoid it.

At last I discovered the source: it was as if I had left just yesterday.

I inspected the table: there was a thin layer of dust, a little too thin for the two years I had been away.

I went to the bathroom to wash the dirt and sweat off my face. When I turned on the light, I could see myself clearly in the mirror. Too clearly. The mirror should not have been that clean. I distinctly remembered going away with my parents during one summer break when I was in elementary school, and although we were only gone a month, when we came back, I could draw a stick figure in the dust on the mirror. Now, when I made a few strokes on the mirror with my finger, nothing appeared.

I turned on the faucet. After two years, the water from the iron tap should have been rusty, but what flowed out was perfectly clear.

I went back to the living room after washing my face and noticed something else: Two years ago, just as I was about to leave, but before I shut the door, I looked over the entire room on the off-chance that I had forgotten something and had noticed a glass sitting on the table. I thought about turning it upside down so it would not collect dust, but with my luggage in hand it would have taken too much effort to go back, so I dropped the idea. I distinctly remembered that detail.

But now, the glass was turned upside down on the table!

Just then, the neighbors came over to see why the lights were on. They greeted me with the sort of kind words one uses with an orphan who has gone off to college, promising that they would take care of renting the place and, if I could not come back after graduation, help me get a good price for it.

"The environment seems to have improved quite a bit since I left," I said casually, as talk turned to how things had changed over the past two years.

"Improved? Get your eyes checked! That power plant over by the distillery just started up last year, and now there's twice as much dust as when you left! Ha! Are things improving anywhere these days?"

I glanced at the table and its thin layer of dust and said nothing. But when I saw them off, I could not help asking whether any of them had a key to the house. They looked at each other in surprise and said they most certainly did not. I believed them, because there had been a total of five keys, three of which still worked. When I left two years ago I took all three: one I had with me now, and two others were far away in my college dorm room.

After the neighbors left, I inspected the windows, all of them tightly sealed with no evidence of break-ins.

The remaining two keys had been carried by my parents. But on that night, they had melted. I will never forget how I'd found those two mis-shapen lumps of metal among my parents' ashes. Those keys, melted and resolidified, were sitting in my dormitory a thousand kilometers away, as mementos of that fantastic energy.

I sat for a while before starting to get together the things that would be stored or taken back with me once the house was rented. I first packed my father's watercolors, one of the few things in the room that I wanted to save. I took down the ones hanging on the walls first, then got others out of a cabinet and packed as many as I could find into a cardboard box. Then I noticed one more painting. It was still lying on the bottom shelf of the bookcase, facedown, which was why I had missed it. When I glanced at it before putting it into the box, it seized my whole attention.

It was a landscape painting of the scenery visible from the door to our home. The surrounding scenery was dull: a few gray four-story walk-ups and several rows of poplars, lifeless from the dust covering them. . . .

As a third-rate amateur painter, my father was lazy. Rarely going out to sketch from the real world, he was content to paint the muddy scenes that surrounded him. He said that there were no flat colors, only mediocre painters. That was the sort of painter he was, but these flat scenes, which acquired another level of woodenness as interpreted through his artless brush, actually managed to capture everyday life in this dingy northern city. The painting I held in my hand was like so many already in the box, with nothing in particular to recommend it.

But I had noticed something: a water tower that was a little more brightly colored than the old buildings surrounding it, standing tall like a morning glory. Nothing special, really, because there was indeed a water tower outside. I looked out the window at the towering structure silhouetted against the lights of the city.

Except, the water tower had not been completed until after I went off to college. When I left two years ago, it had been half-finished and covered in scaffolding.

I trembled, and the painting slipped out of my hand. A breath of cold air seemed to blow through the house on this midsummer night.

I crammed the painting into the box, closed the lid tightly, and then started packing other things. I tried to focus my attention on the task at hand, but my mind was a needle suspended on a filament, and the box was a strong magnet. With effort, I could redirect the needle, but once I let up, it would swing back in that direction.

It was raining. The raindrops tapped softly against the windowpane, but the sound seemed to be coming from the box. . . .

Finally, when I could not stand it any longer, I raced to the box, opened it, took out the painting, and carried it to the bathroom, taking care to hold it facedown. Then I took out a lighter and lit one corner. When about a third of the painting had burned up, I gave in and flipped it over. The water tower was even more lifelike than before, and seemed to poke out of the surface. I watched as it was consumed by flames, which turned strange, seductive colors as the watercolors burned. I dropped the last bit of the painting into the sink and watched it burn out, then turned on the faucet and rinsed the ashes down the drain.

When I turned off the faucet, my eyes were drawn to something on the edge of the sink that I had not noticed when I'd washed my face.

A few strands of hair. Long hair.

They were white hairs, some completely white, so they blended in with the sink, and others half-white, the black portions catching my attention. Definitely not hair that I had left behind two years before. My hair had never been that long, and I had never had any white hair at all. Carefully, I lifted up one long, half-black, half-white strand.

. . . *pluck one, and seven will grow back* . . .

I tossed the hair aside like it burned my hand. As the strand drifted gently downward, it left a trail: a trail made up of the fleeting images of many strands, like a momentary persistence of vision. It did not land beside the sink, but fell only partway before vanishing into thin air. I looked back at the other hairs on the sink: they, too, had vanished without a trace.

I ran my head under the faucet for a long while, then walked stiffly back to the living room, where I sat down on the sofa and listened to the rain outside. It had turned heavy, a storm without thunder or lightning. Rain pounded on the windows, sounding like a voice, or perhaps many people speaking softly, as if they were trying to remind me of something. As I listened, I started to imagine the meaning of the murmuring, which became more and more real as it was repeated:

There was lightning that night, there was lightning that night, there was lightning that night, there was lightning that night, there was lightning that night . . .

Once again I sat in that house until dawn on a stormy night, and once again I numbly left home. I knew I was leaving something behind forever, and I knew I would never return.

BALL LIGHTNING

Classes in atmospheric electricity started that semester, meaning I would finally have to face it.

The subject was taught by an assistant professor named Zhang Bin. He was about fifty, neither short nor tall, wore glasses that were neither thick nor thin, had a voice that was neither loud nor soft, and his lectures were neither great nor terrible. In sum, as average as a person could be, except for a slight limp in one leg, something you would not notice unless you paid close attention.

That afternoon after class, I was left alone in the lecture room with Zhang Bin, who was gathering his things at the podium and did not notice me. A late-autumn sunset sent its golden beams into the room, and a layer of golden leaves covered the windowsill. Ordinarily cold and detached, I suddenly realized that this was the season for poetry.

I got up and walked over to the podium. "Professor Zhang, I'd like to ask you a question completely unrelated to today's lecture."

He looked up at me for a moment before nodding and returning his attention to his things.

"It's about ball lightning. What can you tell me about it?" I uttered the words that I had kept buried deep in my heart, never daring to speak aloud.

His hands ceased their activity. He looked up—not at me, but out the window at the setting sun, as if that were what I was referring to. "What do you want to know?" he asked after a few seconds.

"Everything," I said.

Zhang Bin continued to look at the sun as its light bathed his face. It was still quite bright at that hour. Didn't it hurt his eyes?

"The historical record, for example," I prompted in more detail.

"In Europe, records exist from as early as the Middle Ages. In China, a relatively clear record was set down by Zhang Juzheng in the Ming dynasty. But the first formal scientific discussion only occurred in 1837, and the scientific community didn't accept it as a natural phenomenon until the last forty years."

"Any theories about it?"

"There are many." After this simple sentence, Zhang Bin was silent. He turned away from the setting sun, but did not resume getting his things together. He seemed deep in thought.

"What are the traditional theories?"

"That it's a vortex of high-temperature plasma whose rapid internal rotation exerts a force in equilibrium with outside atmospheric pressure and thus can maintain stability for a relatively long time."

"And?"

"Others believe that it's a chemical reaction within a high-temperature gas mixture, by which it maintains energy equilibrium."

"Can you tell me anything else?" Asking him questions was like try-ing to move a heavy grindstone that barely budged an inch with each push.

"There's also the microwave-soliton theory, which says that ball lightning is caused by an atmospheric maser with a volume of several cubic meters. . . . A maser is like a much less powerful laser, which, in-side a large volume of air, can produce a localized magnetic field as well as solitons, which then create visible ball lightning."

"And the latest theories?"

"There are lots. For example, one by Abrahamson and Dinniss at the University of Canterbury in New Zealand has gained a fair amount of attention. Their theory says that ball lightning is primarily due to the oxidization of a filamentary network of silicon nanoparticles. There are many more. Some people even believe that it is a cold fusion reaction in the air."

He paused, but then came out with more information: "In this country, there's someone at the Institute of Atmospheric Physics at the Chinese Academy of Sciences who has suggested an atmospheric plasma theory. It starts off with magnetic fluid dynamics equations and introduces a vector-soliton resonator model which, under ap-propriate boundary temperatures, is theoretically able to achieve a plasma vortex in the atmosphere—a fireball—and whose numerical analysis explains both the necessary and sufficient conditions for its existence."

"And your opinion of this theory?"

He shook his head gently. "Proving the theory requires nothing more than producing ball lightning in the lab, but no one has suc-ceeded yet."

"Nationally, how many eyewitnesses have there been?"

"Quite a few. I'd say at least a thousand. The most famous was in 1998, when state television was shooting a documentary of the flood-fighting efforts on the Yangtze River and unwittingly recorded ball lightning on film."

"One last question, Professor. In the atmospheric physics community, are there people who have personally witnessed ball lightning?"

Once again, he looked out the window at the setting sun. "Yes."

"When?"

"In July 1962."

"Where?"

"Yuhuang Peak on Mount Tai."

"Do you know where that person is now?"

Zhang Bin shook his head, then raised his wrist and glanced at his watch: "You should head to the cafeteria for dinner." Then he picked up his things and left the building.

I caught up to him and finally asked the question that had been in my mind all these years: "Professor Zhang, can you imagine a fireball-shaped object that can pass through walls, and can reduce a person to ashes instantaneously even though it doesn't feel hot? There is a record of a sleeping couple reduced to ashes in their bed without a single scorch mark on their blanket! Can you imagine it entering a refrigerator and instantly turning all your frozen food cooked and piping hot without affecting the refrigerator's operation? Can you imagine it burning your undershirt to a crisp without you feeling a thing? Can the theories you've mentioned explain all of this?"

"There's no proof for any of those theories," he said, without altering his stride.

"Then, if we leave the confines of atmospheric physics, do you think there is any explanation in the rest of physics, or even in all of science itself, for this phenomenon? Aren't you even the least bit curious? Your reaction is even more shocking than seeing ball lightning itself!"

Zhang Bin stopped and turned to face me for the first time: "You've seen ball lightning?"

". . . I was just speaking hypothetically."

I could not reveal my deepest secret to this unfeeling person before me. Society was plagued by stoicism in the face of the profound mysteries of the natural world: its existence was the bane of science. If science had less of that sort of person, who knows, maybe humanity would have reached Alpha Centauri by now!

He said, "The field of atmospheric physics is very practical. Ball lightning is such a rare phenomenon that neither the IEC/TC-81 international standard for protection against lightning in structures nor China's 1993 Standard for Protection of Structures Against Lightning dealt with it. So there's really no point in devoting any effort to it."

There was nothing I could say to a person like Zhang Bin, so I thanked him and left. And, truth be told, even admitting the existence of ball lightning was already a major step for him. Before the scientific community formally recognized its existence in 1963, all eyewitness accounts were judged hallucinations. One day that year, Roger Jennison, a professor of electronics at the University of Kent, personally witnessed ball lightning on an airplane departing New York in the form of a twenty-centimeter-wide fireball that passed through the wall separating the pilot's cabin and the passenger cabin and down the aisle before disappearing through a wall.

That evening, I performed my first Google search for "ball lightning." I was not particularly hopeful, but I ended up with more than forty thousand search results. For the first time since deciding to devote my entire life to this thing, I felt like the world was paying attention, too.

Another semester began, and then the sweltering summer arrived. For me, summer had an additional meaning: thunderstorms would appear and bring me that much closer to It.

One day, out of the blue, Zhang Bin came looking for me. The class I had with him had concluded the previous semester, and I had practically forgotten him.

He said, "Chen, I've heard that your parents are gone and you're in a tight spot financially. I've got a summer project that needs another assistant. Can you come?"

"What sort of project?" I asked him.

"It's a parameter determination for anti-lightning equipment for a railroad being built in Yunnan Province. And there's one additional goal: in the new national standards for lightning protection currently under deliberation, the plan is to replace the ground flash density of 0.015 from the previous standard with one determined according to individual local conditions. We're doing the observations in Yunnan."

I agreed to go. Although I was not particularly rich, I could still get by. I agreed because this was my first chance for real hands-on lightning research.

The task force consisted of about a dozen people divided into five teams distributed over a large area, with several hundred kilometers between them. The group I was in had three members apart from the driver and experimental assistants: myself, Zhang Bin, and a grad student named Zhao Yu. When we reached our zone, we roomed at the county-level meteorological station.

The weather was quite good the next morning, so we could start our first day of field work. As we were moving the instruments and equipment out to the car from the room we were using as temporary storage, I asked, "Professor Zhang, what are some good ways for exploring the internal structure of lightning?"

He peered at me intently for a moment, as if aware of what I was thinking. "Judging from the current needs of domestic engineering projects, research on the lightning structure is not a priority. The priority right now is large-scale statistical research." Whenever I brought up anything even remotely related to ball lightning, he dodged the question. Evidently the man genuinely detested everything that lacked practical value.

But Zhao Yu answered my question: "There aren't many. Right now, we can't even directly measure its voltage. We have to calculate indirectly from measurements of the current. The most common instrument for studying the structure of lightning is, well, this." He pointed to a tubular object sitting in one corner of the storeroom. "This is a magnetic steel recorder, and it's used to record the amplitude and polarity of the lightning current. The material it's constructed from has a relatively high residual magnetism, and when the inside lead comes into contact with lightning, you can calculate its amplitude and polarity from the residual magnetism left on the device. This one's 60Si2Mn spring steel, but there are also plastic tubes, blade-core, and iron-powder types."

"And we'll be using it?"

"Of course. Why else would we bring it? But that's for later on."

The first stage of our mission was to install a lightning positioning system in the monitoring zone to aggregate signals from a large number of scattered lightning sensors and feed them into a computer that would automatically generate statistics of the number, frequency, and distribution of lightning strikes. It was really only a counting and positioning system and did not involve any physical data, so I was not interested at all. Most of the work consisted of setting up the outdoor sensors, and that was not easy. If we were lucky, we could mount the sensors on electrical poles or transmission towers, but most of the time we had to erect poles ourselves. After a few days, the experimental assistants were complaining incessantly.

Nothing interested Zhao Yu, least of all his major. At work, he constantly procrastinated, and seized every chance he could to slack off. At first he was full of praise for the tropical forest environs, but when the novelty wore off, he seemed dispirited. Still, he was easy to get along with, and we ended up talking quite a bit.

Every evening when we returned to town, Zhang Bin always went back to his room to bury his head in that day's materials, so Zhao Yu took the opportunity to drag me off for a drink on one of the rustic streets. The electricity was usually off on that street, and the candles that flickered in the wooden buildings took me back to an age before atmospherics, before physics, before even science itself, so that I could forget reality for a moment. One day, as we sat, slightly tipsy, in a small candlelit inn, he said, "The people in the forest would have a wonderful explanation for you if they ever saw your ball lightning."

"I've asked the locals," I said. "They've been aware of it for a long time, and they already have an explanation. Ghost lanterns."

"Isn't that enough?" he said, unfolding his fingers. "It's beautiful. All your plasmas and vector-soliton resonators may not be able to tell you anything more than that. Modernity is complex, and I don't like complexity."

I snorted. "Look at you and your attitude. Professor Zhang's the only one who'll tolerate you."

"Don't talk to me about Zhang Bin," Zhao Yu said with a drunken wave. "He's the sort of person who, if he drops his keys, won't look for them in the place the sound came from. Instead, he'll get a piece of chalk and divide the room into a grid and then search section by section. . . ."

We broke down into fits of laughter.

"People like him are suited only to the sort of work that will be done entirely by machines in the future. Creativity and imagination have no meaning for them, and they employ rigor and discipline in their scholarship to cover up their mediocrity. You know the universities are full of them. Still, with enough time, you can find things going section by section, so they manage to do well in their field."

"And what has Zhang found?"

"I believe he was in charge of R&D of an anti-lightning material for use on high-tension lines. It turned out to be quite effective as a lightning deterrent. Putting it on power lines would have eliminated the need for a shield wire along the top. But the cost was too high, and in large-scale use it would have been more expensive than a traditional shield wire. So in the end it had no practical value, and all he got out of it were a few papers and second prize for technological achievement from the province. Nothing more than that."

At last the project advanced to the stage I was waiting for: collecting physical data on lightning. We put out a large number of magnetic alloy recorders and lightning antennae, and each time a storm passed, we retrieved the devices that had been struck, taking care not to jostle them or bring them close to transmission lines or other magnetic sources that could affect their sensitivity by influencing their residual magnetism. Then we used a field strength meter (basically a compass whose needle angle indicated magnetic field strength and polarity) to read the data and a demagnetizer to wipe each device before returning them to their original positions to await the next strike.

The actual work at this stage was as tedious as before, but I was pretty interested. After all, it was my first opportunity to conduct quantitative measurements of lightning. Zhao Yu, that slacker, noticed this and began to slack off even more. It got to the point that when Zhang Bin was not around, Zhao Yu simply dumped his entire workload on me and went off to go fishing in a nearby stream.

As measured by the magnetic alloy recorders, the lightning current averaged around ten thousand amps and peaked at more than a hundred thousand, which meant we could calculate the voltage at one billion volts.

"What could you produce under those extreme physical conditions?" I asked Zhao Yu.

"Produce?" he said dismissively. "The power of an atomic blast or a high energy accelerator is far greater, yet it won't produce the sort of thing you're thinking of. Atmospheric physics is a mundane subject, yet you want to turn it mysterious. I'm the opposite: I'm used to taking sacred things and turning them ordinary." Saying this, he gazed out into the dark green of the tropical rain forest that surrounded the weather station. "Hey, you go chasing after your mysterious fireball. I'm going to enjoy an ordinary life."

His career as a master's student was reaching an end, and he had no desire to continue on to a PhD.

Back at school, classes continued, and I took part in a few more of Zhang Bin's projects outside of class and during the holidays. His methodical fastidiousness sometimes annoyed me, but apart from that he was easygoing enough, and I gained an immense amount of practical experience from him. But more importantly, his specialty was in line with my own quest.

For that reason, when it came time to graduate, I chose to test into the master's program under him.

As I had anticipated, he firmly opposed my choice of ball lightning as a master's thesis topic. In all other matters he was accommodating, including tolerating a lazy student like Zhao Yu, but in this there could be no accommodation.

"Young people should not get wrapped up in imaginary things," he said.

"The existence of ball lightning is recognized by the scientific community. You think it's imaginary?"

"Fine, I'll repeat myself. What point is there to something that is not included in international standards or national regulations? When you were an undergraduate, you could study your own specialty using basic scientific techniques, but now that you are a graduate student, that's no longer acceptable."

"But Professor Zhang, atmospheric physics is pretty much a basic discipline now. It's not just a tool for engineering; it has a duty to help us understand the world."

"But in this country, the priority is to serve the cause of economic development."

"Even so, if the anti-lightning measures at the Huangdao Oil Port had taken ball lightning into account, the 1989 catastrophe might have been avoided."

"The source of the fire in Huangdao is just conjecture. Research on ball lightning itself is full of more conjecture. From now on, you're going to avoid such harmful elements in your studies."

There would be no further discussion of the subject. I was prepared to devote my entire life to that quest, so it was unimportant what I studied for the three years I was in graduate school. So I submitted to Zhang Bin's suggestion and did a project on lightning defense computer systems.

Three years later, my graduate studies reached a smooth and uneventful conclusion.

To be fair, I learned quite a bit from Zhang Bin during those three years, and I benefited substantially from his technical rigor, proficient experimental skill set, and rich engineering experience. But, as I knew three years before, the core of what I required I was unable to find with him.

I also learned a fair amount about his personal life: his wife had died long ago, he had no children, he had lived alone for many years, and he had few social interactions. His humdrum existence echoed my own, but, to my mind, that lifestyle required the presence of an overpowering quest—a "fascination with something," in my dad's words, or what the pretty girl in the library six years ago had called "a sense of purpose." Zhang Bin, with no goals and no fascination with anything, mechanically carried out his boring applied research, treating it as a job rather than a pleasure. His attitude toward fame and fortune displayed a similar rigidity. If that really were how he felt, then life must be a kind of torment for him, and hence I felt a little sympathy.

However, I did not think I was ready to explore the mystery quite yet. No, everything I had studied over the course of six years only made me feel my impotence all the more strongly. My first efforts were primarily in physics, but I eventually discovered that physics itself was a huge mystery, at the far end of which the very existence of the world was called into question. And assuming that ball lightning was not a supernatural phenomenon, only relatively low-level physics would be necessary to understand it: Maxwell's Equations and the Navier-Stokes Equations in fluid mechanics would be sufficient (how superficial and naïve were my initial ideas). But compared to ball lightning, all known structures in electromagnetism and fluid mechanics were simple. If ball lightning was indeed a complicated structure in stable equilibrium constrained by the basic laws of electromagnetism and fluid mechanics, its mathematical expression would have to be incredibly complex, just like simple rules for black and white pieces can describe the intricate positions of Go, the world's most complicated game.

This, then, was what I felt I needed now: first, mathematics; second, mathematics; and third, more mathematics. Complex mathematical tools were absolutely necessary for cracking the secret of ball lightning, tools as unruly as an unbridled mustang. Although Zhang Bin felt that my math skills far exceeded the standard requirements of atmospheric physics, I knew that I was still far from the level required for ball lightning research. As soon as complicated electromagnetic and fluid structures got involved, mathematical descriptions turned savage, involving weird partial differential equations that tangled up like twine, and dense matrices that held blade-filled traps.

With so much to learn before my explorations could truly begin, I knew I could not leave the campus environment immediately, so I decided to study for a PhD.

My doctoral advisor, a man named Gao Bo, had a formidable reputation and had gotten his PhD at MIT. He was the polar opposite of Zhang Bin. What first attracted me to him was his nickname, "Fireball," which I later learned had nothing at all to do with ball lightning. Perhaps it had more to do with his nimble mind and vigorous personality. When I suggested ball lightning as the topic of my dissertation, he acquiesced immediately, at which point I began to have second thoughts: the project would require a large-scale lightning simulator, but there was only one in the country and I would never have a chance to use it.

But Gao Bo disagreed. "Listen, all you need is a pencil and a piece of paper. What you're constructing is a mathematical model for ball lightning. It needs to be internally consistent, innovative, mathematically flawless, and executable on a computer. Treat it as a piece of theoretical art."

Still, I had worries: "Will they accept something that forgoes experimentation entirely?"

He waved his hand. "Are black holes accepted? To date there is no direct evidence of their existence, yet look how far astrophysics has developed the theory, and how many people make a living off it. At the very least, ball lightning exists! Don't worry. If your dissertation meets the requirements I gave you but still doesn't pass, I'll resign and we'll get the hell away from this college!"

Gao Bo was a little too far toward the opposite extreme from Zhang Bin, I thought—I wasn't on a quest for a piece of theoretical art. Still, I was pleased to be his student.

I decided to use the break before classes began to go back to my hometown and visit the neighbors who had been helping me. I could sense that I would have few chances to go back in the future.

When the train reached Tai'an Station, my heart jumped. I remembered what Zhang Bin had said about the atmospheric physicist who had witnessed ball lightning at Yuhuang Peak. I got off mid-journey and began to climb Mount Tai.

I grabbed a taxi to Zhongtian Gate. I had originally planned on taking the cable car up to the peak, but when I saw the long line, I headed upward on foot. The fog was thick, and the trees on either side were indistinct shadows that extended upward before vanishing into white. From time to time, stone inscriptions from past eras loomed into view.

Ever since my trip to Yunnan with Zhang Bin, I always felt a little frustrated whenever I found myself out in the middle of nature. Looking around at the natural world, its mysteries and unfathomable complexity and variability on display, I found it difficult to imagine that humanity could constrain it within the thin bonds of mathematical equations. And every time I thought of this, I would recall how Einstein once said that every tree outside, every flower attracting pollinating bees, escapes all book knowledge.

But my annoyance was soon replaced with physical exhaustion. I could see stone steps stretching endlessly into the fog ahead of me, and the Nantian Gate just below the peak seemed like it was far above the stratosphere.

Just then, I saw her for the first time. She caught my attention because she contrasted with the rest of the people around me. I had seen couple after couple stopped on the path, the woman sitting on a stone step exhausted while the man, breathing heavily, tried to get her to move onward. Whenever I passed someone, or on those rare occasions that someone passed me, I could hear their short, strenuous breathing. I pushed myself to follow a porter in whose broad bronze shoulders I found the strength to continue climbing. It was then that a white figure slipped easily past us, a woman who looked like condensed fog in her white blouse and white jeans. When she passed me on light and springy footsteps, I could not hear her breathing at all. She looked back—not at me, but at the porter—with a serene expression, no sign of fatigue on her face. Her lithe body seemed to have no weight at all, as if climbing this exhausting mountain path was like strolling down an avenue. Before long, she vanished into the fog.

By the time I finally reached the South Gate, it was already floating on a sea of clouds stained red by the sun, which was just setting in the west.

I dragged my heavy feet to the Yuhuang Peak Meteorology Station. Once the people inside learned who I was and where I was from, they acted as if nothing was out of the ordinary: meteorological workers were constantly arriving at the famous station to conduct all sorts of tests. They told me that the station chief had gone down the mountain, so they introduced me to the deputy chief. I almost cried out in astonishment when I saw him: it was Zhao Yu.

It had been three years since our trip down to Yunnan. I asked him how he ended up in this peculiar place, and he said, "I came here in search of peace and quiet. The world down there is too damn frustrating!"

"Then you should become a monk at Dai Temple."

"That's not a peaceful place, either. What about you? Are you still chasing your ghosts?"

I explained my reason for coming.

He shook his head. "1962. That's too long ago. They've changed staff at the station so many times since then, I can't imagine that anyone would know about it."

"That doesn't matter," I said. "I only want to learn about it because it was the first time someone working in meteorology personally witnessed ball lightning in this country. It's not all that important, really. I came up the mountain as a diversion, and who knows, maybe there'll be a thunderstorm. Next to Wudang, this is the best place for lightning."

"Who's got the time to sit and watch lightning? I think you've really gone over the edge! Still, you can't escape thunderstorms up here. If you really want to see something, then stay for a few days and maybe you will."

Zhao Yu took me to his dormitory. It was supper time, so he called the cafeteria to have them send over some food: thin, crispy Taishan pancakes, green onions as big around as shot glasses, and a bottle of Taishan liquor.

Zhao Yu thanked the elderly cook, but as the old man turned to go, a thought occurred to him. He asked, "Master Wang, when did you first start working at the station?"

"It was 1960 that I started, right at this very cafeteria. Those were trying times. You weren't around then, Director Zhao."

Zhao Yu and I shared a surprised smile.

Immediately, I asked, "Have you seen ball lightning?"

"You mean . . . rolling lightning?"

"Right! That's what they call it."

"Of course I've seen it. Over the past forty years, I've seen it three or four times!"

Zhao Yu picked up another glass and we enthusiastically invited Lao* Wang to sit down. As I poured him a drink, I asked, "Do you remember the time it hit in 1962?"

"Sure do. That's the one I remember the best. A guy got hurt then!"

Lao Wang started into the story: "It was at the end of July, maybe a little after seven in the evening. Normally, it would still have been light, but that day the clouds were so thick that you couldn't see anything without a lantern. The rain came in driving sheets, enough to smother you if you stood out in it! Flash after flash of lightning, with no pause between them—"

"Probably a thunderstorm at the head of a passing front," Zhao Yu put in.

"I heard one crack of thunder. The lightning just before it was really bright, enough to almost blind me where I was sitting in my room. Then I heard a voice outside shouting that someone had been hurt, so I ran out to help. At that time, there were four people at the station conducting observations. It was one of them who had been struck. When I hauled the man into the room, one of his legs was smoking and the rain fizzled where it fell, but he was still fully conscious. And then the rolling lightning came in. It entered through the west window, but the window was closed at the time! The thing was about . . . about the size of this pancake, and red, blood red, so that it filled the whole room with red light. It drifted around the room, about this fast . . ." He lifted his glass and gestured in midair. ". . . floating this way and that. I thought I'd seen a ghost, and was so scared I couldn't speak. But those science guys weren't panicked. They just told us not to touch

---

* A respectful form of address for an elder.

it. The thing floated for a while, up to the ceiling, and down across the bed—fortunately it didn't touch anyone—and finally entered the chimney. Right as it got in, it exploded with a bang. All these years on the peak, and out of all the thunder I've heard, I don't remember hearing anything that loud. It set my ears buzzing, and did something to my left ear so bad that I'm hard of hearing now. All of the lanterns in the room went out, and the lantern globes and the glass liners for the hot water bottles shattered and left burn marks on the bed. When we went outside afterward we found that the chimney had exploded!"

"Where did they come from, the four people doing the monitoring?"

"I don't know."

"Do you still remember their names?"

"Hmm. It's been so many years . . . I only remember the one who got hurt. I carried him down the mountain to the hospital with two other people from the station. He was very young, and must've still been a college student. One of his legs was burned to a crisp, and because Tai'an Hospital wasn't all that great back then, he was transferred to Jinan. Geez, it must've made him lame. The guy was named Zhang, I think. Zhang . . . something . . . fu."

Zhao Yu slammed his glass on the table. "Zhang Hefu?"

"Right, yes. That's the name. I looked after him for a couple days at Tai'an Hospital, and after he left, he wrote a letter to thank me. I think it came from Beijing. Then we lost contact, and I don't know where he is now."

Zhao Yu said to Lao Wang, "He's in Nanjing. He's a professor at my old university." He turned to me. "He was our advisor."

"What?" My glass nearly dropped out of my hand.

"Zhang Bin used to go by that name, but he changed it during the Cultural Revolution because it sounded too much like Khrushchev."

Zhao Yu and I sat for a long time without saying anything, until finally Lao Wang broke the silence: "It's not really all that coincidental.

You're in the same field, after all. He was a fine young man, that one. With his legs hurting so bad he bit through his lips from the pain, he just lay in bed reading. I tried to get him to rest for a while, but he said that from then on, there was no time to waste, because his life had just acquired a purpose. He was going to study it, and he wanted to generate it."

"Study and generate what?" I asked.

"Rolling lightning! The ball lightning you were talking about."

Zhao Yu and I stared at each other.

Not noticing our expressions, Lao Wang continued, "He said that he would devote a lifetime to its study, and I could tell that what he had seen on the mountain peak had him fascinated. People are like that—they sometimes become fascinated with something without knowing it and are unable to get rid of it their entire life. Take me: twenty years ago I went out to get some wood for the cooking stove and pulled out a tree root. When I was about to toss it into the fire, I thought it looked a little bit like a tiger, and then after I polished it up and set it down, it really looked rather nice. Since then, I've been fascinated with root carving, and that's the reason that I've stayed on the mountain, even when I retired."

I noticed that Zhao Yu's room did indeed have lots of root carvings of various sizes, which he told me were all Lao Wang's pieces.

We did not speak of Zhang Bin after that. Although we were thinking about him, it was not something easily put into words.

After dinner, Zhao Yu took me for a nighttime tour of the meteorology station. When we passed the only lit window in their small guesthouse, I stopped short in surprise, for in the room was the white-clothed girl. She was alone and apparently lost in thought as she paced back and forth in the middle of the room between two beds and a desk covered in open books and papers.

"Hey, be polite. Don't peep through other people's windows." Zhao Yu gave me a push from behind.

"I saw her on the way up here," I explained.

"She's here to arrange for lightning monitoring. The Provincial Meteorological Bureau notified us before she arrived, but didn't say where she's from. It's got to be some big work unit. They're going to ship equipment to the peak by helicopter."

There were thunderstorms the following day, as it turned out. The way thunder rocked the peak was an entirely different experience from what I'd been through on the ground, as if Mount Tai was a lightning rod for the earth that attracted a universe worth of lightning. Sparks flashing from the rooftops made you tingle all over. With hardly any gap between lightning and thunder, massive rumbles shook every cell in your body until you felt that the mountain beneath your feet had been blown to bits and your soul displaced, flitting terrified between the dazzling bolts with no place to hide . . .

The woman in white stood at the edge of the corridor, wind whipping at her short hair and her slender form frail looking against the web of lightning that flickered within dense black clouds. She presented an unforgettable picture as she stood motionless amid the terrible thunder.

"You'd better stand over here. It's dangerous, and you'll get soaked!" I called to her.

She shook out of her lightning reverie and retreated two steps. "Thanks." She turned to look at me, and beamed. "You may not believe it, but it's only at times like these that I feel any sense of security."

Strange: normally you had to shout to be heard through the thunder, but even though the woman spoke softly, her gentle tones somehow penetrated the peals of thunder so that I was able to hear her words clearly. The mysterious woman captivated me even more than the lightning.

"You're something else." I gave voice to my thoughts.

"So you're into atmospheric electricity," she said, ignoring my words.

By now the thunder had died enough that we could talk freely. I asked, "Are you here to monitor lightning?" I phrased my question carefully, because from what Zhao Yu had said, I got the feeling her background was off-limits.

"That's right."

"What aspects?"

"The formation process. I don't want to insult your profession, but even now there's debate within the field of atmospheric physics over basic things like how lightning is formed in thunderclouds, and how a lightning rod works."

I realized that even if she did not work in atmospheric physics, she had at least dabbled in it. Like she said, there was no satisfactory theory for the principle of lightning formation in thunderclouds, and although every schoolchild knows that lightning rods protect against lightning, the underlying theory was not well understood. In recent years, precise calculations of the charge carried by the metal tip of a lightning rod showed that it was far too low to neutralize the charge that builds up in a thundercloud.

"So your research is very basic."

"Our ultimate goals are practical."

"Based on research on the lightning formation process? Hmm. Lightning elimination?"

"No. Artificial lightning."

"Artificial . . . lightning? What for?"

She smiled sweetly. "Guess."

"Manufacturing nitrogenous fertilizer?"

She shook her head.

"Patching the ozone hole?"

Again, she shook her head.

"Using lightning as a new power source?"

Once again, she shook her head.

"No, it couldn't really be a power source because creating lightning would consume even more power. So there's only one thing left—"

Jokingly, I said, "Killing people with lightning?"

She nodded.

I laughed. "Then you've got to solve the targeting problem. Lightning follows a fairly random broken line."

She sighed slightly. "We'll worry about that later. We haven't even figured out how to produce it yet. But we're not interested in how lightning is formed in thunderclouds. What we want is the rare lightning that forms on cloudless days, but observing that is even more difficult. . . . What's wrong with you?"

"You're serious!" I said, stunned.

"Of course! We've predicted that the most valuable use of this project will be the construction of a high-efficiency air defense system comprising a vast lightning field blanketing a city or some other protected target. Enemy planes will attract lightning when they enter, and under those circumstances the targeting issue you mentioned becomes unimportant. Sure, if land is used as one of the poles, then you could also hit land targets, but there are additional problems with that. . . . We're really only performing a feasibility study for the concept and are looking for inspiration in the most basic areas of research. If it turns out to be feasible, we'll turn to professional organizations like your own for the implementation specifics."

I exhaled. "Are you in the army?"

She introduced herself as Lin Yun, a doctoral student at the National University of Defense Technology, who specialized in air defense weapons systems.

The storm stopped, and the setting sun radiated golden light through the gaps in the clouds.

"Look at how new the world looks, like it's been reborn in the thunderstorm!" She gasped in admiration.

I shared that feeling, although it was unclear whether it was because of the storm or the girl in front of me. At any rate, it was not a feeling I had experienced before.

That night, Lin Yun, Zhao Yu, and I went for a walk. Before long, Zhao Yu got a call to return to the station, so Lin Yun and I continued along the path up the mountain until we reached the Skyway. It was late, and the Skyway was shrouded in a light fog through which streetlamps shone hazily. Nighttime on the mountain was quiet, so still that the clamor of the world below seemed but a distant memory.

When the fog lifted somewhat, a few stars emerged in the sky, their light reflected immediately in Lin Yun's eyes. I gazed spellbound at the reflected starlight before quickly turning to look at the stars themselves. If my life were a movie, then what had been a black-and-white screen had burst into color today on the peak of Mount Tai.

In the night fog on the Skyway, I told Lin Yun my deepest hidden secret. I told her about that nightmarish birthday night so many years before, and I told her about the thing to which I had decided to devote my entire life. This was the first time I had told anyone.

"Do you hate ball lightning?" she asked.

"It's hard to feel hate toward an unknowable mystery, regardless of how much disaster it may bring. At first I was only curious, but as I've

learned more about it, that curiosity has transformed into total fascination. In my mind it became a doorway to another world, a world
where I can see the wonders I have been dreaming about for so long."

A winsome breeze picked up and the fog dissipated. Up above, the
glittering summer star field stretched across the heavens, and far off
down the mountain, the lights of the town of Tai'an formed their own
star field like a reflection in a pond.

In a soft voice, she began to recite a Guo Moruo poem:

> The distant streetlamps are lit,
> Like countless glittering stars.
> Stars emerge in the heavens,
> Like the lighting of countless streetlamps.

I continued:

> I think in the wafting air,
> There must be beautiful street markets.
> And objects laid out on those markets,
> Must be rarities like nothing on earth.

Tears welled. The beautiful night city quivered for a moment through
my tears and then resolved to an even greater clarity. I understood that
I was a person in pursuit of a dream, but I also understood how unimag-
inably hazardous the road I followed was. Yet even if the South Gate
to Heaven never emerged from the fog, I would keep on climbing.

I had no other choice.

ZHANG BIN

Two years as a doctoral student passed quickly while I built my first mathematical model of ball lightning.

Gao Bo was a remarkable advisor, whose forte lay in his ability to induce creativity in his students. His obsession with theory was paired with an extreme distaste for experimentation, which could be insufferable at times. Without any experimental basis whatsoever, my mathematical model became totally abstract. But I did successfully defend my dissertation, and received the assessment, "A novel argument that evinces a strong mathematical foundation and deft technique." The fatal lack of the experimental side of the model naturally provoked considerable debate. As the defense was concluding, one panelist taunted, "One last question: How many angels can fit on the point of a pin?" to a burst of laughter.

Zhang Bin was on the dissertation committee, and he asked a single question on a trivial detail and did not put forth much commentary. In those two years, I had never directly mentioned Mount Tai to him, for a reason I did not know myself, or perhaps I foresaw that it would force him to tell a painful personal secret. But now, since I was about to leave the school, I could no longer hold back from asking about it.

I went to his house and told him what I had heard on Mount Tai. He remained quiet after I finished, looking at the floor and sucking on a cigarette. When I was done, he dragged himself up and said, "Come with me."

Zhang Bin lived alone in a two-bedroom apartment. He occupied one of the rooms, but the door to the other was always shut tight. Zhao Yu once told me that when a classmate from out of town had come for a visit, he had thought of Zhang Bin and asked him whether his classmate could stay there, but Zhang Bin had said there wasn't any room. He wasn't ordinarily so callous, even if he seldom interacted with other people, so Zhao Yu and I felt there was something mysterious about that closed room. After asking him about Mount Tai, he took me through that tightly closed door.

When Zhang Bin opened the door, the first thing I saw was a wall of stacked cardboard boxes, with more of them piled on the floor beyond. But apart from these, there wasn't anything special in the room. On the facing wall hung a black-and-white photograph of a woman in glasses, short-haired in the style of her time. Her eyes sparkled behind the lenses.

"My wife. She died in '71," he said, pointing at the picture.

I noticed something peculiar: the room clearly belonged to a man very concerned with the tidiness of the area around the photograph, since the boxes were some distance away, leaving a semicircle of empty space. But right next to it an old-style rubber-coated dark green canvas raincoat hung on a nail in the wall, looking quite out of place.

"As you've found out, since the day I saw ball lightning in Mount Tai, I've been fascinated with it. I was just an undergrad then, and my attitude was exactly like yours. No more need be said. I first looked for it in natural thunderstorms in tons of places. When I met her later on, it was ball lightning that brought us together. She was an obsessed researcher, and we ran into each other during a huge storm, then went out on searches together. Conditions were poor back then: we had to go on foot more than half the way, and we stayed most nights in local homes, or in crumbling temples or mountain caves, or even slept in the open. I remember once, when we were making observations during an autumn thundershower, we both contracted pneumonia in a remote area where there were no doctors and few drugs. She became seriously ill and nearly died. We crossed paths with wolves and got bitten by snakes, not to mention the frequent hunger. More than a few times, lightning struck the ground quite close to us. These field observations lasted eight years, and it's impossible to sum up the total distance we walked, the pain we endured, and the danger we faced in that time. For the sake of our cause, we decided not to have children.

"Most of the time it was the two of us on the road, but when she was too busy with teaching or research, I would sometimes go out on my own. Once, in the south, I strayed into a military base and was seen carrying a camera and instruments. Since it was the height of the Cultural Revolution and my parents had been to Russia, I was suspected of being a spy gathering intelligence and was locked up, on no charges, for two years. During those two years, my wife continued field observations in thunderstorms.

"I heard of her death from the village elders. She finally found ball lightning in that thunderstorm, and chased the fireball right up to the edge of a raging flash flood. In her haste she touched the raised air terminal of the magnetic field meter to the fireball. Afterward, they said it was an accident, but they didn't understand what it might feel like to finally see the ball lightning you'd spent almost a decade searching for, only to be on the verge of losing the opportunity to observe it."

"I understand," I said.

"According to eyewitnesses, who were quite far away, when the fireball contacted the terminal it vanished, and then traveled the length of the meter and emerged from the other terminal. She was unharmed at this point, but in the end she did not escape: the fireball revolved around her several times, and then exploded directly above her head. When the flash cleared, she was gone. All they found in the place she was last standing was this raincoat, spread untouched on the ground, and underneath it a pile of white ash, most of which was washed away by the rain in thin trickles of white . . ."

I looked at the raincoat, imagining it wrapped around that young, dedicated soul, and said softly, "Like the captain who dies at sea or the astronaut who dies in space, her death was worth it."

Zhang Bin nodded. "I think so, too."

"And the meter recording?"

"Also unharmed. And it was taken immediately to the lab to determine the residual magnetism."

"How much?" I asked nervously. This was the first firsthand quantitative observational data in the history of ball lightning research.

"Zero."

"What?"

"No residual magnetism whatsoever."

"That means no current passed through the receptor conductor. So how was it conducted?"

Zhang Bin waved a hand. "There are too many mysteries about ball lightning that I won't go into here. Compared to the others, this isn't a big one. Now I'd like you to take a look at something even more incredible." As he spoke, he pulled out a plastic-covered notebook from a pocket of the raincoat. "She had this in her raincoat pocket when she died." He placed the notebook on a cardboard box with extreme care, as if it were a fragile object. "Use a light touch when you turn the pages."

It was an ordinary notebook, with a picture of Tiananmen on the cover, blurry now from wear. I gently opened the cover and saw a line of graceful characters on the title page: *The entrance to science is the entrance to hell.—Marx.*

I looked at Zhang Bin, and he motioned for me to turn the page. I turned to page one, and realized why he told me to be gentle: this page was burned, partly turned to ash and lost. Very gently, I turned this burnt page, and the next one was completely intact, its dense data recordings easily visible, as if written yesterday.

"Turn another page," he said.

The third leaf was burned.

The fourth was intact.

The fifth was burned.

The sixth was intact.

The seventh was burned.

The eighth was intact.

As I paged through the notebook, every other page was burned. Some of the burnt pages only had bits close to the binding remaining, but on the neighboring intact pages I could see no burn marks. I looked up and stared at Zhang Bin.

He said, "Can you believe it? I've never shown this to anyone else, since they'd certainly think it's fake."

Looking straight at him, I said, "No, Professor Zhang. I believe!"

Then I told a second person about my fateful birthday night.

After hearing my story, he said, "I guessed you had experience in this area, but I never imagined it would be so terrible. You ought to

know, after all you personally witnessed, that the study of ball lightning is a foolish thing."

"Why? I don't understand."

"I realized this fairly late myself. Over the past thirty years, apart
from seeking ball lightning in naturally occurring thunderstorms,
more of my energies were devoted to theoretical study. Thirty years."
He sighed. "I won't describe that process to you. See for yourself." He
gestured at the large cardboard boxes surrounding us.

I opened two of the heavy ones and found they were filled to the
top with stacks of calculation books! I pulled out two of them and read
the dense differential equations and matrices, then looked around at the
low wall of boxes, and sucked in a breath of cold air at the thought of
the work he had done in thirty years.

I asked, "And experiments—what have you done?"

"Not much. Means were limited. There's no way the project could
get much funding. But more importantly, none of these mathematical
models is worth testing. They were not well-founded, and when I
got further along I'd find out that I'd taken a wrong first step. In
other words, even coming up with a self-consistent mathematical
model is still very far from being able to produce ball lightning in
the lab."

"Are you still carrying out research in this area?"

Zhang Bin shook his head. "I stopped a few years ago. Odd—it was
the same year you first asked me questions about ball lightning. On
New Year's Eve, I was mired in hopeless calculations when I heard the
bells ringing out the new year and the joyous cheers of the students.
All of a sudden I realized that my life was practically over, and a sadness I had never known before came over me and I came here. Like so
many times before, I took the notebook out of the raincoat, and as I
carefully turned the pages, I realized a truth."

"What?"

He picked up the notebook and held it before him. "Look at this, and think about the stormy night of your fourteenth birthday. Do you truly believe that all of this is contained within the existing laws of physics?"

I could say nothing in response.

"We're both mortal men. We may have put far more into the search than other people, but we're still mortal. We can only make deductions within the framework defined by elemental theory, and dare not deviate from it, lest we step out into the airless void. But within this framework, we cannot deduce anything."

Listening to him, I felt the same frustration I had on the foggy mountain road on Mount Tai.

He went on: "In you, I saw another young man like myself, and did my utmost to stop you from going down that dangerous path, although I knew it was of no use. You'll still take that path. I've done everything I can." He finished, and sat wearily down on a cardboard box.

I said, "Professor Zhang, you're being a bad judge of your own work. When you're captivated by something, striving after it is enough. That's a kind of success."

"Thank you for your consolation," he said weakly.

"I'm saying it for myself, too. When I get to your age, that's how I'll console myself."

He gestured to the boxes. "Take these, and some discs too. Take a look if you're interested. If you're not, then forget about it. They're all meaningless. . . . And this notebook—take it too. I get scared looking at it."

"Thank you," I said, a little choked up. I pointed at the photo on the wall. "Could I scan a copy of that?"

"Of course. What for?"

"Perhaps to one day let the world know that your wife was the first person to directly measure ball lightning."

He carefully took the photo down from the wall and handed it to me. "Her name is Zheng Min. Peking University physics department, entering class of '63."

The next day, I moved the boxes from Zhang Bin's house to my dormitory, as if it were a storage unit. Then I read the stuff day and night. Like an inexperienced climber, I had attempted a summit I supposed no one else had reached. But looking around me, I saw the tents of the people before me, and their footprints leading onward. By this point, I had read through the three mathematical models Zhang Bin had constructed, each superbly fashioned, one of which was along the same lines as my PhD thesis, but completed more than a decade before. What shamed me even more was that on the final pages of his manuscript, he pointed out the error of the model, something that I, Gao Bo, and all of the committee members had missed. At the close of the other two models, he likewise pointed out errors. Where I had seen incomplete mathematical models, Zhang Bing had, during their construction, discovered errors.

That night, as I was buried in the pile of manuscripts, Gao Bo dropped by. He looked around at the mountain of calculations and shook his head. "I say, are you really thinking of living your whole life like he did?"

I chuckled, and said, "Professor Gao . . ."

He waved me off. "I'm no longer your professor. With luck, we'll end up colleagues."

"So it's even better that I say this. Honestly, Professor Gao, I've never seen you so brilliant. That's not a compliment. Forgive me for being blunt, but I feel that you lack perseverance. Like how recently, in that structural lightning protection system CAD—a wonderful project—

you spent just a minimum of effort to complete it, and after completing the pioneering work, you foisted the rest of the work onto others because you felt it was too much trouble."

"Ah, perseverance. Spending a lifetime on one thing isn't how things are done any longer. In this age, apart from basic science, all other research should be surgical strikes. I've come to further demonstrate to you my lack of perseverance: Do you still remember what I said? If your dissertation was rejected, then I'd resign."

"But I passed."

"And I'm still resigning. You see now that the promise was a trap!"

"Where will you go?"

"The Lightning Institute at the Academy of Atmospheric Sciences has recruited me as director. I'm tired of universities! What about you? Do you have plans for the future? Come with me!"

I said I'd think about it, and two days later I agreed. I had no particular desire to go there, but it was the country's largest institution of lightning research.

Two nights before leaving the university, I was still reading those calculation manuscripts when I heard a knock at the door. Zhang Bin.

"You're leaving?" He looked over my packed bags.

"Yes. The day after tomorrow. I heard you retired."

He nodded. "It came through yesterday. I've reached an age where all I want to do is rest. I've had such a tiring life."

He sat down. I lit him a cigarette, and we stayed quiet a while before he said, "I've come to tell you another thing, something I'm afraid only you will understand. Do you know what the most painful thing in my life is?"

"I know, Professor. Extricating yourself from this fixation is no easy thing. It's been thirty years, after all. But this hasn't been the only thing you've done in that time. Besides, there are probably more than a few people over the past century who have studied ball lightning their entire lives, and none of them have been as fortunate as you."

He smiled and shook his head. "You misunderstand. I've been through far more than you have, and have a deeper understanding of science and human life. I regret nothing about these three decades of research, much less feel any pain about it. And, like you say, I've exhausted my efforts. It's not a block for me."

So what was it, then? I thought about the many years since his wife died.

As if he could read my thoughts, he said, "Zheng Min's death was a blow, but I think you'll understand that for people like us whose mind and body are occupied so completely that the obsession becomes a part of you, anything else in life will always come second."

"Then what could it be?" I asked in confusion.

Again, he shook his head with a smile. "It's difficult to admit." He went on smoking. My thoughts were jumbled. Was he ashamed of something? Then, due to the common pursuit that made our minds think alike, I realized what it was. "I believe you once said that you've spent these thirty years on an unending search for ball lightning in the field."

He let out a long stream of smoke, and said, "That's right. After Zheng Min died, my health declined and my legs got worse, and I didn't get out as much. But I never interrupted my search, and, at least in the surrounding area, I've practically never let any thunderstorm slip by."

"Then . . ." I paused, realizing in that instant all of his pain.

"Yes, you've guessed it. In thirty years, I've never seen ball lightning a second time."

Unlike other mysteries of nature, ball lightning was not particularly rare. Surveys showed that at least one percent of people claimed to have seen it. But its appearance was accidental and random, following no rules, and it was entirely possible to spend thirty years in an arduous search during thunderstorms and never come across it, with only the cruelty of fate to blame.

He continued, "Long ago I read a Russian story that described a wealthy lord of a manor whose sole joy in life was drinking wine. Once, from a mysterious stranger, he bought a bottle, hauled up from an ancient shipwreck, that still contained a few drops of wine. Once he'd drunk that wine he was intoxicated with it, body and soul. The stranger told him that two bottles had been found in the wreck, but the whereabouts of the second bottle was unknown. At first the lord put no thought to this, but later the memory of that wine kept him up day and night, until at last he sold off the manor and all of his property and went off in search of the second bottle. Through untold hardships he wandered the earth, and grew old. Finally he found it, when he was now an old beggar on his deathbed. He drank the bottle, and then passed away happy."

"He was fortunate," I said.

"Zheng Min was fortunate, too, in a sense."

I nodded, and fell deep into thought.

After a while, he said, "So about that pain—can you still maintain your detached attitude?"

I stood up, went to the window, and looked out at the campus in the darkness. "No, Professor. I can't be detached. What you feel is not just pain, but a kind of fear! If you're trying to show me how evil this road of ours can be, this time you've done it."

Yes, he had done it. I could bear a lifetime of exhausted fruitlessness; I could bear abandoning everything in my life, living out my days alone; I could even sacrifice my life if necessary; but I could not stand it if I never had another glimpse of it. My first encounter determined the path for my entire life, and I could not stand not seeing it again. Other people might not understand, but could a sailor stand never seeing the sea again? Or a mountaineer never seeing a snowcap? Or a pilot never seeing the sky?

"Perhaps you can show it to us again."

Staring blankly out the window, I said, "I don't know, Professor Zhang."

"But this is my final wish in life," Zhang Bin said, standing up. "I have to go. Have you scanned that photograph?"

I recovered myself. "Oh, yes. I ought to have returned it to you before, but I broke the frame while taking it out and wanted to buy a new one, and I haven't had time in the past few days."

"That's not necessary. The old one's okay." He took the photo. "The place feels like it's missing something."

I returned to the window and watched my advisor's figure vanish into the darkness, his leg more hobbled than usual, his footsteps more labored.

When Zhang Bin left, I turned off the lights to go to bed, but couldn't fall asleep, so when it happened, I'm certain I remained absolutely clear-headed.

I heard a soft sigh.

I couldn't tell which direction it had come from; it seemed almost to fill the entire dark space of the dorm room. Alert, I lifed my head from the pillow.

I heard another sigh, very quiet, but audible.

It was a school holiday and the dormitory was practically empty. I sat up sharply and scanned the dark room, but all I saw were those boxes, which in the dark resembled a haphazard pile of stones. I flipped the switch, and as the fluorescent bulb was flickering to light, I saw a faint shadow on the boxes, white. It lasted only an instant before it vanished, so I couldn't make out its shape. I can't be certain it wasn't an illusion, but as the shadow vanished I saw it move in the direction of the window leaving a trail behind it, obviously a stream of fleeting images, like an afterimage.

I thought about that strand of my mother's hair.

With the light still on, I went back to bed, but it was even harder to fall asleep. It would be a long night, so I simply got up, opened one of the boxes, and went on reading Zhang Bin's calculations. After I got through a dozen pages, a page caught my eye: half of the derivations on the page had been crossed out with an X written in ink a different color from the original manuscript. In the white space on the page, a simpler formula had been written, obviously in place of the part that had been crossed out. The formula and the X were written in identical ink. What attracted my attention was the formula's handwriting, delicate and graceful, clearly distinct from Zhang Bin's original. I took out the notebook of alternating burnt pages he had given me, carefully opened it, and compared the handwriting to the formula.

It was an unbelievable outcome, but one that I had expected. Zhang Bin was a meticulous man, and each set of calculations was dated. The date on this portion was April 7, 1983, twelve years after his wife's death.

But this was Zheng Min's handwriting.

I looked closely at the simple formula, which applied to boundary conditions for low-dissipative-state plasma, and realized it replaced the cumbersome crossed-out derivations with a plug-in parameter obtained by a Mitsubishi Electric lab in 1985 while researching the use of plasma streams as a rotor replacement in high-efficiency generators. The project ultimately failed, but one of its by-products was a plasma parameter that had subsequently been widely adopted. But that was after 1985.

At once I opened up the as-yet-unopened boxes and skimmed the other notebooks. I discovered five manuscript pages with edits in the same hand, and I would probably find more if I looked more thoroughly. In each of them, Zhang had done his calculations no earlier than the 1980s.

I sat on the edge of the bed for a long time, quiet enough to clearly hear the beating of my heart. My eyes fell on the laptop on the desk. I turned it on, and opened up the scanned photo of Zheng Min saved on the hard drive. I'd scanned it using the highest resolution available, and now I inspected it carefully, trying to hide from the lifelike gaze of the photo's subject. There seemed to be something there, and so I hurriedly started up a photo editor. I had lots of them installed on this machine because I often had to process a large quantity of lightning photographs; the one I fired up this time could automatically convert black-and-white photos to color. In no time the software had completed the conversion, and although the color was somewhat distorted, it gave me what I wanted. People always look younger in black and white. In this photo, taken a year before Zheng Min was killed, the color revealed the truth that had been hidden by the monochrome: the Zheng Min portrayed in the photo was far older than the age she had been when it was taken.

She wore a white lab coat. The left breast pocket contained a flat object. The pocket fabric was thin enough that it revealed the shape and some of the details of the object within. It caught my eye immediately, and so I cropped that part of the image and opened it in another image program to try and extract more detail. I was fairly adept at this, due to my frequent processing of fuzzy lightning photos, and I soon exposed the outline and details of the object.

What I now saw clearly was a 3½-inch diskette.

It was not until the '80s that 5¼-inch disks became widely used in China, and 3½-inch disks were adopted even later than that. It should have been a roll of black punch tape in her pocket.

I ripped out the computer's power cord, but forgot that it was still powered by a battery, so I had to move the mouse with a trembling hand to shut it down. I closed the case immediately after I clicked the button. It felt like Zheng Min's eyes were piercing the closed computer case to look at me, and the silence of the night clutched me in its giant icy hand.

A BOLT FROM THE BLUE

When I informed Gao Bo of my decision to follow him to the Lightning Institute in Beijing, he said, "Before you make your final decision, I need to make one thing clear: I know that your head is filled with ball lightning, and even though our starting points are different, I'm optimistic about the project too. But you ought to be clear that at the beginning, I can't put a ton of the Institute's resources into your project. Do you know why Zhang Bin failed? He buried himself in theory and couldn't dig out! Still, you can't blame him, given the limitations of his situation. If the past two years have given you the impression that I ignore experimentation, you're wrong—I didn't consider experiments for your PhD because they would have had too high a cost and would have been impossible for us to do well. Inaccurate or false results would have dragged down the theory, and in the end neither theory nor experiment would have amounted to anything. I recruited you so you can do ball lightning research—there's no question about that—but you must acquire all the necessary experimental fundamentals before you can start in earnest. The three things we need now are money, money, and more money. You've got to work with me to get money, understand?"

These words showed me a new side of him. I now saw that he was one of those rare people with a nimble academic mind who was also grounded in the real world—perhaps a characteristic of people who came out of MIT. I was thinking along the same lines: establishing a basic experimental facility was essential for studying ball lightning, since artificially generating it would signify success. These facilities ought to include large lightning simulators, complex magnetic field generators, and even more complex sensing and detection systems, which would require a truly frightening budget. I wasn't entirely stuck in my books, and I knew that realizing this dream would have to start with small steps.

On the train, Gao Bo brought up Lin Yun. It had been two years since Mount Tai, but she had never left my mind, although my focus on ball lightning had kept my thoughts of her well under control. The time I spent with her on Mount Tai was the most treasured of my memories, and it often emerged when I was fatigued, soothing me like soft music. Gao Bo had said once that he envied me in this state, enjoying an emotional life with the detachment necessary to avoid getting pulled in.

He said, "She told you about a lightning weapons system. That interests me a lot."

"You want to do defense projects?"

"Why not? There's no way the military has perfected lightning research, so they'll look to us sooner or later. Projects like that have a stable source of funding, and a very promising market."

Since parting, Lin Yun and I had had no contact. She had given me a mobile number, so Gao Bo told me to get in touch as soon as we reached Beijing.

"You've got to figure out the state of the military's lightning weapons research. Remember, don't ask her for details outright. You could ask her to dinner or to a concert or something, and then when you're on good terms . . . ," he said, looking like a wily old spymaster.

In Beijing, I called up Lin Yun even before settling down. When her familiar voice came on the phone, I felt an inexpressible warmth, and I could hear that she felt pleasantly surprised when she heard it was me. I ought to have suggested meeting up at her workplace, as Gao Bo had instructed, but before I could bring myself to ask, she unexpectedly invited me over.

"Come find me at New Concepts. I've got something to discuss with you!" She gave me an address on the outskirts of the city.

"New Concepts?" What sprung to mind was L. G. Alexander's English-language textbook.

"Oh, that's what we call the PLA National Defense University's New Concept Weapons Development Center. I've worked here since graduating."

Gao Bo pushed me to visit Lin Yun before I'd even reported to my new workplace.

Half an hour's drive beyond the Fourth Ring Road, wheat fields had sprung up along the highway. Quite a few military research institutions were clustered in this area, most of them plain buildings behind high perimeter walls with no signs on the gates. But the New Concept Weapons Development Center was an eye-catching, modern-looking twenty-story building that resembled an office for some multinational corporation. Unlike the nearby agencies, it had no guards at the gate, so people could freely go in and out.

I entered through the automatic door into a large, bright lobby and took the elevator up to Lin Yun's office. The place was like a civilian-side administrative agency. Looking into the half-opened doors lining the corridor, I saw a modern modular office layout, with lots of people busy at computers or amid piles of papers. If they hadn't been in uniform, I would have imagined I had walked into a large corporate office building. I saw a few foreigners, two of whom were wearing their own country's uniforms, talking and laughing with Chinese soldiers in an office.

I found Lin Yun in an office labeled "System Review Dept. 2." When she walked over, wearing a major's uniform and a glittering smile on her face, she rocked my heart with a beauty that transcended fashion, although I was aware at once that she was in the military.

"Different from what you imagined?" she asked me, after we exchanged greetings.

"Very. What is it that you do here?"

"What the name suggests."

"What are new-concept weapons?"

"Well, for example, in the Second World War, the Soviet army strapped explosives onto trained dogs and had them slip beneath German tanks. That was a new-concept weapon, and an idea that still counts as a new concept even today. But there are lots of variations, like strapping explosives to dolphins and having them attack submarines, or training a flock of birds to carry small bombs. Here's the latest thing—" She bent over her computer and pulled up an illustrated article that looked like a page from an entomology website. "Attaching tiny sacks of corrosive fluid to cockroaches and other insects so they can destroy the circuits of the enemy's weapons systems."

"Interesting," I said. Looking at the computer screen, I stood close to Lin Yun and caught an elusive fragrance: a scent stripped of all sweetness, a comfortable, slightly bitter scent that reminded me of a grassy meadow under the first sun after a rainstorm. . . .

"And take a look at this: a liquid that, when sprayed on roads, will turn them slippery and impassible. And this: a gas that can kill the engine of a car or tank. This one's not very interesting—a laser that can scan an area like a CRT's electron gun so that everyone in that area is temporarily or permanently blinded. . . ."

I was a little surprised that they seemed to allow outsiders to see anything pulled up from their information system.

"We're producing new concepts. Most of them are useless, and some might even look ridiculous, but one in a hundred, or one in a thousand, may become a reality, and that's what's significant."

"So this is a think tank."

"You could call it that. The job of the department I'm in is to figure out which of these ideas are workable, and to conduct preliminary research. Sometimes this research can advance quite a ways, like the lightning weapon system we're just about to discuss."

That she brought up Gao Bo's topic of interest so quickly was a good sign, but I still wanted to ask her about something I was very curious about: "What are the Western officers doing here?"

"They're visiting scholars. Weapons research is an academic discipline, and it requires communication. A new-concept weapon is very far from practicality. In this field, we need nimble minds, huge quantities of information, and the clash of a range of ideas. Exchanges are beneficial to both sides."

"So that means you also send visiting scholars to the other side?"

"When I came back from Mount Tai two years ago, I went to Europe and North America and spent three months as a visiting scholar at a leading new-concept weapons development institution called the

Weapons Systems Advanced Evaluation Committee. How have you been the past two years? Still chasing ball lightning every day?"

I said, "Of course. What else can I do? But right now my chase is on paper."

"Let me give you a gift," she said, mousing through directories on her computer. "This is an eyewitness account of ball lightning."

Dismissively, I said, "I've seen a thousand of these things."

"But this one's different." As she spoke, a video clip appeared on screen. It appeared to have been shot in a forest clearing with a military helicopter parked in it. In front of it stood two people: Lin Yun, wearing an Army training uniform, and the other, evidently the pilot, wearing a light flight suit. In the background were several air balloons in mid-rise. Lin Yun said, "This is Captain Wang Songlin, an Army Aviation Corps helicopter pilot."

Then I heard her voice in the recording saying, "Tell it again. I'll record it for a friend of mine."

The captain said, "Sure. I said that what I saw that time is without a doubt the thing you're talking about. It was during the Yangtze River flood of 1998. I flew out toward the disaster area for an airdrop. I was at an altitude of seven hundred meters when I carelessly flew into a thundercloud. Totally a no-fly zone, but for a while I couldn't get out. The air currents in the cloud buffeted the aircraft like a leaf, and my head kept bumping against the hatch. Most of the instruments were jittering randomly, and nothing was clear on the radio. It was pitch black outside. Suddenly a bolt of lightning lit up, and then I saw it: about the size of a basketball, giving off orange light, and when the bolt appeared the static on the radio grew even worse . . ."

"Listen carefully to what he says next," Lin Yun told me.

". . . The ball of light floated around the craft, not too fast, first from the nose to the tail, and then vertically up through the rotors, and then back down through the rotors into the cabin again. It floated for about half a minute, and then it suddenly disappeared."

"Wait. Replay that last part!" I shouted. Like Lin Yun had said, this eyewitness account was unusual.

The video rewound, and after it replayed that section, it continued with Lin Yun asking the question I wanted to: "Were you hovering or flying?"

"Could I hover in a thundercloud? Of course I was flying. Speed at least four hundred. I was looking for an exit from the cloud."

"You must have remembered incorrectly. You must have been hovering. It's not right otherwise."

"I know what you're thinking. That's what's so weird about it. The airflow had no effect on it at all! Even if I'm misremembering, or had the wrong impression at the time and I really was hovering, the rotors were still rotating constantly, and that airflow was enormous. Besides, wouldn't there be wind? But the fireball just turned very slowly around the helicopter. Taking relative speeds into account, it was moving very fast, but it wasn't affected at all by the air."

"This is really important information!" I said. "There's evidence of this in lots of previous records, like eyewitness accounts saying that when ball lightning entered a room through a window or door, wind was blowing in, or other accounts that straight-out describe ball lightning as moving against the wind, but none of them are as believable as this. If the motion of ball lightning really isn't affected by air currents, then the plasma theory is untenable. But that's what the majority of current ball lightning theory is based on. Can I talk to the pilot?"

"Impossible." She shook her head. "Well, let's get down to business. First off, I'd like you to take a look at what we've been doing the past two years." She picked up the phone and seemed to be arranging a tour. Evidently Gao Bo's mission would be easily completed. I took a look around Lin Yun's desk.

The first thing I noticed was a group photo of her and several PLA Marines wearing blue-and-white marine camouflage. Lin Yun was the only woman, and she looked quite young, with a childish face and a submachine gun clutched in her arms like a puppy. A sergeant. Several landing craft were on the water behind them, and there was residual smoke from explosions in the vicinity.

"You went from the army to university?" I asked, and she nodded, still on the phone.

Another photo caught my eye, this one of a young navy captain, handsome, charismatic, against the background of the carrier *Zhufeng*, which appeared so often in the media. Immediately I had the fierce desire to ask Lin Yun who he was, but I held back.

She had finished her call by this point, and said, "Let's go. I'll take you to see the non-results we've come up with in two years."

As we left and took the elevator downstairs, she said, "We've put tremendous effort into lightning weapons these two years. Two subprojects, neither successful, and now the project has been canceled. This weapons system went the furthest and had the highest funding out of all of New Concepts, but it ended badly."

In the lobby, I noticed lots of people smiling at Lin Yun and greeting her, and I sensed that her status exceeded that of an ordinary major.

Exiting the building, Lin Yun took me to a small car. As we sat in the front seats, I caught another whiff of that bitter aroma of grass after the rain, so carefree. Yet this time there was a more ethereal aroma, like the last wisp of cloud in a boundless clear sky, or a fleeting chime in a deep mountain valley. I sniffed once or twice to capture it.

"Do you like this perfume?" she said, glancing at me with a smile.

"Oh . . . don't they stop you from wearing perfume in the army?" I played innocent.

"Sometimes it's allowed."

Wearing that charming smile, she started the car. A small ornament hanging from the windshield caught my interest: it was a piece of bamboo. Two segments, finger-thick, with a length of leaves attached. Quite a fascinating shape. What intrigued me was that the segments and leaves had yellowed, and there were several splits in the bamboo from the dry northern air. Evidently it was quite old, but she kept it hanging in such a prominent position that there must be some story in the bamboo. I reached out to take it for a closer look, but she caught my wrist, her slender white hands surprisingly strong, a strength that disappeared once my hand was pressed back down, leaving only a soft warmth that set my heart beating.

"That's a land mine," she said calmly.

I looked at her in surprise, then looked at the seemingly harmless bamboo in disbelief.

"It's an anti-personnel mine. The structure is simple: the lower segment contains the explosive, and the upper section contains the fuse, which is a flexible striker and a length of rubber band. The bamboo deforms when stepped on, and the striker bends down."

"Er . . . where did it come from?"

"It was seized on the front line in Guangxi in the early eighties. It's a classic design that costs as little as a two-bang firecracker, but it's highly destructive, and since it contains little metal, ordinary mine detectors won't notice it. It's a real headache for engineers, since its exterior is subtle enough that it doesn't need to be buried. Just scattering them on the ground is enough. The Vietnamese spread tens of thousands of them."

"It's hard to believe that something so small can kill someone."

"It won't usually kill, but the explosion can easily take off half a foot or a leg, and a wounding weapon like this can sap the enemy's combat strength far more efficiently than lethal weapons."

It gave me a funny feeling that the first woman I felt something for talked so calmly of bloodshed and death like other women her age talked of makeup. But who could say for certain whether this was an indispensable part of what had attracted me to her?

"Can it still explode?" I asked, pointing to the bamboo.

"Probably. But the striker's rubber bands may have decayed after so many years."

"What? You're saying it's . . . it can still . . ."

"That's right. It's still set, and the striker's taut, so don't touch."

"That's . . . far too dangerous!" I said, staring in horror at the bamboo as it swung beneath the window glass.

She calmly looked straight ahead. It was quite some time before she said in a soft voice, "I like the feeling."

Then, perhaps to break the awkward silence, she asked me, "Are you interested in weapons?"

"I was when I was a kid. My eyes would light up when I saw a weapon. Most boys are like that . . . but let's not talk so much about weapons. Do you know what it feels like for a man to seek information about weapons from a woman?"

"Don't you think they have a transcendent beauty?" She pointed at the mine. "What an exquisite piece of art."

"I'll admit that weapons do possess an indescribable allure, but it's built on top of murder. If this bamboo were just bamboo, that beauty would no longer exist."

"Have you ever thought about why such a brutal thing as murder can bring with it such beauty?"

"A profound question indeed. I'm not much for that kind of thinking."

The car turned onto a narrow road. Lin Yun continued: "The beauty of an object can be completely separated from its practical function. Like a stamp: its actual function is irrelevant in a collector's eyes."

"So then, to you, is weapons research motivated by beauty, or by functionality?"

As soon as the words left my mouth I felt the question too impertinent. But again, she smiled in place of an answer. So many things about her were a mystery.

"You're the sort of person whose entire life is occupied by one thing," she said.

"And you're not?"

"Hmm. Yes, I am."

Then we were both silent.

The car stopped just beyond an orchard, where the mountains that had seemed so distant now appeared right in front of us. A fenced-off area at the foot of the mountains contained mostly weed-covered ground, with a small cluster of buildings in one corner comprising a wide-slung warehouse-like structure and three other four-story buildings. Two military helicopters were parked out front. I realized that this was where the video of the ball lightning eyewitness had been shot. This must be the weapons testing grounds. In stark contrast to the New Concept center, it was heavily guarded. Inside one of the buildings we met the man in charge of the base, an air force colonel named Xu Wencheng, who had an honest face. When Lin Yun introduced him, I realized he was one of the country's specialists in lightning research. I had often seen his papers in domestic and international academic journals, so his name was familiar, but I had never met him in the flesh, much less been aware he was a soldier.

The colonel said, "Xiao* Lin, they're leaning on us to close up shop. Can you work the higher-ups a little more?" I noticed that his attitude

---

* An affectionate form of address for someone younger.

toward Lin Yun was not one of a superior to a subordinate, but something more cautious and deferential.

She shook her head. "I can't speak up in our situation. We must have resolve." Nor was her tone one of a subordinate to a superior.

"It's not a matter of resolve. The General Armaments Department is standing firm, but can't last for much longer."

"New Concepts wants to come up with something as fast as possible—some theory, at least. This is Dr. Chen from the Lightning Institute."

As the colonel shook my hand with enthusiasm, he said, "If our two institutions were already cooperating, things might not have gotten to this point. What we're going to show you today would be eye-opening for anyone in lightning research."

Just then, there was a marked increase in the brightness of the lights in the room, as if some piece of high-energy equipment had just stopped. The colonel obviously noticed this too, and said, "Looks like it's charged. Xiao Lin, take Dr. Chen to have a look. I won't go with you, since, as you put it, I've got to have resolve here. You should get in touch with the Lightning Institute in person afterward, to establish a relationship between our two sides. I know former director Xue. He's retired now, but, just like us, he couldn't turn his experimental results into anything practical."

On the way in, I noticed the fully equipped laboratories and engineering shops. That was another clear difference from New Concepts—this was obviously a place for real work.

Lin Yun explained, "Our lightning research is divided into two parts. What we'll be looking at first is part one: an air-to-ground attack system."

When we exited the large building we saw a pilot and another operator walking toward a helicopter, and two other people gathering up the thick cable that had just been detached from it. The cable ran straight into one of the buildings where several soldiers were loading a bunch of old oil drums into a truck. It was clear that there had been nothing for anyone to do for quite some time, so they all looked excited now.

Lin Yun led me to a sandbag bunker behind an open space the size of a soccer field, where the soldiers were now unloading the oil drums and stacking them into a cabin-like shape inside a red square. Engines roared in the distance, and then, through the dust whipped up by its propellers, the helicopter rose up slowly, angled its rotor slightly, and flew toward the space above the drums. It hovered over the target for a few seconds, and then a glittering shaft of lightning emerged from its belly and struck the drums. The practically simultaneous clap of thunder caught me off guard and startled me, and right on the heels of the thunder were several more dull noises, the explosions and fire from the residual oil in the drums. I stared in shock for a while at the black smoke wrapped around dark flames, and then asked, "What are you using for energy to produce the lightning?"

"The National Laboratory for Superconductivity at CAS has developed high-energy batteries made of room-temperature superconducting material. They can store lots of power simply by flowing current continuously through a large loop of superconducting wire."

Then the helicopter began to discharge to the ground, for a longer duration this time, but at a low intensity. A long, thin arc connected ground and helicopter, snaking through the air like a dancer's graceful curves, or a windblown strand of UV-emitting spider silk.

"This is a low-intensity, continuous release of the superconductor battery's residual energy. The battery is highly unstable and not very safe, so ordinarily it can't store a charge. Let's wait a bit—this will take at least ten minutes. It's a nice sound, isn't it?"

The power release wasn't loud, but it sounded like fingernails on glass, and gave me goose bumps.

I asked, "How many times can you repeat that high-intensity release?"

"That depends on the number and capacity of the superconductor batteries. This helicopter could manage eight to ten, but we can't drain the residual power in that way."

"Why not?"

"People would protest." She pointed to the north, where I saw a group of luxury homes not too far from the base. "The base was originally meant to be farther from the city, but for various reasons it was built here. You'll see later on that noise nuisance isn't the only consequence of this mistake."

When the residual power was drained, she took me to look at the equipment on the helicopter. Unfamiliar with electronics and machinery, I didn't understand much, but I was deeply impressed by the cylindrical superconductor batteries.

"So you say this system isn't successful?" I asked, inwardly amazed at what I'd just witnessed.

"First Lieutenant Yang is an attack helicopter pilot with the Thirty-Eighth Army Aviation Regiment. He is most qualified to draw a conclusion."

I thought about the ball lightning eyewitness, but the man in front of me was a little younger. He said, "The first time I saw this, I was really excited for a while. I felt like I couldn't praise it enough, and that it would greatly increase the ground attack capabilities of our armed helicopters. . . . Basically, I was as excited as a World War I pilot seeing one of today's guided missiles! But I soon realized that it's nothing more than a toy."

"Why?"

"First, the attack range. No more than one hundred meters from its target, or it won't release electricity. A grenade can go a hundred meters."

Lin Yun said, "We tried everything, but that's the range limit."

This was easy to understand. The energy in the superconductor battery was far too insufficient to produce natural lightning in an arc several kilometers long, and even if this energy could be generated by other means, like nuclear reactions, no existing weapons platform—be it armed helicopter or destroyer—would be able to withstand such an energy discharge: when shooting lightning, they'd end up destroying themselves first.

The lieutenant said, "There's another thing that's even more ridiculous . . . but I'll let Dr. Lin explain it herself."

Lin Yun said, "You've probably already thought of it."

This time I had. "You're referring to a discharge pole?"

"Yes." She pointed to the red square area with the oil barrels, still burning. "We gave that red area a negative charge of 1.5 coulombs in advance."

I thought for a moment. "Would it be possible to use another means, like radiation, to induce a negative charge in the target area from a distance?"

"That was one thing we considered from the start, and we began R&D on a long-range electrostatic charger concurrently with this discharge device, but the technology was very difficult, particularly under combat conditions, where effectively fighting a moving target requires completing the charging process within roughly one second. Under current technical conditions, that's practically impossible." She sighed. "Like the lieutenant said, we created a toy. We can demonstrate it to scare people a little, but it has no actual combat value."

Then she took me to see the next project. "You'll probably be most interested in this," she said. "We're producing lightning in the atmosphere."

We entered the high, wide-roofed building, which Lin Yun told me was converted from a large warehouse. A row of floodlights on the high domed ceiling illuminated the vast space, where our footsteps echoed, and Lin Yun's voice produced a pleasant echo as well.

"Ordinary lightning produced by thunderclouds is pretty hard to make artificially on a large scale, so there's little military value. Our research objective is to produce dry lightning—that is, lightning discharged by an electric field produced in electrified air, with no involvement of clouds."

"That's what you said at Mount Tai."

Lin Yun showed me two machines installed along a wall, each the size of a truck, that resembled enormous air compressors and consisted largely of high pressure airbags. "These are electrostatic air generators. They take a large volume of air, charge it, and then expel it. The two machines produce positive and negatively charged air."

A thick tube ran from each generator along the wall at ground level, with thin tubes, more than a hundred in all, extending vertically along it at regular distances to two rows of nozzles affixed to the wall, one high and one low. Lin Yun told me that the one set of nozzles sprayed positively charged air, and the other negatively charged air, to form a discharge field.

Then I saw someone hoisting a small model airplane on a pulley high up into the space between the nozzles. Lin Yun said, "That's the strike target. It's the cheapest kind, only able to fly in a straight line."

Turning around, Lin Yun led me into a small room in the corner of the building—a glassed-in iron cage, really—that contained an instrument panel. She said, "The lightning doesn't usually strike over here, but for safety reasons, we built this shielded control room. It's a Faraday cage." She handed me a plastic bag containing a set of earplugs. "It gets very loud. You'll damage your hearing without earplugs."

When she saw I had the earplugs in, she pressed a red button on the console and the two machines roared to life, their nozzles high up on the wall spraying red and blue mist into the room to form a strange sight under the floodlights shining from the dome.

She said, "Charged air is normally colorless. To see more clearly, the charging process adds a large quantity of aerosol particles."

The blue and red air accumulated, forming two even layers over our heads. On the console, a red number ticked, and Lin Yun told me it displayed the strength of the electric field that was now forming. After a few minutes, a piercing buzzer sounded to indicate that the electric field strength had reached the set value. Lin Yun pressed another button and the small plane that had been hoisted up began to fly. When it reached the space between the red and blue layers, there was a flash of lightning bright enough to white out my vision, and I heard a clap of thunder, still startlingly loud even though I was wearing earplugs. When my vision returned, I saw that the plane was in small pieces, like bits of paper scattered on the floor by an unseen hand, and at its final location, yellow smoke was slowly dissipating.

I was stunned as I surveyed the scene, and I asked, "Did that little plane trigger the lightning?"

"Yes. We brought the atmospheric electric field to a critical point, where any foreign object of sufficient size that enters the vicinity will trigger lightning. It's like an airborne minefield."

"Have you conducted outdoor tests?"

"Lots of them. But we can't give you a demonstration, since a considerable investment is required each time the experiment is run. To release charged air outdoors, pipes with high and low nozzles are hung from tethered balloons that vent positively and negatively charged air. When building an atmospheric electric field, dozens of balloons— more than a hundred, sometimes—are lined up to form two lines of nozzles to produce the two charged air layers. Of course, this is only an experimental system. Other methods may be used in actual combat, such as release from aircraft, or from ground-launched rockets."

I thought about this, and said, "But the air outside isn't still. Currents will blow away the charged air layers."

"That is indeed a major problem. Initially, we thought about continuous release upwind to form a dynamically stable atmospheric field over the defensive target."

"And the results of actual tests?"

"Basically successful. And that success is why the accident occurred."

"What happened?"

"Prior to conducting the atmospheric lightning generation tests, we considered all aspects of safety. Only if the wind direction was safe would we conduct the test. If, at any time during the test, the atmospheric field we created exceeded our expected stability threshold, it would be blown far downwind. During the test, there were constant reports of clear-sky lightning in the area downwind of the base, the farthest from around Zhangjiakou. But that lightning didn't cause any damage, since it was the equivalent of a small thunderstorm. In most directions, the wind was safe. Even in the direction of the city we didn't feel there was any particular danger, apart from one: toward Beijing Capital Airport. The atmospheric field is especially dangerous to aircraft, since, unlike thunderclouds, pilots and ground radar are unable to see it. To increase visibility, we added color, like what you just saw in the inside test, but we later discovered that over long distances the colored air separated from the charged air. Unlike the charged air, the colored air containing heavy aerosol ions dissipated quickly, so the color soon disappeared.

"We set up our own meteorology team to recheck wind direction data with the air force and local meteorological bureaus before each test, but even so, there were many sudden, unexpected changes in wind direction. On the twelfth test, the wind suddenly changed direction after the field was established, and the atmospheric electric field began drifting toward the airport. The airport had an emergency shutdown, and we dispatched five helicopters to track the drifting field. It was difficult and dangerous, since after the colored air dissipated, it was only possible to locate it through the changes in interference on the helicopter radios. One helicopter accidentally entered the field and induced lightning, and exploded when it was struck. The captain who was killed was the ball lightning eyewitness you want to see."

The image of that young pilot came up clearly in my mind. For years, whenever I heard that someone died from a lightning strike, I felt an indescribable fear in my heart, and now this fear grew stronger. Looking at the red and blue fog hanging in midair, my scalp crawled.

"Can you get rid of the field?" I asked.

"That's easy," she said as she pressed a green key. Colorless air immediately issued from the nozzles. "The charge is being neutralized." She pointed to the red digits indicating the field strength, which was dropping dramatically.

But my anxiety persisted. I could feel the invisible electric field everywhere, the surrounding space pulled taut like a rubber band, about to snap, and I found it difficult to breathe.

"Let's go outside," I suggested. Once out of doors, I could finally breathe a little easier. "That thing's frightening!" I said.

She didn't notice anything unusual about me, but said, "Frightening? No, it's a failed system. We ignored one important point. Although we repeatedly measured the dependence curve between the volume of charged air and the volume and strength of the electric field, with promising results, the curve could be determined to within a small range indoors. It wasn't at all applicable to outside space, where creating a large, external atmospheric field consistent with combat conditions meant a geometric increase in the amount of air to measure. Main-

taining a sustained atmospheric electric field by continuously releasing charged air requires an enormous system—one that, even setting
aside economic factors, would be an easy target under combat conditions. So you see now that our two experimental systems were failures. Or maybe, they were partially successful in technical areas, but
have no combat value. As for the reasons they failed, I expect you have
a deeper notion."

"Oh . . . what?" I fumbled for an answer, too distracted to follow
what she was saying.

"You must have realized that the two systems failed due to a physical reason, one that underlying technological problems make it very
difficult to solve. We've arrived at a conclusion: there is no hope for
these two systems."

"Hmm . . . perhaps . . . ," I ventured half-heartedly, as I saw replayed
before my eyes scenes of red-and-blue fields, brilliant lightning, plane
fragments, and burning oil drums . . .

"So we needed to devise a completely new lightning weapon system. Surely you can guess what it is."

. . . drifting atmospheric electric fields, the face of the pilot, an
exploding helicopter . . .

"Ball lightning!" she cried.

I was jerked back to my senses to discover that we had crossed the
open space and had reached the door to the experimental base. I stopped
in my tracks and looked at her.

"If you could really generate that kind of artificial lightning, its
potential far, far surpasses these two systems. It strikes targets with
incredibly selective precision, and can be as accurate as a page in a book,
something absolutely unachievable by any other weapon. And, more
importantly, it isn't affected by air movement—"

"Did you see how lightning struck the helicopter piloted by that
captain?" I interrupted her to ask.

She paused, and then shook her head. "No one saw it. The aircraft was blown to pieces, and we only found part of the scattered wreckage."

"Then have you seen how other people have been killed by lightning?"

She shook her head a second time.

"So you've definitely never seen how a person is killed by ball lightning."

She looked at me with concern. "Are you feeling okay?"

"I've seen it," I said, doing my best to suppress my stomach cramps. "I've seen ball lightning kill. It killed my parents. I watched them turn to ash in a split second, and then the two human-shaped columns of ash collapse at a gentle touch of my finger. Back then I didn't even tell the police, and they filed my parents' case under 'missing persons.' For so many years I've kept it hidden in my heart and haven't told a soul. But that night two years ago on the Skyway on Mount Tai, I told it to you. I'd never have thought you would draw this kind of inspiration from it."

She seemed flustered. "Please let me explain. I didn't want to hurt you. I am truly sorry."

"It doesn't matter. When I go back I'll report to my superiors on what I've learned today and your intention to cooperate, but as for myself, I have no interest in lightning weapons."

Lin Yun and I spent the trip back to the city in silence.

"I never thought you'd be one to have a nervous breakdown!"

Back at the Institute, Gao Bo was highly displeased with me. He did not know about my past, and I did not want to tell him.

"But what you've found out is very valuable. I've learned through other channels that the military has indeed terminated lightning weapons research, but the stoppage was only temporary. Judging from the investment those two experimental systems received, the project remains highly regarded. They're looking for a new research direction, and ball lightning really is an excellent idea. But that project requires an even greater investment, so neither we nor the military can ramp up easily in the short term. Still, we can proceed with theoretical preparations first. I can't give you any money for this project right now, but I can give you time and effort, and you can come up with a few mathematical models with various theoretical perspectives and boundary conditions, so that when conditions are right, we can take all of the promising models and test them at the same time. Of course, the first thing to do is to firm up collaboration with the military."

I shook my head. "I don't want to make weapons."

"I never took you for a pacifist."

"I'm not any -ist. It's not complicated. I just don't want to see ball lightning turn anyone else to ashes."

"You'd rather wait for the day when someone else will turn *us* to ashes?"

"I said it wasn't that complicated! Everyone has their own psychological minefield. I don't want to touch mine. That's all."

Gao Bo gave a sly grin. "The nature of ball lightning determines that research must involve weapons. Are you simply going to abandon the chase you swore you'd devote your life to?"

As the realization hit me, I was at a sudden loss for words.

After work, I went back to my dorm and lay on the bed, my mind a blank. There was a knock at the door, and I opened it to find Lin Yun. She was dressed like a college student and looked far younger than she did in uniform.

"I'm really sorry about yesterday," she said. She looked sincere.

"I'm the one who should say sorry," I said awkwardly.

"With the terrible experience you had, it's understandable that you'd feel such revulsion at my idea. But we must make ourselves strong for the cause."

"Lin Yun, I'm not sure we're working for the same cause."

"Don't say that. All of the major scientific advances this century—aerospace, nuclear energy, computers—are the result of scientists and military personnel, two groups on different paths, combining what their different goals had in common. The common point of our goals is very clear: artificial production of ball lightning. It's just that for you that's an endpoint, and for me it's just the beginning. I didn't come to explain my goals to you, since we're unlikely to find common ground. I came to help reduce your disgust at lightning weapons a little."

"You're welcome to try."

"Okay. Your first thought as far as lightning weapons are concerned is killing—what we call 'destroying the enemy's effective strength.' If you think carefully about this, though, you'll realize that even if the production of lightning weapons is entirely successful, they won't be any more capable than conventional weapons. If the target is a large volume of metal, then a Faraday cage effect will be produced, creating a shield and resulting in a partial or complete reduction in damage to those inside. So lightning weapons aren't as cruel to life as they might appear. In fact, they might be the best weapons system for achieving victory at the least cost to enemy lives."

"How do you figure?"

"What targets suffer greatest damage from lightning weapons? Electronics systems. When the electromagnetic pulse induced by lightning exceeds 2.4 gauss, permanent damage will be caused to integrated circuits, and at greater than 0.07 gauss, there will be interference with computers. The transient pulse induced by lightning is pervasive, and even without a direct strike, lightning can deal a devastating blow to particularly sensitive microelectronics. And it strikes targets with incredible precision, making it a weapon capable of destroying all circuits in the enemy's weapons systems without touching any other parts. If those systems are fried, then the battle is over."

I said nothing, mulling over her words.

"Your revulsion has been reduced a little, I imagine. Next, I'll give you a clearer look at your own goal. The study of ball lightning isn't fundamental science. Weapons systems are its only possible application. Apart from weapons research, who's going to fund your project? You can't possibly believe you can create ball lightning with just a pencil and paper."

"But we've still got to rely on pencil and paper right now." I told her Gao Bo's idea.

"That means we'll be working together?" Delighted, she jumped out of her seat.

"I must congratulate your persuasive abilities."

"It's a work necessity. Every day, New Concepts needs to convince people to accept strange-looking ideas. We successfully convinced the General Armaments Department about lightning weapons, but we've let everyone down so far."

"I see why your position is difficult."

"It's not just a difficult position. The lightning weapons project has been halted, leaving us to fend for ourselves. As you and Director Gao say, we've got to make theoretical preparations. Opportunity will surely come! It's too seductive a weapons system. I refuse to believe that they'll simply terminate it. . . . Have you eaten? Let's go. My treat."

We entered a restaurant with low lighting, few people, and a piano playing soft music.

"The military environment suits you," I said after we sat down.

"Perhaps. I grew up in the army."

As I watched her carefully under the dim lights, my attention was drawn to her brooch, the sole piece of jewelry she wore, a sword the length of a matchstick with a tiny pair of wings on the handle. It was exquisitely beautiful, glistening silver in the dimness like a star hanging from her collar.

"Do you think it's pretty?" she asked me as she looked down at the brooch.

I nodded and said it was, feeling slightly awkward that, as with the perfume the day before, she had noticed that I noticed. A fault of the small circles I moved in. I was unaccustomed to being alone with the opposite sex, or to their refined sensitivity. But to find those feminine qualities so concentrated in a woman piloting a land mine–equipped car was breathtaking.

Then I discovered that the elegant brooch and terrifying bamboo were one and the same.

Lin Yun took off the brooch and pinched the handle of the small sword in one hand, while she picked up a fork and spoon from the table with the other. Holding them together vertically, she swept the sword gently past. To my astonishment, the metal spoon and fork handles severed as if they were wax.

"This is a silicone material produced using molecular arrangement technology, with an edge just a few molecules thick. It's the keenest blade in the world."

Gingerly I took the brooch she handed me and inspected it under the light. The blade was practically transparent.

"Isn't it dangerous to wear something like that?"

"I like the feeling. Just like the Inuit like the cold. It's a feeling that can accelerate your thinking, and give birth to inspiration."

"Inuit don't like the cold. They just don't have any alternative. You . . . you're very special."

She nodded. "I get that sense too."

"You like weapons, and danger. So what about war? Do you like that?"

"In the present circumstances, it's not an issue of whether or not we like war." She adroitly evaded my question, and I knew she was nowhere near opening up. Maybe that day would never come.

But we still talked easily, and had lots to talk about. Her mind was as sharp as her little sword, nicking and slicing and giving me chills; her cool rationality was something I'd never seen in other women.

She never revealed her family background, carefully changing the topic when things moved in that direction. All I knew was that her parents were military.

Before we knew it, it was two in the morning. The candelabra on our table was nearly extinguished, and we were the only ones left in the restaurant. The piano player came over to ask what we wanted to hear, in a clear bid to push us out.

I tried to come up with something obscure, so that we might be able to stay a while longer if he couldn't play it. "There's a movement from *Scheherazade* where Sinbad is voyaging. I've forgotten what it's called."

The piano player shook his head and asked us to choose another piece.

Lin Yun told him, "Play *The Four Seasons*." Then she said, "You must like 'Summer,' the season of thunder and lightning."

We continued to talk through the melody of *The Four Seasons,* on subject matter much less serious than before. She said, "I am convinced that you never spoke to the prettiest girl in your class."

"I did." I remembered the night in the library when the pretty girl asked me what I was looking for, but I couldn't remember what her name was.

When the piece was finished, it was at last time for us to leave, but

Lin Yun smiled and told me to wait. "I'll play that piece from *Scheherazade* for you."

She sat down at the piano and the Rimsky-Korsakov that had accompanied me on countless lonely nights wafted over like a breeze on a spring evening. Watching her lithe fingers dance on the keys, I suddenly realized that I'd wanted to hear this piece because this place was like a harbor. A beautiful major was telling me the story of Sinbad's voyages with music, telling me of the ocean with its storms and calms, of princesses, fairies, monsters, and gemstones, and palm trees and sandy beaches under the setting sun.

On the table before me, in the light of the guttering candles, the world's sharpest sword lay quietly.

Again I began to count the angels on the head of a pin, but this time Lin Yun was counting them with me.

In the process of building a mathematical model, I found that while Lin Yun's mathematical abilities were no match for mine, she possessed vast knowledge and was accomplished in a wide range of disciplines, as her field required. She was strong in computers, so she was the one who programmed the models. Her programs had visualizations for the results. If the mathematics were successful, they would display a slow-motion view of ball lightning on the screen with every last detail visible, capable of clearly showing the release of energy upon the lightning's disappearance as its trajectory was tracked on a three-dimensional axis in a second view. Compared to the dry tables and curves of my earlier program, this was much better, and not just because of visuals and aesthetics: When the earlier data was outputted, it required time-consuming detailed analysis before the success of the simulation could be determined, but now this was done automatically by the computer. The software caused a material change in our study of the theory of ball lightning.

An infinite number of mathematical models could be created for ball lightning, just like an essay prompt. You just have to build a mathematically consistent system compatible with physical laws that uses an electromagnetic field to constrain energy into a stable ball, and that satisfies all known characteristics of ball lightning. But doing this wasn't easy. An astronomer once made an interesting observation: "Take stars. If they didn't exist, it'd be very easy to prove that their existence is impossible." That applied to ball lightning, too. Conceptualizing a means by which electromagnetic waves traveling at the speed of light could be confined into such a small ball was maddening.

But with enough patience, and enthusiasm for a hopeless cause, such mathematical models could be constructed. Whether they would withstand experimental tests was another matter altogether. Truth be told, I was almost certain that experiments would not succeed. The models we had built only exhibited a subset of the characteristics of ball lightning. Some unexpressed by one model were easily found in another, but none exhibited all of its known characteristics.

Apart from the aforementioned confined EM waves, one of ball lightning's most mysterious properties was the selectivity of its release of energy. In the computer, the virtual ball lightning produced by the mathematical model was like a bomb that reduced everything around it to ash when it touched an object or released energy of its own accord. Whenever I saw this, my mind pulled up those charred books on an unharmed bookshelf, and the cooked seafood in the likewise unharmed refrigerator, and the burnt tee shirt next to my skin underneath a completely intact jacket, and the cool surfaces of the oranges beside the spot where my incinerated parents had been sitting. . . . But most deeply imprinted upon my memory was the notebook Zhang

Bin had shown me with the alternating burnt pages: the arrogant demonstration of some mysterious force that had mercilessly destroyed my confidence.

Most of my time was spent working at the Lightning Institute, but sometimes I went to New Concepts.

Most of Lin Yun's colleagues and friends were men—soldiers—and even outside of work I seldom saw her with any female friends. Those young officers were members of the swiftly expanding intelligentsia, and all possessed a masculinity that was rare in contemporary society. This gave me a sense of inferiority that became particularly acute when Lin Yun was engrossed in discussions with them of military affairs, which I knew nothing about. And the navy captain in the photo on her desk was the most impressive of them all.

When I met him, Jiang Xingchen was a colonel, which meant that Lin Yun had known him for quite some time. He was in his early thirties and looked even younger than in his photo. It was rare for a colonel to be so young.

"Jiang Xingchen, captain of *Zhufeng*," Lin Yun said by way of introduction. Addressing him without title, and the brief glance they exchanged, confirmed their relationship.

"Dr. Chen. Lin Yun has spoken of you often, and that ball lightning of yours." As he spoke, his eyes were gently fixed on me, and there was a sincerity in them that put me at ease, not at all how I'd imagined an aircraft carrier captain to be.

My first glimpse of him made me understand that competition was meaningless. He didn't posture or put on aggressive displays of power, but strove at all times to conceal his strength, as a sort of kindness, or a fear that his strength would hurt someone like me. He seemed always to be saying, "I'm really very sorry to make you feel inferior before her. It's not intentional. Let's work to change the situation together."

"Your aircraft carrier cost ten yuan from every ordinary taxpayer," I said in an attempt to relax myself, only realizing how clumsy that sounded after it left my mouth.

"That doesn't even account for the carrier's aircraft and its escort cruisers. So every time we leave harbor, it's like we've got a burden on our shoulders," he said seriously, successfully relieving my tension a second time.

I wasn't as dejected as I imagined I'd be after meeting Jiang Xingchen, but felt instead like a weight had been lifted. Lin Yun had become a microcosm of perfection in my mind, a world I could appreciate, a place I could turn to for relaxation when I was fatigued, but one I was careful to avoid getting trapped in. Something separated our hearts, something that was inexpressible but clearly existed. For me, Lin Yun was like the miniature sword she wore around her neck: crystalline beauty that cut dangerously sharp.

After setting up a few mathematical models, I gradually got the hang of it, and the next models I constructed reflected increasing numbers of the known characteristics of ball lightning. At the same time, the models required an increasing number of calculations, and sometimes my desktop would run for days before completing a model. At New Concepts, Lin Yun networked eighteen machines, and she and I broke the models down into eighteen parts that could execute separately on those machines as close to simultaneously as possible and combine their results, greatly increasing efficiency.

When I finally completed a model that exhibited all of ball lightning's known characteristics, the event Lin Yun had feared had already taken place. This time, she didn't immediately start programming the model when she received it, but spent several days conducting estimates of its computational complexity. When she obtained the results, she let out a long sigh.

"We have a problem," she said. "One round of calculations for this model will need to run for five hundred thousand hours on a single computer."

I was shocked. "That's . . . more than fifty years?"

"Yes. From past experience, every model requires several rounds of debugging before it's operational—more in this case, since it's such a complex model. We can only allow ten days to complete a simulation."

I mentally estimated: "We'd need two thousand computers working simultaneously."

Instead, we started a search for a mainframe, but it wasn't easy. Neither Lightning Institute nor New Concepts had one; their biggest machine was an AlphaServer. The military's mainframes were busy and had tight restrictions, and since ours wasn't a registered military project, Lin Yun could not win us their use despite repeated attempts. So we had to place our hopes on civilian-sector mainframes, where Lin Yun and I had no connections at all. We turned to Gao Bo for ideas.

His situation wasn't good. When he took up his position, he had converted all of the institutional departments into business units that were completely reliant on the market. He had conducted competitive rehiring and laid off a huge number of staff. His HR conduct was more impulsive than careful, and combined with his poor understanding of national conditions and human sentiment, his relationships were tense throughout the hierarchy.

His business failures were even worse. The first thing he did in office was to focus the Institute's main strength on new surge arrestors and eliminators vastly different from conventional anti-lightning systems, including semiconductor eliminators, optimized lightning rods, laser lightning attractors, rocket lightning attractors, and water column lightning attractors. However, right around that time, new surge arrestors and eliminators were under discussion at a conference of the Chinese Society for Electrical Engineering's High Voltage Committee, Overvoltage and Insulation Coordination Subcommittee. Minutes from the meeting showed a decision that, as there had been no theoretical or practical demonstration that these nonstandard products had any superior functionality to ordinary anti-lightning devices, and seeing as many R&D problems still remained, nonstandard anti-lightning products therefore could not be adopted in engineering projects. Due to the group's authority and influence, the conference's viewpoint was destined to be adopted by state-designated lightning projects, meaning that any such technology currently under development would be completely shut out of the market, wasting enormous investment. When I went to Gao Bo to talk about the mainframe, he was looking for me, to ask me to put ball lightning research on hold and concentrate my energy on developing a new lightning location system for power supply systems. He also wanted me to complete the design of an anti-lightning project for the Beijing Capital Theater. Hence the mainframe was a no-go. I had to do ball lightning research in my spare time.

Lin Yun and I tried some other leads, but it turned out that in the era of commoditized computers, mainframes were scarce.

"We're pretty fortunate, really," she said. "Our calculations are nothing next to the world's supercomputing projects. I recently saw the data for a US DOE nuclear test simulation, which their current twelve teraFLOPS is far from satisfying. They're setting up a cluster incorporating twelve thousand individual Alpha processors that can achieve speeds on the order of one hundred teraFLOPS. Our calculations rate as conventional compared to that, so we should be able to find a solution."

She acted like a warrior at all times. No matter the difficulty, she pushed forward, minimizing my stress by understating the difficulties involved. It was something I ought to have been doing for her.

I said, "There are similarities between the digital models of ball lightning and nuclear tests. They're both simulating an energy release process, and in some respects, the former is more complicated. So at some point we'll need the kind of computational power they're using. But even right now, I don't see any way out for us."

For the next few days, I concentrated on the lightning location system Gao Bo had passed down to me, and I didn't have any contact with Lin Yun. One day I received a phone call from her, telling me to look at a website. She sounded very excited.

I opened up the website and saw a black outer space background topped by purple radio waves floating over the Earth. The page title was SETI@home, short for "Search for Extraterrestrial Intelligence at home."

I'd heard of it before: a huge experiment that harnessed the idle power of tens of thousands of Internet-connected computers to search for extraterrestrial intelligence. The SETI@home program was a special screen saver that analyzed data from the world's largest radio telescopes to help in the hunt. When you have a fire hose of data coming at your ears and you need to sift through it to find the information you need, a giant supercomputer is a necessity that comes at a huge cost. Scientists with tight budgets found an expedient solution: rather than use one large machine, they shared the workload among many smaller computers. Every day, data received by Arecibo Observatory in Puerto Rico was recorded onto high-density tapes and sent back to the research base in California, where it was divided into chunks of roughly 0.25 megabytes and distributed by the main SETI@home server to different personal computers. All Internet users around the world had to do was visit the website and download and install the screen saver. Then, when they took a break from work, the screen saver would start running, and a computer that appeared to be at rest would join the ranks of those searching for extraterrestrial intelligence, receiving and analyzing chunks of data from SETI@home, automatically returning the results to base when complete, and then fetching another chunk.

I downloaded the screen saver and started it running. It also had a black background, and in the lower half, the signal received by radio telescope was displayed in three-dimensional coordinates, like a bird's-eye view of a megacity composed of countless skyscrapers, a magnificent sight. The upper left displayed a dynamic waveform—the portion of the signal under analysis—as well as a completion percentage, which, after five minutes, displayed just 0.01 percent.

"Wonderful!" I exclaimed, drawing startled looks from my office-mates. At the realization of how those wealthier scientists had, on encountering the same problem as us, come up with such a creative and frugal solution, I felt a sense of embarrassment. I went to New Concepts immediately, where Lin Yun was seated at a computer and, as I had expected, working on a web page.

"I'm almost done, and we've located a server. The key thing is, under what pretense?"

"Modeling ball lightning, of course!"

"Absolutely not! How many people are interested in that? I say we look for aliens, too."

"We can't trick people."

"It's not tricking them. Ball lightning's behavior is difficult to explain using purely physical laws, but most of the problems are easily resolved if you think of it as a life-form."

"That's going a bit woo-woo."

"I've thought about this before. A world composed of atoms and molecules has evolved life, so if the Big Bang theory is correct, then in the long evolutionary history of the universe, the invisible electromagnetic world would have been in existence far longer than the world of atoms

and molecules. Why wouldn't it have evolved an electromagnetic structure akin to life?"

"That settles it. Let's look for aliens!"

"We've got an advantage over SETI. They're looking for aliens
tens of thousands of light-years away, but we're looking in the atmosphere," she said as she showed me the home page, with SETI@home's
background replaced with blue sky, and the title changed to "SML@
home"—"Search for Magnetic Life at home." The screen saver displayed a faint blue fireball that drifted slowly across the screen, dragging a purple tail of light and emitting a deep hum.

The next thing to do was to divide the model we needed to calculate
into two thousand chunks in parallel. That was a lot of work that took
us half a month—the programming was more complicated than
SETI@home's since the chunks had to transmit data to each other.
Then we hooked the chunks up to the screen saver and put it on the
web page. Finally, we put up the web page and hopefully awaited
the results.

Three days later, we realized we'd been a bit too optimistic. The
website had received fewer than fifty hits, and only four people had
downloaded the screen saver. Two comments were left on our guestbook warning us not to engage in pseudoscience.

"There's only one option left," Lin Yun said. "Subterfuge. We'll up-
load our data to the SETI@home servers. It's no hassle to hack them.
Then, all of those computers that have downloaded their screen saver
will do our work, and the program will send the results back to us."

I didn't object. I had discovered how weak moral constraints seemed
when you crave something. But I rationalized: "They've got more than
a hundred thousand computers working for them. We only need two
thousand, and we'll leave when we're done. It won't affect them much."

Lin Yun's conscience didn't need soothing. She hooked up the broad-
band and quickly got to work. She worked so adeptly I had a hard

time imagining how she'd learned that. Two days later, she had successfully put our data and programs onto the SETI@home server (at UC Berkeley, we found out later).

Lin Yun, I was learning, had far fewer moral constraints than I did, in that she dared to act recklessly to achieve her goals.

Just two days later, all of the two thousand screen savers had been downloaded from the SETI@home server, and the calculation results began streaming into our server. For several days, Lin Yun and I sat for hours watching the data build up, imagining in exhilaration the two thousand computers scattered across the globe working for us.

But on the eighth day, I turned on my computer and logged on to the New Concept server to discover that the updates had stopped. The last transmission was a text file, which read:

We are devoting our meager funds to the service of humanity's greatest endeavor, but find ourselves subjected to such a brazen intrusion. You should be ashamed of yourselves!

Norton Parker

Director, SETI@home

I felt a chill in my heart like I'd plunged into an ice pit, and was too disheartened even to call Lin Yun.

She called instead. "I know. But that's not why I called," she said, and added, "Look at the guestbook on our old web page."

I opened up SML@home and saw another message in English in the guestbook:

> I know what you are calculating. BL. Don't waste your life.
> Come and find me!
> 24th Street, Bldg 106, #561
> Nekrasovsky Naukograd, Novosibirsk, Russia

BL. Short for ball lightning.

SIBERIA

"Ah, the sigh of wind in the pines!" Lin Yun said excitedly. My mind wasn't on aesthetics, but on tightening my coat around me. Through the swirling snow and fog, the distant peaks were vague shadows.

The plane from Moscow took four hours to reach Novosibirsk Tolmachevo Airport, adding an additional layer of strangeness atop the one I felt upon landing in Moscow the week before, except with a modicum of comfort at the thought that this place was closer to China.

After receiving the message, we instinctively felt that there had to be something behind it, but I never dreamed I would ever get the chance to go to Siberia. A week before, Lin Yun informed me that she and I would travel to Russia with a technical advisory group. China and Russia, she said, had basically completed negotiations for in-China assembly of Sukhoi Su-30 fighters, and the advisory group was accompanying low-level representatives to Russia to work out the details. I

would be the group's sole lightning expert. Finding this an odd coincidence, I asked her how she'd found this opportunity, and she said mysteriously, "I exercised a certain privilege, one I didn't use when looking
for the mainframe. This time there was no other way."

I didn't know what privilege she was talking about, but I didn't ask
further.

After reaching Moscow, I found I had absolutely nothing to do in
the delegation's activities, nor did Lin Yun. We visited the Sukhoi
Design Bureau and a few military-industrial assembly plants.

One evening in Moscow, Lin Yun asked for leave from the group
leader and went out, only returning to the hotel late at night. I visited
her in her room, where she was sitting woodenly, eyes red and face
stained with tears, which surprised me because I hadn't thought of her
as the type to cry. She said nothing and I asked nothing, but for the
next three days in Moscow she was depressed. This episode informed
me that her life was far more complicated than I imagined.

When the delegation boarded the plane to fly home, we boarded a
different plane headed in basically the same direction, but for a much
closer destination. Novosibirsk wasn't all that much closer to Moscow
than to Beijing.

We found a taxi to Nekrasovsky Naukograd, which the driver told us
was a sixty-kilometer drive. On either side of the snow-covered roadway was an endless swirl of snow and dark forests. Lin Yun could
speak halting Russian and seemed to have struck up a rapport with
the driver. He twisted his neck to peer at me, shivering with cold in
the back seat, and, as if sympathizing with me being left out of the
conversation, suddenly switched into fluent English and carried on
talking to Lin Yun.

The driver told us Noksbek Naukograd was a Science City. ". . . Science Cities were a romantic idea of the 1950s, brimming with the purity
and innocence of that era, and with idealism for creating a new world.

But they weren't, in fact, as successful as you may have heard. Far from metropolitan areas, transportation difficulties limited the radiant effects of science and technology. Insufficient population meant that metropolitan culture was unable to take shape, violating the human inclination toward urbanism, and, in a futile struggle with larger cities, they could only watch as scientists migrated toward more attractive locations."

"You don't sound like a taxi driver," I remarked.

Lin Yun said, "He's a researcher at the Siberian branch of the Russian Academy of Sciences. He is . . . what did you say your specialty was?"

"I'm engaged in studying comprehensive resource planning of undeveloped areas in the far-east economic region, a project of use to no one in an age of quick bucks."

"Were you laid off?"

"Not yet. Today's Sunday. I make more driving this cab on the weekend than I get in salary for the week."

When the car entered the Science City, buildings from the 1950s and '60s swept past on either side of us in the snow, and I'm certain I even saw a statue of Lenin. It was a city with a sense of nostalgia, something you didn't get from ancient cities and their thousand-odd years of history. They were too old, old enough to have no connection to you, old enough that you lost all feeling. But young cities like these made you think about the era that had just passed away, the childhood and youth you spent there, your own antiquity, your own prehistory.

The car stopped at a five-story building in what could have been a residential area, part of a row of identical-looking buildings. Before the driver drove off, he left us with a memorable line through the window:

"This is the cheapest neighborhood in the city, but the people who live here aren't cheap."

We went through the door into a dark interior of a residential building with '50s-era high ceilings and several election stickers for various local political parties stuck to the lobby walls. Farther in, we had to feel our way forward. We used a cigarette lighter to check the door numbers up on the fifth floor. As we skirted the stairwell entrance in search of number 561, my fingers now getting scorched, I heard a man's deep voice shout in English, "Is that you? For BL? Third door on the left."

We pushed open the door and entered a room that gave two contradictory feelings: at first it was very dark, but then the ceiling lights glared. The room was filled with the stench of alcohol. Books were everywhere, and it looked chaotic, but not to the point of being out of control. A computer screen flashed for an instant before going dark, and the large man sitting at it stood up. He had a long beard, a somewhat pale face, and seemed to be in his sixties.

"When you've lived here for so long, it's easy to tell who's coming up the stairs from the sound. The only strangers paying a visit would have to be you two. I knew you'd come." He took stock of us. "So young—like I was at the start of my tragic life. You're Chinese?"

We nodded.

"My father went to China in the fifties as a hydroelectric engineer, to help you build the Sanmenxia Hydropower Station. I heard it only made things worse."*

Lin Yun thought a moment before replying. "It seems you all didn't

---

* Plans for the Sanmenxia Dam, a gravity dam on the Yellow River in Henan Province near the border with Shanxi Province, were drawn up in the mid-1950s with the help of Soviet engineers. Construction lasted from 1957 to 1960, and the reservoir began to silt up immediately afterward, causing flooding on the Wei River that required decades of renovation work to control.

account for the silt in the Yellow River, so the dam caused flooding up-stream. Even now the reservoir can't be filled to design levels."

"Ah, another failure. The memories left to us from that romantic age are nothing but failure. Alexander Gemow," he said by way of introduction. We introduced ourselves in turn. He took stock of us again, this time with a more meaningful look, and then said to himself, "So young. You're still worth saving."

Lin Yun and I glanced at each other in surprise, and then tried to guess the meaning behind his words. Gemow put a liquor bottle and a glass onto the table, and then began rummaging around for something. We took this opportunity to take a look at the room. I noticed a forest of empties flanking his computer, and realized the source of the peculiar paradox I'd felt upon entering: the walls were papered in black, so it was practically a darkroom, but age and water seepage had faded the color, bringing out white lines and blotches on the black walls.

"Found them. No one ever comes here, damn it." He put two large glasses on the table, then filled them with alcohol, a home-brewed vodka, cloudy white. I declared I couldn't drink that much.

"Then let the lady drink for you," he said coldly, draining his glass and refilling it. Lin Yun did not protest, but drained her glass as I clicked my tongue, then reached over and drank half of mine.

"You know why we've come," I said to Gemow.

He said nothing, simply poured more vodka for him and Lin Yun. They took turns drinking wordlessly for ages. I looked at Lin Yun, hoping she'd say something, but she seemed to have caught Gemow's alcoholism. She downed another half glass and then looked him straight in the eyes. Anxious, I nudged my empty glass on the table beside her. She gave me a look, and then jerked her head toward the wall.

Again I turned my attention to the peculiar black wall, and noticed a few blurry images on the black paper. Going in for a closer look, I found that they were ground scenes of buildings and vegetation, apparently at night, and very blurred, largely showing up as silhouettes. But when I looked back at the white stripes and lines, my blood congealed in my veins.

This huge room was densely covered in black-and-white photos of ball lightning, on all the walls, and the ceiling too.

Different-sized photos, but most of them were three-by-fives, and I could scarcely imagine the total number. One by one I looked at them. There were no duplicates.

"Look over there," Gemow said, pointing toward the door. Hanging on the door we came in through was a large photo that looked to be of a sunrise, the sun just peeking over the horizon and a jungle silhouette in the white orb.

"That was taken seventy-five years ago in the Congo. Its diameter," he said, draining his glass, "was 105 meters. When it exploded, it turned two hectares of forest to cinders and boiled away a small lake. The weird thing is that this superball of lightning appeared during daytime."

I took a glass from beside Lin Yun and poured myself a drink, drained it, and let the craziness of it all begin to spiral. She and I did not speak, but sought to calm our shock. I turned my attention to the pile of books on the table and picked up the closest one, but this time I was disappointed. I couldn't read Russian, but from the photo on the frontispiece of the author with a world map birthmark on his head, I knew what it was. Lin Yun took a look at the book and then passed it back.

"*Perestroika*," she said.

Now I knew why, when we'd come in, the pile of books hadn't seemed too messy: they were all impeccably and identically bound. *Perestroika*, all of them.

Gemow said, "I used to have the materials you're looking for, more than would fit in this building, but ten years ago I torched them. Then I bought tons of books as a new way to make a living."

We looked at him in confusion.

He picked up a volume. "Check out the cover. The lettering is gilded, and gold dust can be washed off with acid. You can procure these books wholesale, then return them to the distributing bookstore as unsold merchandise, only you paint in the lettering with fake gilding. Later on you don't even regild them, since they don't notice anyway. There's a lot of money in this. My only complaint about the author is why the hell he didn't pick a longer title, something like *New Thinking on the Establishment of a New Democratic Institution for the Soviet Socialist Union, Its Integration into a New Democratic Society, and the Possibility of Becoming an Intimate Member.* But the money had only just started coming in when the red flag came off the spire, and then there wasn't any gold on the book cover, and finally the book itself went away. These are from the last lot I bought. They sat in the basement for ten years, and now that the price of kerosene is going up, I remembered that they make pretty good fuel for the stove. Ah, when you've got guests, you really ought to fire up a stove . . ." He picked up a book, lit it with a cigarette lighter, and stared at it a while. "The paper's good quality. A decade and it hasn't yellowed. Who knows—maybe it's made from Siberian birchwood." Then he tossed the book into the stove, followed by two more. The fire kicked up, and the countless balls of lightning in the photos danced in the red light, lending a bit of warmth to the chilly room.

Without turning his gaze from the fire, Gemow asked us a few simple questions about our situation, but didn't touch on ball lightning at all. At last he picked up an old rotary telephone. After he'd dialed, he spoke a few words into the receiver, and then stood up and said, "Let's go."

The three of us went downstairs, and then out into the frozen wind and snow. A jeep pulled up in front of us, and Gemow beckoned us inside. The driver was roughly his age, but burly like an old sailor.

Gemow introduced him: "This is Uncle Levalenkov. He's a fur trader. We use him for transportation."

The jeep drove along a roadway with few cars, and before long we had driven out of the city and into a vast snowy plain. We turned onto a bumpy road, and after another hour or so, a warehouse-like building appeared in the snow and fog ahead of us. The vehicle stopped in front of the entrance. The gate rumbled as Levalenkov pushed it open, and we entered. Pungent animal skins were piled high on both sides inside the warehouse, but right in the middle was an open space where a plane was parked. It was an ancient biplane with a tattered fuselage and some tears in the aluminum skin.

Levalenkov spoke a few words in Russian, which Lin Yun translated: "This used to be used for spraying the trees. I bought it when the forest was privatized. The old fella's a little worn on the outside, but it still works well. Let's strip everything out of it."

And so, from the plane's narrow cabin, we carried out bundles of furs—what animal I couldn't say, but they were clearly of high quality. When all the bundles were out, Levalenkov emptied a canister of oil underneath the plane and lit it, while Gemow explained that the cold had caused the engine pipes to freeze, and that they needed to be roasted a bit before starting up. While they were heating, Levalenkov took out a bottle of vodka and the four of us passed it around, taking swigs. After two sips, I had to sit on the floor and couldn't get up, but Lin Yun continued drinking with them, and I had to admire her alcohol tolerance. When the bottle was drained, Levalenkov waved us up, and then, with an agility that belied his years, jumped nimbly into the pilot's seat. He had not appeared so agile before, but the alcohol was evidently like lubricant for this Siberian. The three of us squeezed through the tiny door into the cabin, and Gemow picked up three heavy fur coats and passed two to us: "Put them on. You'll freeze otherwise."

The plane's engine coughed to life, and the propellers began to turn. Slowly the biplane eased out of the warehouse and into the world of wind and snow. Levalenkov jumped out of the pilot's seat, went back to lock the door, and then sat back at the controls to accelerate the plane across the snowfield. But before long, the engine quit, and then all we could hear was the sound of the snow beating against the window glass. Levalenkov cursed, then clambered around and tinkered for ages before he got the plane started again. When it resumed taxiing, I asked him from my seat in the back, "What happens if the engine stops in midair?"

After Lin Yun translated, he shrugged nonchalantly. "We drop."

He added a few more sentences, which Lin Yun translated. "In Siberia, a one hundred percent guarantee isn't necessarily a good thing. Sometimes you fly all the way only to discover it would have been better to have fallen halfway. Dr. Gemow knows this from experience. Isn't that right, Doctor?"

"That's enough, Captain," Gemow said, obviously pricked by the remark.

"You used to be an air force pilot?" Lin Yun asked Levalenkov.

"Of course not. Just the last guard commander at the base."

We felt a sudden heaviness, and out the window the snowy fields fell away as the plane took off. Now, apart from the engine sound, the snow beat even more urgently on the plane. The air currents blew away the snow that had accumulated in the window troughs. Looking outside beneath the plane, we could see through the dense snow and fog the vast forests slowly slipping past, or the occasional iced-over lake, spots of white dotted through the black forests that reminded me of the photos on Gemow's wall. Looking down at Siberia, I felt immensely gratified that ball lightning had brought me to a place I never imagined I would go.

"Siberia, hardship, romance, ideals, sacrifice . . . ," Lin Yun murmured, her head leaning on the glass as she raptly watched the foreign land.

Gemow said, "You're talking about the Siberia of the past and of fiction. Today all that's left is greed and loss. Everywhere on the ground below us is rampant logging and hunting, and black crude from oilfield leaks flows unchecked."

"Chinese," said Levalenkov from the pilot's seat. "Lots of Chinese. They exchange fake alcohol that turns you blind for our furs and timber. They sell down jackets filled with chicken feathers. . . . But friends of Dr. Gemow I'll trust."

We stayed silent. The storm buffeted the plane about like a leaf, and we wrapped tightly in our coats against the torment of the cold.

After around twenty more minutes of flying, the plane started its descent. Below us I could see a large clearing among the trees, where the plane eventually landed. When we disembarked, Gemow said, "Leave the coats. You won't need them." This baffled us, since the door had opened to a blast of threateningly frigid air, and the world of swirling snow outside was even more formidable. Leaving Levalenkov behind to wait for us, Gemow headed straight out from the plane with us following close behind as the wind ripped through our clothes like gauze. The snow was deep, but the sensation under my feet told me that we were walking along rail tracks. Not far ahead of us was a surface entrance to a tunnel, but from here we could tell it had been sealed up by a concrete wall. We entered the short tunnel portion before the cement wall, which got us out of the wind a bit. Gemow pushed away the snow and heaved aside the large rock he uncovered to reveal a dark hole about one meter in diameter.

Gemow said, "This is a spur tunnel I dug around the cement seal. It's over ten meters long." As he spoke he took out three large rechargeable flashlights, passed one to each of us, and, carrying the third, motioned for us to follow him into the hole.

I was right behind him, with Lin Yun taking up the rear, as we practically crawled through the squat tunnel. It was claustrophobic in the cramped space, and my feeling of suffocation grew the farther in I went. Suddenly Gemow stood up, and I followed. In the gleam of the flashlight I saw we were in a broad tunnel that sloped gently downward into the earth, leading to the train tracks I had sensed outside and off into the darkness. I shone the flashlight on the wall, and saw smooth cement studded with metal pegs and bands, evidently once hung with electrical cables. We followed the tunnel downward, and the chill gradually disappeared as the depth increased. Then we caught the odor of damp, and heard dripping water—the temperature was now above the freezing point.

Space suddenly opened up before us. My flashlight beam lost its target, as if the tunnel had come out into the pitch-black night. But looking carefully I could still see the circle illuminated by the flashlight high up on the ceiling, too high and too dim to make anything out. Our footsteps had multiple echoes, so I couldn't be certain how big the place was.

Gemow stopped and lit a cigarette. Then he began: "More than forty years ago, I was a doctoral student in physics at Moscow State University. I still remember clearly the day that thousands of us watched Yuri Gagarin, just returned from space, cross Red Square in an open-top jeep. He waved flowers, and his chest was covered in medals. Overflowing with passion and harboring a desire to accomplish a grand thing in a brand-new world, I voluntarily requested to join the Siberian branch of the Soviet Academy of Sciences that was just then being set up.

"Once I got there, I told my supervisor that I wanted to work on something completely new, something with no foundation whatsoever, regardless of the difficulty. 'Very well,' he said. 'You'll join Project 3141.' Later I found out that the project code had been chosen based on the value of pi. For days after first meeting the person in charge of the project, the academician Nikolai Niernov, I didn't know what it was about. Niernov was a very unusual person, fanatical even given the politics of the time, someone who secretly read Trotsky and was enamored with the idea of global revolution. When I asked him about the nature of Project 3141, this is what he said: 'Comrade Gemow, I know that recent accomplishments in space flight are particularly attractive to you, but what do they matter? From orbit, Gagarin wasn't able to toss so much as a rock down onto the heads of those capitalists in Washington. But our project is different. If we succeed, it will turn all the conventional weapons of the imperialists into toys, and make their air force flight groups as fragile as butterflies, and make their fleets as flimsy as cardboard boxes floating on the water!'

"And then I came here, with the first group of scientists, and it looked like what you just saw outside. It was snowing that day, and this open area had just been cleared out, and there were still stumps on the ground.

"I won't go into detail about what happened later. Even if we had time, I don't think my mind could take it. All you need to know is that right where we're standing was the world's largest ball lightning research center. The study of ball lightning took place here for thirty years, employing, at its height, more than five thousand people. The Soviet Union's greatest physicists and mathematicians were all involved to varying extents.

"To demonstrate just how much was invested into this project, I'll give you one example. Look at this."

Gemow shone his flashlight behind us, and just beside the tunnel we had come out of we saw another massive tunnel entrance.

"That tunnel is twenty miles long, but for secrecy, all shipments to the base were unloaded on the other end and then brought here through the tunnel. This led to large quantities of goods unaccountably disappearing over there. To keep this fact from attracting attention and questions from the outside world, they built a small city there. Only—likewise for secrecy—the city was not inhabited. It was just a useless ghost town.

"To hide the radiation produced during artificial lightning research, the entire base was constructed underground. We're standing in a medium-sized lab. The rest of the base has been sealed up or demolished, and there's no way to get to it now.

"Large experimental equipment was once installed here, like the world's largest lightning simulator, a complex field generator, and a large-scale wind tunnel, to model the environment producing ball lightning on the largest possible scale and from every angle. Take a look at this."

We had arrived at a massive trapezoidal cement platform.

"Can you imagine a platinum electrode several stories high? There used to be one installed on this platform."

He bent down to pick something up and passed it to me. It was heavy, a metal ball. "It looks like it's from a ball mill," I said.

Gemow shook his head. "During testing of the lightning simulator, metal structures at the top of the tunnel were melted by the lightning, and the drips cooled to form these." I examined the ground with a flashlight and found many of the metal balls. "The lightning produced by the massive simulator in the central lab was an order of magnitude more powerful than natural lightning in the wild, enough for NATO's nuclear monitoring system to detect the shock wave. NATO believed that it was from an underground nuclear test, and the Soviet government admitted to that, taking a major hit in nuclear disarmament talks. When the lightning tests were in progress, the mountains shook, and the ozone produced by underground lightning vented above ground, giving the air within a hundred-kilometer radius an unusually fresh scent. While the simulations were ongoing, the electric field generator, microwave emitter, and large-scale wind tunnels were run to simulate lightning under every condition, and then the results were input into a huge computer system for analysis. Parameters for some of the tests far exceeded the most extreme natural conditions: superpowerful lightning was triggered in a complicated maze of electric fields, or amid microwaves capable of boiling away a pond in a brief period of time. . . . Lightning research continued here for three decades."

I looked up at the trapezoidal platform that had once supported a massive electrode, illuminated by the three beams of our flashlights against the backdrop of the depths of the night, like an Aztec altar in the thick jungle, somehow sacred. We pitiful ball lightning chasers had come here like pilgrims to the highest temple, full of fear and awe. Watching the concrete pyramid, I thought about how many people, over the past thirty-odd years, had been sacrificed here.

"And the final outcome?" I asked. At last, the critical question.

Gemow took out another cigarette, lit it, and took a deep drag, but did not speak. The flashlight didn't give me a clear look at his expression, but he reminded me of how Zhang Bin had looked when describing his unspeakable pain as a ball lightning researcher. So I answered for Gemow. "There was never any success, was there?"

But immediately I realized I was wrong, because Gemow laughed. "Young man, you're thinking too simplistically. Holmes said, 'It is a mistake to confound strangeness with mystery. The most commonplace crime is often the most mysterious.' It would have been very weird if there were not a single success in thirty years of research, weird enough to encourage people to continue. The tragedy was the lack of even that weirdness. All we had was a frustrating boredom. We succeeded, over the course of thirty years, in producing ball lightning twenty-seven times."

Lin Yun and I were stunned, and for a moment had nothing to say.

Gemow laughed again. "I can imagine you are feeling two different things right now. Major Lin Yun is no doubt pleased, since all a soldier cares about is the possibility of making a weapon. You, however, are despondent. You're like Scott reaching the South Pole at last, only to see the Norwegian flag that Amundsen left behind. But neither feeling is necessary. Ball lightning remains a mystery. No more is certain than when we first came here more than thirty years ago. Truly, we came out of it with nothing."

"What does that mean?" Lin Yun asked in wonder.

Gemow let out a slow cloud of smoke and stared at its transformations in the beams of light, sunken into memory of the past. "The first successful generation of ball lightning was in 1962, the third year after research began. I personally witnessed it. After a discharge from the lightning simulator it appeared in midair, light yellow in color, dragging a tail behind it as it flew for around twenty seconds before vanishing without a sound."

Lin Yun said, "I can imagine how excited you must have been."

Gemow shook his head. "Wrong again. To us, that ball lightning was just an ordinary electromagnetic phenomenon. Project 3141 was not intended to be so large-scale at first, so at the time, everyone from the senior leaders in the military and the Academy to the scientists and engineers on the project believed that a country that had sent a man into space merely needed to focus its research efforts and artificial ball lightning would only be a matter of time. In fact, three years without any success already came as a surprise to many people. With the appearance of that ball lightning we felt only a sense of relief. No one could have predicted the ensuing twenty-seven years and the ultimate failure that awaited us.

"Our confidence at the time appeared well-grounded: unlike natural lightning, the conditions and parameters for the lightning we generated had all been recorded in detail. I can write them out perfectly even today. The lightning current was twelve thousand amps, voltage eighty million volts, discharge time 119 microseconds. Entirely ordinary lightning. At the time of discharge, airflow was 2.4 meters per second, microwaves at 550 watts of power, and an external magnetic field. . . . And loads of other parameters, from ordinary ones like air temperature and pressure, to the more particular, like ultra-high-speed imaging of the lightning path, and instrument recordings of the strength and shape of the electromagnetic field and radioactive indices. On and on, all of it recorded into reference material I recall as being at least as thick as *War and Peace*, and all of it top secret. It was right at the time of the Cuban Missile Crisis, and I remember Niernov holding up that stack of material and saying, 'It's no big deal if we recall the missiles. We've got something that will send a bigger shock into imperialism!' We all thought that by repeatedly generating lightning according to those parameters, we could make ball lightning in quantity."

"You couldn't?" I asked.

"I said you were thinking too simplistically. Nobody expected what happened next: when the test was repeated using the same set of parameters, nothing happened. Niernov, extremely irritated, continued the experiments throughout the following year in strict accordance with the recorded parameters, producing lightning fifty thousand times, but there was never any trace of ball lightning.

"I should explain that in the Soviet scientific community in those days, mechanistic determinism held sway over all other approaches. Researchers believed that the natural world was governed by the iron law of cause and effect. This mentality was a product of the political environment.

Renegades like Gamow* were still rare. This was the case even in basic science and pure theory. For ball lightning, which was classified as an applied project at the time, people's minds were even more constrained by traditional linear thinking. They were unable to accept the outcome of the tests, believing that if they successfully produced ball lightning once, they should be able to produce it in subsequent tests using the same parameters. And so Niernov arrived at the obvious conclusion about the fifty thousand tests: the data for the ball lightning test had been recorded incorrectly.

"It wasn't a big deal at first. Entirely solvable within the normal scope of work, and the most anyone would be penalized for would be for dereliction of duty. But Niernov made it political. His dictatorial style had made him lots of enemies, and now he was presented with an opportunity to get rid of dissent. In an alarmist report he submitted to the supreme leadership, he said that Project 3141 had been sabotaged by imperialist spies. And since Project 3141 was a key national weapons research program, his report received swift attention, and a large-scale investigation was launched.

"The investigation team was made up largely of GRU† personnel, with Niernov a key member. To explain the ensuing experimental failures, he came up with a theory inspired by *Dr. Jekyll and Mr. Hyde.* The protagonist of that book prepared a drug that could split a person's personality, but when he made a second batch, the drug was ineffective. He assumed that the new ingredients he had bought were impure, but later he found out that the ingredients in his successful batch had been impure, and it was those impurities that made it a success. Niernov believed

---

* George Gamow (1904–1968), theoretical physicist and cosmologist. He defected in 1933 and ended up in the United States.
† "Main Intelligence Directorate," the foreign military intelligence agency under the General Staff of the Soviet Army.

that in every test, the saboteur had caused the system to deviate from the preset parameters, but as luck would have it, one of the deviations ended up producing ball lightning. Of course, there was no record of what the deviation was, since only the preset parameters were recorded.

"The explanation may have been a little unusual, but it was the only one the investigation team was able to accept at the time. The next issue was which parameter experienced a deviation. Tests had been performed using four systems: the lightning simulator, the external magnetic field, the microwave emitter, and aerodynamics, each of which was formed of mostly independent personnel. This made it unlikely that a saboteur would have been able to penetrate several at once, so at first, deviation in only one system was considered. The mostly unanimous thinking at the time was that the key parameter was the discharge value in the lightning simulation system. The person in charge of the design and operation of this system was none other than me.

"This wasn't the prewar Great Purge era, when unsupported speculation could convict a man. However, right at that time, when attending an academic conference in East Germany, my father defected to the West. He was a biologist, and a staunch geneticist, but genetics still rated as treachery in the USSR. At the time, Lysenko's shadow still loomed large over the academic world, and even though it might not be as dangerous as before if you diverged from the mainstream, it at least meant the termination of your own academic career. My father's viewpoint was suppressed and his spirit was mired in a deep depression. I imagine that was the main factor in his defection. For me, the consequences of his action were disastrous. The investigation focused itself on my person. They soon discovered that during an academic visit to Western Europe, I had had an affair with a British woman. Some of the members of my team, out of self-preservation and at Niernov's behest, directed all manner of false accusations at me. Ultimately, I was convicted of espionage and received a twenty-year sentence.

"But Niernov couldn't handle the technology without me, so he advised the higher-ups to have me returned to the base for the sentence period to continue my former work. Back at work, I led a menial life. No personal freedom, and the scope of my activities was confined to the base. I even had to wear a different color uniform than everyone else. Worst of all was the loneliness. Outside of work, no one wanted to have contact with me, apart from one college graduate who had just been placed onto our team who treated me as an equal. She gave me lots of warmth, and later became my wife.

"As a form of escape, I poured myself entirely into research. My hatred for Niernov is difficult to describe in words. Oddly, I basically agreed with his Jekyll and Hyde hypothesis, although I didn't believe it was deliberate sabotage. I truly thought that a deviation in some unknown parameter was the cause of the experiment's success. This frustrated me, because if I did end up discovering the one or several deviations, it would only make it harder for me to prove my innocence. But I gave this no thought, instead working as hard as I could, looking forward to producing ball lightning a second time.

"The subsequent research path was quite clear: The deviation could not be too large without being detected by other instruments or even the naked eye at the time of discharge. Thus tests ought to be run on minor fluctuations around the recorded value for each parameter in succession. Taking into account the possibility of deviations in multiple parameters simultaneously gave a large combination set that required a huge number of tests. The process only increased my certainty that Niernov was framing me, since if he really believed I'd sabotaged the experiment, he naturally would have tried to find a way to get me to reveal which parameters I had altered. But he never even asked. The others, run ragged repeating experiments without a break, hated me. But at the time, everyone, me included, believed that producing ball lightning again was just a matter of time.

"How things developed was another surprise for everyone: after all of the parametric deviations had been tested, there had still been no success, unexpectedly demonstrating my innocence. This was right as Brezhnev was taking office. He struck a far more cultivated image than that pig farmer who preceded him and was much more acceptable to the intelligentsia. My case was retried, and although in the end I was not cleared of guilt, I was nevertheless released and provided with the chance to return to teach at Moscow State University, a highly desirable opportunity for someone working at this remote base. But I stayed. Ball lightning had become part of my life, and I couldn't leave it.

"Now the one in trouble was Niernov. He had to accept responsibility for the failure of the research, and although he didn't get it as bad as I had, his future in academia and politics was over. He struggled on a while in his Jekyll and Hyde hypothesis, only this time with the notion that the deviation had occurred in one of the other three systems. And so he launched a huge number of tests, far more this time than the last. Who knows how long they'd have lasted, if not for an unexpected interruption.

"Base 3141 had the world's largest lightning simulator, and while ball lightning research was being conducted, it was also being used for some other civilian and military research projects. One test of an anti-lightning project unexpectedly produced ball lightning. The parameters this time were far different from those in our first successful test. No overlap. No external factors like magnetic field and microwave radiation in this test. Just pure lightning.

"And so we started another round of that infernal cycle, repeating their test using their parameters more than ten thousand times. But the outcome was the same as the first round: no ball lightning. There was no question of a saboteur altering the parameters this time, and even Niernov had to admit that his Jekyll and Hyde hypothesis was mistaken. He was transferred to a branch facility in Siberia, where he occupied a nonessential administrative role until his retirement.

"By this point, Project 3141 had been running for fifteen years. After Niernov left, the base changed its experimental direction and began conducting tests using different sets of parameters, producing ball lightning nine more times during the following decade. For each success, at least seven thousand duplication attempts were made, and in some cases tens of thousands. Parameters were different each time ball lightning was produced, diverging quite widely in most cases.

"In the mid-eighties, spurred on by America's Star Wars program, the Soviet Union increased its own investment in high technology and new-concept weapons, including the study of ball lightning. The base was dramatically enlarged and tests multiplied, with the aim of discovering through sheer quantity of tests a rule governing the conditions for ball lightning production. In the final five years, ball lightning was produced a total of sixteen times, but as before, we were unable to discover any rule for its production."

Gemow finished his story, led us to the platform, and shone his flashlight on it. "I made this into a memorial. When I'm tormented by memories of the past, I come here and make inscriptions on it."

I looked at the steps. In the flashlight circles I could see lots of lines, like a pack of slithering snakes.

"In three decades of experiments, ball lightning was produced a total of twenty-seven times. These lines sketch the main parameters for those tests. This line is the lightning's current radiation value. This line, the strength of the external magnetic field . . ."

I looked closely at the lines, each made up of twenty-seven points. They looked like segments of white noise, or the painful spasms of some dying creature. There was no order at all.

We followed Gemow to another side of the platform, which was covered in carved text. "These are the people who sacrificed themselves to Project 3141 over the course of three decades, and who lost their lives to the horrible working conditions. This is my wife, who died after long exposure to discharge radiation gave her a peculiar illness marked by skin ulcers. She died in terrible agony. A fair number of these people died of that condition. This is my son. He was killed by the final ball lightning the base produced, one of three people killed by the twenty-seven times ball lightning was produced here. The stuff can penetrate anything. No one can predict where or when it will release its energy. But we didn't think that conducting these experiments was anything dangerous. Since the chances of producing it were so low, people gradually dropped their guard. And that's when ball lightning would appear, causing a disaster. The final time it appeared, everyone at the test site was unharmed, but it passed through solid rock and incinerated my son in the central control room. He was a computer engineer at the base."

Gemow switched off his flashlight and turned back toward the vast darkness in the cavern. He gave a long sigh. "When I entered the control center, it looked as calm as ever. Under the soft glow of the overhead lights, everything seemed clean and bright. All of the computer equipment was quiet and operating normally. Except, in the middle of a white anti-static floor pad, stood the remains of my son, burned almost entirely to ash, as if he was an apparition projected there from some other place. . . . Right then I surrendered. After thirty years of struggling against this natural or supernatural force, I was completely beaten. My life ended at that moment. What came after was just existence."

When we returned to the surface, the snow had stopped. The setting sun was visible over the crest of the forest in the west, painting the snowscape blood red. On heavy feet I trudged back to the plane, feeling that my life was over.

Back at Gemow's place, the three of us drank through the night. The fierce Siberian wind called outside the window as volume after volume of *Perestroika* turned to ash in the stove. Ball lightning, infinite in number, circled me on the walls and ceiling, revolving faster and faster, as if I was caught in the center of a vortex of white balls of light.

Gemow slurred, "Children, find something else to do. There are lots of interesting things in the world, but you only live once. Don't waste it on an illusion."

When I went to sleep later on a pile of books, I dreamed I was back on the night of my fourteenth birthday, in that small room during the thunderstorm, sitting alone before the birthday cake and lit candles. No father, no mother, and no ball lightning. My dreams of them had ended.

The next morning, Gemow took us straight to the airport. Before he left, Lin Yun said, "I know that you've told us lots of things you shouldn't have. But please rest assured: You have our word that we won't divulge any of it—"

Gemow cut her off with a wave of his hand. "No, Major. The reason I invited you was so you would tell it to the world. I want people to know that in that tragic, romantic era a group of Communist Youth League members went deep into the dense Siberian forest to chase a ghost, and for this sacrificed their lives."

We embraced tightly, tears on our faces.

After takeoff, I sat back in my seat and closed my eyes in exhaustion, my mind a total blank. A passenger next to me gave me a poke and asked, "Chinese?" I nodded, and he pointed to the screen in front of my seat, as if it was weird for a Chinese person not to be watching TV. The news was on. The situation between China and its adversaries was getting tense, and the clouds of war were thickening. I was tired, and my numb heart couldn't care for anything, not even war. I turned toward Lin Yun, who was watching the screen intently. I envied her: ball lightning was just one part of one stage of her life, so losing it would not be a mortal blow. Soon I fell asleep, and when I awoke the plane was about to land.

The spring wind in Beijing that evening was heady and warm, and for the time being the global situation cast no shadow. The snow and ice of Siberia already seemed infinitely far off, like a world that only existed in a dream.

On second thought, my life up till then had been a dream that I was now waking up from.

The streetlights on Chang'an Avenue had just turned on. Lin Yun and I looked at each other without speaking. We were from vastly different worlds, following different roads. It was ball lightning that had brought us together, but now that bond no longer existed. Zhang Bin, Zheng Min, Gemow . . . so many people had been dismembered on that altar that adding me would have little significance. The flame of hope in my heart had already extinguished, but I felt cold water pour onto it, leaving nothing but submerged ash. Farewell, my beautiful major.

"Don't give up," she said, looking at me.

"Lin Yun, I'm just an ordinary person."

"So am I. But don't give up."

"Goodbye." I held out my hand. Under the streetlights I saw the glint of tears in her eyes.

Callously I released her soft, warm hand, then turned and walked off with brisk steps. I did not look back.

PART TWO

LIGHTHOUSE INSPIRATION

I strove to adapt to my new life. I started playing online games, going to ball games, and playing basketball, or playing cards late into the night. I returned all my specialist books to the library, and checked out a pile of DVDs. I started playing the stock market, and thought about getting a puppy. I maintained the booze habit I picked up in Siberia, sometimes alone, other times with the growing number of friends of all sorts I was now making. . . . I even thought of finding a girlfriend and starting a family, although I hadn't found a candidate yet. I no longer had to stare blankly at a pile of differential equations until two in the morning, or tend a computer for ten-plus hours at a stretch, waiting for what was certain to be a disappointing outcome. Where time had once been infinitely precious to me, now I couldn't spend it all. For the first time I knew what it meant to relax and take it easy. For the first time I saw that life was full of richness. For the first time I had the realization that everyone I had looked down on and pitied in the past had it better than me. What they were living was the most reasonable of lives.

More than a month passed. I gained weight. My thinning hair began to grow back. And I frequently counted my good fortune that I hadn't come to my senses too late.

But at times, if only for a few seconds, the past returned like a ghost, usually when I awoke during the night. At those moments, I felt like I was sleeping in that distant subterranean cavern, the trapezoidal platform bearing all of those snaking lines towering in the darkness . . . until the swaying silhouettes of the outside trees cast onto the curtains by the streetlights reminded me of where I was, and then I quickly fell asleep again. It was like having a corpse buried deep in your backyard: though you think you're free of it, you always know it's there, and, more importantly, you always know that you know. Later you learn that to be truly free of it, you have to dig it up out of your backyard, carry it to some faraway place, and burn it, but you don't have the mental energy to do that. The deeper it's buried, the harder it is for you to dig up, since you can't dare to imagine what it may have become while underground. . . .

But after more than a month, the frequency of my past self's resurrection decreased dramatically, because I had fallen in love with a college graduate who had just been assigned to our lab, and I could clearly sense that she had feelings for me. On the first morning of the May Labor Day holiday, I dithered in my dorm for a few minutes before making the decision to ask her out. I got up to head over to her second-floor dorm to find her, but then thought that maybe it would be better to call, so I reached for the telephone . . .

My new life could have continued smoothly forward: I would have fallen into the river of love, had a family, children, and the sort of career success that others would envy. In sum, I'd have had an ordinary, happy life like so many other people. Maybe, in my twilight years, sitting on the sand at sunset, some of my deepest memories would surface. I'd think of the town in Yunnan, the thunderstorm on Mount Tai, the lightning weapons base outside of Beijing, and the blizzard of Siberia; I'd think of the woman in uniform and the sword tied at her neck . . . but those would all be so far away, as if they'd happened in a different time.

But just as my hand touched the receiver, the phone rang.

It was Colonel Jiang Xingchen, asking if I had plans for the holiday. I told him I didn't.

"Interested in taking a ship out into the ocean?"

"Of course. Really?"

"Come on over."

After setting down the phone, I was a little shocked. I'd only had brief contact with the ship captain, and after meeting him with Lin Yun that one time, I hadn't heard from him again. So what was behind his invitation? I pulled some things together to catch a plane for Guangzhou. Asking the girl out would have to wait till I got back.

I arrived in Guangzhou that same day. The climate of war was a bit thicker here than farther inland, and air defense slogans and posters were all over the place. For the captain of the Southern Fleet's carrier to have any leisure at a time like this was astonishing. Still, the next day, I boarded a small sloop in Shekou and set out to sea. With us was another naval officer and a naval aviator. Colonel Jiang enthusiastically taught me the ABCs of sailing, how to read a chart, and how to use a sextant. I found sailing a ship immensely tiring work, and after getting a finger pinched in the rigging, I was unable to help in any way. Most of the time I sat alone at the bow looking at the azure sky and green sea, at the sunlight dancing on the surface, at the undulating reflections of the glistening white clouds, feeling the wonder of being alive.

"You spend all your time on the water. Do you really find sailing relaxing?" I asked Jiang Xingchen.

"Of course not. This trip is for you," he said cryptically.

At dusk, we arrived at a small island, only two football fields in size, utterly empty but for an unmanned lighthouse. We were to spend the night there. Just as we were carrying the tents and other supplies in from the sailboat, we saw a strange sight in the distance.

The sea and sky out to the west were linked by an enormous column, white at the bottom but stained dark red by the setting sun at the top. It twisted lazily in the air like a living creature. The sudden emergence of this giant monster in the placid ocean felt like a bewitching python slithering up to a picnic on the lawn, turning a familiar world strange and savage in the blink of an eye.

"Okay, now we've got something to talk about, Dr. Chen. How big do you think it is?" Jiang Xingchen said, pointing in its direction.

"Hard to say. This is the first time I've seen a tornado. Probably . . . F2," I said.

"Are we in danger here?" the pilot asked nervously.

"Judging from its heading, I don't think so," the colonel said evenly.

"But how do we know it won't turn in this direction?"

"Tornadoes usually move in straight lines."

Off in the distance the tornado moved east. At its nearest point to the island, the sky darkened, and we heard a low rumble. I shivered at the sound. Jiang Xingchen remained calm, watching with what almost looked like admiration, until at last it disappeared. Then he turned his eyes away.

"In meteorology, how far has tornado prediction technology gotten?" the colonel asked.

"I don't think it exists. Tornadoes and earthquakes are the most difficult to predict of any natural disaster."

"The South China Sea has turned into a high-frequency tornado zone as the global climate has changed. This is a major threat to us."

"Really? Aircraft carriers are afraid of tornadoes? Of course, I suppose they'd carry off any planes still on deck."

"Dr. Chen, you're being naïve," the naval lieutenant said. "The carrier's structure can usually only withstand an F2 tornado. If anything larger makes contact, the main deck would be ripped apart. That would be utter disaster!"

The ocean water funneled up by the tornado began to rain down in a short, intense storm. The storm dropped fish onto the island, which we ate for dinner.

That night, the colonel and I walked along the beach under clear stars that reminded me of my night on Mount Tai.

"When you left the ball lightning project, Lin Yun was very upset. The project can't go on without you, so I've taken it on myself to convince you to go back. And I've promised Lin Yun I will succeed," he said.

The sea was dark at night, but I could imagine the colonel's smile. It would take incredible confidence to undertake such a mission for a lover, but perhaps somewhere in him was a disdain for me on Lin Yun's part that he wasn't even aware of.

"Colonel Jiang, it's hopeless research." I sighed deeply toward the night and the ocean.

"Lin Yun told me that you were hit hard by that trip to Russia. But you really shouldn't be frightened by their enormous investment and lengthy time frame. I noticed something in Lin Yun's explanation after she got back: by applying rigid arms research mechanisms to the study of a basic phenomenon of the natural world, the Soviets left no room for innovative thinking. They lacked imagination and creativity."

His comment, though brief, was incisive. And categorizing ball lightning research as a basic question showed a measure of foresight.

"Besides, you were once prepared to devote your entire life to the goal of exploring ball lightning. Or that's what Lin Yun told me, anyway. If that's the case, then you shouldn't give up so easily. Take me, for example. My dream was to be a scholar of military strategy, but for various reasons I ended up on this path. Even though I've reached the position I'm in, in my heart, I'm still a little disappointed."

"Let me think it over," I mumbled.

But our subsequent conversation showed me that things were far more complicated than I had imagined.

"As colleagues for so many years, I'd say I know Lin Yun fairly well. Her thinking contains certain . . . elements of danger. I'd like you to help her avoid that danger."

"Do you mean a danger to herself, or to . . . others?" I asked.

"Both. Let me tell you a story. She could not accept the Ottawa Treaty banning land mines, since she felt mines were anti-invasion weapons. A weapon accessible to the poor. The first year of her doctoral program, she and two classmates developed a new type of mine, using their nano-lab to design it. Her goal was to develop a mine undetectable to soldiers using conventional methods, something strictly banned by the treaty. She accomplished it. Her mine appears very simple."

I interrupted: "I've seen the bamboo segment hanging in her car."

He waved a hand dismissively. "No, no. That's just a toy compared to what she created. She invented a liquid mine. It looks like nothing more than a colorless transparent liquid, but it's actually nitroglycerin altered through nanotechnology to remove the material's sensitivity to vibration and increase its sensitivity to pressure, so the depth at which the material can be stored is strictly limited. It is carried in vessels divided into lots of non-interconnected layers, to prevent the lower layers from detonating due to pressure from above. Deployment means simply pouring out this liquid on the ground, where it will detonate when stepped on, to incredibly lethal effect. Totally undetectable by conventional soldiers. She recommended the mine to her superiors and requested that troops be equipped with it, but naturally she came under heavy criticism. She swore that she would make them see the potential of the mine on the battlefield."

"From what I know of her fascination with weapons, new-concept weapons in particular, that's not hard to imagine."

"But you might when you hear what happened next. In the first half of last year, those mines turned up in the war between Chile and Bolivia and caused considerable harm."

I looked at the colonel in surprise as I realized the implications of this information.

"Even harder to believe is the fact that both the Chilean and Bolivian armies were using the mines."

"What?" I stopped in my tracks, my shock turning to fear. "But she's only a major. Did she even have access to those channels?"

"Apparently she didn't tell you much about herself. She doesn't tell much of this to anyone." He looked at me, and while I couldn't see his expression in the dark, I knew it must have been meaningful. "Yes. She had access."

Back at the tent, I couldn't sleep, so I pulled open the flap to look at the lighthouse, hoping that the regular on-off pulsing would have a hypnotic effect. It did, and as my consciousness gradually slipped away, the body of the lighthouse dissolved into the night, until eventually only the on-off blink remained suspended in midair, visible when it was lit, but leaving only infinite night when it was extinguished. I found it somehow familiar, and a small voice sounded in my brain like a bubble floating up from the ocean depths to burst upon the surface. It said: *The lighthouse is always there, but you only see it when it's lit.*

A spark went off in my mind. I bolted upright and sat there for a long while as the surf sounded around me. Then I nudged Jiang Xingchen awake. "Colonel, can we go back right away?"

"What for?"

"To study ball lightning, of course!"

GENERAL LIN FENG

After landing in Beijing, I gave Lin Yun a call. What Jiang Xingchen had told me had made me inexplicably afraid, but when I heard the major's gentle voice, something in my heart melted, and I yearned to see her.

"Oh, I knew Xingchen would do it!" she said with excitement.

"It's mostly because I suddenly had an idea."

"Really? Come over for dinner with my family."

The invitation caught me by surprise, since Lin Yun had always avoided talking about her family. Even Jiang Xingchen hadn't mentioned anything about it.

As I left the airport, I ran into Zhao Yu. He had resigned from the Mount Tai Meteorology Station and had some things he wanted to do. He had lots of ideas, things like installing lightning attractors on large swaths of farmland to harness it, in order to produce fertilizer or repair the polar ozone holes. He even brought up lightning weapons, which Lin Yun had discussed with him on Mount Tai, but he was of the opinion that they were unlikely to work.

"You're done with taking it easy?" I asked.

"With the current state of things, everyone's nervous, and there's not much fun in taking it easy."

Zhao Yu was a smart man, and if he put in the work, he could accomplish many things. Looking at him, I realized that sometimes a philosophy of life might be set in stone, unchanging throughout one's life, but at other times it could be incredibly weak. The direction of a man or woman's life might be determined by the era they found themselves in. It's impossible for someone to distance themselves very far from the times they live in.

Before we parted, Zhao Yu remembered something: "I paid a visit to school recently, and I saw Zhang Bin."

"Oh?"

"As soon as he saw me, he asked about you. He has leukemia. It's incurable. I suspect it's the result of long-term emotional stress."

As I watched him leave, the words of the Siberian called Levalenkov echoed in my mind:

Sometimes you fly all the way only to discover it would have been better to have fallen halfway.

A fear of the unknown future seized hold of me once again.

I was met at the airport not by Lin Yun but a second lieutenant driving a car common to senior officials.

"Dr. Chen, Major Lin sent me to pick you up," he said after saluting. Then he politely asked me to get into the Red Flag. Along the way, he concentrated on driving, saying nothing. We eventually entered a guarded compound that contained a neat row of residential buildings, all 1950s-style buildings with broad eaves—the sort of building that if you were asked to say the first word that came to mind, it would no doubt be "father." We passed several rows of poplars and parked at the base of a small two-story building in the same style.

The second lieutenant opened the car door for me and said, "They're both at home. If you please." Then he saluted, and watched me as I walked up the steps.

Lin Yun came out the door to greet me. She looked a little more haggard than before, evidently tired from recent work. The change felt sudden, and I realized that in the time we had been apart, I had kept a place in my heart for her, where she lived in her former appearance.

Inside, Lin Yun's father was sitting on a sofa, reading a newspaper. When he saw me come in, he stood up and shook my hand. He was thin but strong, and his hand was powerful.

"So you're the academic who's studying lightning? Greetings! Xiao Yun has talked about you often. Her other friends are mostly from the army, but I say that's not a good thing. Soldiers shouldn't limit themselves to a small circle. Otherwise, in times like these, their thinking will calcify." He turned to Lin Yun, and said, "Auntie Zhang's probably swamped. Why don't I whip up a couple of my specialties for Dr. Chen?" Then he said, "It wasn't just Xiao Yun who invited you today. I did as well. We'll talk in a bit."

"Don't use too much hot pepper, Dad," she called after him as he went off.

I watched him until he disappeared. We'd met for less than a minute, and already I sensed in him some ineffable dignity which, combined with his amiable approachability, lent him a very unusual demeanor.

All I knew about Lin Yun's father was that he was in the military, possibly a general. I had caught a sense of his job from scraps of conversation from the people around her, but military ranks weren't my forte and I couldn't make a good guess, so even now it was completely unknown. But her father's easy manner relaxed me. Sitting on the sofa, I smoked the cigarette Lin Yun passed me and surveyed the living room. It was simply furnished, with very little decoration. An entire wall was practically covered by large maps of China and the world. A large desk caught my eye—definitely a working desk—with two telephones, one red and one white, as well as what appeared to be files. The living room was apparently also an office. My eye finally rested upon a clothes rack set up beside the door on which hung a military uniform; from my vantage point I could see one of the epaulets. I took a closer look, and then dropped my cigarette.

There were three stars on the epaulet.

I hastily snatched up the cigarette and put it out in an ashtray, and then set my hands on my knees, like a schoolboy sitting at attention.

Lin Yun laughed when she noticed my posture. "Relax. My dad's got a science background and gets along well with technical people. He never supported lightning research, and now it looks as if he was right. But when I brought up ball lightning, he was pretty interested."

Now a black-and-white photo on the wall caught my attention. It showed a young woman with a strong resemblance to Lin Yun wearing a plain military uniform.

Lin Yun got up and went over to the photo, and said simply, "My mom. She died in the border war in '81. . . . Let's talk about ball lightning instead. I hope you haven't forgotten it entirely."

"What have you been up to?"

"I had a large-scale computer at a Second Artillery Corps lab run the calculations for our final model. Thirty times, including predictions." She shook her head gently, and I knew that the model had failed. "That was the first thing I did when I returned. But to be honest, I only ran it so that your work wasn't a total waste."

"Thank you. Really. But let's not do any more mathematical models. There's no point."

"I've realized that, too. When I got back from our trip, I followed up through other channels and learned that over the past few decades, it wasn't just the Soviet Union—the major Western powers invested immense sums in ball lightning research, too. Can we gain nothing from any of that?"

"None of them, including Gemow, have disclosed even the slightest bit of technical material."

She laughed. "Look at you in your ivory tower."

"I'm too much of a nerd."

"I wouldn't say that. If you really were, you wouldn't have gone AWOL. But that shows that you've already seen what's most important. The trip could have been a new starting point for us, but you turned it into an end point."

"What did I see?"

"Conventional thinking will never be able to unlock the secret of ball lightning. This conclusion is worth billions!"

"That's true. Even if we managed to twist the equations and force them into a mathematical model, intuition tells me that it wouldn't actually describe reality. You can't explain the sheer improbability of the selectivity and penetration of its energy release using conventional theory."

"So we ought to broaden our thinking. Like you said, we're not supermen, but starting now, we need to force ourselves to think in the manner of supermen."

"I've already thought that way," I said excitedly. "Ball lightning isn't produced by lightning. It is a structure that already exists in the natural world."

"You mean . . . lightning only ignites or excites it?" she rejoindered immediately.

"Precisely. Like electric current lighting a lamp. The lamp was always there."

"Great. Let's organize our thoughts a little. . . . My God! This idea would go a ways toward explaining what happened in Siberia!"

"That's right. The twenty-seven occurrences of ball lightning at Base 3141 and the parameters for artificial lightning that produced them were totally unrelated. The structures just happened to be present on twenty-seven occasions, and that's why they were excited."

"Could the structure penetrate below ground . . . ? Well, why not? People have often seen ball lightning coming out of the ground before earthquakes."

We couldn't contain our excitement, and paced the floor. "That means the error in prior research is all too obvious: we shouldn't be trying to *produce* it, we should try to *find* it! Meaning, when we're simulating lightning, the key factor isn't the nature and structure of the lightning itself, much less any external factors such as EM fields or microwaves. It's getting the lightning to cover as large a space as possible."

"Correct!"

"Then what should our next step be?"

From behind us, General Lin called us to eat. A sumptuous feast was laid out on the table in the living room. "Remember, Xiao Yun, we invited Dr. Chen over as a guest. No work talk over dinner," General Lin said, as he refilled my glass.

Lin Yun said, "This isn't work. It's a hobby."

Then we turned toward some more casual topics. I learned that General Lin had been a top student at PLA Military Engineering Institute in Harbin, where he had studied electronics. But he hadn't touched technology work since that time, transferring to pure military affairs and becoming one of the few senior generals in the army with a technical background.

"I suspect Ohm's Law is the sum total of what you remember of your studies," Lin Yun said.

The general laughed. "You underestimate me. But it's computers, not electronics, that most impress me now. The first computer I saw was a Soviet one, I forget the clock speed but it had 4K of memory—magnetic core memory, mind you, held in a box taller than that bookshelf. But the biggest difference from today was in the software. Xiao Yun loves to boast how awesome a programmer she is, but on that machine, she'd find it hard to code a program for '3+2' without breaking a sweat."

"You used assembly in those days?"

"No, just ones and zeroes. The machine had no compiler, so you had to write out your program on paper and then compile it into machine code, instruction by instruction, a string of ones and zeroes. Hand-coding, we called it." As he was talking, the general turned toward the table behind him, picked up a pencil and paper, and wrote out a string of ones and zeroes for me. "See, this sequence of commands takes the contents of two registers and puts them into the accumulator, and then puts the result into another register. Don't be skeptical, Xiao Yun. It's entirely correct. I once used an entire month to code up a program to calculate pi. From then on I could remember the correspondence between instructions and machine code better than the times tables."

I said, "There's essentially no difference between computers back then and today. Ultimately, what's being processed is still a string of ones and zeroes."

"Right. It's interesting. Imagine the eighteenth century, or even earlier—the scientists who were trying to invent computers would no doubt have imagined that the reason they failed was because their thinking wasn't sophisticated enough. But now we know that it was because their thinking wasn't simple enough."

"It's the same with ball lightning," Lin Yun mused. "Dr. Chen's grand idea just now made me realize we failed because we weren't thinking simply enough." Then she told my new idea to her father.

"Very interesting, and very plausible," he said, nodding. "You really should have thought of it before. What's your next step?"

Lin Yun talked through her thought process: "Build a lightning matrix. To obtain results in the shortest possible time, I'd say that it would have to be . . . an area no smaller than twenty square kilometers. We'd install over one thousand lightning generators in that area."

"Right!" I said excitedly. "For the lightning generators, we could use the lightning weapon you were developing!"

"But that leaves the question of money," Lin Yun said, more soberly now. "At three hundred thousand yuan for a superconducting battery, we'd need a thousand of them."

"That's enough to fit out an entire Su-30 squadron," the general said.

"But isn't it worth it if we succeed?"

"Hey, cut it out with all of the ifs and maybes. How many of those did you have at the start of the lightning weapons project? And how did it turn out? I'd like to say a few words about that project. The General Armaments Department insisted on proceeding with it, and I didn't interfere, but let me ask you: Is the role you're playing in this project within the scope of a major's authority?"

Lin Yun said nothing.

"As for ball lightning, you can't mess around anymore. I'll agree to setting up the research project, but there won't be any money."

Lin Yun was livid. "That's the same as not doing anything. What can we do without money? The Western media says you're one of the most technically minded top brass, but it looks like they have you wrong."

"I've got a technically minded daughter, but can she do anything apart from taking money and washing it down the drain? Isn't your lightning weapons lab on the outskirts of Beijing still around? Why not just do it there?"

"These are two separate things, Dad."

"What two things? They're both lightning, so there's got to be overlap. So much experimental equipment. I can't accept that it's completely useless to you."

"But Dad, we've got to build a large-area lightning matrix."

General Lin shook his head with a smile. "If there's an idiotic idea in the world, it's this one. I really don't get how you two PhDs are missing the obvious."

Lin Yun and I exchanged a confused glance.

"Dr. Chen just came back from the ocean, am I correct? Did the fishermen you saw blanket the ocean in nets?"

"You mean . . . make the lightning mobile? Ah! Dr. Chen's idea got me so excited I lost my mind for an instant."

"How do we make it mobile?" I asked, still confused.

"All we need to do is move the lightning weapon's target from the ground to another helicopter. Then we'll have a discharge arc in the air, and if the two helicopters fly at the same speed, we can sweep the arc through a wide area. It'll have the same effect as a lightning matrix, but it will only require one superconductive battery."

"Like a dragnet in the sky," I said, thrilled to no end.

"A skynet!" Lin Yun crowed.

The general said, "But implementing the plan won't be as easy as you're imagining right now. I'm sure I don't have to remind you of the difficulties."

"First off, there's the danger," Lin Yun said. "Lightning is one of the biggest killers in the air, and lightning areas are no-fly zones. We want to have the aircraft bring lightning along with them."

"Yes," the general said somberly. "You're going into combat."

ATTACK BEES

When we finished eating, General Lin said that he wanted to speak with me alone. Giving the two of us a wary look, Lin Yun went upstairs.

The general lit a cigarette, and said, "I'd like to speak with you about my daughter. When Lin Yun was a girl, I was away working on the front lines and didn't spend much time with my family. She was raised by her mother, and had a strong attachment to her."

He got up and went over to his wife's memorial portrait. "In Yunnan, on the front lines, she was a company commander in the signal corps. Equipment was still fairly primitive at the time, and front-line communications required massive amounts of telephone wire. These wires were one of the objectives of the many detachments of Vietnamese troops that were active on both sides of the line. Their tactic was to cut the wires, and plant mines or lay in ambush near the site of the break. One day, battle erupted between two divisions, and then a key telephone wire was cut. When contact was lost with the first three-member inspection team, she personally led four communications soldiers out to check the line. They were ambushed near the line break. It was a bamboo forest in which the enemy had cut out a clearing. When they entered the clearing, the enemy fired from the surrounding forest. The first volley killed three communications soldiers. This was on our side of the front line, so the small Vietnamese detachment didn't dare stay long, and ran off immediately. She and the remaining communications soldier cleared mines as they approached the break-point. Just as the woman soldier reached the break, she saw the end of the wire wrapped around a foot-long bamboo segment. When she picked up the end of the wire to remove it from the bamboo, it exploded, blowing her face off . . . Lin Yun's mother started to join the wires, but heard a buzzing in the distance. Turning to look, she saw that the Vietnamese soldiers had left behind a small cardboard box that was now spewing a cloud of bees in her direction. She was stung several times, then fled into the bamboo with her head wrapped in camo cloth. But the bees were close behind her, and she had to jump into a shallow pond and submerge herself, only surfacing every thirty seconds to take a breath. The bees swirled above her, refusing to disperse, and she grew anxious, since every minute the communication line was down could mean huge losses for the critical state of the front lines. At last she disregarded all concerns, crawled out of the pond, and returned to the site of the break, chased by the bees. By the time she had repaired the line, she had been stung more times than she could count, and she lost consciousness and was found by a patrol squad. Her skin turned black and festered, her facial features swelled beyond recognition, and a week later she died in immense agony. Lin Yun was five years old when she saw her mother's misery in the hospital in Kunming. . . . For an entire year after that, she didn't utter a word, and when she eventually began to talk again, she had lost her former fluency."

General Lin's story shook me. Memories of pain and sacrifice had grown so distant and strange to me, but here they were so raw and immediate.

He continued: "Perhaps that experience would have different effects on different children. For some, it might give rise to a lifelong aversion to war and all things war-related; to others, it might spark attention and even keen interest in it. My daughter, unfortunately, is the second sort."

"Is Lin Yun's fascination with weapons, and new-concept weapons in particular, connected to this?" I asked, as delicately as I could. I couldn't understand why the general was telling me this, and he seemed to sense my confusion.

"As a researcher, you must know that it's entirely normal, in the course of scientific research, to become fascinated with the subject you're studying. But weapons research is special. If a researcher becomes infatuated with weapons, it poses a potential danger. Particularly with a weapon like ball lightning, which would have enormous power if successful. For someone as overly fascinated with weapons as Lin Yun, with her ends-before-means personality, that danger is even more obvious. . . . I don't know whether you catch what I'm getting at."

I nodded. "I understand, General Lin. Colonel Jiang spoke of it as well."

"Oh, really?"

I didn't know whether the general was aware of the liquid mines, and I didn't dare ask. I guessed he didn't know.

"Jiang Xingchen isn't of much use on this front. His work is pretty distinct from hers. And also—" The general swallowed before quoting, significantly: "They're both standing among those peaks."*

---

* A line from the Su Shi poem, "Inscribed on the Wall of Xilin Temple": "One cannot know the true face of Lushan while standing among its peaks."

"So what can I do?"

"Dr. Chen, I'd like to ask you to monitor Lin Yun during ball lightning weapons R&D, and prevent the occurrence of anything unexpected."

I thought about this for a few seconds, and then nodded. "Very well, sir. I'll do my best."

"Thank you." He went over to the desk, wrote down a phone number, and handed it to me. "If there's a problem, then contact me directly. Dr. Chen, it's in your hands. I know my daughter, and I'm genuinely worried."

The general uttered this last sentence with particular gravity.

SKYNET

Lin Yun and I returned to the lightning research base. As we waited at the gate for a few seconds while the guard checked our documents, I was gratified to realize that I had changed significantly since that evening in early spring half a year ago, when Lin Yun had first revealed her idea of using ball lightning as a weapon.

Once again we met Colonel Xu Wencheng, who was in charge of the base. When he learned that the base would not only continue functioning, but would host a new research project, he was overjoyed. But when we told him the details of our project, he was perplexed.

Lin Yun said, "Our first step is to try to use the existing equipment to search for ball lightning, and show the higher-ups its potential as a weapon."

The colonel gave a cryptic smile. "Oh, I imagine the higher-ups are

well aware of its power. Didn't you know that the most critical location in the country was once subject to a ball lightning attack?"

Lin Yun and I looked at each other in surprise, then Lin Yun asked
him where it happened.

"At the Diaoyutai State Guesthouse."*

I had amassed a large collection of eyewitness accounts of ball lightning through the years, the earliest of which dated to the late Ming or
early Qing dynasties, and I thought I had covered the field relatively
well. But I'd never heard of this incident.

"It was August 16, 1982. Ball lightning simultaneously dropped in
two separate locations at the Diaoyutai State Guesthouse, in both
cases rolling down a tree trunk. One was near the reception hall's eastern wall, where a soldier on guard was taken out immediately. He
was standing in front of a two-meter-high guardhouse, approximately
two to three meters from the tree. The instant the ball lightning came
down the tree, he felt that a fireball was approaching him, and then
everything turned black. When he came to, he had lost his hearing,
but was otherwise unharmed. But several holes were blown in the concrete eaves of the guardhouse and its brick-faced walls, its interior
electric lights were burned out, the light switch was broken, and the telephone line snapped. The other occurred in the southeast corner of the
guesthouse compound, roughly one hundred meters from the guardhouse, also down a tree. About two meters away from the tree was a
wooden storage shed surrounded by three enormous pagoda trees. The
lightning rolled down the eastern tree and entered the shed through a
window, putting two holes in the windowpane. It burned the wooden
wall on the east side and the southeast corner, two inner tubes of a

* The Diaoyutai State Guesthouse is a historic hotel located in Beijing that hosts visiting
dignitaries.

bicycle hanging on a wall, and also all of the plastic circuit breakers in the shed. The wire for the shed's electric light was burned in half, too. . . ."

"How do you know so many details?"

"After the incident, I went as part of an expert team to investigate the scene and study prevention methods. Proposals included installing a lightning cage—that is, grounded metal mesh in a building's doors and windows; stopping up all unnecessary holes in the walls; and installing grounded wire mesh across the mouths of all chimneys and exhaust pipes."

"Was any of that helpful?"

Colonel Xu shook his head. "The window the ball lightning passed through was already covered in a fairly fine metal mesh, which broke in eight places. But those conventional measures were all that was available at the time. If the stuff can really be put to use in combat, it will be immensely powerful. I know a little about the state of ball lightning research overseas, and you're probably the first to have this idea. It sounds reasonable, but your next step . . ." He shook his head. "Lightning is one of the most uncontrollable phenomena in nature. Ball lightning even more so. It not only has lightning's destructive power, but possesses the subtlety of a phantom. No one knows when its fearsome energy will be discharged, or into what. Controlling it will be no small task."

"We can only take it a step at a time," Lin Yun said.

"Indeed. If you're really able to find ball lightning, it will be a great success for science. And a bit of success for our base as well. But I'm worried about safety. I've got an idea: Can't we put the lightning generator into a car, and have cars drive the electric arc along level ground? The arc would still be able to sweep a large space."

Lin Yun shook her head. "We've thought of that. And we've thought of using ships to drag an electric arc over the ocean. But it won't work."

Colonel Xu thought for a moment, and then nodded. "Right. The earth and the ocean surface are both conductors, so the induction effect won't permit a long arc."

"We also considered using fixed-wing aircraft, which would make parachuting out in the event of an accident somewhat easier compared to a helicopter, but that won't work either, since air currents at that speed would blow out the arc. We'll try to adopt as many precautions as possible prior to the actual experiments, like training the pilots to parachute from helicopters under abnormal flying conditions. In addition, naval aviation is introducing an ejection device for helicopters, similar to the kind in fighters, except along the horizontal. We've already requisitioned a few from the General Armaments Department."

Colonel Xu shook his head. "These measures won't have a significant effect. We're taking a big risk."

Lin Yun said, "That is true. But judging from the present situation, with the whole army in second-degree combat readiness, safety isn't our top priority."

Her words may have surprised me, but Colonel Xu tacitly accepted her opinion. He seemed like a nice guy, and couldn't really do anything about Lin Yun and me. On the other hand, with the current state of things, it was time for soldiers to take risks.

The base currently had two domestic-made WZ-9 helicopters. Before the tests formally began, their pilots, two lieutenants, conducted a weeklong parachute training, one of them at the controls doing stunt flying that mimicked plummeting as the other jumped out the rear hatch. They also tried out the ejector, a small rocket affixed across the back of the pilot seat; when triggered, the helicopter would emit a puff of smoke as if it had been hit, and then the pilot would be thrown out of the hatch like a stone for a considerable distance until his parachute opened. It was thrilling to watch.

Once, during a break, a pilot asked Lin Yun, "Major, are we likely to be hit by something? If it's like what happened to Captain Wang, then practicing this is useless, I'm afraid."

"The lightning will be far weaker this time. If the aircraft is unexpectedly hit, it won't cause that extent of damage. The actual test will take place at five thousand meters, so you'll have plenty of time to jump."

The other pilot said, "I've heard that I'm going to be shooting lightning at another helicopter."

"That's right, but the strength is only as high as what you use to drain the residual battery charge."

The lieutenant broke out laughing. "So you want to use this weapon in air combat? A weapon only capable of firing one hundred meters? In air combat?"

"Of course not. Your two aircraft will pull that electric arc through the air like a dragnet to catch—or, rather, excite—a structure that might be present there. If it's discovered, the object might be a powerful deterrent weapon."

"Major, this is all getting really weird. To tell you the truth, I don't have any confidence in you people anymore. I just hope that I can finish this quickly and return to my unit."

When the lieutenant mentioned Captain Wang Songlin, who had been struck by lightning from an artificially charged cloud, my heart tightened. I imagined what I'd be like if I had to face such a danger in flight—no question I'd be consumed with terror. On the other hand, if I were Lin Yun, I'd still be unable to speak frankly about it to the two pilots. But their young faces before me looked unperturbed, as if they were only taking a car on a trip to the suburbs.

Later, we came up with many more ways of increasing the safety of the experiment. The one that seemed the most feasible was hanging the lightning generator from a cable attached to the bottom of the helicopter; if it was long enough, it would completely resolve the safety issue. We cursed ourselves for not coming up with such a simple scheme earlier. Then tests showed it wouldn't work, as the swaying of the suspended generator was severe enough to make precise targeting impossible, and we ultimately had to return to our original, risky plan.

But before that, I grew curious about the principles behind the lightning generator. Even though it had a range of just a hundred meters, using the generator's small electrode to discharge over such a distance was practically impossible, and maintaining an arc harder still. Because of the secrecy involved, it wasn't appropriate to ask too many questions, but when I first saw the outside of the system, I discovered a peculiar piece of equipment. It was a short, thick tube set very close to the electrode. One end pointed in the direction of discharge, and the other was inserted into a large-volume device which—judging from the cylindrical shell and the high-voltage wires that wrapped it—appeared to be a small particle accelerator. I decided that it must be connected in some way to the secret of long-distance discharge. Later I found out it was a beam emitter that fired a stream of charged particles at the target prior to electric discharge. The particles ionized the air to form a discharge path that guided the arc to the target.

The weather was good the day of the first test. There was practically no wind at ground level in the early morning. Everyone involved in the project was at the test site. We were few in number: just twenty-odd engineers, staff, and ground crew. An ambulance was parked not far from the helicopter pad, the medics in their snow-white uniforms conspicuous in the dawn light. I had an odd feeling, and got a vague sense of fear from the two empty stretchers sitting on the grass. But the men who might be carried on those stretchers before long were standing beside them joking easily with the two pretty nurses they'd just met. My sense of inferiority came welling up again. The stormy night that had decided the course of my life had given me a far deeper fear of death than most people.

Lin Yun came over with two yellow jumpsuits for the pilots to put on. "These shielded uniforms are from the municipal power bureau, where they're worn by workmen doing jobs on live high-tension wires. They're shielded using the principle of the Faraday cage and will offer some protection against lightning."

One pilot laughed as he took the shielded uniform and said to Lin Yun, "Don't worry, Major. Your little electric arc won't be any worse than a Stinger missile."

Lin Yun described the test procedure for them: "First, ascend to five thousand meters, and then bring the two craft as close together as is safe. When you're at that distance, ignite the arc, then gradually separate the two craft and hover just under the arc's maximum range. Then fly forward at the speed given by the ground commander. Pay attention to arc stability and hover if you need to—you've done that before. One more thing to watch out for: if the arc goes out, then disengage as fast as possible and turn off the generator. Don't try to reestablish the arc, since if it's ignited at long range, it may strike the aircraft! Make sure you remember that. Don't die a martyr."

According to the plan, the helicopters would fly with the wind to minimize the relative airspeed. Then they would ignite the arc and fly for a while until it went out, at which point they would come back and repeat the process.

The test helicopters quickly ascended to the predetermined altitude. At this point we had to use binoculars to see them. They flew with the wind and drew closer to each other until it looked from the ground like their rotors were practically touching. Then a bright electric arc appeared between the two craft, projecting a dim yet crisp popping sound down to earth. The helicopters slowly separated, and the arc stretched out, its initial straight line becoming more turbulent as the distance increased. At maximum separation, it seemed like a piece of light gauze dancing on the wind, liable to slip its bindings and fly off into the sky. The sun was still below the horizon, and the bright blue-purple electric arc looked unreal against the dark blue of the sky between the helicopters' black silhouettes, like the projection of scratched film on a cinema screen.

I had a sudden chill, my stomach tightened, and I began shivering uncontrollably. I set down the binoculars. With the naked eye, all I could see was a blue dot high in the sky, like a nearby star.

When I picked them up again, the helicopters were flying forward at maximum separation, taking with them that dancing, hundred-meter electric arc. Their speed was so low that it was only by comparing them to the thin high clouds, lit by the sun below the horizon, that you could tell they were moving. As they flew east, their sunlit bodies turned into two orange dots, and the arc dimmed slightly.

I exhaled, but then heard shouts from the binocular watchers beside me. I grabbed up my own pair to catch the scene: on the receptor side, the arc had forked. Its main branch still contacted the electrode, but a smaller branch moved erratically along the helicopter's tail like it was a thin hand searching for something. It lasted only three or four seconds, and then the arc went out altogether.

The situation didn't look scary and seemed unlikely to have any disastrous consequence on the helicopter. But I was wrong. The instant the arc vanished, I saw a bright light in the tail rotor. It vanished immediately, but then smoke appeared at that spot, and shortly after, the helicopter began to rotate, faster and faster. Later I learned that the lightning had struck a control line for the tail rotor, causing it to stop. Since that rotor was used to balance the rotational torque generated by the main rotor, once it lost power, the helicopter began to rotate in the opposite direction from the main rotor. Through the binoculars I saw the rotation accelerate and the helicopter gradually lose lift, then start a shaky fall.

"Bail!" Colonel Xu shouted into the radio.

But just seconds later, it looked like the pilot had restarted the tail rotor. The rotation of the fuselage slowed, as did the speed of descent, until it once again hovered in the air—but only for a split second. Then, like a clockwork toy, it started to turn again and plummet.

"Bail!" Colonel Xu shouted again.

After a short fall, the helicopter again stopped rotating and slowed to a hover. The next instant it began falling again . . . and the cycle repeated. Now it was below the safe altitude for parachuting. We could only pray that it reached the ground when it was near a hover state.

When it landed off to the east, its speed had slowed significantly, but it was still far faster than a normal landing. I looked fearfully in that direction and waited numbly. Luckily, no smoke came from that stand of trees.

When we drove up to the crash spot, the other test helicopter had already landed nearby. The site was in an orchard. The helicopter was tilted, crushing a few fruit trees beneath it, and the tops of several other stocky trees around it had been severed by the blades. The cabin glass had shattered, but apart from that, the fuselage did not appear to be seriously damaged. The lieutenant was leaning against a tree pressing a bleeding arm, impatiently trying to push off the nurse and stretcher carrier, but when he saw Lin Yun he used his unharmed hand to give her a thumbs-up.

"Major, your lightning weapon took out a plane!"

"Why didn't you bail out?" Colonel Xu, who had just arrived, asked in exasperation.

"Colonel, we army aviators have our own rules for when to bail out."

In the car back to the base, I couldn't hold back one nagging question, and said to Lin Yun, "You were the designated ground commander for this test. But it was Colonel Xu who gave the order to parachute."

"It was very possible that Lieutenant Liu would be able to rescue the helicopter," Lin Yun said evenly.

"There was only a fifty percent likelihood of that. What if he couldn't save it?"

"Then the experiment would be suspended for quite some time, and the project might even be canceled."

My stomach turned another somersault. "If you were commanding an attack and there was a minefield in your path, you'd order the soldiers to push through, right?"

"Under the new military regulations, female officers may not serve as front-line battlefield commanders." As usual, she lightly deflected my question. She added—as if by way of apology for perhaps being too curt—"The military has its own form of conduct, somewhat different from yours."

"The colonel isn't military?"

"Of course he is," she said lightly, a faint contempt noticeable in her tone. She held the same contempt for everyone in the base leadership.

That afternoon, the helicopter underwent emergency repairs at the crash site and then flew back to base.

"Until there are effective measures to guarantee safety, the experiment must stop!" Colonel Xu said resolutely at the base meeting that night.

"Let's take it up a few more times. Maybe we'll find a pattern for the arc fluctuations. Then we'd be able to find a flying method that avoids having it strike the fuselage," the pilot who had been injured said, waving a bandaged arm. From his movements and expression, it was evident that his wounded hand hurt, but to show that he could still work the helicopter controls, he didn't have it in a sling and was deliberately making large movements.

"We can't afford to have another accident. There needs to be a reliable guarantee of safety," Lin Yun said.

The other aviator said, "I'd like to ask you all to get one thing straight: We're not taking risks for this project of yours. We're doing it for ourselves. Army aviation needs new weapons now more than ever."

Lin Yun said, "Lieutenant, you misunderstand why we halted the experiment. We did so out of concern for the project. If we have another catastrophic crash like Lieutenant Wang Songlin's, the project is over."

Colonel Xu said, "Let's all use our brains. We've got to come up with workable safety measures."

An engineer said, "Can we consider using remote-controlled aircraft to conduct the experiment?"

An aviator said, "The only craft capable of hovering and low-speed flight that has sufficient carrying capacity is a helium airship developed by Beihang University,* but it's unclear whether it could be controlled precisely enough to guarantee discharge accuracy."

Lin Yun said, "And even if it could, it would only eliminate the risk of loss of life. It doesn't help the experiment itself, since it would still be susceptible to a lightning strike."

I had a sudden thought. "My master's advisor developed an anti-lightning paint for use on high-tension wires, but I've only heard people talk about it, so I'm not too familiar with the details."

"Your advisor was Zhang Bin?" Colonel Xu asked.

I nodded. "Do you know him?"

"I was one of his students. He was just a lecturer back then, and hadn't transferred to your university." Colonel Xu turned melancholy

---

* This elite university was known as Beijing University of Aeronautics and Astronautics until 2002.

for a moment. "I called him up a few days ago. I've wanted to see him but I haven't been able to find the time. I'm afraid he doesn't have much time left. You know of his illness?"

I nodded again.

"He was rigorous in his studies, and he worked diligently his entire life. . . ."

"Let's get back to the paint!" Lin Yun said impatiently.

"I know of that invention. I was on the appraisal committee. It was remarkably effective in protecting against lightning," Colonel Xu said.

"The key thing is whether it needs to be grounded in order to work. If it does, then there's not much point," Lin Yun said. I had always admired her technical mind. The majority of anti-lightning paints needed to be grounded, but the question was not one a non-specialist was likely to ask.

Colonel Xu scratched his head. "Hmm . . . it's been so long that I can't remember. You'll have to ask the inventor for the details."

Lin Yun snatched up the phone and passed it to me. "Give him a call at once and ask him. If it'll work, then have him come to Beijing. We'll need to manufacture a batch of it immediately."

"He's a cancer patient," I said, looking at her awkwardly.

Colonel Xu said, "It's not a problem just to ask."

I took the receiver from Lin Yun's hand. "I don't know if he's at home or at the hospital . . . ," I said, flipping open my address book. His home number was on the first page. I dialed, and then a weak voice sounded on the receiver. "Who is it?"

When I gave him my name, the distant voice instantly became stronger and more excited. "Oh, hello! Where are you? What are you up to?"

"Professor Zhang, I'm working on a national defense project. How's your health?"

"You mean you've made progress?" he asked, ignoring my question.

"It's hard to say on the phone. How's your health?"

"Diminishing by the day. Zhao Yu visited. He may have mentioned it to you."

"Yes. How is your treatment going?" As I spoke, Lin Yun whispered urgently, "Ask him . . . ," but I covered the mouthpiece and snapped, "Get away."

When I returned the receiver to my ear, I heard Zhang Bin say, ". . . I've pulled together another set of research materials and I'm getting ready to send them to you."

"Professor Zhang, I'd like to ask you about something else. It's about the high-tension wire anti-lightning paint you developed."

"Oh. That stuff had no economic value and was shelved long ago. What do you want to know?"

"Does it need to be grounded?"

"No. It doesn't need grounding. Its shielding effect is self-contained."

"We want to use it on aircraft."

"I'm afraid that won't work. The paint produces a fairly thick coating, and definitely won't meet the aerodynamic indicators required for an aircraft surface. Also, the skin of the plane is of an entirely different material from high-tension wires. It might erode the skin it's painted on in the long term."

"None of that matters. I just want to know whether it would have an anti-lightning effect on planes."

"Definitely. Paint it thick enough, and the plane could fly straight through a thunderhead. The paint's been tested for that before, just not on planes. The academy's atmospherics lab once had a project to use sonar balloons to probe the structure of storm clouds. But on several occasions, the balloons and the instrument module suspended from them were destroyed by lightning strikes shortly after entering the clouds. So they looked me up, we put a layer of paint on the instrument module and the balloon, and they ended up entering clouds several dozen times without incident. That might possibly be the sole practical application of the paint."

"Excellent! Is any of the finished paint still around?"

"Sure. It's in the storage room of the atmospheric electricity lab. It should still be usable. There's probably enough to paint a small airplane. The administrator has tried to get rid of those sealed barrels on a number of occasions, since they take up space, but I wouldn't allow it. If they're useful to you, then take them. I've also got a complete set of materials, so it won't be a problem to fabricate more. I've got a question . . . though if it's inconvenient, then of course you don't have to answer: Is this connected to ball lightning research?"

"It is."

"So you've really made progress?"

"Professor Zhang, it's not just me now. Lots of people are involved in it. As for progress, we just might make some."

"Great. I'll come over at once. You'll need me, at least as far as the paint is concerned."

Before I had a chance to speak, Lin Yun covered the mouthpiece. She had heard what Zhang Bin said and was evidently afraid I wouldn't let him come. She whispered, "He can be admitted to 301 Military Hospital once he comes. They're better equipped for treatment than where he is, right? Besides, if his materials are complete, then he won't have to expend much energy."

I looked at Colonel Xu, who picked up the receiver. They were clearly in frequent contact, since without much in the way of salutation, he said, "About how heavy is all of that paint? Roughly two tons? Very well. Wait at home, and we'll come pick you up."

The next afternoon, Lin Yun and I went to Nanyuan Airport to meet Zhang Bin. We parked on the tarmac, awaiting the plane. It was the height of summer, but a storm had just passed, taking with it the oppressive heat of the past few days and leaving behind fresh, cool air. After such a long period of hard work, this was a rare occasion to relax.

"You're growing to dislike me as we work, aren't you?" Lin Yun asked me.

"Do you know what you're like?"

"Try me."

"You're like a ship on the night sea making its way toward a lighthouse. Nothing in the world has any meaning for you but that flashing lighthouse. Nothing else is visible."

"How poetic. But don't you think you're describing yourself as well?"

I knew she was right. Sometimes what we find hardest to tolerate in others is our own reflection. Now I recalled that one late night in the library in my first year of university, when the pretty girl asked me what I was looking for. Her expression, still clearly imprinted in my memory, was the face of someone looking at something strange. I felt certain that there was a boy who had looked at Lin Yun that way. . . . We were people untethered to our time, and untethered to each other, and we would never have a way to merge.

The small military transport plane landed, and Zhang Bin walked out of the tail hatch accompanied by Colonel Xu and another officer from the base. Zhang Bin looked far better than I had imagined, better even than how he had seemed at the university when we parted the previous year, not like he had a terminal illness. When I mentioned this to him, he said, "I wasn't like this two days ago. But when I got your call, I halfway recovered." He pointed at the four steel barrels that were being unloaded from the plane. "That's the paint you wanted."

Colonel Xu said, "We estimate that it will take a barrel and a half to paint a helicopter, so that's certainly enough for two!"

Before getting in the car, Zhang Bin said, "Colonel Xu has already told me about your idea. I can't comment on it at the moment, but I have a feeling that this time you and I might see ball lightning again." He looked up at the clear post-rain sky and let out a long breath. "How wonderful that would be."

Back at the base, we worked through the night to run some simple tests on the paint, and discovered that it was an excellent shield against lightning. Then, in the space of just two hours, we covered the two helicopters in the black paint.

The second discharge test was carried out before dawn. Before the pilots took off, Zhang Bin said to the aviator with the bandaged hand, "Fly without worries, kid. There won't be any problems."

Everything went smoothly. The two helicopters reached five thousand meters and ignited the arc, and then flew with it for ten minutes before landing, to applause from us all.

During the flight, the arc covered an area more than a hundred times larger than Base 3141, but this number was minuscule next to the huge area that needed to be swept.

I told Zhang Bin that the large-area airborne scan would commence in two days.

He said, "Remember to call me over!"

Watching him leave in the car, I felt a hollow emptiness I had never felt before. Facing the two helicopters and their now-still rotors, I said to Lin Yun beside me, "We've placed our bets before the natural world. Are we going to lose everything? Do you really believe the net will excite something in the air?"

Lin Yun said, "Don't overthink it. Let's just see what happens."

The first scan began in the evening two days later. The two helicopters were on an even line with each other, Zhang Bin and I in one, and Lin Yun in the other. The weather was excellent, the stars glittered in the night air, and the lights of the capital were dimly visible on the distant horizon.

The two helicopters slowly drew closer to each other. At first, Lin Yun's helicopter was only locatable by its navigation lights, but as it closed the gap, its outline began to stand out against the night sky, and I could gradually make out the serial number and Ba Yi insignia of the PLA. Eventually, even Lin Yun and the face of the aviator, lit red by the instrument panel, were clearly visible.

After a crisp *crack*, the helicopter was suddenly lit by a blinding blue light that filled our cabin as well. The narrow distance between the two craft meant we could only see a small portion of the arc connecting the electrodes beneath the fuselage, but we still had to avert our eyes from the blue glare. Lin Yun and I waved at each other across the blue-filled space.

"Put on eye protection!" the aviator shouted, reminding me that, during the week of installations and adjustments, the arc had already turned my eyes red and watery. I looked over at Zhang Bin, who wasn't wearing goggles, or even looking at the arc at all. He was watching the light shining on the cabin ceiling, as if waiting, or deep in thought.

The moment I put on the goggles, I could see nothing but the electric arc. As the helicopters gradually separated, the arc lengthened. It was a wonderfully simple universe I saw through my goggles, just endless black emptiness and a long electric arc. In fact, this universe was the actual context for our search, a shapeless cosmos of electromagnetism within which the physical world did not exist. All was invisible fields and waves. . . . What I saw drained away the last of my confidence. It was hard to believe, looking at this scene, that there was anything else in this jet-black universe apart from the electric arc. To escape that feeling, I took off the goggles and, like Zhang Bin, confined my gaze to the cabin. The physical world illuminated by the electric light made me feel a little better.

Now the arc was one hundred meters long. It began to move with the helicopter formation as we accelerated toward the west. I wondered what people on the ground would think at the sudden appearance of this long electric arc against the starry night sky. What would they imagine it to be?

We flew for half an hour, during which time we remained silent apart from short radio communication between the aviators. Now the arc had swept a space more than a thousand times the total space covered by all artificial lightning generated in history, but we had found nothing.

The arc was gradually dimming, the superconducting batteries nearly spent. Lin Yun's voice came over the earpiece: "Attention. Extinguish the arc, disengage, and return to base." In her voice I sensed a note of consolation for us all.

If there was one ironclad rule in my life it was this: if you expect to fail, then you will. There was, of course, almost a month of midair searching to come, but I'd already anticipated the final outcome.

"Professor Zhang, we might be wrong." During the whole flight, Zhang Bin had hardly looked outside the cabin, remaining deep in thought.

"No," he said. "I am more convinced than ever that you're correct."

I exhaled softly. "I don't really have much hope for the next month of searching."

He looked at me. "It won't take a month. My intuition tells me that it ought to appear tonight. Can we recharge back at base and then fly out again?"

I shook my head. "You've got to rest. We'll see about tomorrow."

He murmured, "It's weird. It ought to have appeared. . . ."

"Intuition isn't reliable," I said.

"No. In more than three decades this is the first time I've had this feeling. It's reliable."

Then the voice of an aviator spoke in our earpieces: "Target located! About one-third of the way from Arc 1."

Trembling, Zhang Bin and I pressed ourselves against the window. There, thirteen years after my first sighting, and more than forty years since his, we saw for a second time that life-changing ball lightning.

It was orange in color and pulled a short tail behind it as it drifted in a fluctuating path in the night sky. Its path showed that it was utterly unaffected by the strong wind at this high altitude, as if it had absolutely no interaction with our world.

"Attention! Pull back from the target! Danger!" Lin Yun shouted.

Afterward I had to admire her cool-headedness, since Zhang Bin and I were totally transfixed, unable to think of anything else.

The helicopters separated, and as the distance grew, the arc soon extinguished. Absent the interference of the electric glow, the ball lightning stood out even clearer against the night, lighting the surrounding cloud cover red, like a miniature sunrise. Our first artificially excited ball lightning floated leisurely in the air for about a minute before suddenly vanishing.

When we returned to base, we immediately recharged the batteries and took off again. This time, after just fifteen minutes in the air, we excited our second ball lightning, and by fifty minutes, the third. That last one was a strange color, a peculiar violet, and it remained the longest—around six minutes, letting Zhang Bin and me savor the feeling of fantasy turned reality.

It was midnight when we landed back at base for the night. The helicopter rotors had come to a complete stop. Zhang Bin, Lin Yun, and I stood on the lawn surrounded by the sound of summer insects. It was a peaceful night, the glittering summer stars shining in the heavens overhead, as if they were countless lamps the universe had lit just for the three of us.

"I've finally tasted of the wine, and my life is complete!" Zhang Bin said. Lin Yun looked confused, but I immediately remembered the Russian story he had told me.

THUNDERBALLS

After the success of the first search, I found myself awash in an ecstasy I had never known before. Before my eyes, the world had turned wonderful and new, like I had begun a new life. For Colonel Xu and Lin Yun, however, excitement was tempered by bewilderment, since they had only taken the first of a thousand steps toward their goal. Lin Yun had said that my end point was their starting point. This wasn't entirely correct. My end point was still very far away.

When the aviators talked about ball lightning, they called it a "thunderball," perhaps taking inspiration from the James Bond film of that name. This was the first time anyone had used the term thunderball in domestic lightning research, and it was simpler and catchier than earlier names. More importantly, as we now knew, calling the object "ball lightning" was incorrect. So we all quickly adopted the new name.

After the first breakthrough, our progress stopped in its tracks.

We were consistently able to excite thunderballs with lightning, more than ten times on the most successful days, but we were sorely lacking in techniques for studying it, apart from various long-range scanners like radar of various wavelengths, infrared scanners, sonar, and spectrum analyzers. Touch probing was flat-out impossible, as was sampling the air the thunderball came into contact with, since the wind speed was high enough to disperse any affected air in an instant. As a result, for several weeks we made little progress in understanding thunderballs.

But Lin Yun was disappointed on another front. At one regular meeting on the base, she said, "This ball lightning doesn't seem as dangerous as you said. There's no lethality as far as I can see."

"Right," said an aviator. "Are these fluffy fireballs really useful as weapons?"

"You really won't be satisfied until you see someone burned to a crisp?" I snapped.

"Don't be like that. Our end goal is making weapons, after all."

"You can doubt everything about ball lightning, but don't doubt its lethality. The moment you let your guard down, it will grant you your wish!" I said.

Colonel Xu Wencheng supported me. "I've seen a dangerous tendency right now, an increasing disregard for safety. The observer helicopter has been within the stipulated fifty-meter minimum distance from the target on countless occasions, and once as close as twenty meters! This is absolutely prohibited. I want to remind all team members, particularly aviators, that any further orders to approach the thunderballs closer than the set minimum should be refused."

No one could have anticipated that my ominous prediction would be fulfilled that very night.

The frequency of thunderball discovery remained the same day or night, but because the thunderballs made a better visual effect in the dark, most of the excitement tests were carried out at night. That night, six thunderballs were excited. For five of them, measurements were carried out successfully, including measurements of orbit, radiation intensity, spectral characteristics, and magnetic field strength at the point of disappearance.

When a touch probe was being carried out for the sixth thunderball, disaster struck. When the thunderball was excited, the probe helicopter carefully approached it, flying parallel to its path and trying to maintain a distance of fifty meters. I was in a helicopter a little farther away. After four minutes of flying like this, the thunderball suddenly vanished. But unlike previous occasions, this time we heard a faint explosion, which—taking the helicopter's excellent noise insulation into account—must have sounded deafening outside. Then the probe helicopter gave off a plume of white smoke, right as it lost control. It plummeted, toppling about, and was soon gone from sight. In the moonlight, we saw a white parachute open below us and felt a tiny bit of relief. Not long after that, a fireball appeared, turning the surrounding area into a conspicuous circle of red against the pitch-black ground. Our hearts seized up, and only when we received the report that the helicopter had crashed into a desolate mountain and no one had been injured did we heave a sigh of relief.

Back at the base, the pilot, still shaken, recalled that when the thunderball had exploded in front of his helicopter, an electric discharge had flared from somewhere in the cabin, followed by smoke, and then the craft lost control. The crashed helicopter was burned beyond recognition, making it impossible to determine which part had been struck.

"What makes you sure that the thunderball had anything to do with the accident? Maybe it was a problem with the helicopter that just happened to coincide with the thunderball explosion," Lin Yun said at the accident analysis meeting.

The pilot looked her straight in the eye with the expression of someone who had just awoken from a nightmare. "Major, I'd have agreed with you, except . . . look." And he held up his hands. "Is this a coincidence?"

Apart from his right thumb and the middle finger of his left hand, which had burnt remnants of fingernails, all of the nails on his fingers were gone. Then he took off his aviators' boots. His toenails were entirely missing.

"When the thunderball exploded, I had a weird feeling in my fingers. I took off my gloves and saw my fingernails glowing red, but the next instant the light went out and all ten nails turned opaque white. I thought my hands had been burned, so I raised them to cool them in the air, but at the first wave the fingernails vanished in a cloud of ash."

"And your hands weren't burned?" Lin Yun said, grabbing his hands for a closer look.

"Believe it or not, they didn't even feel warm. Besides, my boots and gloves are completely fine."

The accident gave the project team its first experience of the threat of ball lightning, and afterward, they no longer called it "fluffy." What surprised everyone the most was that the energy discharged by the thunderball acted on an object fifty meters away. Still, this phenomena was not at all rare in the more than ten thousand eyewitness accounts of ball lightning we had compiled.

And so the project reached an impasse. We had by that point excited forty-eight thunderballs, but we had also experienced a major accident; it was impossible for tests and observations to continue in this form. More importantly, everyone knew in their hearts that there was no point in risking it. We had been shaken not by the thunderball's power, but by its almost supernatural strangeness. The aviator's vanished fingernails reminded us that the secrets of the thunderball could not be unlocked through conventional means.

I remembered something Zhang Bin had said: "We're both mortal men. We may have put far more into the search than other people, but we're still mortal. We can only make deductions within the framework defined by fundamental theory, and dare not deviate from it, lest we step out into the airless void. But within this framework, we cannot deduce anything." I included these lines in my report to the GAD leadership.

"Our approach to ball lightning research needs to adopt cutting-edge physics," Lin Yun said.

"Yes," Colonel Xu replied. "We need to bring in a superman."

DING YI

GAD convened a meeting to discuss expanding the ball lightning project. The meeting was attended primarily by representatives of civilian sector research institutions, most of them specialists in physics, including several directors of state physics institutes, as well as the physics department heads at a few well-known universities. The chair of the meeting turned over a stack of forms they had collected, brief introductions of the participants' specialties and achievements, as material for us to use in making our selection.

Neither Colonel Xu nor I was happy after we'd read through the materials.

"These are the country's most outstanding scholars in the field," the head of the Institute of Physics said.

"We believe it. But we need something more fundamental," Colonel Xu said.

"More fundamental? Aren't you doing lightning research? How fundamental does that need to be? You don't expect us to simply fetch Stephen Hawking, do you?"

"Hawking would be wonderful!" Lin Yun said.

The GAD team glanced at each other. Then the academy head said to a physics department dean, "Well, send Ding Yi, then."

"His research is fundamental?"

"The most fundamental."

"How's his scholarship?"

"The best in the country."

"What's his affiliation?"

"He's unaffiliated."

"We're not looking for an outsider physicist."

"Ding Yi holds two doctorates, in philosophy and physics, and a master's in mathematics. I forget which branch. He's been a senior professor and a CAS fellow, the youngest ever, and he once served as senior scientist on the national neutron decay study, for which he was rumored to be nominated for a Nobel in physics last year. Does that sound like an outsider physicist to you?"

"So why is he unaffiliated?"

The academy head and the physics dean both snorted. "Ask him yourself."

Lin Yun and I arrived at Ding Yi's residence in a new apartment building in Haidian District. The door was ajar, and after pressing the doorbell several times with no response, we pushed it open and went in. The large apartment with its three bedrooms and two living rooms was mostly empty and had bare-bones decoration. The floor and windowsills were carpeted white with a large quantity of A4 paper, some of it blank, other sheets covered in formulas and peculiar graphs. Pencils were strewn about everywhere. One room held a bookcase and a computer. There were few books on the bookcase in that room, but it had the largest quantity of paper, rendering the floor barely visible. In a clearing in the center of the room, Ding Yi was sleeping in a deck chair. He was in his thirties, with a thin lanky body, and he was wearing a sleeveless T-shirt and shorts. A strand of saliva hung from his mouth to the floor. Beside the chair was a small table holding an enormous ashtray and an opened pack of Stone Forest brand cigarettes. A few of the cigarettes had been broken open and their tobacco stuffed into a glass. Evidently he had fallen asleep while working. We called out to him a few times, but he did not respond, so we had to forge a path through the paper to the chair and push him awake.

"Hmm? Oh, right. You called this morning?" Ding Yi said, smacking away saliva. "There's tea in the bookcase. Pour it yourself if you want some." After sitting up, he suddenly burst out shouting: "Why did you mess up my calculations? I had them lined up, and now they're out of order!" He got up and busied himself pushing about the paper we had cleared, blocking our retreat.

"Are you Professor Ding?" Lin Yun asked. She was clearly disappointed by her first impression of him.

"I am Ding Yi." He opened up two folding chairs and motioned for us to sit down, then returned to his chair. He said, "Before you tell me why you've come, let me discuss with you a dream I've just had. . . . No, you've got to listen. It was a wonderful dream, which you interrupted. In the dream I was sitting here, a knife in my hand, around so long, like for cutting watermelon. Next to me was this tea table. But there wasn't an ashtray or anything on it. Just two round objects, yea big. Circular, spherical. What do you think they were?"

"Watermelon?"

"No, no. One was a proton, the other a neutron. A watermelon-sized proton and neutron. I cut the proton open first. Its charge flowed out onto the table, all sticky, with a fresh fragrance. After I cut the proton in half, the quarks inside tumbled out, tinkling. They were about the size of walnuts, in all sorts of colors. They rolled about on the table, and some of them fell onto the floor. I picked up a white one. It was very hard, but with effort, I was able to bite into it. It tasted like a manaizi grape. . . . And right then, you woke me up."

With a bit of a sneer, Lin Yun said, "Professor Ding, that's a school-boy's dream. You ought to be aware that protons, neutrons, and quarks would exhibit quantum effects, and they wouldn't look like that."

Ding Yi stared at her for a few seconds. "Oh, of course. You're to-tally right. I tend to oversimplify things. Imagine how wonderful life would be for me if protons and neutrons really were that big. They're so tiny in reality that a knife to cut them open would cost billions. So this is just a poor child's dream of candy. Don't mock it."

"I've heard that the state didn't include the large hadron accelerator and collider in the latest sci-tech five-year plan," I said.

"They said it was a pointless waste of resources, so we physicists have to continue to go cap in hand to Geneva and beg them for a piti-ful scrap of experiment time."

"But your neutron decay project was quite successful. They say you nearly won a Nobel."

"Don't go bringing that up. That's why I'm in the state I'm in today, with nothing to do."

"What do you mean?"

"Oh, just a few innocuous remarks. It was last year at . . . I've for-gotten where. Definitely Europe. On a prime-time talk show, the host asked me for my thoughts as a leading candidate for the Nobel Prize in Physics, and I said, 'The Nobel? It's never been given to superior minds, but favors competence and luck, like Einstein, who won for the photoelectric effect. Today, the Nobel is just a withered old whore, her charm gone, relying on flashy clothing and intricate tricks to win the favor of clients. I'm not interested in her. But the state invested a mint into the project, so I wouldn't reject the prize if it was forced upon me.'"

Lin Yun and I looked at each other in surprise, and then burst out laughing. "That's not cause for termination!"

"They said I was irresponsible, grandstanding, and wrecking it for everyone. Naturally, they all see me as a weirdo. 'Those whose courses are different cannot lay plans for one another.'* So I left. . . . Okay, why don't you two tell me why you've come."

"We'd like to invite you to take part in a national defense research project, to be in charge of the theory portion," I said.

"Research on what?"

"Ball lightning."

"Great. If they've sent you here to insult me, then they've succeeded."

"Why don't you listen to our explanation before forming a conclusion? Maybe you'll be able to use this to insult them," Lin Yun said, opening up the laptop she had brought. She played a recording of the excitation of ball lightning, and explained it briefly to Ding Yi.

"So you're saying that you're using lightning to excite some undiscovered structure in the air?" Ding Yi said, staring at the ball lightning floating faintly on the laptop screen.

Lin Yun affirmed that that was the case. I showed Ding Yi Zhang Bin's notebook with the alternating burnt pages and described its provenance. He took it and looked it over closely and carefully before returning it to me.

He took a bunch of tobacco from the glass, stuffed it into a large pipe, and lit it. He pointed at the loose cigarettes and said, "Take care of those for me." Then he walked over to a wall and began to smoke. And so we extracted the tobacco from the cigarettes and put it into the glass.

---

* *The Analects of Confucius*, Chapter 15: Wei Ling Gong, translation by James Legge.

"I know a place that sells pipe tobacco," I said, looking up at him.

He didn't seem to hear me, but stood there exhaling smoke. His face was practically pressed against the wall, so that the smoke he blew against it seemed to be issuing from the wall instead. His eyes were focused on the distance, as if the wall was the transparent border of another vast world and he was surveying the profound sights it held.

Before long, he finished his pipe, but maintained his posture against the wall. He said, "I'm not as self-righteous as you might imagine. The first task is to prove that I'm qualified for this project. If I'm not, then you can find someone else."

"So you'll join us?"

Ding Yi turned back around. "Yes. Why don't I go with you now?"

That night, quite a few people at the base found it hard to sleep. From time to time they looked out the window at the tiny red star that flashed intermittently on the broad lightning test ground. That was Ding Yi's pipe.

After arriving at the base, Ding Yi looked briefly through the materials we had prepared, and then immediately began calculating. He didn't use a computer, but worked quickly with pencil and paper, and before long the office prepared for him was as covered in paper as his home. He did calculations for two hours straight before stopping, and then moved his chair to the edge of the test ground, smoking his pipe constantly. Its flame, flickering like the summer fireflies, was the light of hope for ball lightning research.

The flame had a hypnotic effect that made me drowsy watching it, so I went to bed. When I woke up, it was two in the morning, and, looking through the window, I could see the tiny star still flashing on the test ground. Now, though, it was moving like a firefly. Ding Yi was pacing. I watched him for a while and then went back to sleep. It was daylight when I awoke, and the test ground was empty. Ding Yi had gone to sleep.

It was almost ten when he got up and declared to us the results of his thinking: "Ball lightning is visible."

We looked at each other with forced smiles. "Professor Ding, you're not just . . . bullshitting us, are you?"

"I mean, unexcited ball lightning. What you called the already existing structure. It's visible. It causes light to bend."

". . . How do you see it?"

"According to my calculations of the light bend, it should be visible to the naked eye."

We looked at each other uncertainly. "So . . . what does it look like?"

"A transparent sphere. It exhibits a round edge due to the bending of light. It looks like a soap bubble, although it lacks a bubble's iridescence, so overall it is not as conspicuous. But it is definitely visible."

"But why hasn't anyone seen it before?"

"Because no one was looking."

"How is that possible? In the whole of human history, think of how many of these bubbles have been floating in the air. And no one saw them?"

"Can you see the moon during the day?" Ding Yi asked.

"Of course not," someone said reflexively.

Ding Yi pulled back the curtain on a crystal clear sky. There in the azure was a crescent moon, snow-white and stunning against the sky, looking conspicuously spherical.

"I've never noticed it before!" the speaker exclaimed.

"Someone did a survey showing that ninety percent of people have never noticed it, but it has often appeared during daytime throughout human history. Do you really expect people to notice a small, indistinct bubble found only once in several cubic kilometers, or maybe even an order of magnitude less than that?"

"That is a little hard to believe."

"So let's prove it. Let's excite a few more thunderballs, and we'll see."

EMPTY BUBBLES

That afternoon, the aircraft that had been grounded for several days took flight once again. They ignited the arc at three thousand meters and excited ball lightning three times. Seven people, including Lin Yun and me, were in the helicopters watching the thunderballs through binoculars until they vanished, but none of us saw the unexcited form.

"Your eyesight isn't good enough," Ding Yi said, after learning the results.

"Captain Liu and I didn't see anything either," said Captain Zheng, one of the helicopter pilots.

"Then you need better eyesight."

"What? We've got perfect vision. You can't find anyone with better eyesight!" Captain Liu, the other helicopter pilot, said.

"Then excite a few more and look more carefully," Ding Yi said, unconvinced.

"Professor Ding, exciting thunderballs is very dangerous. We've got to be cautious," Colonel Xu said.

"I think we should do as Professor Ding says and try once more. Sometimes risks have to be taken," Lin Yun said.

In the less than two days that Ding Yi had been at the base, Lin Yun's attitude toward him had experienced a conspicuous transformation, from initial suspicion to respect, a respect that I had not noticed her showing toward any other individual. After the meeting, I mentioned this to her.

She said, "Ding Yi has lots of ideas. He's contemplating ball lightning on a level far beyond our reach."

"So far I haven't seen any impressive ideas from him."

"It's not something I've seen. It's a feeling I have."

"But his abstruse enigmas are supposed to solve our problems? And his practically pathological stubbornness? I dislike it."

"Ball lightning itself is an abstruse enigma."

And so the next morning another three hours of exciting flight were undertaken. Two thunderballs were excited, but the results were the same as the previous day's. Once they disappeared, there was nothing to be seen.

"I still think you need better eyesight. Could we bring in a few more senior aviators, the kind that fly aircraft with wings?" Ding Yi said.

His question angered the helicopter pilots. Captain Zheng barked, "They're called fighter pilots. And you listen here, the air force and army aviation each have their strengths. One's not higher or lower than the other. And as far as eyesight goes, our requirements are the same as theirs!"

Ding Yi chuckled. "I'm not interested in military issues. Even so, it's got to be because of the distance from the target. No one would be able to see a thunderball at that distance."

"I'm certain that no one could see it from even closer!"

"That is a possibility. It's a transparent bubble, after all. For a target like that, conditions are quite poor for airborne observations. What we need to do is take it back and observe it on the table."

Once again, we looked at each other uncertainly. It was a common expression for us when Ding Yi was around.

"That's right. I've got a plan. We can capture an unexcited ball lightning and store it."

"Is that possible? We can't even see them!"

"Listen to me. While you've been flying, I've been reading the background on these," Ding Yi said, pointing at the two superconducting batteries next to him.

"What's that got to do with ball lightning?"

"They can store unexcited ball lightning."

"How?"

"Simple. Contact the thunderball with a superconducting lead, no thicker than half a centimeter, drawn from the battery's anode, and it will be conducted into the battery and stored like current. It can be released from the cathode in a similar fashion."

"Ridiculous!" I exclaimed. Ding Yi's tricks had become intolerable, and I now regretted inviting him.

"It won't be easy to do," Lin Yun said, entirely serious. "We can't see the bubbles, so how are we supposed to contact them?"

"Major, you're a smart person. Maybe you should think about it a bit?" Ding Yi said with a sly grin.

"Maybe like this? We can see ball lightning in its excited state, so if we extend the lead to that position at the moment it vanishes, we'll contact the bubble."

"You've got to be quick, though, or the bubble will float away," Ding Yi said, nodding. The sly smile remained on his face.

It took us a moment to realize what Lin Yun meant. "That's risking death!" someone shouted.

"Don't listen to his crap, Major," Captain Liu said, pointing at Ding Yi.

"Captain, Professor Ding is a world-famous physicist and a CAS fellow. He deserves respect," Colonel Xu said sternly.

Ding Yi laughed and waved a hand. "Doesn't matter. I'm used to it."

"Oh, I've got an idea! Dr. Chen, I've got to take you someplace right away," Lin Yun said, leading me off.

Lin Yun said she wanted to take a look at something called a "feeler defense system," and that the strangely named system would solve our safety problem. We drove four or five hours in the direction of Zhangjiakou and arrived at a dusty mountain valley crisscrossed by tracks in the ground. She told me this was the proving ground for the Main Battle Tank 2005.

A major wearing a tank soldier's uniform ran over and told Lin Yun that the person in charge of the feeler defense system research group was temporarily indisposed, and asked us to wait.

"Please, have some water!"

He wasn't carrying any. The water came by tank, two glasses held on a tray on the gun muzzle. As the huge vehicle crept slowly toward us, its barrel remained level regardless of how the tank's body rose and fell, as if a powerful magnet was pulling it by the muzzle. Not a drop of water spilled out of the glasses. The armored corps officers nearby laughed merrily at our surprise.

The MBT 2005 was quite different from the tanks I had seen in the past: flat, angular, with practically no curves. The turret and body were stacked flat oblongs that gave an impression of indestructibility.

In the distance, a tank was firing as it moved. The blasts of its shells were painfully loud, and though I wanted to cover my ears, when I saw

Lin Yun and the officers joking beside me, as if the loud noise didn't even exist, I was too embarrassed to do so.

Half an hour later, we met the project director for the feeler defense system. He first took us to watch a demonstration of the system. We arrived at a small multi-barrel rocket launcher, where two soldiers were loading a rocket into the uppermost slot.

The project director said, "Anti-tank missiles cost too much to use for a demonstration, so we'll use this instead. Properly pretested, it's sure to hit the target." He pointed to the rocket's target, an MBT 2005 off in the distance.

A soldier pressed the launch button. Out roared the rocket, leaving a cloud of dust and smoke behind us. It trailed a flat arc of white tail smoke behind it in the air as it headed straight for the target. But just as the rocket was around ten meters above the tank, it appeared to have suddenly hit something, and its heading changed at once, veering off to smack headlong into the dirt less than twenty meters away from the tank. Since it wasn't loaded with a warhead, it merely kicked up a small cloud of dust.

I found my surprise hard to express in words, but asked, "Is there some sort of protection field around the tank?"

Everyone burst out laughing. The project director said through his laughter, "Nothing so outlandish. You're talking about something that's only in science fiction stories. The principles of this system couldn't be any more basic."

I didn't understand what he meant by "basic," so Lin Yun explained: "The principle can be traced back to the time of cold weapons. Cavalry wielded lances that could block the enemy's arrows, if struck correctly."

Seeing that I still didn't get it, the project director said, "We're too far away, and it happened too fast, so naturally you didn't see it clearly." He led me to a nearby display and said, "Take a look at the high-speed camera."

On the screen, the moment before the rocket struck, a thin pole shot like lightning from the top of the tank, like a long fishing pole. It precisely tapped the rocket's nose and diverted its path.

The director said, "In combat, it's sometimes possible to divert an incoming object, but that may cause it to detonate early. For low-speed anti-tank missiles and air-dropped bombs, the efficiency of this defensive system is excellent."

"What an idea!" I said wholeheartedly.

"Hey, this wasn't our idea. The concept of the feeler system was proposed by NATO weapons experts at the end of the 1980s, and the French first tested it successfully on their next-generation Leclerc tank. We're only following in their footsteps."

Lin Yun said, "Even though the principle of the system is simple, its target sensing and positioning system is highly advanced. Not only can the feeler hit the target in the shortest possible time, but it can select the optimum angle. It's basically an intimate scale theater missile defense."

Now I clearly understood Lin Yun's intent. It was like the thing had been custom-made for us.

The project director said, "Major Lin gave us the details of your situation yesterday, and our superiors instructed us to cooperate closely with you. To tell you the truth, in the past I wouldn't have given your research a second thought, but things are different now. When I was first exposed to the idea of the feeler system, I thought it was ridiculous, nothing more. I never imagined the success we've had. On the battlefield of today, only the stubborn will survive."

Lin Yun said, "The biggest problem now is the length of the feeler. How long can you make it? It's very dangerous for the helicopter to get too close to the thunderball."

"The longest the feeler can be at present is ten meters. Any longer and it won't be strong enough. But, for your purposes, there's no strength requirement for contact, and your speed requirements might be one to two orders of magnitude less than ours. In my crude estimation, the feeler could be as long as twenty-five meters. But there's one more thing: it can carry the superconducting lead you need, but apart from that you can't affix anything to the tip."

Lin Yun nodded. "That's basically enough."

On the way back, I asked her, "Do you really intend to do it? Isn't that betting too much on Ding Yi?"

"We've got to give it a try. I think Ding Yi really is the person to make a breakthrough in ball lightning research. We've said before that this mystery won't yield to conventional thinking. Now we've got some unconventional thinking, but you won't accept it."

"The problem now is how to convince Colonel Xu and the aviators."

Lin Yun sighed softly. "If only I knew how to fly a helicopter."

Back at the base, Lin Yun described her plan in a hastily convened meeting.

"You want to poke a thunderball with a long pole? Are you insane, Major?" Captain Zheng said loudly.

"Once again, the pole isn't going to touch a thunderball in an excited state. It will touch the bubble that may possibly exist in that position the instant the thunderball goes out."

"Professor Ding said that the superconducting lead carried on the pole must reach that location within half a second of the thunderball going out, otherwise the bubble will blow away. Is that level of precision possible? What if it's half a second too early?"

"The reaction time of the feeler defense system is faster than our requirements by two orders of magnitude, although that's for the original system's feeler, which moves when the target appears at a specified location. In our improved system, the feeler moves when the target disappears. And our previous observations of EM radiation and visible light have given us data for a precise determination of the ball lightning's disappearance."

"Even if you can do all that, the helicopter still needs to be twenty-five meters from the thunderball. That's half the distance of the last time there was an accident. You've got to be aware of the danger involved."

"I am aware, Captain. But it's a risk we must take."

"I don't agree with the plan," Colonel Xu said, with a tone of finality.

"Colonel, even if you agreed, we wouldn't fly this mission," Captain Liu said. "The two crews are only on loan to the base. Ultimate command authority rests with the army group. We have the power to refuse any command that endangers the safety of the group. Our division leaders reemphasized this point after the last accident."

Lin Yun appeared unfazed. "Captain Liu, if you received a command from the army group ordering you to undertake this mission, would you carry it out?"

"That would change things. Of course we'd carry it out."

"Could I get a guarantee of that?" she said, not moving her eyes from Captain Liu. Her expression frightened me.

"I guarantee it in my capacity as officer in charge of the helicopter group. But, Major, the army group won't give that order."

Lin Yun said nothing. She picked up a phone and dialed. "Hello, I'd like to speak with Senior Colonel Zeng Yuanping. . . . This is Base B436. Yes. That's me. Yes. Thank you!" She passed the phone to Captain Liu. "Captain, the Eighty-Second Aviation Brigade Commander of the Thirty-Eighth Group Army is on the line."

Captain Liu took up the phone. "Speaking. . . . Yes, Commander. I understand. . . . Yes. Certainly!" He put the phone down without looking at Lin Yun. Then he turned to Colonel Xu. "Colonel, we have received orders to fly this mission. The time and number of flights are to be determined by the base."

"No, Captain Liu. Please inform your superior officer that until reliable safety measures are found, the base is halting all observation flights," Colonel Xu said emphatically.

Phone in hand, the captain hesitated, glancing at Lin Yun. Everyone was looking at her.

Lin Yun bit her lip and remained silent for several seconds, then reached for the captain's phone, hung up, and dialed another number. "Hello, sir? This is Base B436. Yes, it's me. About the report I made yesterday. . . . I'd like to know whether the higher-ups have. . . . Good." She passed the phone to Colonel Xu. "Deputy director of the GAD."

Colonel Xu took the phone and listened grimly. He finally uttered two words—"Yes, sir"—and put the phone down. Then he turned to us and said gravely, "The higher-ups have ordered us to proceed with the experiments to capture unexcited ball lightning according to Major Lin Yun's plan. In addition, they have ordered that all other work at the base be suspended so that our energy can be focused on this experiment, and they expect everyone to dedicate themselves to the work in their respective capacities. Would the technical directors for the projects please stay behind after the meeting?"

On the way back from the tank proving ground, Lin Yun had gone to the city on her own and stayed a full day before returning to the base. Now I knew why she had gone there.

No one spoke after that. They left in silence, and the keen edge of that silence was clearly directed at Lin Yun.

"Captains," she called softly after the departing aviators. "Please understand that, in wartime, this would be little different from an ordinary combat mission."

"Do you think we're afraid of death?" Captain Liu said, jabbing a finger into his chest. "We just don't want to die worthlessly, for some experiment that's bound to fail. For a bizarre experiment cooked up by a bizarre individual on the basis of a bizarre theory."

Captain Zheng said, "I think even Professor Ding isn't certain that this will really manage to capture a thunderball."

Ding Yi, who had not said anything during the meeting, was unperturbed by all that had happened. He merely nodded and said, "If everything is carried out precisely as Major Lin has instructed, then I am certain."

The two aviators left, leaving Colonel Xu, Lin Yun, Ding Yi, and me behind. After a lengthy silence, Colonel Xu said severely, "Lin Yun, this time you've gone too far. Think carefully about what you've done ever since coming to this base: You've acted willfully and arbitrarily, stopping at nothing to get what you want. You have a habit of interfering in everything, even when it's beyond the scope of your duties, and you frequently go around the base's leadership to act on your own. This time, by exploiting your privilege through nonstandard channels, you have gone over the heads of several levels of command and delivered your subjective opinion directly to the senior leadership, giving them false information. This is dangerous! Yes, others at the base have previously tolerated you, but they were simply doing their jobs. The army does not exist in a vacuum. We are aware of the part your background plays in this project, and value your connections for communicating conditions up the hierarchy. But you have mistaken this tolerance for indulgence, and are becoming increasingly unreasonable. . . . When this test is finished, I will write an objective report for my superiors explaining your actions. If you have any self-awareness at all, you will leave the base and this project, since it's difficult for any of us to work with you."

Lin Yun bowed her head and placed her hands between her knees. The calm resolve of moments ago was gone, and, like a little girl caught misbehaving, she said softly, "If the experiment fails, I will accept responsibility."

"And if it succeeds, then your actions were correct?" the colonel said.

"I don't think anything's wrong," Ding Yi said. "Extraordinary research must be advanced through extraordinary measures. Otherwise, in this rigid society, science wouldn't budge an inch." He sighed. "If I'd been more alert back then, my accelerator project wouldn't have had its funding pulled."

Lin Yun shot him a grateful glance.

Ding Yi stood up and began pacing to and fro, then his face broke out into that sly grin of his. "As for me, I won't accept any responsibility. We theorists have the task of proposing a hypothesis, and if it doesn't obtain experimental proof, then our responsibility is simply to propose another one."

"But lives are at stake in the proof of this hypothesis," I said.

"Compared to our goals, it's worth it."

"That's easy to say when you're not going to be in those helicopters."

"What?" Ding Yi instantly turned furious. "You mean I'm to be put into the helicopter for the sake of demonstrating some sort of spirit? Not a chance! My life belongs to another master, physics. You listen to me: I'm not going on any helicopter!"

"No one's making you go, Professor Ding," Colonel Xu said, shaking his head.

With the meeting finished, I walked over to an empty space on the test ground, pulled out my phone, and dialed a number. It only rang once before I heard General Lin's deep voice say, "Is that Dr. Chen?"

I was caught a little off guard, but I recounted the meeting to him, and he replied at once.

"We're already familiar with the situation you described. But this is an unusual time and we urgently require the success of this project, so some risks have to be taken. Of course, Lin Yun's approach is unfortunate. Very bad, you might even say. But that's her nature. Sometimes there's nothing you can do. We did not put enough thought into this matter previously. Tomorrow, we'll have GAD send a special commissioner to the base to take charge of communication between the project's front lines and the higher-ups. But thank you for the news, Dr. Chen."

"General, what I'd really like to say is that Professor Ding's theory is really out there. It's incredibly hard to believe."

"Doctor, what area of modern physics isn't out there, or incredibly hard to believe?"

"But . . ."

"We've had other academics and experts look at Professor Ding's theories and calculations, which Lin Yun brought over, and they've given careful thought to her experimental design. In addition, what you may not know is that this isn't the first time that Ding Yi has taken part in a national defense project. We are confident in his abilities, no matter how strange his theories. This is a risk worth taking."

Over the next two weeks, I came to realize the difference between soldiers and civilians. This experiment, for example, was incredibly absurd from a common sense angle. The majority of the project team's members were staunchly opposed to it, and stood in sharp opposition to the minority led by Lin Yun. In a civilian research body, it would be impossible to make smooth progress. Every opponent would slack off, or attempt to secretly undermine the project through any possible means. But it was different here. Everyone put their heart into it. Lin

Yun's orders were resolutely carried out, often by individuals who out-ranked her. Of course, the role her personal charm played couldn't be discounted. Quite a few of the highly educated young officers on the project would have followed her blindly, right or wrong.

With us on the tests were a few engineers who had been transferred over from the feeler defense system. They had upgraded the hardware, lengthened the pole one and a half times, and installed it on the heli-copter. In addition to altering the target identification module, the engineers modified the system's control software to reverse the trigger mechanism so that it would whip out the pole the instant the thunder-ball disappeared.

On the day of the formal test, with everyone on base gathered at the launch site, I was reminded of the first air discharge test more than a month ago. Like on that occasion, it was a clear day with no wind. Now, the only people who seemed truly relaxed were the two aviator captains who were about to risk their lives. As usual, they were chat-ting up the nurses beside the ambulance.

Lin Yun, wearing a combat uniform as she had done on every previous flight, headed toward the helicopter carrying the feeler sys-tem. But Captain Liu stopped her. "Major, the feeler system works automatically. Only a pilot is needed on board."

She pushed aside his arm without saying a word and climbed into the rear seat. The captain stared at her for a few seconds, then climbed into the cabin and silently helped her strap on the parachute. His burnt-off fingernails had still not grown back.

Ding Yi began to make a fuss, afraid that someone would drag him onto a helicopter. He again declared, without a thought for the looks of withering disdain he received from those around him, that his life belonged to physics. He added that he had done additional calculations to further prove the correctness of his theory. A thunderball was cer-tain to be captured! Now the image of the man before us was no more than an itinerant con artist. Apart from him and Lin Yun, no one held out any hope of success for the experiment. They just prayed that those aboard the two helicopters would escape with their lives.

The helicopters took off with a roar. When the arc crackled to life, tension seized the hearts of everyone on the ground. The plan was that after the thunderball was excited, the arc would go out at once and the feeler system–equipped helicopter would close to a distance of twenty-five meters from the target. When the thunderball extinguished, the pole would whip out, carrying a superconducting lead connected directly to a drained superconducting battery on board the helicopter, into contact with the spot where Ding Yi believed the bubble to be.

The helicopters slowly flew farther out, and the arc turned into a sparkle against the blue sky. What happened next we only heard about later on.

Around twenty-four minutes into the flight, ball lightning was excited. The arc went out, and the feeler-equipped helicopter approached the thunderball to a distance of roughly twenty-five meters, then aligned the feeler. This was the first time a helicopter had been so close to the thunderball since the first one was excited. Tracking flight was difficult, because the thunderball was unaffected by air movement and no one knew what determined the path of its drift, which was volatile and random-seeming. Most dangerously, it might suddenly approach the helicopter. From recordings after the incident we discovered that the helicopter had drawn as close as sixteen meters to the thunderball. It was an ordinary thunderball that glowed orange yellow, and was inconspicuous in the daylight. It remained excited for one minute and thirty-five seconds before it disappeared, at a point 22.5 meters from the helicopter, with an explosion that Lin Yun and

Captain Liu could hear clearly from inside. The feeler system triggered, and the twenty-odd-meter pole brought the tip of the superconducting lead to the precise point of disappearance. The recording showed that the time from the thunderball's disappearance to the arrival of the lead was just 0.4 seconds.

That was immediately followed by a loud noise next to Lin Yun, as if something on the aircraft had exploded. The cabin quickly filled with scalding steam. But the helicopter maintained a normal flight attitude all the way back.

The helicopter landed amid cheers. Like Colonel Xu had said, in this experiment, a safe return was a victory.

Upon inspection, it was a bottle of spring water left under the seat by one of the ground crew that had exploded. The thunderball had released its energy into the water, turning it instantly to steam. Fortunately, since it was under the seat and ruptured without fragmenting, the only injury was a light burn to Lin Yun's right calf where the steam had penetrated her combat uniform.

"We're lucky the helicopter is oil-cooled. If it had a water tank like in a car, it would have turned into a bomb," Captain Liu said with a shudder.

"You're overlooking another, even bigger way you were lucky," Ding Yi said, coming over with a mysterious smile, as if none of this had anything to do with him. "You're forgetting that there was water on the helicopter apart from that bottle."

"Where?" Lin Yun asked, but then answered immediately, "My God! Inside of us!"

"Yes. Your blood, too."

We all took a chilly breath. The prospect of all the blood in their bodies turning to steam in the blink of an eye was too much to imagine.

"That means that when ball lightning selects a target to release its energy, the target's boundary conditions are very important," Ding Yi said thoughtfully.

Someone said, "Professor Ding, you ought to be thinking about thunderballs that have already released their energy. What were they called? Bubbles? There ought to be one in the battery."

Ding Yi nodded. "The capture process was carried out with high precision. It ought to be in there."

We all grew excited, and began to take the superconducting battery off the helicopter. There was more than a bit of irony in this excitement, since most people had already guessed what the outcome would be. The proceedings were a relaxing comedy to celebrate the helicopters' safe return.

"Professor, when can you bring out the bubble and give us all a look?" someone asked after the heavy battery was finally out. We all expected that Ding Yi would secrete the battery in the lab so that as few people as possible would witness his failure, but his answer caught us by surprise: "Right away."

Cheers sounded in the crowd, like we were a group of deviant onlookers awaiting a beheading.

Colonel Xu took a step up the ladder of one of the helicopters, and said loudly, "Listen up. Extracting the bubble from the battery requires care and full preparation. The battery will now be taken to Lab 3 and we will inform you of the results presently."

"Colonel, everyone's put in so much effort, particularly Captain Liu and Major Lin, who risked their lives. I think they have the right to be compensated," Ding Yi said, to another chorus of cheers.

"Professor Ding, this is a significant experimental project, not a children's game. I order the battery to be returned to the lab immediately," Colonel Xu said firmly. I sensed his kindness, and knew he was doing his best to preserve Ding Yi's dignity.

"Colonel, don't forget that the bubble extraction portion of the experiment should be my sole responsibility. I have the right to decide what steps to take for this experiment and when to take them!" Ding Yi said to Colonel Xu.

"Professor, I suggest you calm down," the colonel said to him quietly.

"And what's Major Lin's opinion?" Ding Yi asked the silent Lin Yun.

With a toss of her hair, she said decisively, "Do it now. Whatever it is, it's better that we face it sooner rather than later."

"Precisely." Ding Yi waved his hand. "Next, I'd ask the engineers from the superconductivity department to come forward."

The three engineers in charge of operating the superconducting battery pushed forward, and Ding Yi said to them, "I'm sure you're quite clear on the extraction procedure we discussed yesterday. Have you brought the magnetic retaining field assembly?" Receiving an affirmative answer, he said, "Then let's begin."

The cylindrical battery was situated on a workbench. One engineer strung a superconducting lead, with a switch attached, to the cathode. Ding Yi pointed at it. "When that switch is pressed, the lead will be connected to the battery, and the bubble within it will be released."

At the other end of the lead, two engineers set up a device composed of several spools of wire set at equal distances. Ding Yi said to the crowd, "When the bubble is released, no vessel will be able to contain it. It can pass through all matter and move of its own accord. But the theory predicts that the bubble will bear a negative charge, so it can be constrained by a magnetic field. This device produces a containment field to hold the bubble in place for you to observe. Good. Now turn on the field."

An engineer flipped a switch and a small red light on the field device came on.

Ding Yi took out a square object from behind him. "I brought this along so you'll be better able to see the bubble." To our great surprise, it was a Go board.

"Next, let's welcome this historic moment." Ding Yi went over to the superconducting battery and placed a finger on the red switch. With everyone's attention focused on him, he pressed it.

Nothing happened.

Ding Yi's expression remained dead calm as he pointed at the space within the field generator and declared solemnly, "This is ball lightning in an unexcited state."

There was nothing there.

For a moment there was silence, other than the faint hum of the field generator. Time passed sluggishly like sticky paste, and I ached for it to flow faster.

A sudden burst behind us made us jump, and we turned around to see Captain Liu doubled over. He'd taken a drink of water, but couldn't hold back his laughter, and had sprayed it out.

Through his laughter he said, "Look at Professor Ding! He's basically that tailor from 'The Emperor's New Clothes'!"

It was an apt analogy, and we burst out laughing at the humor and sheer audacity of the physicist.

"Simmer down and listen up!" Colonel Xu said, waving his hand to suppress the laughter. "We ought to have a proper understanding and attitude toward the entire experiment. We knew that it would fail, but we arrived at the common understanding that a safe return of the experimental personnel would be a victory. Now that outcome has been satisfied."

"But someone's got to be responsible for the outcome!" someone shouted. "More than a million yuan has been put into it, and a helicopter and two lives were gambled on it. Is this farce all that we get in return?" The remark drew immediate rejoinders from the crowd.

Then Ding Yi raised up the Go board to a level higher than the generated magnetic field. His movement caught people's attention, and the hooting quickly died down. When there was complete calm, Ding Yi eased the board downward until the bottom made contact with the generator.

People drew closer to look at the board, and what they saw turned them as still as statues.

Some of the squares on the board were deformed. There was a clear curve to their edges, as if the board had been placed behind an almost perfectly transparent crystal ball.

Ding Yi removed the board, and everyone bent down to peer straight on at the space. Even without the aid of the board, the bubble was visible, a faint circular outline vaguely described in the air, like a soap bubble lacking all markings.

Captain Liu was the first of the frozen crowd to move. He extended a trembling, fingernail-less hand to touch the bubble, but pulled it back in the end without making contact.

"Don't worry," Ding Yi said. "Even if you stuck your head in, it wouldn't matter."

And so the captain really did stick his head into the bubble. This was the first time that a human had looked at the outside world from within ball lightning, but Captain Liu saw nothing unusual. What he saw was a crowd cheering once again—only this time, their cheers were genuine.

MACRO-ELECTRONS

The base was close to the Kangxi Grasslands northwest of the city. To celebrate the experiment's success, we took a trip to have roast whole mutton. Dinner was outdoors on the edge of that fairly small grassland.

Colonel Xu gave a small speech: "In olden days, there must have been a day when someone had a stroke of inspiration and understood that they were surrounded by air. Later, people learned that they were constrained by gravity, and that their surroundings were an ocean of electromagnetic waves, and that cosmic radiation passes through our bodies at all times. . . . Now we know something else: that bubbles are there around us, floating nearby in space that appears empty. Now, let me speak for us all, and offer Professor Ding and Major Lin my well-deserved admiration."

Again, everyone cheered.

Ding Yi went over to Lin Yun, raised up a large saucer (he was a boozer as well as a smoker), and said, "Major, I used to have a prejudice against soldiers. I thought you were the epitome of mechanical thinking. But you have changed my ideas."

Lin Yun looked at him wordlessly. I had never seen that expression in her eyes before toward anyone—not even, I'm willing to believe, Jiang Xingchen.

And then I realized that in the midst of all of the uniforms, Ding Yi stood out. In the hot summer wind on the grassland, he seemed formed of three flags: one, his wind-tossed long hair, and the two others his large sleeveless T-shirt and shorts that whipped constantly about his thin stalk of a body, like flags hung on a flagpole. Next to him, Lin Yun cut a lovely figure in the evening light.

Colonel Xu said, "Now you all must be brimming with anticipation for Professor Ding to tell us just what ball lightning is."

Ding Yi nodded. "I know that lots of people have poured immense effort into unlocking the secret of nature, including the likes of Dr. Chen and Major Lin. They devoted their life's energies to taking the EM and fluid equations and twisting them to mind-shattering degrees, until they nearly broke. Then they put in one patch after another to plug the holes, adding extra struts to support the teetering edifice, ultimately coming up with something far too huge and complicated, and incomparably ugly. . . . Dr. Chen, do you know where you failed? It wasn't that you weren't complex enough. It was that you didn't think simply."

It was the same thing I'd heard from Lin Yun's father. Two uncommon men in two different fields had come up with the same profound observation.

"How simple could it be?" I asked, mystified.

Ding Yi disregarded my question and went on: "Next, I will tell you what ball lightning is."

At this moment, the few scattered stars that had begun to appear in the heavens seemed to stop their twinkling, as if listening for God's last judgment.

"It is nothing more than an electron."

We looked at each other, each of us trying to wrap our minds around this. Eventually we focused our attention back on Ding Yi. His answer was so weird that we lacked the ability to take it any further.

"An electron the size of a soccer ball," he added.

"An electron the . . . What makes it like that?" someone stammered.

"What do you think an electron ought to be like? An opaque, dense little ball? Yes, that's the picture of an electron, proton, or neutron in most people's minds. First I'll tell you about the picture of the universe painted by modern physics: the geometry of the universe is not physical."

"Can you be a little less abstract?"

"What if I put it this way: in the universe, apart from empty space, there is nothing."

Again we lapsed into silence and contemplated what our minds couldn't grasp. Captain Liu was the first to speak. He waved half a lamb leg in the air and said, "What do you mean, nothing? It's all empty space? This roast whole mutton is totally tangible. Are you telling me that I've just eaten emptiness?"

"Yes. All of what you've eaten is empty space, as are you, since you and the mutton are made of protons, neutrons, and electrons, particles that, on a microscopic level, are curved space." He cleared aside a few plates and drew on the tablecloth with a finger. "Suppose that space is this cloth. Atomic particles are the minute wrinkles in it."

"That's something we can understand a bit better," Captain Liu said thoughtfully.

"It's still quite different from our conventional picture of the world," Lin Yun said.

"But it's the picture that's closest to reality," Ding Yi said.

"So you mean that electrons are like bubbles?"

"Closed curved space," Ding Yi agreed, nodding gravely.

"But an electron . . . how is it so big?"

"In the briefest period after the Big Bang, all of space was flat. Later, as energy levels subsided, wrinkles appeared in space, which gave birth to all of the fundamental particles. What's been so mystifying for us is why the wrinkles should only appear at the microscopic level. Are there really no macroscopic wrinkles? Or, in other words, are there no macroscopic fundamental particles? Now we know there are."

My first thought at this point was that I could breathe at last. My mind had been asphyxiating for more than a decade, and all that time it felt like I'd been immersed in water that was murky at every turn. Now I had burst to the surface, and I took my first breath of air, and saw the vast sky. A blind man probably has the same feeling on regaining his sight.

"We're able to see the bubbles because the curved space bends the light that passes through, forming visible edges," Ding Yi went on.

"But what makes you believe they're electrons, and not protons or neutrons?" Colonel Xu asked.

"Good question. But the answer is quite simple: throughout the process of being excited by lightning, turning to ball lightning, and then returning to bubbles, the bubbles are actually electrons being excited from a low potential to high potential state, and then returning back to a low potential state. Of those three particles, only electrons can be excited in this way."

"And because it's an electron, it can be conducted through superconducting leads, and run ceaselessly through a superconducting battery, like a loop current," Lin Yun said, as understanding dawned.

"What's weird, though, is that its diameter is about the same as that battery."

"With macro-electrons, the wave form is dominant in the wave-particle duality, so the significance of its size is completely different from what we generally expect. They also have some pretty unbeliev-able characteristics, which we'll gradually observe, and which I believe will change everyone's view of the world. But right now, we need to choose a name for these large electrons. They're electrons on a mac-roscopic scale, so let's call them macro-electrons."

"Then do macro-protons and macro-neutrons also exist?"

"They ought to. But since they can't be excited, we'll have a hard time finding them."

"Professor Ding, your dream has become reality," Lin Yun said, but apart from Ding Yi and me, no one really understood the meaning of her words.

"Yes, yes. There really are watermelon-sized fundamental particles lying on the table of physics. Our next step must be to study their in-ternal structure—a structure formed from curved space. It will be dif-ficult. But innumerable times easier, I believe, than studying the structure of microscopic particles."

"Then, are there macro-atoms too? The three macro-particles ought to be able to combine into atoms!"

"Yes, there ought to be macro-atoms."

"The bubble—I mean, the macro-electron—that we caught: is it a free electron, or does it belong to a macro-atom? And if so, where's its nucleus?"

Ding Yi chuckled. "You've got me there. But there's an immense amount of space in an atom. If a macro-atom is the size of a theater hall, the nucleus would be about the size of a walnut. So if this macro-electron does belong to a macro-atom, then the nucleus would be quite far from here."

"My God. One more question: If there are macro-atoms, then is there macro-matter, and a macro-world?"

"Now we're into grand questions of philosophy," Ding Yi said to the questioner with a smile.

"So is there or isn't there a macro-world?" the questioner followed. We were like a group of children in the thrall of a story.

"I believe there's a macro-world. Or a macro-universe. But what it's like is an unknown unknown. Maybe it's completely different from our own world. Maybe it corresponds exactly, like the posited matter and antimatter universes, and there's a macro-Earth with a macro-you and -me. In that case, my brain in the macro-world would be large enough to contain our universe's entire solar system. . . . It's a parallel universe, in a way."

Night had fallen, and we looked up at the glittering summer sky, each of us straining our eyes into the vast star field, hoping to find, somewhere in the cosmic downy empty depths of the Milky Way, the enormous outlines of Ding Yi's brain. That macro-atom-made ultra-head was, in my mind, crystal clear. We were amazed that our thoughts had turned so profound all of a sudden.

After the dinner ended, we strolled tipsily on the grassland. I saw Ding Yi and Lin Yun close together, talking intimately. Ding Yi's three flags looked dashing in the night breeze, and I knew that this thin beanstalk of a guy would easily defeat the full-on masculine appeal of the carrier captain. This was the power of the mind. For whatever reason, my heart was filled with an inexpressible bitterness.

The stars in the heavens were as brilliant as they were on Mount Tai. In the night of the grassland, countless ghostly macro-electrons were drifting by.

WEAPONS

From the first successful capture of a bubble, research blazed a new trail, and forward progress smoothed out as results came in one after another. It was a little like riding a roller coaster. Once I proposed the excitement hypothesis for ball lightning, and Ding Yi used theory to describe the existence of macro-electrons, Lin Yun's technical genius began to play a critical role.

The next step in the research was naturally to collect macro-electrons. Ding Yi did not need many for his theoretical research, but the base required an enormous number for weapons research. This initially seemed like a difficult task, since the conventional electric arc collection method was highly dangerous and could hardly be used again.

People dreamed up all kinds of solutions, but the one that received the most support was remote aircraft. Although this would solve the safety problem, it would be costly and highly inefficient to use it to collect the huge number of macro-electrons needed.

Instead, Lin Yun considered detecting unexcited macro-electrons directly, believing that if they were visible to the naked eye up close, they ought to be detectable by highly sensitive optics from farther away. She designed an atmospheric optical detection system that could detect transparent objects that refracted light over a vast range of space. The system used two lasers perpendicular to each other to scan the atmosphere, while on the ground there was a highly sensitive image capture and recognition system that turned the refractions of the lasers in the atmosphere into a 3-D image, similar to how a CT scanner works.

For a while, the base was crawling with non-uniformed personnel: software engineers, optics specialists, pattern-recognition experts, and even a telescope maker.

When the system was complete, rather than macro-electrons, the screen displayed atmospheric turbulence and gas streams, movement that was ordinarily invisible, but was clear as day to the sensitive system. The atmosphere typically appeared as calm as still water, when in actuality it was astonishingly agitated, like water sloshing in a gigantic washing machine. I realized that the system would be quite useful in meteorology, but since our focus was on detecting macro-electrons, I didn't put much thought in that direction. The macro-electrons showed up amid the complicated airflow disturbances, but since they had a round shape, the pattern-recognition software could easily pick them out of the chaos. And so a large number of macro-electrons were located in the air.

Collection was far easier once we began locating them this way, since, unexcited, they posed no danger. The feeler was no longer necessary, and was replaced by a net formed out of superconducting wires, and we switched to capturing macro-electrons by blimp to save money. Sometimes multiple macro-electrons were collected at once, like trawling for fish in the sky.

Now it was far easier to capture ball lightning and turn it into a human collectible. Looking back on humanity's arduous process of studying it, the people like Zhang Bin who spent a lifetime on it without anything to show for it, and the grand tragedy of Base 3141 in the Siberian forest, we felt the heartache of knowing that we had taken such a long and winding road that had ended up being an enormous detour.

Colonel Xu said, "That's what scientific research is. Every step you've taken, no matter how absurd, is a necessary one."

He said this while sending off the helicopter group. After we began using blimps to capture the macro-electrons, the base no longer had any use for helicopters. We bade farewell to the two aviators who had been with us through hardship and danger. Those endless nights of towing the blinding arc would become one of our lives' most treasured memories and, we believed, part of scientific history.

Before leaving, Captain Liu said to us, "Work hard! We'll be waiting to install your thunderball machine gun!"

The aviators had come up with another new term, which we actually used in the field of ball lightning weapons.

The success of optical detection of unexcited macro-electrons kindled our hopes for more progress, but turned out only to demonstrate the shallowness of our physics knowledge. After the system's first success, Lin Yun and I made a beeline for Ding Yi.

"Professor Ding, now we should be able to find the nuclei of macro-atoms!"

"What gives you that impression?"

"We haven't been able to find them because macro-protons and macro-neutrons aren't excitable like macro-electrons. But now we can locate bubbles directly by optical means."

Ding Yi laughed and shook his head, as if forgiving two school pupils for their error. "The primary reason we can't find macro-atom nuclei isn't because they aren't excitable, but because we have no idea what they're like."

"What? They're not bubbles?"

"Who told you they were bubbles? The theory postulates that their shape is completely different from macro-electrons, as different as ice and fire."

I had a hard time imagining that other forms of macro-particles could be floating around us. It lent an eerie feeling to the surrounding space.

Now we were able to excite ball lightning in the lab. The excitement apparatus started off with a bubble contained inside a superconducting battery. When it was released, it was accelerated in a magnetic field, and then passed through ten separate lightning generators. The total power of the lightning produced by these generators was far greater than that of the arc that excited airborne thunderballs. The amount of lightning to produce was determined by the needs of the experiment.

As for weapons production, what we now needed to know was how to make use of the high target selectivity of the macro-electron's energy release, the most perplexing, terrifying, and devilish aspect of ball lightning.

Ding Yi said, "It concerns the wave-particle duality of macro-particles. I've established a theoretical energy-release model, and have designed an observation experiment that will show you something truly unbelievable. It's a simple experiment: observe the thunderball's energy release slowed down by a factor of 1.5 million."

"1.5 million?"

"That's right. It's a crude estimate based on the smallest-volume macro-electron we currently have stored. That's roughly the factor."

"But that's . . . 36 million frames per second! Where are we going to find recording equipment that's that fast?" someone asked.

"That's not my concern," Ding Yi said, as he lit the pipe he hadn't touched for some time in a leisurely fashion.

"I'm sure the equipment must exist!" Lin Yun said firmly. "We'll find it."

When Lin Yun and I entered the laboratory building of the State Defense Optics Institute, our attention was immediately captured by a large photograph in the lobby: a hand holding a gun whose massive barrel was aimed directly at the photographer; red flame light inside the barrel and tendrils of smoke just beginning to issue from it. The most eye-catching focal point of the photo was a ball suspended in front of the gun, coppery and smooth: the bullet that had just been fired.

"This is a high-speed photo taken during the Institute's early days. It has a temporal resolution of roughly one ten-thousandth of a second. Using today's standards, it's just ordinary fast photography, not high-speed photography. You can find that standard of equipment at any specialty camera store," a director at the Institute said.

"So who was the martyr who snapped the picture?" Lin Yun asked.

The director laughed. "A mirror. The photo was taken using a reflected light system."

The Institute had convened a small meeting with several engineers. When Lin Yun put forward our request, that we needed ultra-high-speed camera equipment, several of them grimaced.

The director said, "Our ultra-high-speed equipment is still a ways away from international levels. It's highly unstable in actual operation."

"Give us an idea of the numbers you require, and we'll see what we can do," an engineer said.

Shakily, I told them our number: "We need to take around 36 million frames per second."

I had imagined they would shake their heads, but to my surprise they burst out laughing. The director said, "After all of that, and what you're looking for is just an ordinary high-speed camera! Your notion of ultra-high-speed photography is stuck in the fifties. We're up to as much as four hundred million frames per second now. The top standards at the world level are around six hundred million."

After we'd relaxed a bit, the director led us on a tour of the Institute. He pointed to a display and said, "What does this look like to you?"

We looked at it a while, and Lin Yun said, "It looks like a slowly blooming flower. But it's strange—the petals are glowing."

The director said, "That's what makes high-speed photography the gentlest of photography. It can turn the most violent of processes gentle and light. What you see is an armor-piercing shell exploding as it strikes its target." He pointed to a bright yellow stamen in the flower, and said, "See, this ultra-high temperature, ultra-high-speed jet is piercing the armor. This was taken at a rate of around six million frames per second."

As we neared Lab 2, the director said, "What you'll see next ought to satisfy your high-speed photography requirements. It shoots at fifty million frames per second."

In this photo, we seemed to be looking at a still water surface. A small, invisible stone had landed on the surface, kicking up a bubble, which fractured, sending liquid particles in all directions as waves spread out in rings on the surface. . . .

"This is a high-energy laser striking a metal surface."

Lin Yun asked inquisitively, "Then what can you film with a hundred million frames per second ultra-high-speed camera?"

"Those images are classified, so I can't show them to you. But I can tell you that the cameras often record the controlled nuclear fusion process in a tokamak accelerator."

High-speed imaging of thunderball energy release progressed quickly. Macro-electrons were passed through all ten lightning stages and were excited to very high energy states, with energy levels far higher than any ball lightning ever excited in nature, allowing their energy release process to be somewhat more noticeable. The excited thunderballs entered the target area, which had targets of various shapes and compositions: wooden cubes, plastic cones, metal balls, cardboard boxes filled with shavings, glass cylinders, and so on. They were distributed on the ground or on cement platforms of varying height. Pure white paper was laid out under each, giving the whole target area the feel of an exhibition of modern sculpture. After a thunderball entered the target area, it was slowed by a magnetic damper, so it drifted about until it discharged or went out on its own. Three high-speed cameras were set up on the edges of the target area. They were massive and structurally complicated, and unless you knew what they were, you wouldn't think they were cameras. Since there was no way of knowing beforehand which target the thunderball's energy would strike, we had to rely on luck to capture the target.

The test started. Since it was highly dangerous, all of the personnel exited the area. The whole test procedure was directed by remote control from an underground control room three hundred meters from the lab.

The monitor showed the superconducting battery releasing the first bubble, which contacted the first arc. The monitoring system transmitted a distorted rushing sound, but the loud crack carried across the three hundred meters from the lab. The excited ball lightning moved slowly forward under the influence of the magnetic field, passing through nine more arcs as thunder rumbled ceaselessly from the lab. Every time the ball lightning contacted an arc, its energy levels doubled. Its brightness didn't increase correspondingly, but its colors changed: from dark red, it turned orange, then yellow, then white, bright green, sky blue, and plum, until at last a violet fireball entered the acceleration area, where it was whipped by an acceleration field into a torrent. In the next instant, it entered the target area. Like plunging into still water, it slowed down, and began to drift among the targets. We held our breath and waited. Then, after a burst of energy and a flash of light, a tremendous noise came from the lab that shook the glass cases in the underground control room. The energy release had turned a plastic cone into a small pile of black ash on white paper. But the high-speed camera operators said that the cameras had not been trained on that target, and so nothing had been recorded. Another eight thunderballs were subsequently fired off. Five of them discharged, but none of them struck the targets the cameras were trained on. The last energy release struck a cement platform supporting a target, blowing it to bits and causing an immense mess in the target area, so the experiment had to be halted until the lab, which now smelled heavily of ozone, was set up again.

Once the target area was reset, the tests continued. One macroelectron after another was fired at the target area to play a game of cat and mouse with the three high-speed cameras. The optics engineers worried about the safety of their cameras, since they were the equipment nearest to the target area, but we pressed on. It wasn't until the eleventh discharge that we captured an image of a target being struck, a wooden cube thirty centimeters on a side. This was a wonderful example of a ball lightning discharge: the wooden cube was incinerated into ash that retained its original cubic form, only to collapse at a touch. When the ash was cleared, the paper beneath it was completely unaffected, with not even a burn mark.

The raw high-speed image footage was being loaded into the computer, since if we were to play it back at normal speed, it would be more than a thousand hours long, of which only twenty seconds would show the target being struck. By the time we had extracted those twenty seconds, it was late at night. Holding our breath and staring at the screen, we pulled back the veil on that mysterious demon.

At a normal twenty-four frames per second, the whole clip lasted twenty-two minutes. At the time of discharge, the thunderball was around 1.5 meters from the target; fortunately, both the thunderball and the target were in frame. For the first ten seconds, the thunderball's brightness increased dramatically. We waited for the wooden cube to catch fire, but to our surprise, it lost all color and turned transparent, until it appeared only as a vague outline of a cube. When the thunderball had reached maximum brightness, the cube's outlines had totally vanished. Then the thunderball's brightness decreased, a process lasting five seconds, during which the position formerly occupied by the cube was completely empty! Then the outlines of the transparent cube began to take shape again, and soon it regained corporeality and color, only gray white—it was now a cube of ash. At this point, the thunderball was entirely extinguished.

Dumb as wooden chickens, we took a few seconds to recover and think of replaying the video. We now went through it frame by frame, and when we reached the point where the wooden cube was a transparent outline, we paused the video.

"It's like a cubic bubble!" Lin Yun said, pointing at the outline.

As we continued the playback, only the dimming thunderball and the empty white paper beneath it were visible on screen. We advanced the frames, staring at each of them for ages, but there really was nothing on the paper. Advancing further, the outlines returned, now surrounding a cube of ash. . . .

A cloud of smoke covered the screen. Ding Yi had lit his pipe at some point, and was exhaling at the screen.

"You have just witnessed the dual nature of matter!" he said loudly, pointing at the screen. "In that brief moment, the bubble and the wooden cube both exhibited a wave nature. They experienced resonance, and in that resonance the two became one. The wooden cube received the energy released by the macro-electron, and then they both regained their particle nature, the burnt wooden cube coalescing into matter at its original position. This is the puzzle that has vexed you all, and the explanation for the target selectivity of the thunderball's energy release. When the target is struck by the energy, it exhibits a wave state and is not at its original position at all. Thus the energy will naturally have no effect on the object's surroundings."

"Why is it only the target object, the wooden cube here, that exhibits a wave nature, and not the paper beneath it?"

"This is determined by the object's boundary conditions, through a mechanism similar to how image processing software can automatically pick out a face from an image."

"There's another puzzle that now has an explanation: ball lightning's penetrative power!" Lin Yun said excitedly. "When macro-electrons exhibit wave nature, they can naturally penetrate matter. And if they encounter slits roughly their size, they will be diffracted."

"When ball lightning exhibits a wave state, it can cover a large range. So when a thunderball discharges, it can affect objects at a distance," Colonel Xu said, as realization dawned.

And so the cloud of mystery surrounding ball lightning gradually dissipated. But these theory-based accomplishments did not have much direct application to the development of ball lightning weapons. As far as weapons development was concerned, a large quantity of lethal macro-electrons needed to be collected first, and theory was useless for that purpose. However, the base had captured and stored more than ten thousand macro-electrons already, and that number was swiftly growing, which gave us the liberty to use crude techniques that did not rely on any theory. We already knew that the target selected for energy discharge was determined by the nature of the macro-electron, and unrelated to the lightning that excited it. This was the basis upon which we chose our experiment.

We began conducting a large number of animal tests. The procedure was simple: take animals similar to human targets, such as rabbits, pigs, and goats, place them into the target area, and then release and excite ball lightning. If the ball lightning blast killed an animal target, then that macro-electron was selected for the weapons stockpile.

It was impossible for your spirit not to be affected by watching ball lightning turn group after group of test animals to ash every day, but Lin Yun reminded me that dying from ball lightning was far less painful for the animals than dying in a slaughterhouse. She had a point, and my heart was steadier after that. But as the tests went on, I realized that things weren't quite so simple: the target selectivity of the ball lightning's energy release was so precise that oftentimes a macro-electron discharge would incinerate an animal's bones, or vaporize its blood, but not harm its muscles or organs. Animals suffering those attacks died in a horrible fashion. Fortunately, Ding Yi made a discovery that put an end to that nightmarish experiment.

Ding Yi had been studying ways of exciting ball lightning through means other than lightning. His first thought was lasers, but that was unsuccessful. Then he thought of using high-powered microwaves, to no success. But during the course of a subsequent experiment, he discovered that microwaves were modulated into a complex spectrum after passing through a macro-electron, different spectra for different macro-electrons, like a fingerprint. Macro-electrons that discharged into like targets had like spectra. And hence, recording the spectra of a small number of macro-electrons with a suitable target selectivity made it possible to find many more similar macro-electrons using spectral recognition, without excitation experiments. And so animal testing became unnecessary.

Work on a ball lightning emitter for use in combat was proceeding at the same time. In fact, using previous work as a foundation, the technological fundamentals were basically in place. The thunderball gun consisted of several parts: a superconducting battery to store the bubbles; a magnetic field accelerator rail, which was a three-meter-long metal cylinder with EM coils set at regular intervals that could invert the instant the bubble passed, using the magnetic field created to push and pull it along the series of coils and accelerate it to speed; an excitation electrode, a row of discharge electrodes that would produce lightning to excite the thunderball as it passed; and subsidiary mechanisms, including a superconducting battery to power the system, and a machine gun targeting system. Since it used existing test equipment, the first thunderball gun required only two weeks to assemble.

Once the spectral recognition technology was in place, the search for weapons-grade macro-electrons proceeded much more quickly, and soon we had more than a thousand of them. In an excited state, their energy only discharged into organic life. This quantity of macro-electrons was enough to kill all of the defenders of a small city, without the need to break so much as a dish in a cabinet.

"Doesn't your conscience bother you even a little?" I asked Ding Yi. We were standing in front of the first ball lightning weapon, which looked not so much like an attack weapon as a radar or communications device, since the acceleration rail and excitation electrode looked like a sort of antenna. Atop it were two superconducting batteries, meter-high metal cylinders in which those thousand-odd weapons-grade macro-electrons were stored.

"Why don't you go ask Lin Yun?"

"She's a soldier. You?"

"I don't care. What I study is on a scale of less than a femtometer, or more than ten million light-years. At those scales, the Earth and human life are insignificant."

"Life is insignificant?"

"From a physics perspective, the form of matter movement known as life has no more meaning than any other movement of matter. You can't find any new physical laws in life, so from my standpoint, the death of a person and the melting of an ice cube are essentially the same thing. Dr. Chen, you tend to overthink things. You should learn to look at life from the perspective of the ultimate law of the universe. You'll feel much better if you do."

But the only thing that made me feel better was that the ball lightning weapon didn't seem as fearsome as it did at first. It was possible to defend against it. Macro-electrons could interact with magnetic fields, and if they could be accelerated by fields, they could also be deflected. It was quite possible that the weapon's power would be exhibited only briefly after its introduction in combat, so the military worked hard on the project's secrecy.

Not long after the birth of the ball lightning weapon, Zhang Bin came to the base. He was in much weaker health, but he still stayed the entire day. In a trance, he watched the macro-electrons confined by the magnetic field, and watched as each was excited into ball lightning. He was thrilled, as if an entire lifespan was concentrated in that one day.

After meeting Ding Yi, he said excitedly, "I knew that someone like you would solve the riddle of ball lightning. You and my wife, Zheng Min, graduated from the same department. She was a genius like you. If she were still alive today, these discoveries wouldn't have been yours to make."

Before leaving, Zhang Bin said, "I know I don't have much time left. My only wish now is to be cremated by ball lightning when I die."

I wanted to say some words of comfort, but, realizing that he didn't need any, I just nodded silently.

OBSERVERS

A ball lightning weapons force was established, only a company at first, under the leadership of an unflappable lieutenant colonel named Kang Ming. The force was code-named Dawnlight, a name Lin Yun and I came up with, since the first excitation of ball lightning had been an unforgettable moment, when it turned the surrounding wisps of clouds red like a miniature sunrise.

Dawnlight began intensive training immediately. The core of the training was live fire target practice. To get as close as possible to actual combat conditions, training was conducted outdoors, but it had to be carried out on overcast days to prevent satellite detection. For this reason, several target ranges were chosen in the rainy south, and exercises switched constantly among them.

Across those target ranges flew lines of ball lightning fired from thunderball guns, in lines or fanned out toward their target. The balls made noise as they flew, like a shrill trumpet, or a gale across the wilderness. The sound of the thunderball explosion was very peculiar, with no directionality, as if it came from all of space, or even from within your own body.

One day, we followed Dawnlight as it moved to a new target range. Ding Yi had come; but as he was in charge of theory, there was nothing much for him to do here.

"I came to prevent you from making an error, and to demonstrate something weird," he said.

As the force was preparing for live firing, Ding Yi asked us, "Do you often engage in philosophical speculation?"

"Not much," I said.

"Never," Lin Yun said.

Ding Yi glanced at Lin Yun, and said, "Not surprising. You're a woman." When she glared back at him, he added, "It doesn't matter. Today I'm going to force you to think philosophically."

We looked around us. The target range was a damp forest clearing under an overcast sky. At the other end were temporary buildings and junked vehicles that served as targets. We couldn't see anything that could be connected to philosophy.

Lieutenant Colonel Kang came over dressed in camos, and asked Ding Yi about his requests for the shooting.

"They're simple. First, shut down all monitoring equipment at the site. Second, and most importantly, during the firing, close your eyes as soon as you aim at the target, and don't open them until my command. This applies to everyone, including the commanders."

"You . . . may I ask you why?"

"I will explain, Lieutenant Colonel. First I'd like to ask you a question. At this distance, what is the target hit rate of the ball lightning you fire?"

"Nearly one hundred percent, Professor. Since thunderballs aren't affected by air movement, their paths are steady after acceleration."

"Very good. Now begin. Remember, after aiming, everyone must close their eyes!"

When I heard the shout "Target set," I closed my eyes. Soon afterward, I heard the crackle of the excitation arcs in the thunderball acceleration rails, which caused my flesh to crawl. Then the thunderballs started whistling. It felt like they were being fired at me, and my scalp tightened, but I fought to keep my eyes closed.

"Good. Now you all can open your eyes," Ding Yi choked out through the ozone produced by the ball lightning explosions.

I opened my eyes and felt a momentary lightheadedness, and listened to the target reporter's voice on the radio: "Shots fired: ten. Hits: one. Misses: nine." Then in a softer voice, "What the hell!" A number of soldiers, I noticed, were scrambling to put out brush fires started by the errant ball lightning explosions.

"How did that happen?" Lieutenant Colonel Kang demanded of the shooter behind the thunderball weapon. "Didn't you aim properly before you shut your eyes?"

"We did! The aim was dead-on!" the sergeant said.

"Then . . . inspect the weapon."

"That's not necessary. There's nothing wrong with the weapon or the shooter," Ding Yi said with a wave of his hand. "Don't forget, ball lightning is an electron."

"You mean it exhibits a quantum effect?" I asked.

Ding Yi nodded. "Indeed it does. In the presence of an observer, its state collapses to a determined value. This value is consistent with our experience in the macro-world, so it strikes the target. But without an observer, it exhibits a quantum state where nothing is determined, and its position can only be described as a probability. In such circumstances, all of this ball lightning exists in the form of an electron cloud—a probability cloud. And a strike on the target location is very improbable."

"So you mean that the thunderballs can't strike anything we can't see?" the lieutenant colonel asked in disbelief.

"That's right. Wonderful, isn't it?"

"It's a little too . . . anti-materialistic," Lin Yun said, shaking her head in confusion.

"See, now that's philosophy. It may have been forced, but you've done it." Ding Yi made a face at me, and then said to Lin Yun, "Don't try to school me in philosophy."

"Right. I'm not qualified. The world would be a terrible place if everyone shared your ultimate line of thinking," Lin Yun said, shrugging.

"You surely know a little bit of the principles of quantum mechanics," Ding Yi said.

"Yes, I do. More than just a little. But . . ."

"But you never expected to see it in the macro-world, right?"

The lieutenant colonel said, "Do you mean to say that if the thunderballs are to strike a target, we must watch them from start to finish?"

Ding Yi nodded, and said, "Or the enemy could watch them. But there must be an observer."

"Let's do it again, and see what a probability cloud looks like," Lin Yun said excitedly.

Ding Yi shook his head. "That's impossible. The quantum state is only exhibited in the absence of an observer. Once the observer appears, it collapses into our experienced reality. We will never be able to see a probability cloud."

"Can't we just put a camera onto a drone?" the lieutenant colonel said.

"A camera is an observer, too, and will likewise collapse the quantum state. This is why I had all of the monitoring equipment shut off."

"But the cameras don't have consciousness," Lin Yun said.

"Now who's being anti-materialistic? The observer doesn't need consciousness." Ding Yi grinned devilishly at her.

"This can't be right," I said, feeling like I'd found a flaw in his thinking. "If it's as you say, then wouldn't anything in the vicinity of ball lightning be an observer? Just like they leave an image of themselves in the camera's photoreceptive system, ball lightning also leave ionized traces behind in the air. The light they give off causes a response in the surrounding plants, and their sound vibrates the sand. . . . The surrounding environment retains traces of them to some extent. There's no difference between this and the images taken by the camera."

"Yes. But there's a huge difference in the strength of the observer. A camera recording an image is a strong observer. Sand vibrating in place on the ground is a weak observer. Weak observers can also cause the quantum state to collapse, but it is very unlikely."

"This theory is too bizarre to accept."

"Without experimental evidence, it would be. But the quantum effect was proven at the microscopic level early on in the last century. Now we've finally observed its macroscopic manifestation. . . . If only Bohr were alive, or de Broglie, or Heisenberg and Dirac . . ." Ding Yi grew emotional, and paced back and forth as if sleepwalking, muttering to himself.

"It's a good thing Einstein is dead," Lin Yun said.

Then I remembered something: Ding Yi had insisted on installing four surveillance systems in the lab where macro-electron excitement had been carried out, in addition to the high-speed cameras. I asked him about it.

"Right. That was out of safety concerns. If all of the systems failed, the ball lightning would be in a quantum state that would engulf a good portion of the base in an electron cloud. Ball lightning could suddenly appear at any location."

And then I understood why, in so many eyewitness accounts throughout history, ball lightning had appeared mysteriously and drifted randomly, always popping up out of nowhere, with no nearby lightning to excite it. This quite probably was because the observer was within a macro-electron probability cloud, and the chance observation caused the ball lightning's quantum state to collapse.

I exclaimed, "I thought I already more or less understood ball lightning. I never imagined—"

"There's lots you haven't imagined, Dr. Chen. You can't imagine the sheer oddity of nature," Ding Yi said, cutting me off.

"What else?"

"There are things I can't even bring myself to discuss with you," Ding Yi said in a low voice.

This didn't sink in at first, but after a second of thought, I shuddered. I looked up at him, and saw him staring at me with a snakelike gleam in his eye that made my whole body shiver. Deep in my consciousness was a dark and shadowy place that I had striven to forget, and had nearly succeeded—a place I did not now dare to touch.

In the next two days of experiments, ball lightning's macro-quantum effect received further confirmation. When observers were removed, the ball lightning shot from the thunderball weapon missed by wide margins, and hit targets at a rate of only one-tenth of that when an observer was present. We brought in additional equipment and performed more complicated tests, chiefly in an attempt to determine the size of the probability cloud of a macro-electron in a quantum state. Using a strict quantum mechanics definition, this terminology wasn't entirely correct, since an electron (whether macro or micro) has a probability cloud the size of the entire universe, so it was possible that ball lightning in a quantum state might appear in the Andromeda Nebula, although the probability of that was infinitesimally small. We used "probability cloud" in engineering terms, to refer to a fuzzy boundary beyond which the chance was so low as to be insignificant.

But on the third day, the unexpected happened. Without any observer present, the ten shots from the thunderball gun all struck the target. They were a class of macro-electrons that released energy into metal and had been excited into a high-energy state. A third of the junked armored vehicle serving as the target was liquefied.

"Something must have been overlooked and left behind an observer. Maybe one of the cameras wasn't turned off. Or, more likely, some soldier snuck a peek, to see what a macro-electron cloud looks like," Ding Yi said decisively.

And so before the next test, the two cameras were dismantled, and all of the personnel on the target range were removed to a shielded basement cut off from the outside world. With the range empty, the already-aimed thunderball guns were switched to automatic fire mode.

But every one of the fifteen shots of ball lightning struck the target.

I was pleased that something had stumped Ding Yi, even if it was only a momentary difficulty. Looking over the results, he did seem worried, but his worry was different from what I imagined, and he didn't seem overly perplexed. "Stop all tests and live fire training immediately," he told Lin Yun.

Lin Yun looked at him, and then glanced up at the sky.

I said, "Why do we have to stop? There was no quantum effect this time despite the complete absence of an observer. We have to find the reason."

Lin Yun looked up and shook her head. "No, there was an observer."

I looked up at the sky, and realized that at some point the clouds had parted, and a thin strip of blue was visible through the crack.

We returned from the south to a Beijing autumn where the nights were already chilly.

The temperatures dropped, and with them the military's enthusiasm for ball lightning weapons. Back at the base, we learned from Colonel Xu that the General Staff Department and the General Armaments Department were not planning on equipping troops with these weapons in large numbers, and Dawnlight would not be expanded in size. This attitude on the part of the higher-ups was primarily motivated by the probability that the enemy would build defenses against ball lightning weapons. The weapons we had come up with were their own nemesis: ball lightning could be both accelerated and deflected in a magnetic field, so the enemy could use a reverse magnetic field to defend against it. Once the weapon made it into a combat situation, it would quickly meet an effective defense.

The next stage of research at the base followed two forks: a search for a way to breach the magnetic field defense, and a reorientation of ball lightning's target from personnel to weapons equipment, particularly high-tech weapons.

The first idea was to collect macro-electrons that would melt wiring. This would be an effective way to disable the enemy's high-tech weapons. But a serious problem was discovered during experiments: ball lightning that would melt wiring would also discharge into large metal objects, and since melting large metal objects required immense amounts of power, most of the energy in this form of ball lightning was discharged into the metal object, with little released into the wire. Efficiency was poor, and potential damage to the weaponry was very limited.

Our very next thought, naturally, was that electronic chips might make an excellent target for ball lightning weapons. First of all, unlike wires, chips were made of a unique material for which nothing similar yet nonessential existed to split the ball lightning's energy. Additionally, chips were small, so a relatively minor discharge could destroy a large number of them. Chip destruction was absolutely fatal to modern high-tech weaponry. But macro-electrons that discharged into chips (we called them chip-eating macro-electrons) were very rare, like pearls in the imperial crown of ball lightning. To collect a sufficient quantity of them required capturing a huge number of macro-electrons to subject to spectral recognition, for which substantial funds were needed. But the higher-ups had stopped further investment in the project.

To gain their attention, and to win research funding, Colonel Xu decided to conduct an attack exercise using the chip-eaters we had already collected.

———

The exercise was conducted at the MBT 2005 test base, where Lin Yun and I had gone to learn about the feeler defense system. Now all was quiet here. Weeds grew in the vehicle tracks. All we could see were two MBT 2005s that had been brought here the day before for use as test targets.

Initially, only General Armaments Department personnel were supposed to watch the tests, but a notice sent two hours beforehand doubled the number of observers. Most of them were from the General Staff Department, and included a major general and a lieutenant general.

We first took them on a tour of the target area. Apart from the two tanks, the targets to be fired upon included several armored vehicles equipped with military electronic equipment. One vehicle held a frequency-hopping radio, another held a radar assembly, and a third held several hardened military-use computers. The computers were switched on, their screens displaying various images on screen saver mode. One additional target was an obsolete surface-to-air missile. The vehicles and equipment were set up in a line.

After showing them the target equipment, we specifically opened the electronic control portion to show them the unharmed chips on the circuit boards.

"Young man, are you telling us that your new weapon will completely destroy these ICs?" the lieutenant general asked.

"Yes, General. But the other parts will remain unharmed," I answered.

"The ICs will be fried by lightning-produced induction, is that correct?" the major general asked. He was quite young, and evidently a technical officer.

I shook my head. "No. EM induction from ordinary lightning would be drastically weakened by the Faraday cage effect of the tank's metallic exterior. Ball lightning will penetrate the armor and turn the chips to ash."

The two generals glanced at each other and smiled, then shook their heads, clearly unconvinced.

Then Lin Yun and Colonel Xu brought us all to the firing site five hundred meters away and showed them the thunderball gun. It was installed on a truck that had once been used for transporting rockets.

The lieutenant general said, "I have a sixth sense about weapons. An immensely powerful weapon, regardless of what it looks like, will have an invisible edge to it. But I can't see any edge to this thing."

Colonel Xu said, "Sir, the first atomic bomb looked like a big iron barrel. You wouldn't have seen any edge on it, either. Your sixth sense is only applicable to conventional weapons."

The general said, "I hope so."

Out of safety concerns, we erected a simple cover for the observers out of sandbags. When firing was about to commence, the visitors all filed behind it.

Ten minutes later, firing began. The thunderball gun was operated much like a conventional machine gun, with a trigger-like firing device and sight that were nearly identical to a machine gun's. In the initial design, firing was carried out via computer, using a mouse to drag the crosshairs across the screen to lock on a target; the thunderball gun would automatically train the launcher on the target. But this required a complicated electro-mechanical system, and the thunderball weapon didn't need to be aimed particularly precisely—that is, even with a certain amount of deviation, the ball lightning would still incinerate the target. So we decided to use a more primitive means of controlling this advanced weapon, partly because of tight time constraints, but also to make the weapon as streamlined and reliable as possible. Now it was operated by a sergeant, a distinguished marksman from the force.

First we heard a series of deafening crackles, a sound produced by the artificial lightning used for excitation at the head of the launcher, closely followed by the emergence of three lightning balls, glowing orange red. They flew off in the direction of a tank with a shrill whistle, spaced roughly five meters apart, and disappeared when they struck the target, as if melting into the tank. Then, from the tank, came the sound of three explosions, clear and sharp, as if the detonations had not been inside it but right next to our ears. Then the other targets were fired upon, two to five shots of ball lightning apiece. The crackle of the excitation arc, the whistle of the ball lightning, and then the explosion when they struck the target sounded in turn. In the target area five hundred meters away, two balls that had missed their targets or passed through without exploding drifted about. . . .

When the last thunderball struck the surface-to-air missile, calm descended. The two misses floated above the target area for a while before disappearing silently in succession. One armored car was smoking, but the other targets sat there calmly, as if nothing at all had happened.

"What did those signal flares of yours do?" a colonel asked Lin Yun.

"You'll find out!" she said, full of confidence.

Everyone exited the shelter and walked the five hundred meters to the target area. Although confident about the results we were about to witness, I couldn't help but feel a little nervous at being surrounded by all of the senior officers who would decide the fate of the project. Ahead of us, the armored car was no longer smoking, but there was a crisp odor in the air that grew stronger the closer we got. One general asked what it was.

Lin Yun said, "Ozone, emitted in the ball lightning discharge explosion. It might replace the smell of gun smoke on the battlefield of the future, sir."

Lin Yun and I brought them to the armored car first. The observers circled it, peering at it closely, evidently thinking they would find burn traces, but there was nothing to be found. The vehicle body was unchanged. When we opened the door, a few of them stuck their heads in for a look, but apart from a stronger smell of ozone, there was no trace of damage. The four military computers were still lined up inside the vehicle, but it would not have escaped notice that one thing was different: all of the screens were dark. We pulled one of the computers out onto the ground, and Lin Yun quickly opened up its dark green case. I held it up at an angle, and dumped out a white ash intermingled with a few black fragments from the interior. I held the case up high to let them all see the interior, and I heard gasps from the crowd.

On the motherboard, two-thirds of the chips were gone.

The gasps continued. In the MBT 2005, the observers saw that the communications equipment and the radar had more than half of their chips burned to ash. When we finally opened up the nose of the surface-to-air missile, the gasps reached a crescendo, since the missile's guidance module had been turned into a reliquary for cremated chips. The two soldiers from the missile corps in charge of removing the warhead looked up at Lin Yun and me with fear in their eyes, then looked through the gaps in the crowd to the distant thunderball weapon, looking like they'd seen a ghost.

The lieutenant general declared, "It can take out the main strength of an entire army!"

The observers applauded enthusiastically. If ball lightning weapons were to have an advertising slogan, there was nothing more appropriate.

After returning to base, I noticed a loss of my own: the notebook computer I had taken with me to the exercise wouldn't turn on. I took it apart, and discovered its insides were covered in a fine white ash. I blew on it, and it took flight and sent me coughing. Taking another look at the motherboard, I saw that the CPU and two 256 MB sticks of ram were missing, turned into the dust now drifting about me. During the firing demonstration, I was in a position half the distance from the ball lightning ignition point that the others were so as to observe and record, but I was still much farther than the customary fifty-meter safe distance.

It should have occurred to me before, really. The chips were so small in size that each could absorb only a small amount of the energy discharged by the ball lightning, leaving the remainder to act at a much larger distance. For tiny targets such as chips, ball lightning's threat radius was greatly expanded.

One night under a brilliant moon, Lin Yun, Ding Yi, and I strolled easily along a path on base discussing how the ball lightning weapon could defeat the magnetic defense problem.

"Now we can be certain that, so long as we use charged macro-electrons, the problem is unsolvable," Lin Yun said.

"That's my opinion, too," Ding Yi said. "Recently I've been trying to use the motion state of macro-electrons to locate the nucleus of the atom they belong to, but the theory is extremely knotty, and there are certain obstacles that are practically impossible to overcome. It's a long road, and I fear that humanity won't make any breakthroughs this century."

I looked up at the stars, thinned out now due to the full moon, and tried to imagine what an atom five hundred to a thousand kilometers in diameter would be like.

Ding Yi went on, "But on second thought, if we can find a macro-nucleus, that would mean we can obtain chargeless macro-neutrons, which would be able to penetrate EM barriers."

"Macro-neutrons can't be excited like macro-electrons, and don't have energy release. How would they be weaponized?" Lin Yun asked the question I was about to.

Ding Yi was about to answer, but then Lin Yun put a finger to her lips. "Shh—listen!"

We were walking next to the ball lightning excitation lab. Before the advent of spectral recognition, it was here that large numbers of animal tests were performed with select weapons-grade macro-electrons, turning hundreds of test animals to ash. It was the same building that Lin Yun had taken me to on my first visit to the base to demonstrate the lightning weapon. Under the moonlight it looked like an enormous shadow, without definition. Lin Yun motioned for us to stop, and when our footsteps ceased, I heard a sound coming from the lab.

It was the bleat of a goat.

There were no goats in the lab. Animal tests had stopped two months ago, and during that time, the lab had been sealed.

I heard the sound again, unmistakably a goat's bleat: faint, and a little bleak. Oddly, the sound reminded me of ball lightning explosions, since the two shared the same quality: even though a listener could determine the direction of the sound's source, it nevertheless seemed to fill all space, and sometimes seemed to be coming from inside your body.

Lin Yun headed toward the lab entrance, Ding Yi following close behind, but my feet were like lead and I stood rooted in place. It was the same old sensation, a whole body chill, as if I were in the grip of an icy hand. I knew they wouldn't find any goat.

Lin Yun pushed open the lab door, and the heavy iron rumbled loudly as it rolled back on its track, drowning out the faint bleats. When the door sound had subsided, the goat's bleats were gone as well. Lin Yun turned on the light, and through the doorway, I could see part of the building's vast interior. A square pen formed from two-meter-high iron fencing had once held the targets for excitation experiments. Several hundred test animals had been incinerated by ball lightning there. Now, the space was completely empty. Lin Yun looked inside the huge lab for a while, but as I had predicted, she found nothing. Ding Yi stood at the entrance, the light casting a long, thin shadow behind him on the ground.

"I clearly heard a goat!" Lin Yun called, her voice echoing in the cavernous interior.

Ding Yi didn't respond, but turned and walked toward me. When he reached me, he said softly, "Have you come across anything in all these years?"

"What do you mean?" I said, striving to keep my voice from trembling.

"Some . . . things it would be impossible for you to encounter."

"I don't understand." I forced a laugh, which must have sounded ridiculous.

"Forget it." Ding Yi clapped me on the shoulder. He had never done that before. The action gave me a smidgen of comfort. "In the natural world, the unusual is just another manifestation of the normal." As I was considering this, he shouted toward Lin Yun in the lab, "Stop looking and come out!"

Lin Yun turned off the light before she came out, and just as the door was closing, I saw a shaft of moonlight from a high window light up the now-dark lab, casting a trapezoid of light on the floor, right in the center of the pen of death. The building felt cold and sinister, like a long-forgotten tomb.

THE NUCLEAR POWER PLANT

Actual use of ball lightning weapons took place much earlier than we anticipated.

It was around midday that Dawnlight received an emergency order for immediate departure, fully equipped for combat. The order added that this was not a drill. One platoon carrying two thunderball guns left by helicopter, and Colonel Xu, Lin Yun, and I went along. After a short flight of not much more than ten minutes, we landed. It wouldn't have taken much longer to go by car on a convenient highway, so this was clearly an emergency situation.

We disembarked and realized immediately where we were. In front of us was a white complex gleaming in the sun, one that had appeared countless times on television. An enormous columnar structure stood conspicuously in the center of the complex. This was a large-scale nuclear reactor, newly built as the largest nuclear power plant in the world.

From our vantage point, the plant appeared exceedingly calm and devoid of people. But our surroundings were bustling. Groups of heavily equipped People's Armed Police leaped out of the military vehicles that had just pulled up. Three officers next to a military jeep peered in the direction of the plant through binoculars for quite a long while. Beside a police car a group of police officers were putting on bulletproof vests, their submachine guns lying in disarray on the ground. I followed Lin Yun's gaze to several snipers on a roof behind us, rifles trained on the reactor.

The helicopters had landed in the yard of the plant's guesthouse. Without saying a word, a PAP colonel led us to a conference room inside that evidently served as the temporary command center. Several PAP commanders and police officers were clustered round a black-suited official looking at a large paper chart that appeared to be an internal blueprint of the plant. Our officer guide informed us that the official was the operational commander. I recognized him from his frequent television appearances. That such a high-ranking official was here indicated the gravity of the situation.

"What are regular troops doing here? Things are getting overcomplicated!" a police officer said.

"Oh, I asked GSD to bring them in. They've got new equipment that might be useful," the operational commander said. This was the first time he had raised his head since we came in. I noticed in his expression none of the tension and anxiety of the military and police officers around him, but rather the faint fatigue of routine that, in this situation, was an expression of inner strength. "Which of you is in charge? Ah, hello, Colonel," he said to Xu Wencheng. "I have two questions. First, can your equipment destroy a live target without damaging any of the facilities inside the structure?"

"Yes, sir."

"Second . . . hmm, why don't you take a look at the site conditions first and then I'll ask you. Let's continue," he said, and he and the group around him turned their attention back to the large chart.

The colonel who had led us in motioned for us to follow him, and we went from the conference room to the door of an adjacent room. It was ajar, and a large number of temporary cables were running through it. The colonel gestured for us to remain in place.

"There's little time, so I'll give you only a brief rundown of the situation. At nine o'clock this morning, eight armed terrorists took over the power plant's nuclear reactor. They entered by hijacking a bus taking elementary school students on a plant tour, and in the course of occupying the reactor, they killed six plant security guards. Now they have thirty-five hostages: twenty-seven students and teachers from the bus, and eight plant engineers and operating personnel."

"Where are they from?" Lin Yun asked.

"The terrorists? The Garden of Eden."

I knew about that international terrorist organization. Even an utterly benign idea could be dangerous if taken to an extreme, and the Garden of Eden was a classic example. It had originated as a group of technological escapists who had established an experimental microsociety on an island in the Pacific Ocean in an attempt to break free from modern technology and return to nature. Like many similar organizations throughout the world, it was closed off in the beginning, a community with no aggressive tendencies at all. But as time passed in seclusion, the mentality of these isolationists turned radical, and their flight from technology turned into a hatred of it, their removal from science into an opposition to it. Some extreme diehards left the island they called the Garden of Eden and, with a mission to obliterate all of the world's modern technology and bring it back to nature, began engaging in terrorist activities. Unlike other stripes of terrorists, the Garden of Eden attacked targets that were bewildering to the public: they blew up the European Synchrotron, burned down the two largest genetics labs in North America, destroyed a large neutrino detection tank deep within a mine in Canada, and even assassinated three Nobel Physics laureates. The group found repeated success at research facilities where scientists were minimally defended, but this was its first attack on a nuclear reactor.

"What measures have you taken?" Lin Yun asked.

"None. We've set up an observational perimeter at a distance, but we haven't dared approach. They've put explosives on the reactor and can blow them up at any time."

"As far as I'm aware, these large nuclear reactors have a very thick and sturdy shell. Several meters of reinforced cement. How much explosive material could they have brought in?"

"Not much. They only took in a small vial of red pills."

The colonel's words sent a chill through Lin Yun and me. Garden of Eden may have hated technology, but they would use any means necessary to achieve their goals. It was, in fact, the world's most technologically sophisticated terrorist organization, and a significant number of its members were top-flight scientists. The red pills were their own creation, enriched uranium, clad in some nanomaterial. Under sufficient impact force, fission detonation was possible without the need to achieve supercritical mass by other means of compression. Their typical method was to weld the muzzle of a large-bore gun shut, place several red pills inside it, and chamber a flattened-down bullet. When the gun was fired, the bullet would strike the red pills, triggering a nuclear explosion. When the Garden of Eden used this gadget to successfully break the world's largest synchrotron, which was several kilometers underground, into three segments, it threw the world into terror overnight.

Before the colonel led us into the room, he gave us a warning: "Be careful what you say in there. We have set up bidirectional communication."

After entering, we saw several military and police officers staring at a large screen displaying a surprising scene. For a moment I thought there must be some mistake, for we were watching a teacher leading a class for a group of students. Behind her was a wide control panel with lots of display screens and flashing instruments, probably one of the reactor's control rooms. It was the teacher who caught my attention. She was in her thirties, plainly dressed, with a gaunt face that made the delicate glasses dangling from a gold chain around her neck look particularly large. A keen intelligence showed in her eyes. Her voice was soft and gentle, and it soothed some of my fear and anxiety to listen to it. My heart immediately filled with respect for the teacher, who had taken her students to visit a nuclear plant and maintained composure in the face of danger, and now was soothing them with a laudable sense of duty.

"She's the head of the Asian branch of Garden of Eden and is the primary architect and director of this act of terrorism. In North America last March, she assassinated two Nobel laureates in one day and escaped capture. She's the third most wanted Garden of Eden fugitive in the world," the colonel whispered to us, pointing at the teacher on the screen.

I lost all grip on the world around me, like I'd been bashed in the head. I twisted around to look at Lin Yun, who didn't seem particularly surprised. Looking back at the screen, I noticed something unusual: the children were crowded close together and were looking fearfully at the teacher, as if she were a monster who'd popped up out of nowhere. I soon discovered the reason for their fear: a boy was lying on the ground, the top of his skull shattered. His eyes, wide open, stared across the floor with a bemused expression at the abstract painting formed of brains and blood. The teacher's bloody footprints were on the ground, too, and her right sleeve was spattered with blood. The gun she had used to shoot the kid in the head was lying on the control station behind her.

"Now, children, my dear children. You have been very good in class, and it's time for a new stage. I'll ask a question: What are the basic building blocks of matter?" The teacher continued her lesson, her voice still soft and gentle, but I felt like a cold, supple snake had wrapped itself around my throat. The children must have been feeling the same thing, only ten times worse.

When no one responded, the teacher said, "You. You answer," pointing at a girl. "Don't worry. There's nothing to be afraid of if you're wrong," she said gently, a kind smile on her face.

"A . . . atoms," the girl said, in a trembling voice.

"Very good. See: you're wrong, but it doesn't matter. Now I'll tell you the correct answer. The basic building blocks of matter are—" She emphasized each word with a stroke of her hand. "Metal. Wood. Water. Fire. Earth. Good. Now repeat that ten times. Metal, wood, water, fire, earth."

The children recited the elements ten times.

"Very good, children. That's right. The world has been made complicated by science, and we're going to make it simple again. Life has been raped by technology, and we're going to make it pure again! Have you ever seen an atom? How do they have anything to do with us? Don't let those scientists trick you. They are the filthiest, most foolish people in the world. . . . Now, please wait a moment. I've got to finish this lesson before negotiations can continue. I can't let the children get behind in their lessons." The last bit was evidently directed at us.

She must have had a display there that allowed her to see us, since she glanced in a different direction when she spoke to us. Then something caught her attention.

"Oh? A woman? Finally you've got a woman there. How wonderful!" she said, clearly referring to Lin Yun. Then she clasped her hands together in an expression of sincere surprise.

Lin Yun nodded at the teacher, an icy smile on her face. I realized

I felt a certain dependence on Lin Yun now. I knew that the teacher's ruthlessness wouldn't frighten her, since she was similarly ruthless, and had the emotional power to combat the teacher. I lacked that power, and the teacher had casually flattened my spirit.

"We have a common language," the teacher said with a smile, as if talking to a close friend. "Women are intrinsically opposed to technology, not like nauseatingly robotic men."

"I'm not opposed to technology. I am an engineer," Lin Yun said evenly.

"I was too, once. But that doesn't prevent us from seeking out a new life. Your major's emblem is very pretty. It's a remnant of ancient armor, that, like humanity, has been so eroded by technology that there's only a smidgen left. We ought to treasure it."

"Why did you kill that child?"

"Child? Was he a child?" The teacher looked with frightened eyes at the corpse on the ground. "Our first lesson was about life guidance. I asked him what he wanted to be when he grew up, and do you know what the little idiot said? He said he wanted to be a scientist. His little brain was already polluted by science. Yes, science pollutes everything!" Then she turned to the other children, and said, "Good children, let's not be scientists. Let's not be engineers or doctors either. Let's never grow up. We're all little herders riding on the back of a big water buffalo playing a bamboo flute as we traipse across the green grass. Have you ever ridden a water buffalo? Have you ever blown a bamboo flute? Do you know that there was once a purer and more beautiful age? In those days, the sky was so blue and the clouds were so white. The grass was so green you'd cry, and the air was sweet. Every brook was clear as crystal, life as leisurely as a nighttime serenade, love as intoxicating as the moon . . . but science and technology stripped away all of that. Now ugly cities blanket the ground, the blue sky and white clouds are gone, the green grass has withered, the brooks have turned black, and the buffalo has been penned up on a farm and turned into a robot making milk and meat. The bamboo is gone, and there's only maddening rock music played by robots. . . . What are we doing here? Children, we want to bring humanity back to the Garden of Eden! First, we need to let everyone know how vile science and technology are. And how can we do that? If you want to make people realize how disgusting a boil is, what do you do? You cut it open. Today we're going to cut open this technological boil, this huge nuclear reactor, and spill out its radioactive pus. Then people will see the true face of technology—"

"Can you grant me one request?" Lin Yun cut in.

"Of course, my dear."

"Let me be your hostage in place of those children."

The teacher smiled but shook her head.

"Let me replace just one of them."

Still smiling, the teacher shook her head again. "Major, do you think I don't know what you are? Your blood is as cold as mine. After you come in, in point five seconds you'll have taken my gun, and then you'll put a bullet through each of my eyes, point two five seconds apiece."

"From the way you talk, you really do seem like an engineer," Lin Yun said with a chilly laugh.

"All engineers can go to hell," the teacher said, still smiling. Then she turned and picked up the gun from the control station, trained it on the camera, and advanced until we could see the rifling inside the barrel. We heard half a gunshot, which the microphone picked up as a hiss, and then the camera cut out and the screen went white.

I left the room and let out a long breath, as if I'd just come up from a cellar. The colonel briefly explained the structure of the reactor and control room, and then we returned to the conference room, in time to hear a police officer say, ". . . If the terrorists had proposed conditions, we would have agreed to everything for the safety of the children, and then figured something out. But the problem is that they haven't given any conditions. They came to blow up the reactor, and the only reason they haven't done so yet is because they are attempting a live broadcast to the outside using a small satellite antenna they brought with them. The situation is already critical. They could blow it up at any time."

Noticing us coming in, the operational commander said, "Now that you know the situation, I'll ask my second question. Can your weapon distinguish between adults and children?"

Colonel Xu said that it couldn't.

"Can't they avoid the control room where the children are, and only attack the reactor area? That's the section where the terrorists are working with the bombs," a police officer said.

"No!" said a PAP senior colonel, before Colonel Xu had a chance to reply. "The teacher brought a remote control with her." Apparently they had already adopted the nickname "teacher" for this terrible monster of a woman.

"It wouldn't work, in any case," Colonel Xu said. "The reactor and the control room are part of the same structure, and the weapon attacks the structure as a whole. Walls don't stop it. Given its size, no matter where the weapon is aimed, the entire structure will be in lethal range. Unless the children are brought out and taken far away from the reactor structure, they'll definitely be injured or killed."

"What is that weapon, anyway? A neutron bomb?"

"I'm sorry. I can only provide further details after authorization from GAD leadership."

"There's no need," the senior colonel said, turning to the operational commander. "It looks like it won't work."

"I think it will work," Lin Yun said, speaking out of turn and making me and Colonel Xu nervous. She went over to the operational commander's desk, placed her hands flat on the surface, and directed a scorching look at him. He met her stare with a calm face. "Sir," she said, "I think the present situation is as clear as one plus one equals two."

"Lin Yun!" Colonel Xu snapped.

"Let the major finish speaking," the operational commander said, unperturbed.

"I've finished, sir." She dropped her gaze and retreated to the back.

"Very well. Apart from the emergency command center personnel, the rest of you comrades can wait outside," the commander said. He dropped his gaze too, but he wasn't looking at the blueprint any longer.

We came to the roof of the guesthouse, where the other Dawnlight members had convened. Two thunderball guns had been set up on the edge of the roof, each covered by a green tarp. Near them were four superconducting batteries, two charged up for the immense power required to excite ball lightning, and the other two containing two thousand anti-personnel macro-electrons.

Two hundred meters away, the huge column of the nuclear reactor stood quietly under the sun.

When the PAP colonel left, Colonel Xu said to Lin Yun in a low voice, "What are you up to? You're well aware that the main risk of ball lightning weapons right now is that if there's a leak the enemy can easily build effective defenses against it. Then where's our battlefield advantage? With tensions as high as they are, the enemy's surveillance satellites and spies have their attention focused on anything unusual in any part of the country. If we use it—"

"Colonel, this right here is a battlefield! The reactor has a volume ten times that of Chernobyl. If it's blown up, you'll have a no-man's land hundreds of kilometers in diameter. Hundreds of thousands of people might die from the radiation!"

"I'm fully aware of that. If the higher-ups gave the order to use ball lightning, I would resolutely carry it out. The problem is that you shouldn't have overstepped the scope of your position to influence the director's decision."

Lin Yun remained silent.

"You really want to use that weapon," I said, unable to hold back.

"So what if I do? There's nothing abnormal about that attitude," Lin Yun said quietly.

Then we all stopped speaking. The hot wind of early autumn blew across the roof, and the sound of cars screeching to a halt came up from the foot of the building, closely followed by the rapid footfalls of soldiers exiting the vehicles, and metallic clashes of weapons against armor. Apart from a few short commands, there was no talking. But within these sounds I sensed a terrifying deathly silence overwhelming all the other sounds striving madly to escape, and crushing them in its giant palm.

Not much time had passed before the PAP colonel came back. Everyone on the roof stood up, and he said simply, "Would the military commander of Dawnlight please come with me?" Lieutenant Colonel Kang Ming stood up, adjusted his helmet, and followed. The others barely had time to sit back down before he came back in again.

"Prepare to attack! We will determine the number of shots ourselves, but we must ensure that all living targets inside the reactor structure are destroyed."

"Let Major Lin decide the number of shots to fire," Colonel Xu said.

"Two hundred dissipative shots, one hundred from each gun," Lin Yun said, evidently having thought it over already. All of the macro-electrons currently loaded in the weapons were dissipative. Once all of the targets in the structure had been destroyed, the remaining ball lightning would drain their energy in the form of EM radiation, going out gradually, no longer destructive. Other varieties of ball lightning would release excess energy as an explosion, causing random damage to targets other than their selective target type.

"First and second shooting teams, come forward," Lieutenant Colonel Kang said as he pushed through the group. He pointed ahead and said, "The PAP squad will advance on the reactor, up to the hundred-meter safe line. They will stop there, then we will commence firing."

My heart seized up as I looked out at the huge nuclear column reflecting the blinding white light of the sun, preventing me from looking at it directly. For a moment I heard voices, as if the sound of the children was being blown over the roof by the wind.

The tarps were taken off the two thunderball guns, and the metal shells of their accelerator rails gleamed in the sunlight.

"Allow me," Lin Yun said, taking the shooter's seat at one of the thunderball guns. Lieutenant Colonel Kang and Colonel Xu exchanged a glance, but did not oppose her. I saw in her expression and movement an excitement she could not suppress, like a child finally getting her hands on a coveted toy. It gave me the chills.

Down on the ground, the PAP's skirmish line had started moving toward the reactor. It already seemed tiny against that massive structure. The line moved quickly, rapidly approaching the reactor's hundred-meter safety line. Then the thunderball guns ignited the excitement arcs in their accelerator rails, the crisp crackle turning heads down below the building, and even causing the PAP troops to glance backward.

When the line was a hundred meters from the reactor, they halted, then two lines of ball lightning flew off the roof toward the reactor. The deadly hurricane whooshed across two hundred meters. As the first ball lightning struck the reactor structure, more ball lightning was issuing in an unending stream from the accelerator rails, joined into a continuous thread by fiery tails that connected the guesthouse and the reactor with a river of flame.

I watched a video recording afterward of what happened in the control room.

At the time the ball lightning flew in, the teacher had already stopped her class and was stretched across the control station messing with something, while the children, still clustered together, were being guarded by an assault-rifle-wielding terrorist. The ball lightning was unobserved for a short time after it entered the structure and entered a probability cloud state. By the time the reappearance of an observer caused the probability cloud to collapse, the ball lightning had lost its speed and now drifted slowly on a random path. Everyone looked up in fear and confusion at the wandering fireballs, which screamed the cries of a multitude of ghosts as their tails painted a complicated, shifting picture in the air. In the images recorded by the cameras in the control room, the teacher's face was the clearest. Her glasses reflected the yellow and blue of the ball lightning, but, unlike the others, there was no fear in her eyes, only confusion. She was even smiling, perhaps to let herself relax, or maybe because she genuinely found the fireballs interesting. That was the last expression she wore in this world.

When the first ball lightning exploded, a strong EM pulse cut off the camera image. When it returned several seconds later, the place was empty, except for a few remaining excited lightning balls that drifted until they gradually went out. As their energy levels dropped, their sound grew less terrifying and more mournful, requiem-like.

On the roof of the guesthouse, I heard the explosions from the reactor. The sound rattled all of the glass in the building, but we heard it not through our ears, but in our very organs. It was so nauseating that it must have had infrasonic elements.

I felt like I wouldn't be able to hold myself together if I entered the reactor room, but I still went in alongside Lin Yun, my psyche so weak that my legs shook and I could scarcely stand still. More than a decade after seeing my parents turned to ash, I stood among the ashes of children. Apart from a very few charred remains, the majority of the deceased had been burned up entirely, but their clothing was basically unharmed. Ball lightning had incinerated them in an instant, with an internal temperature of more than ten thousand degrees and a matter wave resonance that caused its energy to release evenly into every cell.

Several police officers ringed the teacher's ashes, searching for something in her pockets. The other seven terrorists had also been tidily taken care of, including the two who were preparing to detonate the red pills.

I stepped gingerly among the children's ashes. Those blooms of life were now white piles beneath as many sets of children's clothing. Many of them retained the shape of children fallen on the ground, heads and limbs clearly distinguishable. The control room floor had become a huge painting, a work of art describing life and death executed by ball lightning. For a moment I even sensed something transcendent and ethereal.

Lin Yun and I stopped before a small pile of ash which, judging by the undamaged clothing, must have been a girl. Her final position was preserved excellently in ash, and it looked as if she had leaped into a different world with a dance of joy. Unlike the other ash piles, part of her body had escaped destruction: a hand. Her hand was small and white, the wrinkles on each finger unmistakable, as if it still belonged to a living body. Lin Yun squatted down and gently lifted the hand, then held it in both palms. I stood beside her, and we remained motionless; time had stopped for us. I genuinely wished I could become an unfeeling statue and remain with the ashes of the children forever.

After a while, I realized that there was someone else beside us, the operational commander. Lin Yun noticed him too, and gently set down the hand before standing up. "Sir, let me visit the children's parents. I was the one who conducted the weapon attack."

The commander slowly shook his head. "The decision was mine. The consequences are not your responsibility. They aren't the responsibility of any comrade who took part in the action. You did well. I will request commendation for Dawnlight. Thank you all. Thank you."

After saying this, he took steady footsteps toward the door. We knew that no matter what assessment this operation received from various quarters, his political career was over.

After a few steps, he stopped, and without turning around, uttered a sentence that Lin Yun was sure to remember for the rest of her life: "Also, Major, thank you for your counsel about the situation."

I handed in my resignation as soon as we returned to base. Everyone tried to make me stay, but my mind was made up.

Ding Yi said, "Chen, man, you've got to think about this rationally. Without ball lightning weapons, those kids would have died anyway. And they'd have died far more horribly, taking tens of thousands of other people with them. Deaths from radiation sickness and leukemia. And the next generation would have deformities. . . ."

"That's enough, Professor Ding. I don't have your pure scientific rationality. Or Lin Yun's military cool. I don't have anything. So I've got to leave."

"If it's because of something I did . . . ," Lin Yun said slowly.

"No, no. You did nothing wrong. It's me. Like Professor Ding says, I'm too sensitive. Maybe it's because of what I experienced as a child. I just don't have the courage to see anyone else get burned to ash by ball lightning. No matter who they are. I don't have the emotional strength that's needed for weapons research."

"But we're still collecting chip-burning macro-electrons. Those weapons will end up reducing personnel casualties on the battlefield."

"They're the same thing, as far as I'm concerned. At this point I don't ever want to see ball lightning again."

I was in the records room, returning all of the confidential material I had used in the course of my work. I had to sign my name onto each document, the last bit of paperwork I had to complete before leaving the base. With each name I signed, I took another step away from this world unknown to the outside where I had spent the most unforgettable period of my waning youth. I knew that when I left this time, I would never return.

When I left, Lin Yun accompanied me for quite a ways. When we parted, she said, "Research on civilian uses of ball lightning may start quite soon. We may have another opportunity to work together then."

"It will be nice when that day comes," I said. It was indeed a comforting thought. But a different feeling prompted me not to wait for that possible future reunion, and instead say the words I had long wanted to tell her.

"Lin Yun, the first time I met you on Mount Tai, I felt something I'd never felt before. . . ." I looked off at the distant mountains separating us from Beijing.

"I know . . . but we're too different." She followed my gaze. We remained like that for a while, not looking at each other, but watching the same spot in the distance.

"Yes. Too different . . . Take care."

With the clouds of war growing thick and foreboding, she surely understood what I meant by the last two words.

"You too," she said lightly.

The car had driven a fair distance when I looked back and saw her standing there still. The autumn wind had blown a carpet of leaves at her feet, so it seemed like she was standing in the middle of a golden river. This was the last impression that Major Lin Yun left me with.

After that, I never saw her again.

When I returned to the Lightning Institute, I fell into a deep malaise. I spent my days in a stupor, passing the time getting drunk in my apartment. One day Gao Bo visited. He said, "You're an idiot. That's the only way to describe you."

"What for?" I asked lazily.

"Are you under the impression that you're a saint simply because you left weapons research? Any civilian technology can be put to military use. Likewise, any military technology can benefit the public. As a matter of fact, practically all of the major scientific advances of the past century, in aerospace, nuclear energy, computers, and on and on, were the product of cooperation between scientists and soldiers following different paths. Is even this simple truth too hard for you to understand?"

"I have unique experiences and wounds that others don't. Besides, I don't believe you. I'll be able to find a research project that saves and benefits lives and has absolutely no use as a weapon."

"Impossible, I'd say. The scalpel can kill, too. On the other hand, it wouldn't be a bad thing if you found something to do."

It was already late when Gao Bo left. I turned off the light and lay down on my bed. Like every night recently, I entered a state of non-sleep, more exhausting than being awake, since the nightmares came one after another. They rarely repeated, but all of them shared the same background noise, the wailing of ball lightning in flight, like a lonely *xun* flute blowing endlessly in the wilderness.

A sound woke me. *Deet.* Just one brief note, but it stood out from the noise of my dream, and I was clearly aware that it came from non-dream reality. I opened my eyes and looked at the strange blue light enveloping the room. The light was dim and flickered occasionally, and rendered the ceiling cold and dark, like the roof of a tomb.

I sat up halfway and noticed that the light was coming from the LCD screen of my laptop, which was sitting on the table. That afternoon, as I was unpacking a travel bag I had been too lazy to open up for the many days I'd been back from the base, I found my old laptop and connected it to a network cable so I could go online. But when I pressed the switch, the screen remained black but for a few lines displaying an error message from the ROM self-check. Then I remembered that it was the machine I'd taken to the ball lightning weapons test exercise, and that its processor and memory had been torched by the ball lightning discharge, the CPU and two RAM sticks turned to ash. And so I just left it there and focused on other things.

But now the computer was running! A computer sans CPU and

memory had started up! The Windows startup logo appeared on the screen. Then, with a soft clicking of the hard drive, the desktop popped up, the blue sky so empty and the meadow such a brilliant green that they seemed to belong to a strange other world, as if the LCD screen was a window onto it.

I forced myself out of bed and went to turn on the light, the violent shaking of my hands making it hard to reach the switch. The brief moment from when I flipped the switch until the light came flooding in felt like a suffocating eternity. The light snuffed out the weird blue, but did nothing to lessen the fear that gripped my whole body. I remembered the words Ding Yi had left me with when we parted: "If you come across anything, give me a call," he had said, meaningfully, looking at me with that peculiar expression of his.

So I picked up the phone and dialed Ding Yi's cell phone in a fluster. He was evidently not asleep, since the phone only rang once before he answered.

"Come to my place at once! The faster the better! It . . . it's turned on. It's running. I mean, the . . . the notebook computer is running. . . ." I found it hard to be coherent, given the circumstances.

"Is this Chen? I'll be right over. Don't touch anything until I get there," Ding Yi said in a voice that sounded perfectly calm.

After I set down the telephone, I looked back at the laptop. As before, it was quietly displaying the desktop, as if waiting for something. The desktop's blue-green odd-eyed stare left me unable to remain in the room, so without even getting dressed, I went outside. The hall of the bachelors' apartments was quiet enough to hear the snoring of my neighbor, and I felt much better and breathed more easily. I stood in the doorway and waited for Ding Yi to get there.

He arrived quickly. Ball lightning theoretical research was to be transferred to the Institute of Physics, so he had been in the city for the past few days in connection with that.

"Shall we go in?" he said, after a glance at the tightly closed door behind me.

"I . . . I won't. You go in," I said, turning aside to let him pass.

"It might be something incredibly simple."

"Maybe for you. But me . . . I can't take it anymore," I said, pulling at my hair.

"I don't know whether or not supernatural phenomena exist, but what you've seen is certainly not that."

His words calmed me down a bit, like an adult's hand grabbed by a child in the terrifying dark, or the firm ground beneath a drowning man's feet. But this feeling immediately made me depressed. Before Ding Yi, my mind was weak; before Lin Yun, my actions were weak. I was such a fucking weakling—no wonder I placed after Ding Yi and Jiang Xingchen in Lin Yun's heart. Ball lightning had molded me into this form; from that night of terror in my youth, the shape of my psyche had been determined. I was destined to live my whole life with a terror no one else could feel.

Biting the bullet, I followed Ding Yi into my room. Past his thin shoulder I saw that the computer on the table had entered screen saver mode, the star field. Then the screen went dark. Ding Yi moved the mouse and the desktop came up again. I had to avert my eyes from the strange grass.

Ding Yi picked up the computer and, after inspecting it, passed it to me. "Take it apart."

"No." I pushed it aside. When I made contact with its warm case, my hand jerked back as if shocked. Something about it felt alive.

"Fine. I'll take it apart. You look at the screen. And find a Phillips screwdriver."

"You don't need one. I didn't put the screws back after the last time."

And so he began feeling around the laptop. They were ordinarily hard to dismantle, but mine was a late-model modular Dell, so he was easily able to open the bottom of the case. As he worked, he said, "Do you remember the first time we used the high-speed camera to record the ball lightning's energy discharge? We played it back frame by frame, and when we reached the point where the incinerated wooden cube was a transparent outline, we paused the image. Do you remember what Lin Yun said then?"

"She shouted: 'It's like a cubic bubble!'"

"That's right. . . . Pay attention to the screen as I look inside," he said, then bent at the waist and peered into the interior of the open computer.

At that moment, the screen went black, except for two lines displaying a self-check error message, indicating that no CPU or memory had been found.

Ding Yi flipped over the computer to show me the motherboard, where the CPU and RAM slots were empty.

"The moment I observed this, the quantum wave function collapsed." He set the computer carefully down on the table. Its screen remained black.

"Do you mean that the incinerated CPU and memory sticks exist in a quantum state, just like the macro-electrons?"

"Yes. In other words, when the chips experience matter-wave resonance with the macro-electron, they turn into a macro-particle in a quantum state. Ball lightning's energy release is essentially the full or partial superposition of the probability clouds of it and its target. The chips' state is indeterminate—they exist between two states, destroyed and undestroyed. Just now, when the computer started up, they were in the latter state, the CPU and memory completely unharmed and plugged into their slots in the motherboard. But when I observed them, their quantum states collapsed back into a destroyed state."

"In the absence of the observer, when will the chips exist in an undestroyed state?"

"That's undetermined. They only exist as the probability of an event. You can consider the chips in this computer to be within the probability cloud."

"Then the animals that were burned up—are they in a quantum state, too?" I asked nervously, with the premonition that I was nearing an unbelievable truth.

Ding Yi nodded.

I didn't have the courage to ask my next question, but Ding Yi looked calmly at me, and clearly knew what I was thinking.

"Yes, the people too. All the people who have been killed by ball lightning exist in a quantum state. Strictly speaking, they haven't really died. They're like Schrödinger's cat, and exist indeterminately in two states, living and dead." Ding Yi stood up and walked to the window and looked out at the deep night. "To them, to be or not to be is indeed a question."

"Can we see them?"

Ding Yi waved a hand at the window, as if resolutely dismissing the idea from my brain. "Impossible. We'll never be able to see them, since their collapsed state is death. They exist alive for a certain probability of the quantum state, but when we appear as observers, they immediately collapse to a destroyed state, to their urns or graves."

"Do you mean they're alive in some parallel universe?"

"No, no. You've misunderstood. They live in our own world. Their probability cloud might cover quite a large area. Perhaps they're even standing in this room, right behind you."

The skin crawled on my back.

Ding Yi turned around and pointed behind me. "But when you turn around to take a look, they immediately collapse to a destroyed state. Trust me: neither you nor any other person will ever be able to see them. That includes cameras and other observers. Detection of their presence is impossible."

"Can they leave traces behind in the real world that are not in a quantum state?"

"They can. I suspect you've already seen such traces."

"Then why don't they write me a letter!" I shouted, losing control. By "they," I meant only two people.

"Compared to an object like a computer chip, a conscious being in a quantum state, particularly a human, behaves in a far more complicated manner. How they interact with us in the non-quantum-state world is an unanswered mystery, one that contains many logical and even philosophical traps. For example: maybe they *have* written, but how large is the probability that those letters would have a non-quantum state for you to read them? Also, is the real world in a quantum state for them? If it is, then they will have a very hard time finding this state of you in your probability cloud. For them, the road home is long and uncertain. . . . But that's enough. These are things that can't be figured out in a short amount of time. Get stuck down a blind alley and you'll burn out. Take your time to think things over later."

I said nothing. How could I *stop* thinking?

Ding Yi picked up a more than half-filled bottle of Red Star erguotou from the table, and poured us each a glass. "Come on. This might push those thoughts from your mind."

With the fiery spirit burning in my blood, the chaos in my brain did clear out a little. I tried to think of other things instead.

"How's Lin Yun doing? What's she up to?" I asked.

"Still collecting chip-attacking macro-electrons. I'm not too sure about the details. Some unfortunate incidents came between us."

"What happened?"

"I secretly installed a miniature video camera in her apartment."

I waited.

"She found it and called me a pervert. If it had been any other man, she would have forgiven me, but on the surface I look like someone who's never had an interest in women. And that is indeed the case: my mind is fully occupied by abstract theory, and naturally I'm obtuse when it comes to these irrational matters. The camera didn't even capture anything, anyway. It recorded, and then erased the recording. I explained this repeatedly, but she wouldn't listen."

"You were trying to install an . . . observer? Are you worried about the terrorists?"

"Particularly that teacher. She's got to hate Lin Yun's guts."

"Can people in a quantum state attack people who aren't?"

"I don't know. From a logical standpoint, there's too much that's unclear. But it's better to be safe than sorry."

"Didn't you explain your motivation to her?"

"I did. But she said I was bullshitting. With the quantum effect on a macro level, the world has become strange and uncanny, and it's hard for ordinary people to believe. I couldn't offer much by way of explanation, and before further research is in, I don't want to sow confusion on base."

"My mind is already confused to the extreme," I said, dropping to the bed in a daze.

"You should find something to do."

PART THREE

TORNADOES

I soon found the thing I needed to do. It was the kind of research I'd spoken of to Gao Bo, which would save and benefit lives, but could not be put to military uses: predicting tornadoes. Witnessing a tornado from the small island with Jiang Xingchen the past summer had left a deep impression on me. The optical system for detecting macro-electron bubbles clearly displayed atmospheric disturbances on the screen as it operated, which had given me the idea that it might provide a key breakthrough in tornado forecasting. Modern atmospherics had a thorough understanding of the aerodynamic mechanisms giving rise to tornadoes. By building an improved mathematical model of the process of tornado formation and linking it to the atmospheric disturbances observed by the bubble detection system, we would be able to identify the ones that might develop into tornadoes, and thus be able to predict them.

Gao Bo solved the biggest obstacle to the project: transferring technology behind the bubble optical detection system over for civilian use. When he contacted the military, he discovered that it was easier than he had imagined: since the system had no direct connection to ball lightning, the military readily agreed to the technology transfer.

When Gao Bo returned from GAD, he had me set up direct connections with the two units working on the development of the bubble detection system: namely, the software and hardware researchers, both of which were non-military and had no more ties with the base. I asked Gao Bo about conditions at the base, and he said he only spoke with the GAD project management department, and had not interacted with the base at all. He had heard that secrecy had been tightened substantially, and that practically all contact with the outside world had been cut off. This was understandable, in light of the present global situation, but I still found myself worrying about my old colleagues from time to time.

My research made swift progress. Since the precision required for detecting atmospheric disturbances was far less than what was necessary to detect bubbles, the optical detection system could be used in its present state, and its detection range correspondingly increased by an order of magnitude. What I needed to do was to use an appropriate mathematical model to analyze existing images of atmospheric disturbances, and recognize which ones might give rise to tornadoes. (Later, specialists in the field would call such disturbances "eggs.") In my early days doing ball lightning research, I had put an enormous amount of energy into mathematical modeling. It was a road I had no desire to look back upon, but at least it seemed like it wasn't a total waste of time. I had the skills to construct models in fluid and gas dynamics, skills that were immensely useful in my present research, allowing the software portion of the tornado detection system to be completed quite quickly.

We tested the system in Guangdong Province, a frequent site for tornadoes, and successfully predicted several of them, one of which grazed a corner of urban Guangzhou. The system gave ten- to fifteen-minute advance warnings—enough time to safely evacuate personnel before the tornado's arrival, but not long enough to avert other losses. But in atmospherics circles, this was already a remarkable achievement. Besides, according to the principles of chaos theory, long-term prediction of tornadoes was basically impossible anyway.

Time moved quickly while I was immersed in my work, and, in the blink of an eye, a year had passed. In that year, I attended the World Meteorological Congress, held once every four years, and was nominated for the International Meteorological Organization Prize, known as the Nobel in Meteorology. In part because of my academic background, I ultimately didn't win, but I still attracted the attention of the meteorological world.

To demonstrate the achievements of tornado research, a conference sponsored by the organization—the International Workshop on Tropical Cyclones—specifically selected Oklahoma to host. The region, known as "Tornado Alley," was the setting for the movie *Twister*, which depicted tornado researchers.

The main motivation for the trip was to see the world's first practical tornado forecasting system. Our car drove along the flat plains, Oklahoma's three most common sights alternating outside the window: livestock farms, oil fields, and vast wheat fields. When we had almost reached our destination, my travel companion, Dr. Ross ordered the windows covered.

"I have to apologize. We're entering a military base," he said.

I felt crushed. Was I really unable to escape from the military and army bases? I got out of the car and noticed that most of the buildings around us were temporary structures, along with several radar antennas in large radomes. I could also see a vehicle carrying a device that resembled a telescope, but was no doubt actually a high-powered laser transmitter, probably for atmospheric optical observation. In the control room was a familiar sight: a row of dark-green military computers and operators wearing fatigues. The only thing a little unfamiliar was the large, high-resolution plasma display, usually unaffordable back home, where projection screens were used instead.

The big screen displayed images of atmospheric disturbances captured by the optical observation system, a technology transfer that had netted Gao Bo's Lightning Institute a nice sum. What appeared as ordinary disturbance images on the small screen were quite impressive when blown up to this size, chaotic turbulence like a group of crystalline pythons dancing wildly, tangling into balls, and then flinging out again in all directions, disorienting and frightening at the same time.

"You look at the air and it seems so empty, not a crazy world like this," someone exclaimed.

There's even wilder stuff you haven't seen yet, I said to myself, and then looked closely at the chaotic turbulence on the screen, trying to get a glimpse of a macro-electron bubble. I couldn't, of course, but there was definitely more than one of them hiding in such a large area, only recognizable by the still-classified pattern-recognition software.

"Will we be seeing any eggs today?" I asked.

"That shouldn't be a problem," Ross replied. "Tornadoes have been common in Oklahoma and Kansas lately. Just last week, 124 tornadoes occurred in Oklahoma in the space of a single day. A new record."

So as not to waste time, our hosts had set up a conference room on the base so the symposium could take place while we waited for the eggs to appear. Before the attendees had even taken their seats, an alarm sounded. The system had found an egg! We rushed back to the control center, but the screen still rolled with the same translucent chaos, little different from how it was before. The egg had no fixed shape; it was only discernible through the model recognition software, which then marked it on the image with a red circle.

"It's 130 kilometers away, at the border of Oklahoma City. It's very dangerous," Ross said.

"How long until it produces a tornado?" someone asked nervously.

"Around seven minutes."

"It will be difficult to evacuate all personnel," I said.

"No, Dr. Chen. We're not doing any evacuation!" Ross said loudly. "This is the surprise we want to give you today!"

A small square region on the big screen displayed a missile roaring off the launcher and into the sky. The camera tracked it, showing its thin white tail painting a giant parabola across the sky. Roughly one minute later, the missile crossed the peak of the parabola and began to descend, and after one more minute, at an elevation of roughly five hundred meters, it exploded in a blistering fireball that looked like a blooming rose against the sky. In the section of the screen showing the atmospheric disturbance, a rapidly expanding crystal ball appeared at the spot marked by the red circle egg. Then the transparent sphere transformed and disappeared, its position filled in by the chaos of the disturbance. The red circle vanished, and the alarm ceased. Dr. Ross declared that the egg had been annihilated. This was the ninth egg wiped out by the "Tornado Hunter" system that day.

Dr. Ross explained: "You all know that tornadoes are usually born out of strong thunderstorms. When the hot, wet air of a thunderstorm rises and crosses the upper layer of cold air, it gradually cools. Water vapor condenses into raindrops or hailstones, which are borne downward when the cooled air begins to sink, only to be pushed back up again by factors like the warm lower layer and the rotation of the Earth. Ultimately, these layers form a tornado. The process of tornado formation is unstable, but the sinking of the cold air represents a critical energy flow. This mass of sinking cold air is the heart of the egg. The

Tornado Hunter system fires a missile carrying an oil firebomb that detonates in a precision strike on the sinking cool air, instantly releasing an immense amount of heat energy that increases the temperature of the mass of air and breaks the tornado's formation. It strangles it in the cradle.

"As we're all aware, the technology for missile strikes and oil firebombs is not new. This isn't really a precision strike, either, since the precision we require is a level less than is used for military uses. That lessens the cost. What we're using are all obsolete, decommissioned missiles. The key technology in the Tornado Hunter system is Dr. Chen's atmospheric optical detection system. That's the innovation that allows us to determine the advance positioning of the egg. It's what makes the artificial destruction of tornadoes possible. Let us pay him our deep respect!"

The next day, Oklahoma City, the state capital, made me an honorary citizen of the city. When I accepted the citation from the governor, a young blonde woman presented me with the Oklahoma state flower, mistletoe, which I had never seen before. She told me that a tornado had taken her parents the previous year. It had been a terrifying night. An F3 tornado had ripped off the roof of her house and flung everything inside more than a hundred meters into the air. She had only survived because she had landed in a pond. Her account reminded me of the night I lost my parents, and gave me a sense of pride in my work. It was this kind of work that finally rid me of the shadow of ball lightning, and let me start on a new life in the sun.

After the ceremony, I congratulated Dr. Ross. Even though I had been the one to make the breakthrough in forecasting tornadoes, they had been the ones who ultimately conquered them.

"It was TMD that finally conquered tornadoes," he said absently.

"Theater missile defense?"

"That's right. It was adopted practically without modification. It was only a matter of replacing the system's incoming missile identification module with your egg positioning system. TMD seems purpose-built to destroy tornadoes."

I realized then that the two were indeed similar: they both automatically identified targets, and then used guided missiles for precise interception.

"My original field of study had nothing to do with meteorology. I was in charge of TMD and NMD software systems for many years. When I realized that the weapons systems I'd developed could be used to benefit society, I felt a joy I'd never had before. Dr. Chen, you have my special thanks for that."

"I feel the same way," I said sincerely.

"Swords can be made into plowshares," Ross said. But then in a much lower voice, he added, "But some plowshares can be cast back into swords. Weapons researchers like us sometimes have to accept blame and loss for this in the course of carrying out our duties. . . . Can you understand that, too, Dr. Chen?"

I had heard similar words from Gao Bo, and so I nodded silently, but my mind grew wary. When he said "us," did he include me? Did they really know about the work I used to do?

"Thank you. You have my sincere gratitude," Ross said. He was looking at me with a peculiar expression, which betrayed a glimpse of sorrow. Later I realized I was thinking too much, and that his words had nothing to do with me. I only learned later what his expression really meant.

I was among the final group of visiting scholars to go abroad. Ten days after I returned home, war broke out.

ZHUFENG

Life grew tense. Apart from daily attention to the war, work also took on a new level of meaning, since the joys and cares that had previously occupied a primary position in my life no longer seemed so important.

One day I received a telephone call from the military instructing me to attend a meeting. A naval ensign would come to pick me up by car.

As the war escalated, I sometimes thought about the ball lightning weapons project. These were unusual times, and if the research base needed me to go back, I would abandon all of my personal feelings and do my utmost to fulfill my duty, but I never heard from them. The war news I read never had anything related to ball lightning weapons. This should have been the best opportunity for them to come out, but it was as if they had never even existed. I tried calling the base, but found that all their numbers were disconnected. Ding Yi was similarly nowhere to be found. All that I had been through was like a dream, and it had left no traces behind.

It was only after I arrived at the military meeting and discovered that most of the people there, none of whom I recognized, were from the navy that I realized that this had nothing to do with ball lightning weapons. Everyone looked grim, and the atmosphere of the meeting was depressive.

"Dr. Chen, first off we'd like to explain to you something that happened in naval combat yesterday," a senior colonel in the navy said, getting down to business without any opening remarks. "You don't need to know the specific location and circumstances of the battle, so I'll only tell you the pertinent information. At around three p.m. yesterday, the *Zhufeng* carrier battle group was attacked by a large number of cruise missiles—"

My heart jumped when I heard the name.

"—Forty of them. The group immediately switched on defensive systems, but they soon discovered the method of attack was peculiar: under ordinary circumstances, cruise missiles attacking a sea target will fly close to the surface of the ocean to break through anti-missile defenses, but these flew at an altitude of one thousand meters, as if they didn't care about being shot down. And sure enough, the missiles didn't directly attack targets in the group. Instead, all of them exploded outside our defensive perimeter at altitudes of five hundred to one thousand meters. The force of each explosion was small, just enough to disperse a large quantity of white powder. Please have a look at the recording."

Empty sky appeared on the projection screen. There were lots of clouds, and it looked about to rain. Then lots of small white dots appeared and gradually expanded, as if dripping dozens of drops of milk onto the water.

"Those are the cruise missiles' explosion points," the senior colonel said, pointing at the expanding dots on the screen. "What's strange is that we really didn't know what the enemy was doing. That white material—"

"Were there any other unusual signs at that location?" I interrupted, a foreboding fear rising in my heart.

"What do you mean? There was nothing that seemed relevant."

"Unrelated, then. Can you take a look?" I asked urgently.

The colonel and several other officers exchanged glances, and a be-spectacled lieutenant colonel said, "An enemy early warning aircraft flew through that airspace. That doesn't seem unusual."

"Anything else?"

"Hmm . . . the enemy emitted a high-energy laser at that region of the ocean from a low-orbit satellite, perhaps to coordinate submarine detection with the plane. . . . Is that related to the missile attack under discussion? Dr. Chen, are you okay?"

I hope to God it's submarine detection. May the lord make it submarine detection. My heart prayed in a panic as I said, "Not really. . . . That white powder, do you have a rough idea of what it was?"

"I was about to tell you," the senior colonel said as he flipped the scene on the screen. Now it was an image formed from a small number of brilliant colors, like a well-used painter's palette. "This is a false-color infrared image of that region of space. See, the explosion points are rapidly turning into low-temperature zones." He pointed at a patch of brilliant blue, and said, "So we guess that the white powder might be a highly efficient refrigerant."

I felt like I had been struck by lightning, and the world had turned upside down. I had to grip the table to bring myself to earth. "Hurry! Get the fleet out of there!" I said to the senior colonel, while pointing at the screen.

"Dr. Chen, this is a recording. The event took place yesterday."

Dazed by the facts, I was struck dumb for a while before I realized what he meant.

"This was recorded on *Zhufeng*. Have a look."

Sea and sky appeared on screen. A small escort destroyer flickered in and out at one corner. A thin funnel took shape in the sky, its tail extending down toward the ocean as a long thin thread. Upon contact with the surface, the thread turned white as it began sucking up water. At first this thread connecting sea and sky was narrow, and it rocked and swayed gently, and seemed almost to snap in half at its thinnest point. But it soon grew thicker, turning from thin gossamer hanging from the sky into a towering column standing on the water, holding up the heavens. It turned black, with only the swirling seawater on its surface still reflecting the sun.

I had thought of this before, in fact, but didn't believe anyone would do it.

The disturbances capable of giving birth to a tornado—the eggs—were very numerous in the atmosphere. The sinking cold air at the heart of the egg could be warmed to stop its descent, thereby wiping out the egg that would evolve into a tornado, like I had seen in Oklahoma. Similarly, if a coolant were used to further chill that mass of air, "incubating" an egg that would otherwise have disappeared, it could be spurred to form a tornado. Since the eggs were so plentiful, under appropriate climatic conditions, tornadoes could be manufactured at will. The technological key was in finding potential eggs, and my tornado forecasting system made that possible. Even worse, the system could be used to find opportunities for two eggs nearby, or even superimposed. If multiple eggs were incubated at once, it could focus atmospheric energy into the generation of super-tornadoes that had never existed in nature.

Now before me was one of those tornadoes, more than two kilometers in diameter, twice as large as any naturally occurring tornado.

The largest tornadoes in nature were F5s, and their size had won them the name "the hand of God." But this artificially incubated tornado was at least an F7.

On screen, the tornado crept toward the right. *Zhufeng* was clearly executing an emergency turn in an attempt to avoid it. Tornadoes usually advance in a straight line at a speed of around sixty kilometers per hour, or roughly the same as the carrier's top speed. If *Zhufeng* could accelerate and turn quickly enough, it had a chance of missing it.

But just then, in the air on either side of the huge black column, two more white threads dropped down and then swiftly thickened and evolved into another two huge black columns.

The three super-tornadoes were separated by less than their diameter, not even a thousand meters. Together they formed a nearly eight-kilometer-wide, slowly approaching earth-to-sky fence of death. *Zhufeng*'s fate was sealed.

The tornado columns now filled the entire screen. Mist from the roiling waves surged ahead of them like an approaching waterfall, the columns themselves the dark abyss behind. The picture jostled violently, and then cut out.

As the senior colonel explained, a tornado had crossed *Zhufeng*'s front half, and, just like the lieutenant colonel had predicted on that small island, its deck snapped. Half an hour later it sank, carrying more than two thousand officers and sailors, including their captain, to a watery grave. As the tornadoes neared, the captain had issued a decisive order to fully seal off the two pressurized water reactors to reduce any nuclear leak to the minimum possible, but this left *Zhufeng* dead in the water. Two escort destroyers and one supply ship were also sunk. When the super-tornadoes had swept the ships, one of them continued onward for two hundred kilometers before expiring, twice as far as any tornado had traveled in recorded history. During its journey, it retained enough power to scour an island fishing village and kill more than one hundred people, including women and children.

"Was Jiang Xingchen captaining *Zhufeng*?"

"Yes. Did you know him?"

I didn't speak. I was thinking more of Lin Yun now.

"We asked you here firstly because you are the most successful tornado researcher in the country, and secondly because the attack on *Zhufeng* was carried out by a meteorological weapon system codenamed Aeolus. Our intelligence indicates it is related to your research results."

I nodded heavily. "That's true. I'm willing to accept responsibility."

"No, you've misunderstood. We didn't ask you here to assign blame. And you don't have any responsibility. The Lightning Institute's publication and transfer of the project's results passed through multiple levels of review by the relevant departments and was entirely legal. Of course someone must be held responsible, but it isn't you. We're not as sensitive about the use of advanced technology as the enemy."

I said, "The weapon can be defended against. All you need to do is link up the fleet's missile defense system with our atmospheric optical detection system. I've seen how a missile shooting an oil firebomb can wipe out a tornado, but there's an even faster and more effective method: use high-energy microwaves or lasers to heat up the descending cold air mass."

"Yes, we're putting all our energies into developing that kind of defensive system. And we'd like your full assistance." The senior colonel sighed gently. "But, honestly speaking, it will probably have to wait until the next war to be used."

"Why is that?"

"The loss of the *Zhufeng* carrier battle group was a huge blow to our sea power. For the rest of this war, we no longer have the ability to engage the enemy in a large-scale sea battle. We have to rely on shore-based firepower for coastal defense."

After I left the Naval Warfare Center, shrill anti-aircraft sirens sounded in the air above the city. The streets were empty, and I walked through the emptiness with no particular destination in mind. A civil defense warden ran at me shouting something, but I pretended not to hear him. The wardens came over to grab me, but I shook them off unfeelingly and continued to sleepwalk along, and they left me on my own like the lunatic they imagined I was.

Now all of my hopes were dashed, and I ached for a bomb to bring my tormented life to an end. But the explosions remained distant. Nearby, the silence only grew.

After I'd walked for I don't know how long, the sirens seemed to have stopped, and people gradually returned to the streets. In total exhaustion I sat down on the steps of a city garden, and realized that my empty brain was now occupied by a feeling, the feeling of understanding someone at last.

I understood Lin Yun.

I took out my mobile and dialed the number of the base, but no one answered. So I got up and looked for a cab. They were rare in wartime, and it took half an hour before I found one, then we drove off to the base at once.

It was around three hours later that we arrived at the base, only to discover that I had wasted my time. It was completely empty, personnel and equipment removed. I stood on my own for a long while in the center of the excitation lab, a shaft of weak light from the setting sun piercing the broken window to illuminate me, gradually fading until night descended. Only then did I leave.

After returning to the city, I made inquiries into the fate of the ball lightning project team and Dawnlight, but no one could tell me anything. They seemed to have evaporated from the world. I even dialed the number that General Lin had left, but there was no answer there, either.

There was nothing I could do but go back to the Lightning Institute and start researching the use of high-powered microwaves to dispel tornadoes.

CHIP DESTRUCTION

The war dragged on, and another autumn arrived. People gradually grew accustomed to life during wartime, and air-raid sirens and food rationing, like concerts and cafés before them, became a normal part of life.

For my part, I threw myself entirely into developing a tornado defense system, a project overseen by Gao Bo's Lightning Institute. Work went at a feverish pace, so for a while I forgot everything else. But one day, what seemed like an endless stalemate in the war was finally broken.

That afternoon at roughly 3:30, I was discussing technical details of shipboard high-energy microwave emitters with a few engineers from the Institute and the military. The device could emit a highly focused microwave beam of around one billion watts of power at frequencies from ten to one hundred hertz, frequencies at which the power could be absorbed by water molecules. Several of these beams added together could produce a regional power density of one watt per square centimeter, comparable to a microwave oven, that would raise the temperature of the falling mass of cold air in the egg and eliminate it in an embryonic state. When the device was paired with the atmospheric optical detection system, they would form an effective defense against tornado weapons.

Just then there was a sudden, strange noise outside, a little like the drumming of a squall of hail on the ground. Starting off in the distance, the sound grew closer, until it finally reached the room we were in. Then there were snapping sounds all around us, as close as the left side of my chest! As this was going on, something strange was happening to the computers: lots of objects flew out of the towers, but left their cases untouched. On closer inspection, they turned out to be complete CPUs, memory chips, and other chips. For a moment, the floating chips grew incredibly dense in the air. I waved a hand and brushed against several of them with the back of my hand, so I knew they weren't an illusion, but eventually they all disappeared without a trace, leaving the air empty again. Then the computer screens changed, showing blue screens, or simply going dark.

I felt an intense heat on the left side of my chest and felt for the source. My mobile, in my shirt pocket, was burning up, so I plucked it out. My companions were doing the same thing. Our phones emitted white smoke, and when I took mine apart, a small quantity of white ash dispersed. The chips inside had been incinerated. We opened up the computers and found that nearly a third of the chips on the motherboards had been burned up. White ash and a peculiar stench filled the office for a while.

Then the rest of the computer screens and the lights went dark. The power had gone out.

My first thought was that we had been attacked by ball lightning that released its energy into computer chips, but something wasn't right: all of the nearby buildings were research units where chips were plentiful. This would weaken the ball lightning energy discharge enough to reduce its effective radius to no more than one hundred meters. At that distance, we'd definitely have heard the unmistakable explosion it made when discharging, but we had heard nothing apart from the popping of burning chips, so I was nearly certain that no ball lightning had been present nearby.

The first thing we had to do was to determine the scope of the attack. I picked up my phone from the table, but it was dead, so we went downstairs together to check things out. We soon learned that chips had been attacked in two of the Institute's office buildings and one lightning lab, and about a third of them had been destroyed. Separately, we visited the neighboring Institute of Atmospheric Physics and the Meteorological Modeling Center, and found that the chips in those two units had suffered an attack identical to ours. It would have taken dozens of ball lightning strikes to do the damage we were now aware of, but I hadn't seen the slightest trace of it.

Immediately after that, Gao Bo sent a few younger people off on bicycles to check out the situation, while the rest of us waited anxiously in the office. He and I were the only ones at the Lightning Institute who knew about ball lightning weapons, and we exchanged glances from time to time, with a panic somewhat worse than other people's. Half an hour later, the bicyclists came back, terror on their faces, like they'd seen a ghost. They had all ridden for three to five kilometers. Everywhere they went, all electronic chips, without exception, had been attacked by some mysterious force, and had been destroyed in the same ratio, around one-third. They panicked and didn't dare ride any farther, reporting back to the Institute instead. We were a little unaccustomed to being without mobile phones and landlines.

"There's no hope for us if the enemy really has such a devilish weapon!" someone said.

Gao Bo and I exchanged another glance. My mind was a jumble.

"How about we take four of the Institute's cars and drive off in four directions so we can check out things in a wider area?"

I drove a car through the city to the east. All of the buildings I saw along the way were dark, with people clustered in small groups outside talking nervously. Many of them still held their clearly useless mobile phones. I knew what the situation was in these places without even having to get out of the car, but I still got out a few times, mostly to ask people whether they had seen signs of ball lightning. But no one had seen or heard anything.

Outside of the urban area, I continued to drive, all the way to a distant county seat in the far suburbs. Here, even though the power was out, there were far fewer signs of panic than downtown. I felt a surge of hope in my heart, a hope that I was approaching the edge of the ring of destruction, or at least that I would see fewer signs of damage. I parked the car outside a web café and rushed inside. It was dusk, and the café was very dark without power, but I smelled that familiar burnt odor at once. I grabbed a machine, took it outside, and carefully inspected the motherboard. In the light of the setting sun I saw that the CPU and several other chips were missing. The computer dropped out of my hands and smashed onto my foot, but I didn't feel the pain. I only shivered heavily in the cold late autumn breeze, and then jumped in the car and went back.

Not long after I got back to the Institute, the other three cars also returned. The one that went the farthest had taken the expressway for over a hundred kilometers. Everywhere they went, things were the same as here.

We urgently searched for information of the outside, but we had no TV or Internet, and no phone. Only the radio worked. But all of the deluxe digitally tuned radios were driven by integrated circuits, and all of them were now junk. It wasn't easy, but we eventually found a usable vintage transistor radio that an old mail clerk kept in the reception office, which received three fuzzy southern provincial stations, as well as three in English and one in Japanese.

It was only late that night that these stations began to have reports on this bizarre disaster, and from those fragmentary broadcasts, we learned the following: the chip damage zone was centered somewhere in the northwest of China. It covered a circular area with a radius of 1,300 kilometers, or around one-third of the land in the country, an astonishingly large area, but the chip damage rate gradually tapered off the farther you got from the center. Our city was located near the edge of the region.

For the next week, we lived in a pre-electricity agricultural society. It was a difficult time. Water had to be trucked in and rationed out in amounts that were barely sufficient to drink. At night we relied on candles for illumination.

During this period, rumors about the disaster flew thick as cow hair. In the public chatter as well as in the media (which for us was limited to radio), the most popular explanation had to do with aliens. But in all of the rumors, there was no mention of ball lightning.

Out of the mess of information, we could conclude one thing: the attack was unlikely to have come from the enemy. It was obvious that they were as confused as we were, which let us breathe a little easier.

I came up with a hundred different possibilities during that time, but none of them was convincing. I was convinced that this was connected to ball lightning, but I was also certain that ball lightning wasn't that powerful. So what was?

The enemy's behavior was also mystifying. Our territory had been dealt such a blow that our defensive capability was basically gone, yet they halted their attack. Even the routine daily airstrikes disappeared.

The world media had a fairly convincing explanation: in the face of such a strong, unknown force that could easily destroy the entire civilized world, no one wanted to act rashly before figuring out what it was.

In any event, it gave us the most peaceful period since the start of the war, albeit an ominous and chilly one. Without computers or electricity, we had nothing to do, and no way to dispel the terror in our hearts.

One evening, as an icy autumn rain began to fall outside, I sat by myself in my chilly apartment listening to the raindrops. It felt as if the outside world had been swallowed up by an infinite darkness, and the lonely flickering candle in front of me was the only light in the entire universe. An infinite loneliness crushed me, and my all-too-brief life played back like a movie rewinding in my mind: the abstract painting made up of children's ashes in the nuclear plant, Ding Yi putting the Go board behind the bubble, long electric arcs in the night sky, Siberia in the blizzard, Lin Yun's piano playing and the sword at her neck, the thunderstorm and starry sky on Mount Tai, my university days on campus, and finally back to that stormy birthday night. . . . I felt like my life had gone in a huge circle, bringing me back to my point of origin, only now there was no sound of thunder in the rain, and there was only one candle left in front of me.

Then there was a knock at the door. Before I could get up to answer it, someone pushed it open and came in. He took off a wet raincoat, his thin body shivering from the cold, and when I made out his face in the candlelight, I cried out for joy.

It was Ding Yi.

"Do you have anything to drink? Preferably something hot," he said, through chattering teeth.

I passed him half a bottle of Red Star erguotou. He held it over the candle flame to warm it, but he soon grew impatient and tossed back a few mouthfuls. Wiping his mouth, he said, "No beating around the bush. I'll tell you what you want to know."

AMBUSH AT SEA

This is the account that Ding Yi gave me of what happened at the ball lightning research base after I left:

Because the nuclear plant operation was such a big success (from the military's point of view, at least), the sidelined ball lightning weapons project began to receive renewed interest, followed by substantial investment. This investment was mostly put toward collecting chip-striking macro-electrons, as highly selective strikes on integrated circuits were believed to be the area of ball lightning weapons with the greatest potential. After a large amount of work, there were finally more than five thousand of these rare macro-electrons in storage, enough to constitute a combat-capable weapons system.

When war broke out, the base entered a state of nervous excitement. Practically everyone there believed that ball lightning would be to this war what the tank was to the First World War and the atom bomb to the Second, a history-making weapon. Overflowing with enthusiasm, they prepared to make history, but their instructions from the higher-ups were just two words: *await orders*. And thus Dawnlight was the idlest of all the units in the war. At first, people imagined that High Command might want to use the weapon in the most critical position at the most critical moment, but Lin Yun learned through her channels that they were thinking too highly of themselves; High Command had a fairly low opinion of the weapon. They believed that the nuclear plant operation had been a special case and did not prove the weapon system's battlefield potential. None of the branches had much of an interest in putting the weapon to use. Hence, investment in the project dried up again.

After the destruction of the *Zhufeng* carrier battle group, the base was fraught with anxiety. The staff were baffled that the demonstration of the enormous power of a different new-concept weapon had done nothing to shake up old attitudes toward ball lightning. They felt that their weapon was the only hope left for turning the tide of the war.

Lin Yun repeatedly asked her father to give Dawnlight a battle assignment, but each time she was refused. On one occasion, General Lin told his daughter, "Xiao Yun, don't let your fascination with weapons develop into superstition. Your thinking about war needs to be deeper, more holistic. The notion that the entire war can be won by relying on one or two new-concept weapons is, frankly, naïve."

Here Ding Yi said, "As a believer in science, my faith in the weapons was even stronger than Lin Yun's. I firmly believed that ball lightning could determine the outcome of the war. At the time, I ascribed High Command's attitude

toward ball lightning weapons to rigid thinking that was impervious to
reason, and I was far more annoyed than most of the people at the base. But
the way things developed ultimately demonstrated our naïveté."

At last there was a turning point. The base and Dawnlight received
orders to carry out an exploratory attack on an enemy carrier group
in coastal waters.

The headquarters of the South Sea Fleet convened a war meeting.
Personnel in attendance were not of high rank, so clearly the higher-
ups did not place much value on this combat operation. Two senior
colonels chaired the meeting: one the director of the fleet's Operations
Division, the other from the army, the second commander of the Southern Military Region's coastal defense system. The other twenty-odd
officers mostly hailed from submarine units and the coastal force of
the South Sea Fleet.

The defense commander started off by describing the battlefield
situation: "You are all aware of recent events that have seriously
weakened our blue-water sea power. The enemy's naval forces are
encroaching on our coastal waters. The enemy fleet has on several
occasions come within range of our shore-based anti-ship missiles, but
our strikes have failed. Their missile defense systems have successfully
intercepted the vast majority of our anti-ship missiles. If we can destroy
or partially destroy the systems' early warning capability, then our
land-based missiles will be able to effectively attack the enemy. The primary mission of the present operation is this: the electronics in the
enemy fleet's missile defense system will be destroyed using 'Maple
Leaf,' partially or totally crippling the system to give our land-based
defenses an opportunity to attack."

Maple Leaf was the code name for the ball lightning weapon. This gentle name in part reflected the attitude the higher-ups had about the weapon.

The operations director said, "Let's first agree on a general framework for drafting the battle plan, then each branch can work out specific details on their own."

"I have a question," an army colonel said, standing up. He was the commander of a shore-based missile unit. "I've heard that Maple Leaf can only be used for line-of-sight attacks. Is that the case?"

Colonel Xu Wencheng answered in the affirmative.

"Then what's the use of your gadget? A basic requirement for modern weaponry is the ability to strike from beyond line-of-sight. Maple Leaf isn't any better than a premodern weapon."

"Colonel, I'd say it's your mind that's premodern," Lin Yun snapped, drawing disapproving looks.

"Well then, would Maple Leaf's commander please discuss their ideas for a battle plan?" the operations director asked.

"We plan to use a submarine as a launch platform for Maple Leaf," Colonel Xu said.

"Can Maple Leaf strike underwater?" a submarine colonel asked.

"No."

"To conduct a line-of-sight surface attack, even under ideal conditions, will require approaching to within eight to ten thousand meters of the target. If a submarine surfaces that close to the enemy's antisubmarine center, isn't that basically suicide?" the submarine commander said angrily.

"Colonel, a very short time after Maple Leaf strikes, the enemy's electronics systems will be destroyed. Its antisubmarine system will be completely disabled and no longer pose a threat to you," Lin Yun said.

The submarine commander snorted almost imperceptibly, but he clearly had no regard for the female major. He shot a glance at the operations director, and his meaning was clear: *Do you trust this girl's assurances?*

The operations director shook his head firmly. "Vetoed. This idea won't work."

After a heavy silence, a naval lieutenant colonel proposed another plan: "Let high-speed torpedoes lie in wait outside the line of sight of the enemy fleet, and, when the target approaches, speed into line-of-sight and attack."

"That won't work, either," another naval officer said. "Torpedoes can't be hidden. Have you forgotten that the enemy has aerial reconnaissance? They have very strong aerial patrols cruising coastal waters. Stealth only applies to radar. And since this operation will strike the entire fleet at the same time, it will need a considerable number of torpedoes, which will form a target that will definitely be detected from the air. Unless the torpedo ambush is set up outside the enemy's three hundred kilometer aerial patrol radius, it won't have any use in combat."

An army senior colonel looked around the room. "Is there no one from the air force? Can't we consider an air strike?"

Colonel Xu said, "Maple Leaf does not have any airborne models. Besides, line-of-sight attacks are even more dangerous in the air."

Another heavy silence. The members of the ball lightning unit could feel the unspoken accusation of the other participants: *What a piece of junk.*

The operations director said, "Let's focus our thinking on a single problem: Is there anything that can get to within sight of the enemy fleet?"

Lin Yun said, "There's only one thing: a fishing boat."

A few chortles sounded in the meeting room.

"According to our observations, the enemy fleet generally ignores fishing boats near its sea routes. Even more so for small-tonnage fishing boats. So we can use fishing boats as a launch platform for Maple Leaf, and get even closer to the enemy than just within sight."

There was more laughter. The shore defense commander shook his head and said, "No need to be patronizing, Major. We're just coming up with ideas, aren't we?"

Colonel Xu said, "No, this is a plan we're actually working on. And it's the plan we believe is the most workable. Before we received this battle order, we had already been thinking about it for quite some time, and we sent a task force to carry out research."

"But it's just—" a naval officer started to say, before a gesture from the operations director cut him off.

"Don't say it. It really looks like a plan! They've evidently put some thought into it."

The missile unit commander that Lin Yun had attacked laughed. "It really is a premodern plan."

"Not even premodern," the submarine commander said. "Have you heard of anyone using fishing boats to attack warships in Jutland or Tsushima?"

"If we had Maple Leaf back then, we would have," Lin Yun said.

"It just doesn't seem like naval warfare. It's more like piracy. If it gets out, won't we look ridiculous?" asked a navy captain.

"So what? If we can give shore-based firepower a chance to strike, then we can be thieves, not just pirates," one of the battle plan's drafters, a shore-based defense system commander, said.

The operations commander said, "The flaws of the fishing boats are, one, they have no defensive weapons, and two, they are slow. But in the face of the total attack power of the enemy fleet, the difference between fishing boats and torpedoes on those two points can be ignored."

No one spoke. The meeting attendees thought over this plan carefully, several naval officers occasionally exchanging views in low voices.

"For the time being, it looks basically workable. However . . . ," a naval officer said.

Again there was silence, silence for the "however," since everyone knew what it implied: if the attack failed, or if it succeeded but the land-based missiles did not arrive in time, then those small fishing boats would have no chance of escaping from the powerful fleet.

But as soldiers in wartime, they knew that there was no need of further discussion of that "however."

After a brief, whispered exchange with the shore defense systems commander, the operations director said in a loud voice, "Very well. Teams for each branch should draw up detailed battle plans based on this framework at once."

The next day, Dawnlight, fully equipped, took three military transport planes to a small airfield in the Fujian theater. Ding Yi and Lin Yun disembarked first. On the runways to either side of them, fighters and bombers were landing in succession, while on a runway a little farther away, a large number of transport planes were landing, depositing a stream of tanks and soldiers in fatigues. More planes were circling, their engines thundering as they waited to land. On a road in the distance, an iron river of military vehicles sped through the dust, with no end in sight.

"Deployment against a land invasion has begun," Lin Yun said darkly.

"Ball lightning will make it unnecessary," Ding Yi said to console her. At the time, he believed it too.

At this point, Ding Yi said, "After I said that, Lin Yun looked at me for a few seconds, with the face of a woman looking for comfort. I had the wonderful feeling that, for the first time, I was not just a thinker, but a strong, powerful man."

"Do you really believe that you're stronger emotionally than she is?" I asked.

"She has her weaknesses, too. She can even be fragile. After Zhufeng sank and Jiang Xingchen died, that fragility became increasingly apparent."

Lin Yun pointed out a grassy area not far off that was closely guarded. Heavily armed soldiers stood watch over tall stacks of goods, all of them in dark green metal containers half the size of a standard freight container. A large number of military trucks were constantly loading them and carrying them off.

"It's all C-805 missiles. Probably in preparation for this operation," she said softly. Ding Yi knew she was referring to the "Chinese Exocet" anti-ship missile, the most powerful weapon in China's shore-based defense system, but he was shocked by the sheer quantity.

The first set of thunderball guns arrived, and were immediately shipped to the harbor and installed on the requisitioned fishing boats that were waiting there. The boats were small, the largest having a displacement of no more than one hundred tons. Each thunderball gun's superconducting batteries were placed in the cabin, but the launchers were too long and had to be placed on deck, covered with a tarp or fishnet. Naval sailors and engineers took the place of fishermen, more than one hundred in all to pilot the fifty fishing boats.

Leaving the harbor, Lin Yun and Ding Yi headed toward the Coastal Defense Command Center, where Xu Wencheng and Kang Ming had assembled Dawnlight. In the war room, a navy colonel was describing the enemy on a large screen.

". . . the core of the enemy fleet consists of three carriers: *Carl Vinson*,

John C. Stennis, and *Harry S. Truman*, all of them top-of-the-line nuclear supercarriers first launched in or after the 1980s. Also in the battle group are the following: three cruisers, fourteen destroyers, twelve frigates, and three supply ships. Thirty-five surface vessels altogether. Submarine numbers are uncertain—we believe around ten. Next is a diagram of the fleet formation."

An image came up on the screen that resembled a complicated chess position made up of lots of oblong pieces.

"This is our ambush formation."

A line of dots appeared on either side of the central fleet's heading, twenty-five in each line.

"Using this diagram, you can easily determine the target you're responsible for. Know that although the enemy may change formation when it reaches coastal waters, it's already in a classic coastal defensive formation, so any changes are expected to be minimal. Fire points should adjust their targets according to actual conditions.

"Let me particularly stress the focus of the attack. I asked around just now and found unanimous agreement that the carriers were the focal point. I can forgive my army comrades for this, but for my naval comrades to have the same idea is ridiculous. Remember: ignore the carriers. Attack the cruisers! They are the backbone and control center of the electronics parts of the Aegis defense system. And after them, target the destroyers, an integral part of that defense system. With them disabled, the entire fleet is a hunk of meat on the chopping board. Also, those ships will be closest to our positions. Ignoring the periphery to attack the center will have disastrous consequences. Once more: the carriers are the meat, the cruisers and destroyers are the bones! At least eight hundred shots should be taken at every cruiser, and one hundred and fifty to two hundred per destroyer."

On the screen appeared a longitudinal section of a warship showing a dizzyingly complicated internal layout. Then a green line extended from the bridge and twisted through the bowels of the ship like a roundworm.

"This is a Ticonderoga-class cruiser. The green line is the path of the thunderball sweep."

Small circles appeared at different points along the line, each accompanied by a number.

"These are the key strike points. The numbers next to them are the recommended number of thunderballs for that point. The booklet you have just been given contains longitudinal sections and sweep lines for every ship. There's no way to memorize all of them in the time we have, so remember your own targets for the key strike points. Army comrades may find it more difficult to read the diagrams, so just commit them to memory. Let me simply say that the key strike points are the Aegis computer systems on the cruisers and destroyers. Now, let's have the head of weapons technology elaborate on some details."

Lin Yun went up front and said, "I already said all I need to say back at the Beijing training center. Here I'd just like to remind everyone that according to the average speed of the thunderball guns, you'll have to fire on each target for anywhere from forty seconds to one minute before finishing. This is a relatively long time, so don't panic. The thunderball paths are clear. Fire just like you'd fire ordinary tracer rounds. Get a stable path going, and then begin the sweep.

"The fleet's wake is a major issue. Our vessels are small, so their rocking will definitely affect your shooting. When the enemy has entered the ambush area completely, the wake won't have reached the front section of the ambush line, and it will already have calmed for the back section. So shooting in the middle section will be affected the most. We have deployed our toughest fireteams there. They've had marine training and are experienced at firing on the waves. . . . We should have had a longer training period, but there's no time. We're relying on your performance on the battlefield!"

"Don't worry, Major. Do you think a gunner who's firing on a carrier will fail to perform?" a second lieutenant said.

"Let me repeat yet again: the carriers are not within our attack scope! Stop thinking about them! Anyone who wastes ammo on them will be held responsible!" the navy colonel said.

After dark, Dawnlight went to a shooting range where a peculiar simulated fleet was set up. Dozens of ship profiles had been cut out from large cardboard sheets, each set on two small rollers so they could move slowly across the range if pushed by a soldier. Each shooter trained a light machine gun, a laser pointer affixed to the barrel, on their designated target to indicate the point of impact, and then strove to move the red dot along the prescribed sweep path. The exercise continued late into the night, until everyone was entirely familiar with the shooting process for their own target. The ship silhouettes moving slowly in the dark and the red dots moving equally slowly along them formed a mysterious, abstract painting, hypnotic enough to make everyone drowsy by the end.

The rest of the night they spent asleep in naval barracks. It was said that the night before the Normandy invasion, a psychologist observed the sleeping conditions of the soldiers, imagining that they would have difficulty falling asleep on the eve of a bloody battle. To the contrary, all of them slept soundly, a fact he attributed to an instinctive response of the group to the huge energy expenditure they were about to experience. Dawnlight also fell asleep quickly. It was a night without dreams.

As morning broke, Dawnlight arrived at the dock. The sun was still at the horizon, and the fifty fishing boats in the harbor rocked gently in the morning mist.

Before they boarded, Lin Yun drove up in an open-top jeep carrying several camouflage bags, which she took out of the vehicle and opened up. They were stuffed with uniforms. Dawnlight had left them behind at camp after they changed into a fishing company's work clothes that stank of the sea.

"What are you doing, Lin Yun?" Lieutenant Colonel Kang Ming asked.

"Have the soldiers put their uniforms on under the work clothes. When the operation is finished, they can strip out of the work clothes."

Kang Ming was silent for a while, then slowly shook his head. "I appreciate your good intentions, but Dawnlight has its own rules. We won't be captured. Let the naval soldiers wear uniforms."*

"Those rules may apply to lieutenant colonels and higher ranking officers, but the soldiers executing this mission are just thunderball gunners. They don't know much. I've made inquiries, and the higher-ups have given their tacit permission. I'm telling the truth. Please believe me."

Lin Yun was correct. In the early stages of Dawnlight's training, Kang Ming had wanted to conduct all-round training in both operation and repair of the thunderball gun, but she had staunchly opposed the idea, and had pushed successfully for the strict separation of personnel for weapons operations and engineering services. The thunderball gunners were not permitted to dismantle the weapons, nor did they have any opportunity to come into contact with the principles of the weapon or other technical information. Their only concern was its use. Up until they boarded the fishing boats, none of the gunners knew that what they were firing was ball lightning. They believed, as the commander had told them, that they were firing EM radiation bombs.

---

* Only combatants wearing the uniform of their country enjoy the rights of captured soldiers under the Geneva Convention.

Looking back, Lin Yun's decision was made not merely for confidentiality purposes, but also out of kindness.

"This kind of mission is seldom seen in modern warfare. If the attack fails, we require nothing from these soldiers other than the immediate destruction of their weapons," she said urgently.

Lieutenant Colonel Kang hesitated for a few seconds, then waved a hand at the unit. "Very well. Put these uniforms on at once. Be quick about it!" Then he turned toward Lin Yun and extended a hand. "Thank you, Major Lin."

Ding Yi interrupted his story to remark, "You can see where she had become fragile."

The following account Ding Yi pieced together after the fact.

Ten minutes later, the fifty fishing boats filed out of the harbor, a classic scene of fishermen heading out to sea at dawn. No one would have imagined that the humble craft were en route to attack the most powerful fleet on the planet.

After leaving the harbor, Kang Ming and the naval commanding officers—a lieutenant commander, a lieutenant, and two junior lieutenants—held a meeting on a larger fishing boat that served as a command craft for the hundred-odd helmsmen and engineers piloting the fishing boats.

The lieutenant commander said to Kang Ming, "Colonel, I suggest your people stay hidden belowdecks. You clearly don't look like fishermen."

"We can't stand the fishy stench down there," Kang Ming said with a grimace.

The lieutenant said, "Our orders are to pilot the fishing boats to the designated region, and to accept your instructions only when enemy ships appear. Our superiors said this mission is extremely dangerous, and asked for volunteers. That's highly unusual, you know."

A junior lieutenant said, "I'm the navigator of a Luda-class destroyer. It would be more than a little pathetic if I sank on this leaky boat."

"Even if this leaky boat is headed to attack a carrier battle group?" Kang Ming asked.

The junior lieutenant nodded. "That would be more heroic. Yeah, back in school, attacking a carrier was our biggest dream. The second was to be a ship captain. The third was to find a woman able to put up with us being at sea all the time."

"We've been tasked with targeting a cruiser. If we succeed, the enemy carrier will be sunk in a matter of minutes."

Four naval officers stared in astonishment. "Colonel, you've got to be kidding!"

Kang Ming said, "Why act so surprised? Have you lost the courage of your predecessors? Back when the country was founded, the navy once sunk a destroyer with wooden boats."

"Sure, and we ought to do them one better and assault a mobile off-shore platform with surfboards!" the lieutenant commander said.

A junior lieutenant said, "Even so, we've got to have weapons, right? All we've got aboard this vessel are a few handguns."

Kang Ming asked, "What do you think that equipment on board was?"

"Those are weapons?" the lieutenant commander asked, looking at the other three officers.

The lieutenant said, "It looks like radio or radar. Isn't that an antenna there on the deck?"

"That, I can tell you, is the weapon we're going to use against the carrier group," Kang Ming said.

The lieutenant commander laughed. "Comrade Colonel, you're making it hard for us to be serious."

A junior lieutenant pointed at the two superconducting batteries and quipped, "I've got it. Those are depth charges, and the two iron frames are launch rails."

Kang Ming nodded. "I can't tell you the weapon's real name, so let's just call them depth charges." He showed the officers a red button on one of the batteries, and said, "This is the self-destruct button. If things get tight, the first thing we've got to do is press this, and then toss the thing into the ocean. Whatever happens, we can't let it fall into enemy hands."

"Don't worry, our superiors have stressed that repeatedly. If there's nothing else, then we should get to work. This old boat leaks oil all over."

They reached the ambush point around noon and began a long wait, during which Kang Ming had little to do apart from scanning the ambush line and checking the state of each vessel's thunderball gun. The boat he was on had a radio, which he used to contact headquarters just twice, once to report that all vessels were in place, and a second time to resolve a technical issue: he had reservations about the plan's stipulation that all boats operate under a blackout after dark. He felt it was pointless, and would only serve to raise the enemy's suspicion. Headquarters concurred, and instructed all vessels to run with normal lighting. No information was provided about the enemy's movements.

Their anxiety and excitement quickly burned away in the blistering sun, and they no longer trained their binoculars constantly on the northern horizon. So as not to attract attention, the vessels occasionally moved back and forth in a small area, futilely tossing the nets out and bringing them back in again. The lieutenant was skilled at this, and managed to catch a few fish. Kang Ming learned that he hailed from a fishing village in Shandong.

More of their time was spent on the deck, playing cards or chatting about all sorts of topics with their backs to the sun. The only thing they didn't mention was their mission, and the fate of the tiny ambush fleet.

By nightfall, the team had grown a little lax, after so long a wait. It had been over eight hours since their last contact with headquarters, and since then there had been nothing but static on the radio. Kang Ming had not slept well for several nights, and the monotonous rhythm of the ocean waves made him drowsy, but he fought to stay awake.

Someone nudged him gently. It was the lieutenant commander. "Look ahead to the left, but don't be too obvious," he said softly. A reddish moon had just risen over the horizon, rendering the ocean surface clear. In that direction, Kang Ming first saw a V-shaped wake, then, at its head, a thin black vertical rod with a spherical object at its tip. It reminded him of a photo he had seen somewhere of the Loch Ness Monster, its long neck extending from the murky water.

"Periscope," the lieutenant commander whispered.

The thin rod moved quickly. As it cut through the water's surface it whipped out an arc of spray that was audible as a light *whoosh*. Then it gradually slowed, and the spray lessened and vanished. The periscope, now directly ahead of their vessel around twenty meters away, was motionless.

"Ignore it," the lieutenant commander said, a slight smile on his face, as if he was absorbed in conversation with Kang Ming.

Just before he turned away, Kang Ming clearly saw the glint of light reflecting off the glass spherical object at the top of the rod. Then the lieutenant and the two junior lieutenants emerged from the cabin carrying a netting shuttle, and sat right on the tarp covering the weapon's launch rail to mend nets under the moonlight. Kang Ming watched the captain's skilled hands and followed his movements, but his mind concentrated on the strange eye behind him that was staring at them from the ocean, stabbing into his back.

The lieutenant said, "I'll throw this one over, and with any luck it'll get tangled in their damn propeller." He wore an expression of lazy fatigue, as if complaining about having to work so late at night.

"Then toss over those two depth charges," a junior lieutenant said, chuckling. Then he turned to Kang Ming. "Say something." But Kang Ming couldn't come up with anything.

The lieutenant pointed at the net and asked him, "How's my mending look?"

Kang Ming held the mended section up against the light coming from the cabin, inspected it, and said to him, "Let's give them a look at your handiwork."

The lieutenant commander said, "It's moving again."

The lieutenant warned Kang Ming, "Don't look back."

After a while, they heard the whooshing sound again, and when they looked behind them, the rod was heading away from them at increasing speed, lowering as it went, until it was entirely underwater.

The lieutenant threw down the net, stood up, and said to Kang Ming, "Colonel, if I were commanding that sub I'd have seen through us. You held the net all wrong!"

Then the radio received a short message from headquarters telling them that the enemy fleet had reached the ambush area, and to prepare for attack.

Before long, they heard a faint rumbling sound that quickly grew loud. They looked off to the northern sky and saw a line of black dots appear—five of them, one smack in the middle of the moon's disc, so its whirling rotors were visible. The five helicopters came in fast and rumbled overhead, red beacons flashing on their bellies. One dropped a long object that hit the water not far from them in a plume of white; a short distance later, another helicopter dropped another long object. Kang Ming asked what they were, and the lieutenant commander's voice answered from the cabin: "Sonar buoys for submarine detection. The enemy takes great care with its antisubmarine measures."

The helicopters soon vanished into the southern night sky, and stillness returned once more. Now Kang Ming's micro-earpiece, tied in to the radio in the cabin, chirped with a voice from headquarters.

"The target is approaching. All vessels to shooting state. Over."

The moon was now blocked by clouds, darkening the ocean surface, but a glow had appeared in the northern sky, the same glow that was visible from the base each evening in the direction of the city. Kang Ming raised his binoculars, and for a moment had the impression he was looking at a glittering shoreline.

"We're too far forward!" the lieutenant commander shouted, putting down his binoculars and dashing into the cabin. The fishing boat's turbines rumbled to life and it reversed course.

The glow in the north grew brighter, and when they turned back to look at it, the "shore lights" on the horizon were visible even without binoculars. With them, they could make out individual ships. The voice in Kang Ming's earpiece said, "Attention all vessels. The target formation is basically unchanged. Proceed according to original plan. Over."

Battlefield command, Kang Ming knew, had now been transferred to their vessel. If everything had developed as expected, they had only to wait for the cruisers at the head of the enemy fleet to advance directly in front of their small craft, then give the order to fire, since they knew from their intel of the enemy's fleet formation that the fleet would be entirely encircled at that point. Now they made their final preparations before firing: putting on life jackets.

The fleet approached quickly. When individual ships became visible to the naked eye, Kang Ming looked for targets he could identify only to hear the lieutenant shout, "That's *Stennis!*"—perhaps because the ship's shape had been imprinted in his brain at the naval academy. As he shouted, he looked at Kang Ming with a challenge: *Let's see what you do now.* Kang Ming stood at the bow, silently watching the swiftly approaching fleet.

Enormous ovals cast by the fleet's searchlights danced chaotically on the water ahead of them. Occasionally the beams caught a fishing boat in a beam and threw a long shadow onto the surface, but they soon moved away. The small boats apparently did not attract attention. The enormous fleet now filled their whole field of vision. Details of the two cruisers at the front were clearly visible under the moonlight and the ships' running lights, while the six destroyers on either side were black silhouettes, and the enormous bodies of the three carriers in the center of the formation cast giant shadows on the water. The sailors on the fishing boats heard a sharp, scalp-tingling whistle overhead that grew dramatically louder, as if the sky were being cut open. They craned their necks upward in time to see four fighters pass by. And then they began to hear the rolling crash of surf, the sound of those metal hulls plying the waves. The thin white cruisers passed by, followed by the gray iron destroyers—which, though smaller than the cruisers, appeared much larger, since they were on the nearer side of the formation. They dazzled with intricate superstructures and towering antennae. A few sailors were visible moving about on board. Soon the carriers were in front of them, partially obscured by the destroyers: three nuclear-powered floating cities, three death-bringing iron mountains whose outlines seemed beyond the work of human hands. For the troops on the fishing boats, this massive fleet was a surreal sight, as if they had suddenly landed on a strange planet whose surface was covered in enormous iron castles.

Kang Ming took out a tiny wireless mouthpiece from his lapel, and the two Dawnlight gunners who had stayed in the hold the entire time lifted the tarp off the thunderball gun, lay down on it, and aimed directly at the cruiser passing ahead of them, tracking it with the launch rail. Kang Ming said in a soft voice, "All fire points, commence firing."

Ball lightning issued from the tip of the rails, strands of pearls issuing an ear-splitting crackle and lighting up the surrounding ocean with an intensely flickering blue electric light. A string of red thunderballs flew across the ocean, close to the surface, trailing long tails and whistling sharply. Gracefully, they swept by the stern of the first destroyer and the prow of the second, heading toward the cruiser.

Lines of ball lightning shot at the fleet by the other fishing boats looked from this distance like bright rays of light. When ball lightning was fired along an unvarying trajectory, the ionized air formed a fluorescent trail that would continue to glow after the lightning itself moved on. These trails fanned out from each fishing boat and expanded as the ball lightning moved about. The battleground was a giant net made out of strings of ball lightning and their far more numerous fluorescent trails.

They seemed on the cusp of a grand moment in the history of warfare.

But just as the first group of ball lightning was about to reach the target, their trajectories were diverted by a giant, invisible hand. The ball lightning shot up into the air, or plunged into the ocean, or veered off to either side, passing far from the prow or stern of their targets. And when the diverted ball lightning flew near neighboring ships, the same thing happened. It was as if every ship in the fleet was enveloped in a giant glass enclosure that ball lightning could not penetrate.

"A magnetic shield!"

This was the first thought that entered Kang Ming's mind. Something that had come up countless times in the nightmares of ball lightning researchers had come to pass in the real world.

Kang Ming shouted the command: "All strike teams, abort firing! Destroy your weapons!"

On each boat, a Dawnlight sergeant pressed a red button on the thunderball gun, then, together with the other crew members, shoved it into the ocean. Not long after, the sound of muffled explosions carried up from the depths, and the surface of the ocean roiled, rocking their boats. The superconducting batteries that powered the guns had been shorted out and exploded with a power equivalent to a depth charge. The thunderball guns were now in pieces underwater.

The streams of ball lightning from the fishing boats had been severed simultaneously. Now a large mass of ball lightning floated above the fleet, absent any targets, weaving a shining carpet in the air with their fiery tails. Their sound changed from a uniform whistle to a chaotic buzz or shrill moaning.

Kang Ming saw a flash from a gun on the destroyer, but only in his peripheral vision. When the shell struck the command ship, he was staring straight ahead at the sea, where the ball lightning that had fallen into the water continued to glow faintly, like a school of effervescent fish.

The sound of guns grew thick, and in the ocean on either side of the fleet, huge columns of water bearing pieces of the fishing boats rose and fell. When the firing stopped after three minutes, forty-two of the fifty fishing boats had been taken out. They were so small that most of them hadn't even sunk, but had been blown to pieces by direct hits from the large guns. The eight remaining ships were locked in a circle of searchlights, as if taking a lonely curtain call at the close of this tragedy on the ocean stage.

The ball lightning released its energy as electromagnetic radiation, and soon went out, ionized air forming a fluorescent canopy in the air above the fleet. The radiation's effect on the ocean covered it in a layer of thick white steam. Some long-lasting balls of lightning slowly floated away, their sound growing fainter and more ethereal, like lonely ghost lanterns carried by the wind.

How the enemy knew of ball lightning's existence, and how it had built a system to defend against it, were unanswered questions. But there were some scattered clues: at the test target range in the south the previous year, ball lightning shot from the thunderball gun hadn't entered a quantum state even in the absence of our observers, which meant that there was another observer present. It was known that the nuclear plant operation could lead to a leak, but it was deemed to be worth the risk. The enemy could hardly have learned the fundamental principles of ball lightning or the technical details of the weapon from observing, but they too had been studying that natural phenomenon for many years. They may even have conducted large-scale R&D, like Project 3141 in Siberia, and if so would not have found it difficult to guess the truth beneath those scattered intelligence reports. And the effect of magnetic fields on ball lightning had long been known to science, independent of the nature of ball lightning itself.

On the transport plane back to base, Lin Yun squatted silently in a corner holding her helmet, her slender body curled up into a ball, looking alone and helpless like a girl lost in the wilderness in the dead of winter. Ding Yi felt a sudden compassion for her, so he went over and sat down next to her with words of comfort:

"You know, our success has been pretty great. Through macro-electrons, we can view the most profound mysteries of matter on a macro scale, something that was once only possible by entering the microscopic world. Compared to this achievement, the military use of ball lightning is insignificant—"

"Professor Ding, do people burned up by ball lightning remain in a quantum state?" Lin Yun interrupted him with a mindless question.

"Yes. Why?"

"You once said that the teacher would come to attack me."

"That was just random nonsense. Besides, you didn't believe me, did you?"

Lin Yun rested her chin on the helmet lying on her knees, and looked straight ahead. "After you mentioned it, I slept with a gun with the safety off. I really was afraid, but I was too embarrassed to let anyone know."

"I'm sorry I frightened you."

"Do you think it's really possible?"

"Theoretically . . . perhaps. But the probability is so low that it's not going to happen in the real world."

"But it is possible," Lin Yun murmured. "And if the teacher can attack me, then I can attack the enemy carrier."

"What?"

"Professor Ding, I can take another fishing boat close to the enemy fleet."

". . . and do what?"

"Incinerate myself with ball lightning. Wouldn't that turn me into a quantum soldier?"

"What are you talking about?"

"Think about it. In a quantum state, I can sneak into the carrier, and the enemy will have no way to find me, since the moment they notice me, my quantum state will collapse, just like you said. There's a large arsenal on board, and thousands of tons of fuel. So as long as I can find those, I'll be able to easily destroy the carrier. . . . Oh, and I can find Lieutenant Colonel Kang Ming and the other Dawnlight personnel. We could become a quantum unit . . ."

"This loss has turned you into a child, I see."

"I never was very old."

"You should go rest. We still have two hours until Beijing. Get some sleep."

"Is what I described possible?" Lin Yun turned to look at Ding Yi, with a look of entreaty in her eyes.

"Okay. Let me tell you what a quantum state really is. In a quantum state, you—ah, supposing you've already been incinerated by ball lightning—you are just a probability cloud. In that cloud, everything you do is indeterminate. You lack the free will to decide where you will appear. Your position in the probability cloud, and whether you will be alive or dead when you appear, is indeterminate, decided only when God rolls his dice. If you are burned up on the fishing boat, then the probability cloud for quantum-you will be centered on that boat. In the surrounding space, you have a very small probability of appearing in the carrier's arsenal or fuel storage. You will most likely appear in the water, and if you're in a live state at that time, you will very quickly drown. Then your quantum state will no longer include the probability of being alive; you will be dead in every probability. Taking a huge step back, even if you hit the probability jackpot and appear in some critical part of the enemy carrier, will you be alive then? How long can you stay there? An hour, or a tenth of a second? Also, the moment one enemy, or one of the enemy's cameras, catches sight of you, you will immediately collapse into that pile of ash in the center of the probability cloud to await your next jackpot. And when that opportunity comes, the carrier will be eighteen thousand kilometers away and there may no longer be any war left on Earth. . . . Finally, you've forgotten one point: those Dawnlight soldiers died from artillery shells, not ball lightning. Before their sacrifice, the ball lightning weapons were destroyed and sent to the bottom of the sea, so the soldiers did not turn quantum. . . . Lin Yun, you're like the little match girl, seeing all kinds of illusions. You really need to rest."

Lin Yun abruptly flung aside her helmet, then leaned against Ding Yi's shoulder and started crying as if heartbroken. She cried sorrowfully, her slender frame trembling in Ding Yi's embrace, as if letting out all of the anguish in her life at once. . . .

"You can imagine how I felt at the time," Ding Yi said. "I thought I was the sort of person for whom all emotions apart from rational thought were nonessential, and that impression has been reinforced on several prior occasions. But now I know that something else in addition to rationality can occupy a person's entire mind. . . . Lin Yun seemed to have shrunk down. The old unshakable, goal-oriented major was now a fragile, helpless little girl. Was that who she really was?"

"Maybe a combination of the two. I understand women even less than you," I said.

"Jiang Xingchen's death already weighed heavy on her, then the failure of the mission smashed through the limit of what her psyche could endure."

"That's not a good state to be in. You should get in touch with her father."

"Listen to yourself. How could I contact someone so high up?"

"I've got General Lin's phone number. He gave it to me himself, and asked me to look after Lin Yun."

I noticed that Ding Yi had not moved, and was staring at me. "It's no use."

His words frightened me. It was only then that I realized: Ding Yi's story was cloaked in a shroud of sadness.

He stood up, walked to the window, and looked quietly out at the chilly night. It was a long while before he turned around again. He pointed at the empty bottle on the table. "Got another one?" I rummaged around for another bottle, opened it, and poured him half a glass. He sat down, looked squarely at the glass, and said, "There's more. More than you ever would have imagined."

STRINGS

After their mortal failure in battle, ball lightning weapons research and deployment work came to a halt. Most personnel were transferred away, and even though the unit had not been disbanded, the base was a depressing place. It was then that Zhang Bin passed away.

"Zhang Bin was, after all, one of the pioneers of domestic ball lightning studies, so we decided to honor his wishes and conduct a ball lightning funeral. This would have to be kept confidential, and since you were an outsider then, we didn't notify you," Ding Yi explained.

I sighed softly. It was an unusual time, and my feelings were not overly stirred up by my advisor's passing.

The funeral was conducted on the base at the lightning test ground. It was overgrown with weeds, so they cleared a patch in the center for Zhang Bin's remains. When everyone had retreated to the one-hundred-meter safe line, a single excited high-energy ball of lightning flew from one corner of the test ground at slow speed. It floated slowly over Zhang Bin's body, whistling that deep *xun* music, as if narrating the unfortunate life of this ordinary explorer. Ten minutes later, the ball disappeared with a bang, and white smoke rose from the body. The white sheet covering it collapsed; underneath, all that was left was fine bone ash.

Since work at the base had stopped, Ding Yi had returned to the Institute of Physics in the city to continue theoretical research on macro-electrons. He had missed Zhang Bin's funeral, but he had seen the papers of calculations left behind in Zhang Bin's effects and had been stunned by the sheer amount of work in them. In his eyes, Zhang Bin had not been granted the imagination or opportunity for theory, but had lived a life of wandering uncertainly through the muddy wilderness; he deserved respect as well as pity. Ding Yi felt he ought to visit the grave of that pioneer.

Zhang Bin's grave was in a public cemetery near Badaling. Lin Yun drove Ding Yi out there one afternoon. They followed the stony path to the cemetery that afternoon, a carpet of golden leaves under their feet, and a stretch of the Great Wall peeking out of the distant mountains blanketed in red. Another autumn had come, the season of dying, of parting, and of writing poetry. A shaft of light from the setting sun reached through a gap in the mountains to touch the lines of headstones.

Ding Yi and Lin Yun stood before Zhang Bin's plain headstone, pondering their own thoughts until the sun had completely set.

Lin Yun murmured a Frost poem:

> *Two roads diverged in a yellow wood,*
> *And sorry I could not travel both . . .*
> *I took the one less traveled by,*
> *And that has made all the difference.*

Her voice was like a woodland spring.

"Have you ever thought of taking a different road?" Ding Yi asked.

"Is there one?" she said softly.

"Leave the army after the war, and come study macro-electrons with me. I've got the theory skills, and you're an engineering genius. I'll build the ideas, and you'll be in charge of experiments. It's very possible we'll make the greatest breakthrough in modern physics."

She smiled at him. "I grew up in the army. I don't know if I could entirely belong anywhere else." She hesitated before adding, "Or to anyone else."

Ding Yi said nothing. He walked up to the gravestone and placed the fresh flowers he had brought on the pedestal. As he did so, something on the stone caught his attention, and for a long while, he didn't straighten up. Eventually he squatted down and peered closely, his face practically pressed against the stone.

"My God. Who drafted the inscription?" he exclaimed.

His question caught Lin Yun by surprise, since at Zhang Bin's request, nothing had been put on the stone but his name and his dates, since he felt that there was nothing worth saying about his life. Lin Yun came over for a closer look, and then froze in shock. In addition to the large inscription, the face of the marker was densely covered with small carved letters. Lettering was on the top and sides of the stone, too, along with formulas and calculations. It was as if the gravestone had been dipped in a liquid made of formulas.

"Oh, they're fading. They're disappearing!" Lin Yun shouted.

Ding Yi roughly pushed her away. "Turn around! With one less observer they'll collapse more slowly."

Lin Yun turned around and wrung her hands anxiously. Ding Yi leaned on the stone and began reading the text line by line. "What is it? Can you see anything?" she asked.

"Keep quiet!" he said loudly, still focused on reading.

Lin Yun rummaged in her pockets. "Should I go back to the car for a pencil and paper?"

"There's no time. Don't bother me!" he said, reading the text with astonishing speed. His eyes were locked fiercely on the stone, as if trying to pierce through it.

Now the last bit of light in the west painted the gravestones an eerie blue, and the surrounding woodland was immersed in a sea of darkness. The few gleaming stars that had emerged hung unblinkingly in the sky. From time to time there was the faint whisper of leaves rustling in the gentle breeze, which soon stopped, as if some unknown power was holding its breath. Stillness enveloped everything, like the whole world was focusing its attention along with Ding Yi on the quantum inscription.

Ten minutes later, Ding Yi had finished reading the front of the gravestone, and, after a quick scan of the top and sides, began reading the back. It was completely dark now, so he took out a lighter and read rapidly in the light of its weak flame.

"I'll get a flashlight!" Lin Yun said, running off along the path between the ranks of gravestones to the car. When she returned with a flashlight in hand, the lighter flame had gone out. She found Ding Yi sitting with his back against the gravestone and his legs stretched out in front of him, looking at the stars.

On the gravestone, the inscription had vanished without a trace. The smooth marble surface reflected the flashlight beam like a mirror.

At the light from the flashlight, Ding Yi regained his senses like a man waking from a dream. He reached out, pulled Lin Yun around to the back of the gravestone, and pointed to its base. "Look at that. There's one line left. It's not in a quantum state, and it's the only line of the inscription in Chinese." Lin Yun crouched down and read the elegantly carved text:

> Bin, inciting F requires a speed of just 426.831 meters per second. I'm very afraid.

"I know that handwriting!" Lin Yun said, staring at the words. On more than one occasion, she had read Zhang Bin's notebook, its alternating pages burned by ball lightning.

"Yes. It's Zheng Min."

"What did she carve?"

"A mathematical model. A complete description of macro-atoms."

Lin Yun sighed. "We really should have brought a digital camera."

"It doesn't matter. I've got it all in my head."

"You do? All of it?"

"Most of it I'd derived already. But my theoretical system was stuck on a few points that she cleared up."

"It must be a very important breakthrough!"

"Not just that. Lin Yun, we can find macro-nuclei!"

"The nuclei of macro-atoms?"

"Yes. By observing the movement of a macro-electron in space, we can use this model to precisely determine the exact location of the macro-atom it belongs to."

"But how can we detect those macro-nuclei?"

"The same as with macro-electrons, and just as surprisingly simple: we can see them with the naked eye."

"Wow . . . what do they look like? I remember you said that the shape of macro-nuclei would be completely different from the shape of macro-electrons."

"Strings."

"Strings?"

"Yes, strings. They look like a length of string."

"How long? How thick?"

"They're in basically the same class as macro-electrons. They're about one to two meters long, depending on the atom. And they're infinitely thin. Every point is a dimensionless singularity."

"How can we see an infinitely thin string with the naked eye?"

"Because light bends in its vicinity."

"So what does it look like?"

Ding Yi half closed his eyes, like someone who has just woken up attempting to recall a dream. "It'll look like . . . a transparent crystalline snake. Or a hanging-proof rope."

"That second one's a strange analogy."

"That's because the string is the smallest building block of macro-matter. It's impossible for it to be cut."

On the way back, Lin Yun said to Ding Yi, "One more question: You're the cutting edge of theoretical physics in this country. It's hard to believe that decades ago, another ball lightning researcher was as well. There's certainly an element of subjectivity in Zhang Bin's assessment of his wife, but was Zheng Min really capable of making those discoveries?"

"If humanity lived in a frictionless world, Newton's Three Laws might have been discovered even earlier by someone even more ordinary. When you yourself become a macro-particle in a quantum state, you might have a far easier time understanding that world than we do."

And so the base started working on collecting macro-atomic nuclei.

They began by using the bubble optical detection system to make precise observations of the free-motion state of macro-electrons in the air, understanding now that the complicated floating path followed by a macro-electron, or the ball lightning that resulted when it was excited, was in fact an endless succession of atomic electron transitions—quantum leaps—that appear to us like continuous motion. If that macro-electron did indeed belong to a macro-atom, the magnificent mathematical model that had appeared on Zhang Bin's gravestone could determine the position of a macro-atom's nucleus through a complicated calculation involving various parameters of the atomic transition.

The first set of ten free-moving macro-electrons observed were discovered at a height of five hundred meters. A macro-electron had to be observed continuously for half an hour to obtain enough raw data for the calculation. The results showed that, of those ten macro-electrons, two were free electrons, and the other eight each belonged to a different macro-atomic nucleus, between three hundred and six hundred kilometers away. This was very close to Ding Yi's initial estimate of the size of macro-electrons. Three of the nuclei were beyond the atmosphere in space, one was deep in the Earth's crust, and of the four in the atmosphere, two were outside the country. So the researchers set off in search of one of the in-country macro-atomic nuclei, which was 534 kilometers away from the observed macro-electron.

It was wartime, so it was impossible to requisition a helicopter, but fortunately the base had three helium blimps they had used for capturing macro-electrons. These were easy to use, and cheap to fly; their one flaw was that they moved very slowly, at maximum speed no better than a car on an expressway.

Skies were blue in northern China that day, an excellent time for capture. They flew westward for more than four hours, crossing the Shanxi border. Below them was the unbroken line of the Taihang Mountains. The position of macro-nuclei was relatively constant compared to macro-electrons, but they still moved slowly, meaning the base had to continuously monitor the macro-electron and notify the capture blimp of the latest calculations of the macro-nucleus position. After the observation team on base notified the blimp that it had reached the target's location, the aviators turned on the blimp's optical detection system, whose pattern recognition software had been modified to detect a length of string rather than a round shape. There was a roughly one-hundred-meter margin of error for locating the macro-nucleus, so the optical detection system carried out fine observations of that area of sky to quickly locate the target.

The blimp descended slightly, and the aviator said that the target was several meters off the front left side of the cabin.

"Maybe we can see it directly!" Ding Yi said. Macro-electrons were hard to see without particularly keen eyesight, but Ding Yi had predicted that the shape of macro-nuclei was clearer to the naked eye, and their movement was slower and more regular, so they could be tracked more easily.

"It's over there," the aviator said, pointing down and to the left. All they could see in that direction was a rolling mountain range.

"Can you see it?" Lin Yun asked.

"No. That's based on the data," the pilot said, pointing at the detection system's screen.

"Take us down a bit more, so we can use the sky as a background," Ding Yi said to him.

The blimp descended slightly. The aviator watched the screen as he worked, and soon the blimp came to a standstill again. He pointed up and to the right. "It's over there. . . ." But this time, he didn't pull his hand back. "My God! There really is something! Look over there! It's moving upward!"

And thus, after the discovery of the macro-electron, humanity saw a macro-atomic nucleus for the first time.

The string was indistinct against the background of the blue sky. Like the bubbles, it was transparent, with a shape formed from its refraction of the light around it. Motionless, it would be invisible to the naked eye, but the string bent and contorted continuously in the air in a strange dance, unpredictable, but full of a wild vitality that exerted a strong attraction and hypnotic power on the observer. Later, theoretical physicists gave it a poetic name: "stringdance."

"What are you thinking?" Ding Yi asked, without taking his eyes off the macro-nucleus.

"It's not a crystalline snake or a hanging-proof rope," Lin Yun answered. "It reminds me of Shiva, the eternally dancing god of Hinduism. When her dance stops, the world will be destroyed with a bang."

"Brilliant! You seem to have found a sensitivity for abstract beauty."

"I've lost my focus on the beauty of weapons. An emptiness needs to be filled with some other sort of feeling."

"You'll refocus on weapons soon enough."

At Ding Yi's statement, Lin Yun turned away from the macro-nucleus outside the cabin to look at him in wonder. Until that point, she had not connected the string dancing in midair to weapons.

When she turned back to look at the macro-nucleus, finding it again took a lot of effort. It was hard to imagine that the dancing transparent string and the far-off crystalline bubble formed an atom with a radius of more than five hundred kilometers. How big would a macro-universe formed from those atoms be? The mere thought was enough to drive you crazy.

Capturing macro-nuclei worked similarly to capturing macro-electrons. Since the protons in a macro-nucleus bore a positive charge, they were attracted to magnetic fields. But unlike macro-electrons, they would not flow through superconducting wires. The blimp hatch opened, and a feeler with a powerful electromagnetic coil attached to its end gingerly extended toward the string. The balancing presence of the macro-electrons gave the macro-atom itself a neutral charge, but the blimp was now deep inside it, near the unneutralized nucleus. When the coil at the tip of the feeler neared the string, the rhythm of its dancing slowed. It rotated once, bringing one end into contact with the coil, as if it knew which end was supposed to be connected. Then it continued its senseless dance, only fixed in place this time.

Lin Yun and Ding Yi carefully drew the feeler back into the cabin. *It's a little like fishing,* they thought. The string danced in the cabin. It was around one meter long, and looked like a shimmer of hot air on the summer blacktop, rendering the cabin wall behind it slightly wavy. Lin Yun reached out to it, but, like the helicopter pilot who paused before the first macro-electron, she stopped, then watched uncomfortably as Ding Yi passed his hand casually across the center of the string without affecting its dance in the slightest.

"No big deal. It doesn't have any interaction with the physical matter of our world." Then, after staring at the string with Lin Yun for a minute, Ding Yi let out a long sigh. "Frightening. A terror of the natural world."

Lin Yun asked, "It can't be excited like macro-electrons, so what's so terrible about it? It looks like the most harmless thing in the world."

Ding Yi sighed again, and then stepped away, seeming to leave behind the unspoken words, *Just you wait.*

———

It wasn't long before the detection team at the base located another macro-nucleus three-hundred-odd kilometers away from the blimp. They continued on, and three hours later, in the sky over Hengshui, Hebei Province, captured their second macro-nucleus. Another three were located in quick succession, the farthest some four hundred kilometers away, the nearest just over one hundred. The problem was that the blimp was only equipped with two magnetic coils, each of which had a string stuck to it. Lin Yun suggested that they stick two to a single coil, and use the other coil to capture new strings.

"Are you crazy?" Ding Yi shouted sharply, startling Lin Yun and the pilot. He pointed at the two coils and their strings. "I'll say it again: the coils must be kept at least five meters apart. Do you understand?"

Lin Yun looked at Ding Yi thoughtfully for a few seconds, and said, "There's something you're not telling me about macro-nuclei . . . for example, you've never been willing to explain what that last line on the gravestone means."

"For something this important, I wanted to go directly to the higher-ups," Ding Yi said, avoiding Lin Yun's eyes.

"You don't trust me?"

"That's right. I don't trust you." Finding his resolve, Ding Yi looked straight at Lin Yun and said, "I can trust Colonel Xu and the others at the base, but I don't trust you. The other person I don't trust is myself. We're actually quite alike. Both of us might use macro-nuclei without considering the consequences, albeit for different reasons. I would act out of a burning curiosity about the universe, but you—you would act out of an infatuation with weapons, driven by your failures."

"Again with the weapons," Lin Yun shook her head in confusion. "This pliable, infinitely thin string can pass through our bodies without us feeling anything, and it can't be excited into a high-energy state. It's got nothing to do with weapons. . . . Your refusal to explain is affecting our work."

"With your training, you should be able to figure it out."

"I don't get it. Why is putting two of them together so frightening?"

"They'll get tangled."

"So what?"

"Think about what happens to two atomic nuclei that get tangled up in our world."

Ding Yi knew he had peeled back the last layer of wrapping, and he watched her closely, hoping to see signs of shock and terror on her face. There were traces at first, but they were quickly replaced by excitement—the excitement of discovering a new toy.

"Fusion!"

Ding Yi nodded in silence.

"Would it release a lot of energy?"

"Of course. A ball lightning discharge is like a chemical reaction in the macro-world. Fusion would yield at least a hundred thousand times the energy of a chemical reaction of the same number of particles."

"Macro-fusion—that's what we'll call it. Would its energy release have target selectivity like ball lightning?"

"In theory, yes, since they have identical energy release channels. They both experience quantum resonance with our world."

Lin Yun turned back to look at the two hanging strings. "That's brilliant. We used to require temperatures of a billion degrees for fusion, but now we can achieve it simply by tangling two strings!"

"It's not that simple. The separation I'm insisting on is merely a cautionary measure. If you put those two strings together, they wouldn't get tangled, since electrical repulsion would prevent them from coming into contact." Ding Yi extended a hand to rub an incorporeal dancing string. "Combining strings requires a certain amount of relative speed to overcome that repulsion. You should now be able to understand the inscription from the gravestone."

"Inciting F requires a speed of just 426.831 meters per second. . . . F is fusion?"

"That's right. Two strings need to strike each other at that relative speed in order to become entangled. That's fusion."

Lin Yun's engineering mind began working at top speed. "Since the strings carry a positive charge, it wouldn't be hard to get each of them to two-hundred-some meters per second on two EM accelerator rails of sufficient length."

"Don't head off in that direction. Our primary task now is to think of a safe way to store them."

"We should begin building two accelerators immediately—"

"I said, don't go in that direction!"

"I'm just saying, we should make preparations. If we don't, we won't be ready when the higher-ups decide on macro-fusion tests . . . ," Lin Yun said. Then, suddenly she got angry, and paced urgently inside the narrow cabin. "What's the matter with you? You're so neurotic and shortsighted. It's like you're a different person compared to when you first came!"

Ding Yi gave a strange laugh. "Major, I'm just carrying out my pitiful little duty. Do you think I really care? I don't. No physicist really cares about anything. Last century, when they turned over the formulas and techniques for atomic energy release to engineers and soldiers, then struck a pose of injured innocence at the price paid by Hiroshima and Nagasaki? Such hypocrites. They wanted to see the results, believe me. They wanted a demonstration of the power they had discovered. It was determined by their nature—by our natures. The only difference between them and me is that I'm not a hypocrite. I really want to see what will happen when those two strings of singularities get tangled together. Do I care about anything else? Hell no!"

Ding Yi had begun to pace as he spoke, and now the blimp rocked from their restless movement. The pilot turned back curiously to watch them fight.

"Then let's go back and build rails," Lin Yun murmured, her head down. She seemed momentarily drained of energy, as if something Ding Yi said had hurt her. And he soon found out the answer. On the flight back to base, sitting with him between the two dancing strings, Lin Yun said softly, "Do you really not care about anything apart from the mysteries of the universe?"

"Oh, I . . . ," Ding Yi stammered. "I just meant that I don't care about the consequences of macro-fusion tests."

THE SPECIAL LEADING GROUP

After the first successful capture of macro-nuclei, the base delivered a research report to the higher-ups that had the immediate effect of re-focusing attention on the forgotten ball lightning weapons project.

Not long after, the base received a relocation order moving it from Beijing to a region in the northwest. The first things to move were the captured macro-nuclei, which by this point numbered twenty-five. Keeping them near the capital was highly dangerous, no question about it.

Relocating the base took a month. During that time, work on macro-nuclei capture (they referred to them as strings now) continued uninterrupted; by the time the move was complete, nearly three hundred strings had been captured and stored. Most of them were light-weight nuclei. It appeared that in the macro-universe, as in ours, lighter elements like hydrogen were most plentiful. But Ding Yi staunchly opposed defining them using terms like "macro-hydrogen" and "macro-helium," since it was now known that the elemental system of the macro-universe was completely different. It had an entirely unknown periodic table whose elements were not in one-to-one correspondence with our own.

The captured strings were stored in simple, hastily assembled warehouses in the Gobi Desert, stuck to magnetic coils in a grid separated by at least eight meters, and subject to an isolation field to guarantee that they were kept safely apart. From a distance, these warehouses resembled greenhouses, so, to the outside world, the base was the Research Center for Anti-Desertification Plants.

The higher-ups specifically named safety concerns as the reason for relocating the base, but its location clearly suggested another possibility.

This was the spot where China had detonated its first atomic bomb. Here, just next to the base, were remains of metal towers twisted by the atomic blast and a small, nearly forgotten commemorative plaque. A short journey would take you to the nuclear weapon proving ground: buildings and bridges constructed to observe the effects of the nuclear explosion on them, and a large number of old armored cars used as test targets. Geiger counters no longer clicked incessantly here—radiation left by the explosion had been drained by time—and it was said that a fair number of those abandoned objects had been carted off by local farmers for sale as scrap.

A major meeting to discuss the discovery of strings was held in Beijing. It was attended by senior leaders, including the premier. Lin Yun's father chaired the meeting. The fact that he was able to take a full day away from vital war command to hold the meeting demonstrated the strings' importance.

After listening to two hours of technical reports by Ding Yi and the other physicists who had just been added to string research, General Lin said, "These reports have been rigorous and comprehensive. Now I'd like to ask Professor Ding to clear up a few questions for us in the plainest language possible."

Ding Yi said, "My understanding of the physical laws of the macro-world is still very superficial. Our study of strings has only just begun. For some questions, I'll only be able to give a very vague or even uncertain answer. I hope that you all will understand."

General Lin nodded. "First, when two strings from light atoms collide at critical velocity, how certain are we that they will undergo fusion? As far as I am aware, only two hydrogen isotopes and He-3 can cause a fusion reaction in our world."

"Sir, it's hard to compare the physical elements of the macro-world with ours. The unique string structure of macro-nuclei makes it relatively easy for them to combine, so fusion reactions between macro-atoms can be accomplished with much less effort than for our atoms. And macro-particles move at velocities a great many orders of magnitude slower than our particles. That means that, from the perspective of the macro-world, a collision speed of four-hundred-odd meters per second is equivalent to fusion temperature in our world. So we can be certain of producing fusion if we achieve a collision at that critical velocity."

"Excellent. The next, and most important, question: What will the size and effect scope of fusion energy be?"

"Sir, this question involves many variables, so it's difficult to be certain. This is the question that I'm most concerned with, too."

"Can we try to come up with a relatively conservative estimate, like the equivalent of fifteen or twenty megatons of TNT?"

Ding Yi shook his head with a smile. "Definitely not that high, sir."

"For safety's sake, we'll base our thinking on that, then. That is roughly the biggest thermonuclear yield that humanity has detonated. In the mid-twentieth century, during US ocean tests and Soviet land tests of that yield, the destructive radius was around fifty kilometers, well within controllable range. So what's your worry?"

"Sir, I'm afraid you're forgetting one thing: the high selectivity that macro-particle energy discharge has for its target. Conventional nuclear fusion releases its energy without any selectivity at all. It acts upon all matter in its surroundings—air, stone, earth, and so forth—which swiftly drains it away. So while conventional fusion may be high-yield, its area of effect is limited. But macro-fusion is different. The energy it releases acts on only one specific type of matter, and all other matter is completely transparent to it. If there's only a very small amount of that matter type, the energy drain will be small, but the area of effect will be large indeed. I'll give you an example: a twenty megaton release of energy without selectivity would turn the region within a fifty kilometer radius to cinders, but if that energy only acted upon hair, it would be enough to turn everyone in the world bald."

It was an amusing example, but no one laughed. The climate of the meeting remained serious and oppressive.

"Are you now able to determine a string's specific energy release target?"

"Yes. We discovered a while ago that microwaves are modulated into a complicated spectrum when passing through a macro-electron—different spectrums for different macro-electrons, as if they were fingerprints. Macro-electrons having the same discharge targets share a spectrum. Theoretically, this method will also apply to strings."

"But obtaining the spectrum of a particular class of macro-electron at first required discharge tests. You now believe that strings that share a spectrum with macro-electrons will also share a discharge target. Is there a theoretical basis for this?"

"Yes. We are able to prove this."

"So what are some of the targets of the three-hundred-odd strings you have captured?"

"All kinds. The most dangerous are those that target living organisms. Fusion of those strings would have unimaginable destructive power."

"One final question: Are there strings that release into electronic chip targets?"

"As in the case of macro-electrons, these are very rare. At the moment, we have collected only three of them."

"Good. Thank you." General Lin concluded his questioning, and the meeting fell into silence.

"The situation, I think, has been fully explained," said the premier, who had kept silent until this point. "Everyone not in the leading group is dismissed."

A thousand kilometers away, the ball lightning research base was engaged in intense preparation for macro-fusion tests.

The string accelerator rails, each of them more than ten meters long, were complete. They resembled two model railroad bridges, and, indeed, their code names were "Bridge 1" and "Bridge 2." The two strings would be accelerated to 250 meters per second on these bridges before colliding and undergoing macro-fusion.

The strings to be used in this experiment were those with the greatest practical significance: strings that released into electronic chips.

The bulk of the work went into setting up the target area. The base began importing huge quantities of electronic waste from overseas, most of it junked computer motherboards and network cards. Under the wartime economic blockade, e-waste was among the few products it was possible to import, and it was acquired in large quantities from third parties or even directly from the enemy. It was collected domestically as well. Ultimately, eighty thousand tons of e-waste were amassed and piled into unnatural mountains in the Gobi Desert. The boards and cards, bearing a huge number of chips, were arranged in three target circles around the central fusion point, the innermost at a radius of ten kilometers, and the outermost at one hundred kilometers, which included two small county towns on the edge of the Gobi. Small yellow surveying flags were used in this region, under each of which was anchored a black sealed bag holding several boards.

At the final work meeting, Ding Yi said, "I'll warn you of one thing: since the energy density will be high in the vicinity of the point of macro-fusion, there will be no target selectivity. Everything within a radius of two hundred meters will be incinerated. That means the rails will be single-use, and test personnel must maintain a safe distance of at least two thousand meters from the fusion point and ensure that they have no electronic equipment on their person."

Everyone waited, but Ding Yi said nothing more. "Is that all?" Colonel Xu asked.

"I've said everything I need to say to the people I need to say it to," he said, without emotion.

"Are you anticipating something unpredictable?" Lin Yun asked.

"As of this moment, I have not found anything predictable about macro-fusion."

"It's just two nuclei. They may be macro-nuclei, but it's only two of them. In micro-fusion in our world, a hydrogen bomb with a mass far greater than those two strings has a yield of only a few megatons."

Ding Yi said nothing, but just shook his head—whether to express his own lack of understanding or his helplessness at Lin Yun's naïveté, it was hard to say.

The next day, a battalion of soldiers from a local garrison arrived to strengthen security at the base. This caused excitement, since it was a sign that the test was about to start.

"Even if the fusion energy only destroys chips in the first target circle, we will have acquired an unstoppable weapon. Think of it: How can a fleet defend against an explosion ten kilometers away? An explosion that cripples all of its electronics?" Lin Yun enthused.

Her mood was shared by everyone on base. Their first failure had robbed them of the chance to make history, but now a second chance was in front of them, and it was even more palpable.

Late that night, Lin Yun and a few engineers were still making final adjustments to the bridges. To avoid detection from the air, the two bridges had been set up in a large tent the size of a gymnasium. During the test, the tent would be the first thing destroyed by the fusion energy. Ding Yi called Lin Yun outside, and they walked in the cold Gobi wind.

"Lin Yun, leave the base," Ding Yi said, suddenly breaking his silence.

"What are you talking about?"

"I want you to leave the base. You can apply for a transfer, or take a vacation. Just leave at once. Ask your father for help if you need to."

"Are you crazy?"

"You're the crazy one if you stay."

"Is there something you're not telling me?"

"No. It's just a feeling."

"Can't you think of my feelings? How can I leave at a time like this?"

In the dark, Lin Yun heard a long sigh. "I fulfilled my duty at the meeting in Beijing last week. Now I've done my duty as far as you're concerned." He waved both hands at the darkness, as if casting something aside. "There. Since you're not going to leave, then let's make preparations to watch the spectacle together. A spectacle beyond our wildest dreams!"

Under the moonlight across the vast sand of the Gobi, in a carpet of white temporary warehouses, three hundred strings spun their silent, endless dance.

———

The next morning, the base received notice that a special leading group would arrive that day to take over. The news pushed excitement to new heights, for this was an unmistakable sign that the macro-fusion test was a go.

That afternoon, the leading group arrived in two helicopters. Heading the group was a major general named Du Yulun. He wore glasses and cut a cultivated figure, a scholar-general. The group was warmly welcomed at the landing site by base leadership and the entire ball lightning project team. When Colonel Xu's introductions reached Lin Yun, Ding Yi noticed that General Du's smile vanished, and when Lin Yun saluted, he clearly heard her call him "teacher." General Du just smiled thinly and gave a slight nod before moving on to the next person.

On the way to the office building, Ding Yi overheard Colonel Xu talking to General Du.

"You seem to know Major Lin, sir?"

"Hmm. I was her doctoral advisor."

"I see." Colonel Xu did not inquire further. Clearly he had also noticed their unusual interaction. But Du Yulun did not change the topic.

"I did everything I could to stop her from getting her degree," he said, turning his head to look at Lin Yun following far behind them.

"Why? Major Lin was exemplary in her discipline."

"In her discipline, I'll acknowledge that she was the most exemplary student I've ever advised. Her technical gifts were without peer. But in our area of research, I place the same value on a person's morality as on their talent."

Colonel Xu was evidently a little surprised. "Oh . . . yes. Lin Yu's personality is a little abrasive, a little headstrong—"

"No, no." The general waved a hand. "It's not about temperament.

I believe that someone who treats guns like drugs is unfit for weapons research. Particularly cutting-edge and new-concept weapons."

Colonel Xu said nothing, but turned slowly to look back at Lin Yun.

"Colonel Xu, you've probably heard of the liquid mine incident."

"Yes. The Discipline Inspection Commission at Headquarters told me about that. . . . What? Did the investigation find anything?"

The general nodded. "She sold the technology to Chile and Bolivia simultaneously. That's deplorable, and she must be held responsible."

Colonel Xu, his expression grim now, looked back at Lin Yun again. She was engrossed in conversation with some young technical officers.

"Lin Yun will be isolated for investigation. Starting now, she is not to be permitted to have contact with any of the materials or equipment pertaining to string research. I must specifically state that this is the wish of General Lin Feng. He knows his daughter even better than I do."

"But . . . she is the key tech on base. Without her, the fusion test can't proceed."

General Du looked meaningfully at Colonel Xu, but said nothing more.

They all realized that the atmosphere wasn't right as soon as the meeting started, but what General Du led with came as a shock.

"Colonel Xu, what sort of show are you running here? You attended the meeting in Beijing. You ought to understand the intent of the higher-ups. You ought to know that there has never been a plan to go forward with macro-fusion tests, much less any sort of decision to do so! We ordered you to proceed with preparations only as a precautionary measure."

Colonel Xu sighed. "Sir, I have made this clear to the comrades on the base time and again, but . . . they have their own ideas."

"It's because of your permissiveness of a certain dangerous line of thinking on base that they have been misled."

A murmur passed through the meeting room.

"Now I will read out the order that's been handed down." General Du adjusted his glasses, and began. "First, immediately cease all preparations for macro-atomic fusion tests and seal up all experimental equipment. Second, cease all experimental research on macro-nuclei, all experimental projects involving macro-nuclei, and strictly restrict research on macro-nuclei to the confines of pure theory. Third, release the vast majority of collected macro-nuclei currently in storage back into the atmosphere, retaining only one-tenth for future research use. Fourth, the special leading group will take over all facilities on base. Apart from a small number of personnel to keep guard, all members of the ball lightning project team are to vacate immediately and return to Beijing to await orders."

Silence descended on the meeting room, but the icy stillness did not last very long. It was Lin Yun's voice that broke it.

"Teacher, why are you doing this?"

"I am not your teacher anymore. And as a base-level technical officer, your only right at this meeting is to listen."

"But I have a soldier's duty. With the war in such a dire state, we're going to abandon a chance for victory out of a few vague fears?"

"Lin Yun, you're at your most shallow and naïve when you believe that any one new-concept weapon will win the war. Think about your actions. Are you still qualified to talk about duty?" General Du looked straight at her as he spoke, then swept his gaze around the whole room. "Comrades, the war is indeed in a grave situation, but even greater than our responsibility to the war is our responsibility to human civilization!"

"Those are some lofty words," Lin Yun challenged him, jumping up.

"Lin Yun!" Colonel Xu snapped. "You cannot talk to a superior that way."

General Du stopped Colonel Xu with a wave of his hand, then turned and said to Lin Yun, "I am carrying out a lofty order, an order given by people wiser, more moral, and more responsible than you. Your father is among them."

Lin Yun said nothing more. Her bosom heaved and tears had welled up in the corners of her eyes, but her expression was as fiery as before.

"Now, Colonel Xu, get going with the handover. But let me note that the base's handover team may not include Major Lin Yun. She has been transferred off of the ball lightning project team, and will leave the base by helicopter immediately after the meeting," Major General Du said, looking meaningfully at Lin Yun. "This is also your father's wish."

Lin Yun sat slowly back in her seat. When Ding Yi looked back at her a little while later, he was surprised to discover that she seemed an entirely different person. The tumult in her heart seemed to have vanished in a flash, and her expression was as calm as water. She was silent for the remainder of the meeting.

The meeting continued for another half hour, focusing mainly on the details of the handover. When it was dismissed, Lin Yun passed through the exiting crowd to the front of the building, where she said to General Du, "Teacher, have someone accompany me."

"Where?" he asked, confused.

"To the fusion point. I need to pick up some personal items," she said simply.

"Oh, right," Colonel Xu said. "She's been staying out by the bridges doing calibrations."

"You go with her," General Du said to a lieutenant colonel next to him.

Lin Yun saluted, then turned and left, disappearing into the blood-red Gobi sun outside.

Following the meeting, the members of the special leading group remained behind with several of the base's technical directors to discuss the issue of storing the small number of macro-nuclei that were to be kept. They agreed that the strings would be stored in an underground facility to mitigate the risk of air strikes and other dangers.

Colonel Xu inquired again about the ultimate fate of the ball lightning project team, and General Du said, "I may have been too severe at the meeting. The higher-ups are well aware of the excellent achievements the project team has made, and even though string research will be suspended for the time being, macro-electron research can still continue."

"Sir, ordinary macro-electron weapons have reached a dead end," Colonel Xu said, grimacing.

"Is it really that serious? It was just one failed attack on a fleet. And a fleet is the most heavily defended target in modern warfare. But on land? The enemy can't equip every single soldier with a magnetic shield, and I'd wager it would be pretty difficult to do so for every tank and armored vehicle. So there's still a bright future for the weapon. The key is where you use it. Also, the higher-ups are now very interested in pure dissipation ball lightning."

"Pure dissipation? But that's useless junk," Colonel Xu said uncertainly. That type of ball lightning did not have an explosive release of energy at all. After excitement, it gradually discharged its energy through ordinary EM radiation. It was the gentlest macro-electron, and had been deemed to be the least useful, militarily.

"No, Colonel. Haven't you noticed the EM radiation that they release? It blankets practically all communication wavelengths, and is very strong. Right now, the military has adopted a double-blind warfare strategy and is carrying out full-spectrum jamming of the enemy, but our jamming sources frequently get located and destroyed, so we are investigating pure dissipation ball lightning as a jamming source."

"That's true! When it drifts through the air, wireless communications cut out over a fairly large area. And it's long-lived, with a discharge that lasts for up to two hours!"

"And it's not easily destroyed. We've done tests in which ball lightning in flight hasn't been affected even after being bombed."

"That's right, sir. We should have come up with that idea before."

"You did come up with the idea, Colonel. You've submitted so many technical reports that it's quite likely you just didn't notice it."

Ding Yi said, "I knew about it. Lin Yun was the one who proposed it."

At the mention of Lin Yun, they fell into silence.

Just then, the sound of a gunshot came from the fusion point.

The test location was roughly one thousand meters away, so the sound was faint, but Ding Yi knew it was a gunshot from the soldiers' sudden alertness. It was followed by several more in quick succession.

Everyone in the meeting room rushed outside and looked off toward the fusion point.

A swath of empty land lay between the fusion point and the office building. They could see someone running across that space from the tent holding the acceleration bridges. As he got closer, they could make out the lieutenant colonel who had gone with Lin Yun to the fusion point. Closer still, and they saw that his left hand was clutched to his shoulder, and his right held a gun. When he reached the office building, they could see the blood running down and dripping off the barrel of his gun.

The lieutenant colonel pushed aside someone who tried to treat his wound and went straight up to General Du. In a hoarse voice, he said, "Major Lin Yun . . . she's going to conduct the macro-fusion test by force!"

Time froze. They looked across at the fusion point, and for a moment, everywhere else in the world vanished from sight, leaving only the huge tent towering alone.

"Who fired?"

"I did. There were too many of them. If I didn't shoot first, it would have been too late." The lieutenant colonel set down his bloody gun and sat down heavily.

"Any other casualties?" Colonel Xu asked.

"I definitely hit one of them. A captain, I think. Injured or dead, I don't know."

"And Lin Yun?" General Du said.

"Unharmed."

"How many of them are there?"

"Six, including Lin Yun. Three of the others are three majors and two are captains."

"So many people are on her side?" General Du said, eyeing Colonel Xu.

"Lin Yun had considerable appeal to some of the more nationalistically inclined young people on base."

"And the atomic nuclei for the fusion test?"

"The two strings are already on the bridges."

Every eye drew back from the tent in the distance to focus on General Du Yulun.

"Order base security to attack and occupy the fusion point immediately," General Du instructed the guard commander who had just run up.

"Sir, I'm afraid that's impossible!" said the deputy director of the special leading group, a senior colonel named Shi Jian, as he walked quickly over to General Du. "The strings are already on the bridge. Fusion might take place at any time. We need to take more decisive action."

"Carry out the order," Du Yulun said, without expression.

Senior Colonel Shi stared at him in anxiety verging on panic, but ultimately said nothing.

"Professor Ding, we ought to go and dissuade her," Colonel Xu said.

Ding Yi shook his head. "I won't go. It wouldn't do any good. Besides, I understand her." His frankness drew odd looks from the others. He added, "I might be the only one here who understands her."

"Let's go!" Colonel Xu said, and, without a second look at Ding Yi, he hurried off with the guard commander.

"Don't shoot rashly," General Du called after them as they left. The guard commander turned back with a hasty, "Yes, sir."

"It's no use. Trying to persuade her won't work. I still don't understand her . . . ," General Du murmured to himself. He looked like he had aged considerably in the blink of an eye, perhaps blaming himself for allowing emotion to trump reason, for it was clear to all now that Lin Yun had been his most prized student.

The security force quickly surrounded the fusion point and began drawing their line tighter around the tent. They moved in silence, neither side opening fire. When the line reached the tent, Colonel Xu shouted through a megaphone, but he was clearly no longer thinking straight. His attempts at persuasion were jumbled and unconvincing, nothing more than entreaties to "calm down," and "think of the consequences."

As if in answer, the sharp electric hum of a thunderball gun was heard in the tent, followed immediately by a whistling string of cool blue ball lightning, which whipped over the line like a gale. The soldiers reflexively hit the ground. The ball lightning exploded just behind them in a short bang, and a few stands of tamarisks and two nearby piles of crates turned instantly to ash, producing no flame, but giving off black tendrils of smoke. The ball lightning had released its energy into wood and vegetation.

"That was a warning. Your last warning." From the tent, Lin Yun's voice came over a megaphone, calm as water.

"Lin Yun, you . . . you'd really try to kill your comrades in arms?" Colonel Xu shouted in despair.

There was no answer.

"Pull the forces back at once," General Du said.

"We should immediately carry out a ball lightning attack on the tent, sir. We can't delay any longer!" Senior Colonel Shi said.

"No," a base officer said. "Lin Yun's group is using the latest-model thunderball gun. It has a built-in EM shield system that will deflect all ball lightning shot by other thunderball guns at fifty meters."

General Du thought for a few seconds, then picked up a phone and dialed the number for Lin Yun's father, General Lin Feng.

"Sir, this is Du Yulun. I'm calling you from the Project B436 base. When the special leading group was about to take over the base, there was an unexpected incident. Lin Yun and five other young officers forcibly occupied the fusion test point, and are now going to carry out the macro-fusion test by force. The two atomic nuclei are in the accelerators, and fusion could take place at any time. They are armed with a thunderball gun. Would you . . .”

The other end was quiet for two seconds, but only two seconds. Then General Lin said evenly, “You are fully capable of giving the order yourself.”

“But, sir—”

“You have been relieved. Hand the phone to Senior Colonel Shi Jian.”

“Sir!”

“Quickly.”

General Du passed the phone to Shi Jian, who snatched it up at once, clearly eager for the opportunity to talk to the brass. He was about to speak when General Lin gave a short, decisive order: “Destroy the fusion point.”

“Yes, sir.”

The senior colonel then set down the phone and turned to a major: “What’s the nearest class two or higher fire point?”

“Red 331. It’s around 150 kilometers away.”

“Immediately transmit the fusion point coordinates to them. Four-point precision. Send them the attack authorization, and connect me with the commander of Red 331.”

The missile base commander was soon on the line. The senior colonel said into the receiver, “Yes. Right. Have you received the coordinates and the attack authorization? Right. Immediately! Good. Treat it as a type-four land target. . . . You determine that yourselves. Just ensure it’s destroyed. Immediately. I won’t hang up. . . .”

“Hey, don’t we have any other choices? Where macro-fusion is concerned . . . ,” Ding Yi said, pushing forward.

Phone in hand, Senior Colonel Shi Jian turned a fierce glare on Ding Yi, and gave a decisive sweep downward with his other arm, either to say there was no other choice, or to stop Ding Yi from talking at all.

"Good. Acknowledged," he said into the phone, then set it down. His movements slowed, the anxiety dissipated. He let out a long sigh, like he was free at last of a heavy burden, but also like fear had struck him.

"The missile is in transit. It will arrive in three minutes," he said.

"Sir, maybe we should pull back a little," an officer said to General Du.

"No." General Du waved a hand tiredly and did not raise his bowed head.

Very soon they were able to see the missile. Its white tail traced it in the southern sky like an airplane's contrail, but far faster.

Lin Yun's voice sounded through the megaphone from the tent, still calm, as if everything that was happening was nothing more than a fluid piece of music she was playing. Now she was declaring that it had come to an end.

"You're too late, Dad."

Macro-fusion is quiet. In fact, the majority of eyewitnesses said that it was quieter than usual at the time of fusion, as if all other sounds in nature had been screened out so that the whole process could be conducted in an incomprehensible silence. As one eyewitness put it, the process of macro-fusion looked like "the rising and setting of a blue sun." At first, the tent emitted blue light. Then people could see the ball of light, still small, as the tent turned transparent like a sheet of cellophane hanging over the tent poles. But soon it collapsed, as if melting. The collapse strangely drew every part of the tent into the fusion's center, where it was absorbed into the ball of light as if being sucked into a whirlpool, leaving behind no remains or traces of any kind. After the tent disappeared, the ball continued to grow, and soon emerged in the Gobi Desert like a blue sun. By the time it stopped expanding, its radius had grown to around two hundred meters, the distance at which Ding Yi had predicted that ball lightning's target selectivity would start. Within that distance, the extreme density of the energy meant that everything was destroyed.

The blue sun remained at its largest state for around half a minute. It was stable during that time, but an eerie stillness enveloped the world, so that the brief period felt like an eternity, as if nothing had changed since the birth of the world. The blue sun outshone the real sun, which was half below the western horizon. It drowned the entire Gobi in its blue light and rendered the world weird and unfamiliar. It was a cold sun, and even close by, no one could feel any heat from it.

Then came the strangest marvel of all: from its ghostly depths, the blue sphere radiated a multitude of glittering small stars that turned immediately into objects of various sizes when they reached its surface. The onlookers were shocked when they realized what the objects were: tents, in a state of quantum superposition! They appeared entirely corporeal, not illusory. The largest was bigger than the original tent and hovered in the air like an enormous black shadow. The smallest was pebble-sized, but was complete and whole, like an exquisite model. The tents soon collapsed under the gaze of the observers into a destroyed state, trailing a series of superimposed images before vanishing into the air. But more quantum tents kept flying out from the center in a tent probability cloud that permeated the nearby space. The blue sun was enveloped within the cloud, its expansion arrested by the presence of observers.

At last a sound broke the stillness: a faint snap from a computer on the desk, and then from everyone's mobile phone. The sound of electronic chips frying. At the same time, a multitude of small objects passed through the unharmed outer case of the computer and radiated outward—objects that, on closer inspection, turned out to be complete CPUs, memory sticks, and other chips, each in a quantum superposition, existing simultaneously in an unknown number of positions.

The flying chips were so numerous that the office building was momentarily choked in a thick chip probability cloud. Then, like an invisible broom, observation returned these chips to a destroyed state and they vanished, dragging tails behind them, collapsing to ash inside the computer case. Soon the air was empty again.

There was a louder noise, a thunder that carried through the air. It was the incoming missile, chips fried, spiraling downward in a huge fireball.

Peace was restored. The blue sun shrank rapidly down to a single point near the ground, then disappeared into the spot where, just one minute before, two macro-nuclei had collided off their bridges at five hundred meters per second and two strings of singularities twisted together in the blink of an eye. Now, in the unimaginable macro-universe, two atoms were gone, but a new one had been born, an incident unnoticed by any observer in that world. As in our world, only when billions and billions of nuclei were tangled together would they produce an effect that could be called an incident.

The setting sun quietly shone its light on the Gobi Desert and the base. A few birdcalls sounded from the tamarisks, as if nothing at all had happened.

Base personnel gathered at the fusion point, where the tent and everything within it had vanished without a trace. Before them was a smooth mirror roughly two hundred meters in radius lying flat on the sands, formed when the silicon of the ground instantly liquefied and then solidified. Like other objects melted by ball lightning, the ground had not emitted an appreciable amount of heat when it melted, but had been transformed while in a wave state in some other space. It was now cool to the touch. Its surface was astonishingly smooth, and reflected their faces with great clarity. Try as he might, Ding Yi found nothing to indicate how the ground had solidified, or by what mechanism this part of the Gobi had been made so flat and smooth after melting. The people stood around the huge mirror in silence, looking at the beautiful reflection of the sunset in the western sky, then the stars that came out one by one in the reflection of the heavens.

Meanwhile, the macro-fusion wave of energy was propagating outward. It passed all three target circles, turning all eighty thousand tons of chips in the hundred-kilometer radius to ash, then kept going. It expanded to more than a thousand kilometers before the volume of chips it passed along the way was enough to weaken it, thereby dragging one-third of the country back to an agricultural age.

LIN YUN II

The rain had stopped at some point, and outside the window, the first light of
dawn was coming.

As on that birthday night in my youth, I was no longer the person I was
the day before. I had lost too much—although, for the moment, I wasn't sure
of what I had lost, only that I had been reduced to a weak, hollow shell.

"Do you want to keep listening?" Ding Yi, his eyes bloodshot, said drunkenly.

"Hmm? No, I don't want to listen anymore."

"It's about Lin Yun."

"Lin Yun? What more is there to say about her? Go on."

On the third day after macro-fusion, Lin Yun's father arrived at the
fusion point.

By this point, most of the more than three hundred captured macro-nuclei had been released into the air. When the electromagnets that attracted them cut out, the strings danced away fairly quickly, and soon disappeared without a trace. The thirty-odd strings kept for research use were transferred to a safer storage point. Base personnel had mostly dispersed, and stillness returned to this part of the Gobi Desert that had witnessed two massive energy discharges in two separate centuries.

Only Colonel Xu and Ding Yi accompanied General Lin to the fusion point. The general looked more haggard and far older than he had at the meeting in Beijing not long before, but he maintained an indomitable spirit that made him appear unbroken.

They reached the edge of the huge mirror created by macro-fusion. The mirror's surface was covered in a thin layer of sand, but it was still smooth and bright and reflected the clouds that swirled overhead, like a patch of sky fallen into the Gobi, or a window into another world. As General Lin and the other two stood there in silence, time in their world seemed to have stopped. In the world of the mirror, it raced breakneck forward.

"This is a unique monument," Ding Yi said.

"Let the sand slowly bury it," General Lin said. A few wisps of white hair that had appeared on his head wafted in the wind.

And then Lin Yun appeared.

The clunk of a security officer pulling back a rifle bolt alerted them. When they looked up, they saw Lin Yun standing on the other side of the mirror—four hundred meters away, but even at that distance, they all recognized her. She strode across the mirror toward them. General Lin and the others quickly realized it was the real Lin Yun, not an illusion, since they could hear the light crunch of her feet on the surface like the tick of a second hand, and they could see the footprints she left in the thin layer of sand. The clouds continued their tumble across the

mirror as she walked atop them, at times raising a hand to brush away
her short hair where the Gobi wind had blown it onto her forehead.
When she had nearly reached them, they could see her uniform was
trim, like new, and although her face was a little pale, her expression
was clear and calm. Finally, she stood in front of her father.

"Dad," she said softly.

"Xiao Yun, what have you done?" General Lin said. His voice wasn't
loud, and it was tinged with a deep sorrow and despair.

"Dad, you look tired. Why don't you sit down."

A security officer carried over a wooden crate that had once held
experimental equipment, and General Lin sat down on it slowly. He
did seem exhausted. Perhaps for the first time in his long military
career, he let his exhaustion show.

Lin Yun nodded at Colonel Xu and Ding Yi in greeting, and gave a
familiar smile. Then she said to the guard, "I'm unarmed."

General Lin waved at the guard, who lowered the assault rifle, but
kept a finger next to the trigger.

"I really didn't imagine that macro-fusion would have so much force,
Dad," Lin Yun said.

"You've rendered a third of the country defenseless."

"Yes, Dad," she said, lowering her head.

"Xiao Yun, I don't want to criticize you. It's too late for that. This is
the end of everything. The only thought in my mind the past two days
has been: Why did you take this step?"

Lin Yun looked at her father, and said, "Dad, we came here together."

General Lin nodded heavily. "Yes, child. We came here together, and
what a long road it's been. Perhaps it began with your mother's sacrifice." The general squinted at the blue sky and clouds in the mirror, as
if staring at past time.

"Yes, I remember that night. It was the Mid-Autumn Festival. A

Saturday. I was the only one left behind out of all the kids in the military kindergarten. I sat on a stool in the compound, clutching a mooncake an auntie had given me, but instead of looking up at the moon, I was staring at the gate. She said, 'Poor Yunyun, your dad's with the troops and can't come back to pick you up. You'll sleep at the kindergarten tonight.' I said, 'My dad never comes to pick me up. My mom does.' She said, 'Your mom's not here. She gave her life in the south. She won't be coming to pick you up anymore, Yunyun.' I knew that already, but now the dream I had tended for a month was completely dead. The big kindergarten gate often appeared before me in my waking hours and my dreams. The difference was that, in my dreams, Mom always came through the gate, but when I was awake, it remained empty. . . . That Mid-Autumn Festival night was a turning point in my life. My lonely melancholy turned all at once to hatred, hatred for the people who had taken Mom's life, making her leave me alone in the kindergarten even on the night of the Mid-Autumn Festival."

General Lin said, "I came to get you a week later. You were always holding a little matchbox with two bees inside. The women were afraid you'd get stung, and wanted to take the matchbox from you, but you cried and howled and wouldn't give it to them. Your ferocity frightened them."

Lin Yun said, "I told you that I wanted to train those bees so they'd sting the enemy, like they'd stung Mom. I proudly described to you all my ideas for killing the enemy . . . like how I knew that pigs liked to eat, so we should put lots and lots of pigs where the enemy was living and let the pigs eat all of their provisions so the men would starve to death. I thought a small speaker placed outside the enemy's homes could produce an eerie sound at night to frighten them to death. . . . I constantly came up with ideas like these. It became a fascinating thought exercise for me that amused me to no end."

"I was alarmed to see that in my daughter."

"Yes, Dad. After I finished telling you my ideas, you looked at me in silence for a while, then took out two photos from a briefcase. Two identical photos, except that the corner of one was singed, and the other had brown marks on it that I later learned were blood. They were photos of a family of three. Both parents were military officers, but their uniforms were different from yours, Dad, and they wore epaulets that you and the others didn't have back then. The girl was around my age and pretty, her pale skin a little pink, like fine porcelain. Growing up in the north, I had never seen skin like that. Her hair was so black and so long, down to her waist. So cute. Her mother was pretty, too, and her father was so handsome that I envied the entire family. But you told me that they were enemy officers who had been killed by our artillery fire, and the photos had been recovered from their bodies when the battlefield had been swept. Now the pretty kid in the photographs didn't have a mom or dad anymore."

General Lin said, "I also told you that the people who killed your mom weren't bad. They did it because they were soldiers and had to carry out their duty to the fullest. Like your father the soldier, who also had to carry out his duty to kill the enemy on the battlefield."

"I remember that, Dad. Of course I remember. You need to understand that it was the 1980s. The way you educated me was pretty alternative and unrecognized back then. If it had gotten out, it would have spelled the end of your political career. You wanted to dig out the seed of my hatred to keep it from germinating. That showed me how much you loved me, and I'm still grateful for that."

"But it didn't help," General Lin said, with a sigh.

"Right. Back then I was curious about a thing called duty, which made it possible for soldiers to kill but not hate each other. But not for me. I still hated them. I still wanted to have them stung by bees."

"It pained me to listen to you. Hatred born out of the lonely melancholy of a child who lost her mother doesn't go away easily. The only thing capable of wiping out that hatred is a mother's love."

"You understood that. For a while there was a woman who came over often and was kind to me. We got on well. But for some reason she didn't end up as my new mother."

The general sighed again. "Xiao Yun, I should have paid more attention to you."

"Later, I slowly got used to life without Mom, and the naïve hatred in my heart faded with time. I never stopped the fascinating thought exercises, though, and I grew up with all kinds of fantasy weapons. But it wasn't until that summer holiday that weapons became a real part of my life. It was the summer of second grade. You had to go to the south to work on building up the PLA Marine Corps, and when you saw how disappointed I was that you were going, you took me along. It was a fairly remote unit, and with no other kids around. My playmates were your colleagues and subordinates, all of them officers in the field army, most of whom didn't have children. Bullet casings were what they usually gave me to play with. All kinds of casings. I used them as whistles. One time I saw a man eject a bullet from a magazine and I started fussing for it. He said, 'That's not for children to play with. Children can only play with headless ones.' I said, 'Take off the head and give it to me!' He said, 'Then it'll be just like the casings I gave you before. I'll give you some more of those.' I said, 'No, I want that one with the head taken off!'"

"That's just how you were, Xiao Yun. Once you got something in your sights, you didn't care about anything else."

"I gave him such a hard time that he said, 'Fine, but this one's hard to take off. I'll shoot it for you instead.' He shoved it back into the magazine, carried the rifle outside, and fired once at the sky. Then he pointed at the casing that bounced onto the ground and said, 'Take it.' Rather

than picking it up, I asked with wide eyes, 'Where did the head go?'
He said, 'It flew away, way up high.' And I said, 'Was the sound right
after the crack the sound of it flying?' He said, 'You're really clever, Yunyun.' Then he aimed at the sky and fired again, and again I heard the
sound of a bullet whistling in flight. He said it flew fast enough to
puncture thin steel plates. I rubbed the rifle's warm barrel, and all the
weapons I had fantasized about in my thought exercises instantly
seemed weak and impotent. The real weapon in front of me held an
irresistible attraction."

General Lin said, "The rough army guys thought it was adorable
that a little girl loved guns, so they continued to amuse you with them.
Ammunition was far less strictly supervised back then, and lots of ex-
soldiers took dozens of rounds away with them, so they had plenty for
you to play with. Eventually it got to the point where they let you fire,
at first helping you hold the gun, and eventually letting you do it on
your own. By the time the summer holiday ended, you could drop to
the ground with an assault rifle and fire bursts all by yourself."

"I held the gun and felt the vibrations of it firing the way other girls
cradled singing dolls. Later on, I watched light machine guns firing
on the practice range. To me it was a song of delight, not a painful
sound. . . . When summer was over, I no longer covered my ears for
hand grenade explosions or recoilless rifles."

"I took you to the front-line troops for subsequent holidays, mostly
with the thought that I'd be able to spend more time with you, but also
because I felt that, even though the army wasn't a place for a kid, it was
at least a fairly innocent place that wouldn't do you much harm. But I
was wrong."

"I had more contact with weapons during those holidays, since the
enlisted officers and troops liked to let me play with them. They were
proud of their weapons. In their childhood memories, guns were always their favorite toys. Teaching me to shoot was a pleasure for them,

so long as they kept things safe. Other kids only had toy guns to mess around with, but I was lucky enough to play with the real thing."

"Right. I remember this was just after the marines had been established, so there were frequent live-fire exercises, and you also got to see live firing of heavy equipment. Tanks, artillery, and ships. On that seaside hill, you watched warships shell the shore, and bombers drop column after column of bombs on sea targets. . . ."

"What made the deepest impression on me, Dad, was the first time I saw a flamethrower. I watched in excitement as the whooshing flame left a pool of fire on the beach. A marine colonel said, 'Yunyun, do you know what the scariest thing on the battlefield is? Not a gun or a cannon, but this thing. On the southern front, it licked the ass of one of my buddies, and his skin fell right off and put him in a living hell. In the field hospital, when no one was paying attention, he took a gun and offed himself.' I remembered my last sight of Mom in the hospital, all the skin on her body festering, her blackened fingers so swollen there was no way for her to turn a gun on herself. . . . Such an experience might turn some people off of weapons, but for others, it made them even more fascinating. I was in the latter group, for whom those fearsome machines possessed the intoxicating power of a drug."

"I did have a sense of the power weapons had over you, Xiao Yun, but I didn't pay much attention. At least until that exercise on the beach range, which involved a machine-gun squadron firing on near-shore targets. It was a difficult exercise, since the targets were rocking on the water and the light machine-gun tripods were liable to sink into the sand on the beach, so the performance of the soldiers was unimpressive. Then the captain in command shouted, 'You're pathetic! Look at yourselves! You're worse than a little girl! Come here, Yun, and show these rejects how it's done.'"

"And so I lay on the sand and fired two magazines, both of them to outstanding success."

"I watched the flashing rifle pulse steadily in the soft, pale hands of my twelve-year-old girl, the blowback from the chamber tossing your bangs on your forehead, the reflection of the muzzle fire in your child's eyes, and the look of rapturous excitement on your face . . . and I was frightened, Xiao Yun, truly frightened. I didn't know how my daughter had become like that."

"You dragged me away. Dragged me away amid the cheers of the marines, and furiously told all of them, 'You are not to let my daughter touch a gun!' That was the first time I had ever seen you so angry, Dad. From then on you stopped taking me with you to the army, and you took more time to be with me at home, even if it was detrimental to your career. You introduced me to music, art, and literature—at first just for the novelty of it, but later going deep into the classics."

"I wanted to find a normal aesthetic sense for you, to steer your sensibility away from those frightening tendencies."

"You did so, Dad. You were the only one who could. None of your colleagues back then had that ability. I've always admired your erudition, and I'm grateful beyond words for the amount of effort you devoted to me. But Dad, when you planted that flower in my heart, did you ever stop to look at what the soil was like? There was no way to change it. Yes, growing up, I may have had more appreciation for beauty in music, literature, and art than most girls, but the greatest significance it held for me was the deeper appreciation it gave me for the beauty of weapons. I realized that beauty for most people is characterized by fragility and powerlessness. True beauty needs to be supported by an internal strength, and develop itself through sensations like terror and brutality, from which you can both draw strength and meet your death. In weapons, this beauty is expressed to the full. From then on—it must have been around high school—my fascination with weapons reached the level of aesthetics and philosophy. You shouldn't feel bad about this change, Dad, since you helped me accomplish it."

"But Xiao Yun, how did you take that step? Weapons could turn you unfeeling, but did they need to turn you mad?"

"We spent less and less time together after I went to high school, Dad. And then after I joined the army and went to college, we had even fewer opportunities for contact. You have no idea about lots of things that happened during that time. There's one incident having to do with Mom that I never told you about that had a huge effect on me."

"With your mom? But she had been dead for over a decade, then."

"That's right."

And then, in the chilly wind of the Gobi, between the sky streaked with clouds and its reflection in the enormous mirror, Ding Yi, Colonel Xu, and General Lin listened to Lin Yun's story:

"You may be aware that the bees that killed Mom on the southern front weren't indigenous. They came from a habitat at a far higher latitude. It was strange: the tropical environment of the southern front had a wealth of bee species, so why weaponize this species from the distant north? It was an ordinary bee, not one prone to swarming and stinging, and not particularly toxic. Similar attacks occurred a few more times on the southern front, causing some casualties, but the war ended quickly after that, so it didn't attract much attention.

"When I did my master's, I used to hang out on an old BBS, Jane's Defence Forum. Three years ago I met a Russian woman there—she didn't reveal anything more about herself, but her language indicated she was no amateur weapons enthusiast, more likely a well-qualified expert. She was in bioengineering—not my field at all, but she had sharp ideas about new-concept weapons, and we got on well. We stayed in contact, often chatting online for hours. Two months later, she told me she had joined up with an international expedition to Indochina to survey the long-term effects of US chemical weapons from the Vietnam War on the region, and she invited me along. I was on break, so I went. When I saw her in Hanoi, she was nothing like I'd imagined: in her forties, thin—nothing of a Russian woman's stockiness—with that kind of timeless beauty, Eastern and deep-seated, that made me feel warm and comfortable when we were together. With the expedition team, we began an arduous survey of the Ho Chi Minh Trail, where the US army had sprayed defoliants, and the Laotian jungles where traces of chemical weapons had been found. I found her highly professional, always working with a sense of mission and dedication. Her only fault was drinking: she drank to desperation. We were good friends in no time, and on several occasions, after she got drunk, she told me bits of her own experiences.

"I learned from her that as early as the 1960s, the Soviets had established a new-concept weapons institute under the General Staff called the Long-Term Equipment Planning Commission, where she and the man she later married worked in the biochemistry department. I wanted to find out what work the department had done, but I discovered that, even when drunk, she kept a clear head and said not a word about any of it. It was obvious she had spent a long time in key military research organizations. Later, after my persistent questioning, she told me about one project: the agency had once conducted research on a large number of people with so-called psychic abilities to see if they could find NATO nuclear submarines deep in the Atlantic. But this had been declassified long ago, and was the butt of jokes in the world of serious research. Still, it showed that her agency had adopted a dynamic approach, a clear contrast to the ossified thinking of Base 3141.

"The agency was dissolved after the end of the Cold War. Due to the poor conditions of the military in those days, researchers turned to jobs in the private sector, where they immediately ran into problems, and then their Western counterparts exploited the opportunity to trawl for talent. After her husband left the service, he accepted a high-paying position from DuPont, which promised her the same treatment if she was willing to come along, provided she brought her new-concept weapons research with her. They fought bitterly over this, and she laid it out for him: she wasn't totally divorced from reality, and she wanted a better future, to own a comfortable detached home with a swimming pool, holiday in Scandinavia, and give a good education to their only daughter; and the superlative liberal research conditions were a definite attraction as well. If she had been on a civilian project, or even an ordinary military project, she would not have hesitated at all. But their research had been on new-concept weapons that could not be openly discussed. It was highly advanced technology nearing practical application, and the tremendous military power it held might decide the balance of power in the next century. She was dead set against seeing the fruits of half a lifetime of R&D put to use against her homeland. Her husband said she was being ridiculous. He was from Ukraine, and she was from Belarus. The homeland she had in mind had splintered into many countries, some of which were now enemies of each other.

"In the end, her husband left, and her daughter left with him. Her life was a lonely one from then on. Many aspects of this woman's personality and demeanor were familiar, and it occurred to me that they were there in my hazy memories of Mom.

"In Laos, the team stayed in a village in the jungle. A strain of malaria transmitted by mosquito had already killed two children there. The team's doctor was powerless to do anything: he said the onset of the virus was so fierce that there was no way to treat it locally. But the virus had an incubation period, and if it were possible to discover certain indications that might show up during that time, the entire village could undergo a physical exam, and those found to be infected treated.

"When she heard that, she went out at once and came back a couple of hours later carrying a bag made of mosquito netting full of mosquitoes she had caught. She stuck an arm into the bag and tied it tight around her elbow. When she took her arm out again, it was covered

in welts from mosquito bites. She had the doctor observe her for symp-
toms, but he saw nothing, until she came down with that strain of
malaria five days later and was evacuated to a hospital in Bangkok.

"I spent the last few days of my holiday sitting with her in the hospital. I felt even closer to her then. I told her about my mom dying in
the war when I was six, and how I had lived with my mother in my
memory, and how she had stayed forever young in my mind until a
short while ago, when, with the realization of the passing of time, my
mind began to sketch the outlines of an older image of her, but one I
was unable to fully imagine. But when I saw the Russian woman, the
image suddenly clarified and I became convinced that if Mom were still
alive, she would be much like her.

"When I said this, she hugged me and began to cry, and told me
through her tears that six years before, her daughter and her daughter's
boyfriend had overdosed and were found dead in a luxury Las Vegas
hotel.

"We parted with an added sense of worry about each other. That's
why, on my trip to Siberia to study ball lightning with Dr. Chen, I paid
her a visit when we passed through Moscow.

"You can imagine her surprise upon seeing me. She still lived alone,
in a chilly retirees' apartment, and she drank even more heavily. She
seemed to spend her days in a half-inebriated state. She kept saying, 'Let
me show you something. Let me show you something.' She brushed
aside a stack of old newspapers concealing an oddly shaped sealed container, which she said was a super-cooled liquid nitrogen storage tank.
A large part of her meager income was spent on periodically refilling
the liquid nitrogen. That she had such a thing at home surprised me,
and I asked her what it contained. She said it was the distillation of
more than twenty years of efforts.

"She told me, 'In the early 1970s, the Soviet Union's new-concept weapons institutes had conducted a survey, global in scope, that brought together scattered ideas and implementations for new-concept weapons projects. Ideas first, collected from a truly broad range of sources. Intelligence agencies, naturally, but personnel going abroad on business were given these tasks as well. Sometimes things got ridiculous: researchers in some departments watched James Bond films over and over, to try and glean traces of the West's new-concept weapons from the fancy gadgets he carried. Another angle was collecting the applications of new concepts on the battlefield from regional conflicts then in progress. The Vietnam War was their first choice, of course. Bamboo traps and the like set up by the Vietnamese people were carefully observed for their effectiveness on the battlefield. The first thing my department came across were some guerrillas in the south who used bees as weapons. We learned of it from news reports, and so I took a trip to Vietnam to investigate. It was at the time that the US was planning to abandon South Vietnam: the Saigon regime was teetering, and the Vietcong's guerrilla war in the south had evolved into a proper war that was growing larger by the day. Naturally, the peculiar ways of fighting I wanted to investigate were no longer to be found. But I made contact with lots of guerrilla groups and learned details about their combat effectiveness—which it turned out the news reports had greatly exaggerated. All of the guerrillas I spoke to who had used bees said they had practically no lethal effect as weapons. Any use they might have had was purely psychological: they heightened the American soldiers' feeling that this land they were in was unfamiliar and eerie.

"'But I found inspiration there anyway. When I came home, we started using gene technology to modify bees. It might have been the earliest application of genetic engineering. Little was accomplished the first few years, since molecular biology was still primitive throughout the world, and also because the political suppression of genetics in the Soviet Union a short while before had caused technology of that sort to lag behind. But by the early eighties we finally made a break-through in breeding highly toxic, highly aggressive bees. Marshal Dmitry Yazov personally observed a test in which one attack bee stung a bull to death. The marshal was greatly impressed, and I, as director, was awarded the Order of the Red Star. Money poured into the project, and further studies were made of the possibility of combat use of attack bees. Our first breakthrough came in target discrimination. New bees were bred to be highly sensitive to certain chemicals, which our forces could apply in minute amounts to their bodies to avoid accidental harm. The next development was in bee toxicity: joining the initial highly toxic variety that could kill instantly was a new breed, equally deadly, but with mortality delayed by five to ten days, so as to increase the burden on the enemy. . . .

"'This storage tank contains one hundred thousand attack-bee embryos.'"

Here Lin Yun sighed, and her voice trembled. "You can imagine how I felt when I heard this. My eyes darkened and I nearly collapsed, but, still holding out hope, I asked her if they had ever been used in combat. But I had already guessed the answer. Without noticing my expression, she told me even more excitedly that, due to the war with Cambodia and border conflicts with China, Vietnam was constantly asking the Soviets for weapons, causing headaches for the Politburo, which gave them only perfunctory replies. When Lê Duẩn visited, the general secretary prom-ised to provide the most advanced weapons systems to Vietnam— meaning none other than the attack bees. She was sent to Vietnam with one hundred thousand attack bees. You can imagine how incensed the Vietnamese were when the advanced weapons systems they had been dreaming about turned out to be a beehive. They said that the Sovi-ets had engaged in shameless deception toward their comrades while standing on the front lines of a bloody war against imperialism.

"While it was true that the Soviet leadership was giving them the brush-off, she personally believed that no one had been cheated. Although the Vietnamese didn't realize the attack bees' power at first, they did put them into action, deploying a special forces division from the General Department for Military Intelligence to handle it.

"Before they did, the Russian woman took the division through a weeklong training and then went with them to the front lines. Trembling, but still clinging to a pitiful thread of hope, I asked her, 'Which front lines? Cambodia?' She said, 'Not Cambodia. The Vietnamese army had the absolute advantage on that front. It was the northern front. Against you.' I looked at her in terror, and said, 'You . . . you went to the Vietnam-China border?!' She said she had—not to the farthest front lines, of course, but to Lang Son, and she had watched every time the five-man teams of wiry young guys applied an identification agent to their collars and ran off to the front carrying two thousand attack bees . . .

"Finally noticing the state I was in, she asked, 'What's wrong? The whole time, all we conducted were experimental attacks. We'd hardly gotten any of your people by the time the war ended.' She said it so casually, like talking about a ball game.

"If we were only chatting between two soldiers, then I was out of line, since I ought to have been able to remain relaxed even when discussing the Zhenbao Island Incident.* But I didn't want to tell her the cause of Mom's death, so I ran out, leaving her staring in shock. She chased me and caught up to me and begged me to tell her what she'd done wrong, but I struggled free and ran aimlessly through the frozen streets.

"It snowed that night, and for a moment I felt the grim face of the world. Later, a police patrol van rounding up drunks took me back to the hotel. . . .

---

* Zhenbao Island, also known as Damanskii Island, was the site of a border clash in March 1969 during the seven-month undeclared conflict that marked the height of the Sino-Soviet Split.

"When I got home, I received an e-mail from the Russian woman that read, 'Yun, I don't know how it is I've hurt you. After you left, I spent many sleepless nights, but couldn't think of anything. I am certain, though, that it's connected to my bee weapons. If you were just an ordinary young woman, I wouldn't have let the slightest hint of it slip out, but you and I are alike. Both of us are soldiers researching new-concept weapons, and we have common aims, which was why I told you everything. When you left in tears that night, it was like a knife in my heart. Back at my residence, I opened the lid of that container and watched the liquid nitrogen evaporate into white fog and disperse into the air. During the chaos of the Institute's dissolution, more than a million attack-bee embryos died due to poor management, and the container you saw held the last remaining ones.

"'I wanted to sit there all night until the liquid evaporated entirely; even in the bitter cold of the Russian winter, the cells would die quickly. I was destroying two decades of hard work, destroying the dreams of my youth, all because a Chinese woman dearer to me than even my own daughter hated them. As the nitrogen fog dissipated, my cold home turned even colder. The cold clarified my thinking, and all of a sudden I understood that the material inside the container did not belong to me as an individual. It had been developed at the cost of billions of rubles eked out by the hard labor of the Soviet people. At this thought, I replaced the lid and closed it tightly. Then I protected it with my life, and at last gave it to the appropriate people.

"'Yun, for the sake of our ideals and our faith, for the sake of our homeland, we two women have trodden a lonely road no woman ought to follow. I have been on it longer than you, so I know a little more of its dangers. All the forces of the natural world, including those that people believe are the most gentle and harmless, can be turned into weapons to destroy life. The horror and cruelty of some of these weapons is beyond imagination, unless you have seen them yourself. But I, a woman you believe resembles your mother, can tell you that we are not on the wrong road. Fearsome things may fell your countrymen and your family, or strike the tender flesh of the child in your arms, but the best way to prevent this from happening is to create them yourselves, before the enemy or potential enemy has that chance! So I have no regret for the life I've lived, and I hope that you won't either, when you reach my age.

"'Child, I've moved to a place you don't know, and I won't contact you anymore from now on. Before I say goodbye, I won't offer any vacant blessings, which are useless for a soldier. I'll just leave you with a warning: beware the attack bees! Instinct tells me that they will appear on the battlefield again, and the next time it won't be just one swarm of a thousand or two, but a mega-swarm of tens or hundreds of millions, blotting out the sky and covering the sun like a storm cloud, enough to annihilate an entire field army. May you never meet them in battle. This is the only blessing I can give you, child.'"

Now that Lin Yun had opened up about the psychological world she had long kept deeply hidden, she appeared to feel some sort of release, even as her listeners remained in shocked silence. The sun was setting. Another dusk had come to the Gobi. The glow reflected in the mirror plated everyone standing near it with a layer of gold.

"What's happened has happened, child. All we can do about it is to accept our own responsibility," the general said slowly. "Now take off your badge and epaulets. You're a criminal now, not a soldier."

The sun dipped beneath the horizon and the mirror darkened, like Lin Yun's eyes. Her sorrow and despair were no doubt as boundless as the Gobi at night.

As Ding Yi looked at her, he heard the words she had said at Zhang Bin's gravesite: *I grew up in the army. I don't know if I could entirely belong anywhere else. Or to anyone else.*

Lin Yun raised her right hand and reached over to the major's epaulet on her left shoulder—not to take it off, but to rub it.

Ding Yi noticed that her finger dragged an afterimage behind it.

When Lin Yun's hand touched the epaulet, it was as if time stopped. This was the final image she left in the world. Her body began to turn transparent, swiftly turning into a crystalline shadow, and then the quantum-state Lin Yun vanished.

> *Two roads diverged in a yellow wood,*
> *And sorry I could not travel both . . .*
> *I took the one less traveled by,*
> *And that has made all the difference.*

VICTORY

It was bright outside when Ding Yi finished his tale. The war-ravaged city had welcomed another morning.

"You tell a good story. If the purpose was to comfort me, then you succeeded," I said.

"Do you think I'd be able to invent all that you just heard?"

"How did she remain in a quantum state for so long without collapsing with all of you observing her?"

"There's one thing I've been pondering ever since I first posited the existence of the macro-quantum state: a sentient quantum individual is different from an ordinary non-sentient quantum particle in one important way, and we overlooked an important parameter for the wave function describing the former. Specifically, we overlooked an observer."

"An observer? Who?"

"The individual itself. Unlike ordinary non-sentient quantum particles, sentient quantum individuals can engage in self-observation."

"Okay. But what does self-observation imply?"

"You've seen it. It can counteract other observers, and maintain the
quantum state uncollapsed."

"And how is that self-observation conducted?"

"No doubt by some highly complicated emotional process that we're
unable to even imagine."

"So will she return again like that?" I asked, full of hope for the
answer to this critical question.

"Probably not. Objects that experience resonance with macro-fusion
energy will, for a period of time after the resonance is complete, have
an existence-state probability higher than their destroyed state. That's
why we were able to see all of those probability clouds of chips as the
fusion was going on. But the quantum state will decay as time moves
onward, and eventually the destroyed state will be more probable than
the existence state."

"Oh—" I exclaimed, the sound coming from deep within my heart.

"But the existence-state probability, no matter how small, is still
there."

"Like hope," I said, doing my best to throw off my fragile emotional
state.

"Yes. Like hope," Ding Yi said.

As if to answer him, we heard a commotion out on the street. I went
to the window and looked down to see lots of people outside. More
were streaming out of the buildings, gathering excitedly in threes and
fives. What surprised me most were their expressions: everyone was
beaming like the sun had risen early. This was the first time I had seen
this sort of smile since the start of the war, and now it was on so many
faces.

"Let's go down," Ding Yi said, picking up the half-finished bottle of Red Star from the table.

"What's the booze for?"

"We might need it when we get down there. Of course, in the unlikely event I'm wrong, don't laugh at me."

We had just exited the building when someone from the crowd ran over to us. It was Gao Bo. I asked him what was up.

"The war is over!" he shouted.

"We surrendered?"

"We won! The enemy alliance dissolved, and they've declared unilateral ceasefires. One by one, they've begun to pull back. Victory!"

"You're dreaming." I turned from Gao Bo to Ding Yi, who didn't seem surprised at all.

"You're the one who's dreaming. Everyone's been focused on the progress of the talks the whole night. Where have you been? Zonked out?" Gao Bo said, then ran off joyfully to join an even bigger crowd.

"Did you anticipate this?" I asked Ding Yi.

"I don't have that foresight. But Lin Yun's father predicted it. After Lin Yun disappeared, he told us that macro-fusion would probably end the war."

"Why?"

"It's simple, really. When the truth about the chip burn-out catastrophe got out, the whole world was frightened."

I smiled, but shook my head. "How? Not even our thermonuclear weapons frighten anyone that much."

"There's a difference between this and thermonuclear weapons— a possibility you may not have realized."

I looked at him, baffled.

"Think about it. If we detonated all of our nuclear bombs on our own soil, what would happen?"

"Only an idiot would do that."

"But supposing that we have lots of macro-nuclei that can fry chips, a hundred or more, and we keep conducting macro-fusion on our own territory. Is that still idiotic?"

At Ding Yi's prompting, I soon understood his point. If a second, identical macro-fusion took place on the same spot, the fact that the first had fried all the chips in the vicinity would mean the energy of the second would not be drained. It would pass through the region cleared by the first and destroy chips in a larger region beyond that until it, too, was drained by the chips it encountered. Proceeding in that manner with multiple macro-fusions on the same spot, fusion energy could propagate throughout the world. The Earth would be transparent to it. Perhaps fewer than a hundred strings of that type would be enough to temporarily return the entire world to an agricultural age.

There was one other important point: indiscriminate use of conventional nuclear weapons would take humanity out with them, so under no circumstances would politicians with even a shred of reason make such a decision. And even if some crazed strategist gave an order, it was unlikely to be executed. But macro-fusion was different. It could achieve strategic objectives without killing a single person. Hence the decision to use it was a relatively easy one, compared to conventional nukes, and when a country was backed into a corner, it was very likely to do so.

Chip-frying macro-fusion would reformat the world's enormous hard drive, and the more advanced the country was, the harder it would be hit. The road to recovery back to the Information Age would lead to an undetermined new world order.

Now that I understood this, I knew I wasn't dreaming. The war really was over. As if a string on my body had been plucked out, my legs crumpled beneath me and I sat on the ground watching the sky dumbly until the sun rose. In the deceptive warmth of the first ray of sunlight on that day, I covered my face and wept.

Around me, the sounds of celebration rolled on in waves. Still crying, I stood up. Ding Yi had disappeared into the reveling crowd, but someone immediately hugged me, and then I went and hugged someone else. I lost count of the people I hugged on that grand morning. As the dizzy joy ebbed somewhat, I found myself hugging a woman. When we let go, we happened to look each other over for a moment, and I froze.

We knew each other. She was the pretty student who had said I had a strong sense of purpose on that late night in the university library so many years ago. It took me a while, but I remembered her name: Dai Lin.

Two months later, Dai Lin and I got married.

After the war, people's lives turned far more traditional. Single people got married, and childless families had children. The war had made people cherish things they used to take for granted.

During the slow economic recovery, times were hard, but they were warm. I never told Dai Lin of my experiences after graduation, and she never spoke of hers. Clearly all of us had a past in those lost times that it was hard to look back on. The war told us what was truly valuable: the present and the future.

Half a year later, we had a child.

———

During that time, the only interruption to this plain but busy life was a visit from an American. He introduced himself as Norton Parker, an astronomer, and said I ought to recognize him. When he mentioned the SETI@home project, it came to me at once: he had been in charge of the project to search for extraterrestrial intelligence whose distributed processing server Lin Yun and I had invaded to swap in the mathematical model for ball lightning. That experience seemed a world away. Now that the early research on ball lightning was known to the world, it would not have been hard for him to find me.

"There was also a woman involved, I believe."

"She's no longer on this earth."

"Dead in the war?"

". . . You could say that."

"Damn the war. . . . I came to tell you about an applied ball lightning project I'm heading up."

With the secret of ball lightning now unlocked, collecting macro-electrons and exciting them into ball lightning had become an industrialized operation, and research on civil applications was making swift progress. It had many unbelievable uses, including burning away cancer cells in sick patients without harming other organs. But Parker said his project was more surreal.

"We're searching for and observing a particular phenomenon of ball lightning: sometimes it maintains a collapsed state, not a quantum state, even without an observer."

I was unimpressed. "We encountered that a number of times, but ultimately we were able to find one or several undetected observers. The one I remember most clearly was on a target range. We later learned that the observer was a reconnaissance satellite in space that had caused the ball lightning to collapse."

Parker said, "And that's why we chose to conduct tests in places where all observers could absolutely be screened out. Places like abandoned deep mines. We removed all personnel and observation equipment, so there shouldn't have been any observers inside. We set the accelerators to automatic, conducted target tests, and then used the hit rate to ascertain whether or not the ball lightning was in a collapsed state."

"And the results showed . . . ?"

"We have performed tests in thirty-five mines. The outcome of the majority of them was normal. But on two occasions, the ball lightning reached a collapsed state in the mine without any observer."

"So do you think that the outcome raises doubts about quantum mechanics?"

Parker laughed. "No, quantum mechanics isn't wrong. But you've forgotten my specialty. We're using ball lightning to search for aliens."

"What?"

"In the mine tests, there were no human observers, and no man-made observation equipment, but the ball lightning remained collapsed. This can only mean that there was another, nonhuman, observer."

This immediately piqued my interest. "It would have to be a very powerful observer to see through the earth's crust!"

"That's the only reasonable explanation."

"Can those two tests be repeated?"

"Not anymore. But the collapsed-state outcome of the tests remained for three full days before the tests started producing quantum-state outcomes again."

"There's an explanation for that, too: the super-observer must have detected that you had detected it."

"Perhaps. So we're planning even larger-scale tests now, to find more of this phenomenon for study."

"That's significant research indeed, Dr. Parker. If you are really able to prove that a super-observer is watching our world, then human activity becomes very indiscreet. . . . You could say human society is in a quantum state, and a super-observer will force it to collapse to a state of reason again."

"If we'd found that super-observer a little earlier, maybe war could have been averted."

Parker's research prompted me to pay a visit to Ding Yi. To my surprise, he was living with a lover, a dancer who had lost her job in the war. She was clearly a simpleminded type, and I couldn't say how they ended up together. Evidently Ding Yi had learned how to enjoy life apart from physics. A person like him wouldn't bother with marriage, of course, but fortunately the woman wasn't looking for that, either.

When I arrived, Ding Yi wasn't at home, just the woman. His three-bedroom apartment wasn't as spare as it was before: to his calculation papers, she had added lots of cute decorations.

The moment the woman heard I was Ding Yi's friend, she asked me whether he had any other lovers.

"Physics counts as one, I guess. No one can hold the top place in his heart so long as physics is there," I said frankly.

"I don't care about physics. I mean, does he have any other women?"

"I don't think so. He's got so much stuff in his head I don't think he could make room for two people."

"But I heard that during the war, he and a young major were close."

"Oh, they were just colleagues and friends. Besides, that major isn't here anymore."

"I know that. But you know what? He looks at that major's photograph every day, and rubs it."

I had been distracted, but this surprised me. "A photo of Lin Yun?"

"Oh, so she's called Lin Yun. She looks like a teacher, or something. Are there teachers in the army?"

This shocked me even further, and I insisted on seeing the photo. She led me to the study, opened up a drawer in a bookshelf, and took out an exquisite silver-inlaid picture frame. Then, she said, "It's this one. Every night before he goes to sleep he steals a look at it and dusts it off. Once I told him, 'Put it on the writing desk, I don't mind,' but he still doesn't leave it out. He just gives it a stealthy look and dusts it off."

I took the frame and held it facedown in my hand. With eyes half-closed, I steadied my heart—the woman must have been looking at me in amazement—and then I jerked the photo around and stared at it.

At once I understood why the woman had thought Lin Yun was a teacher: she was with a group of students.

She was standing in their midst, more beautiful than ever, still wearing that trim major's uniform, with a beaming smile on her face. Looking at the children around her, I immediately recognized them as the group that had been incinerated by ball lightning at the nuclear power plant. They, too, were smiling sweetly, and were obviously very happy. I noticed in particular a little girl that Lin Yun was holding tightly, an adorable child smiling so hard her eyes were slits.

But what caught my attention was the girl's left hand.

It was missing.

Lin Yun and the children were standing on a well-manicured lawn where there were a few small white animals. Behind them, I could see a familiar structure: the macro-electron excitation lab, where we had heard the bleat of a quantum goat. But in the photograph, the warehouse's long exterior wall was painted in colorful cartoon animals, flowers, and balloons. The brilliant colors made the building look like an enormous toy.

From the photograph, Lin Yun looked at me with her touching smile, and in her limpid eyes I read things I had not seen while she was alive: a happy belonging and a peace from somewhere deep within.

It reminded me of a distant, long-forgotten still harbor in which a small boat was moored.

I gently returned the photo to the drawer and walked out to the balcony, unwilling to let Ding Yi's lover see the tears in my eyes.

Ding Yi never spoke of the photo. He never even mentioned Lin Yun, and I never asked. It was a secret deep in his heart.

And I soon had a secret of my own.

It was two in the morning one night in late autumn. I was at my desk working, and when I looked up, the amethyst vase on the desk caught my eye. It was a lovely wedding gift from Ding Yi, but the flowers that had been placed in it had dried up at some point. I took them out and tossed them into the wastebasket and thought, with a bitter smile, *Life's responsibilities keep getting heavier. I don't know when I'll find the time to put fresh flowers in the vase.*

Then I leaned back in my chair, shut my eyes, and sat thinking about absolutely nothing. Late every night I would sit for a while at the stillest moment of the day, when it seemed like I was the only one awake in the whole world.

My nose caught a hint of freshness.

It was an aroma absent any sweetness: comforting, slightly bitter, bringing to mind the first sunlight on green grass after a storm has passed, the last wisp of cloud in a clear blue sky, the fleeting chime in a deep mountain valley . . . only more ethereal this time. By the time I noticed its existence, it had already disappeared, only to reappear once I turned my attention away from my nose.

Do you like this perfume?

Oh . . . don't they stop you from wearing perfume in the army?

Sometimes it's allowed.

"Is it you?" I asked softly, without opening my eyes.

There was no answer.

"I know it's you," I said, eyes still closed.

But there was still no answer, only a great stillness.

I opened my eyes with a jerk, and there, in the amethyst vase on the desk, was a blue rose. But no sooner had I seen it than it vanished, leaving the vase empty.

Every detail of the rose had been imprinted on my mind, so full of life, with such a cold aura.

I closed my eyes and opened them again, but the rose did not reappear. But I knew she was there, sitting in the amethyst vase.

"Who are you calling?" my wife asked sleepily, as she sat up in bed.

"It's nothing. Go back to sleep," I said gently. I got up and picked up the vase, then carefully filled it halfway with clean water and set it back on the table. Then I sat in front of it until morning.

My wife saw there was water in the vase and brought back a bouquet of flowers on her way home from work. I stopped her as she was about to put it in the vase.

"Don't. There's a flower in there."

She looked at me strangely.

"It's a blue rose."

"Oh, the most expensive kind," she said, laughing, clearly thinking I was joking. Then she reached out to put her flowers in again.

I grabbed the vase from her and returned it gently to the desk, then snatched the flowers out of her hands and tossed them in the wastebasket. "I said there's a flower in there. What's wrong with you?"

She stared at me for a moment, then said, "I know you've got a place of your own deep in your heart. I have one, too. It's been so many years, after all. . . . You can keep it, but you shouldn't bring it into our lives!"

"There really is a flower in that vase. A blue rose," I stammered, in a much softer voice.

My wife ran out, covering her tears with her hand.

And so the invisible rose in the amethyst vase caused a fracture between Dai Lin and me.

"You've got to tell me what imaginary person put that imaginary rose in the vase, or I'm not going to be able to take it!" my wife said many times.

"It's not imaginary. There really is a rose in the vase. A blue one," I answered every time.

Eventually, when the rift between us was almost beyond being patched over, it was our son who saved our marriage. Early one morning, he woke up, yawned, and said, "Mom, that amethyst vase on the writing desk has a rose in it, a blue one. It's pretty! But it's gone as soon as you look at it."

My wife looked at me in alarm. The first time we had argued about it, he hadn't been born yet, and our later quarrels hadn't been in front of him, so he couldn't have known about the blue rose.

A few days later, my wife fell asleep at the desk while writing a paper late at night. When she awoke, she roused me with a nudge, and there was fear in her eyes. "I woke up just now and I smelled . . . the scent of a rose. It came from that vase! But when I tried to smell it more closely, it disappeared. I mean it. There's no mistake. It really was a rose scent. I'm not lying to you!"

"I know you're not lying. There really is a rose there. A blue rose," I said.

From then on, my wife never brought up the matter again, just left the vase there. Sometimes she would carefully wipe it, keeping it upright, as if she was afraid the rose inside would fall out. And on several occasions, she filled it with distilled water.

I never saw the blue rose again, but it was enough to know it was there. Sometimes in the still of the night I would move the amethyst vase to the window, then stand with my back to it. On these occasions, I could always smell that ethereal aroma, and I knew the rose was there. With my heart's eye I could clearly see every detail, I could caress every petal, I could watch it sway slightly in the night breeze from the window. . . .

It was a flower I could only see with my heart.

But I still held out the hope of getting another glimpse of that blue rose in my lifetime. Ding Yi said that, from the perspective of quantum mechanics, death is the process of transitioning from a strong observer to a weak observer, and then to a non-observer. When I become a weak observer, the rose's probability cloud will collapse to a destroyed state more slowly, giving me the hope of seeing it again.

When I come to death's door and open my eyes for the final time, all of my intellect and memories will be lost into the abyss of the past, and I will return to the pure feeling and fantasies of childhood. At that moment, I'm sure the quantum rose will smile at me.

AFTERWORD

It was a stormy night. When blue arcs of electricity flashed, you could perceive individual raindrops outside the window for the briefest instant. The thunder and lightning had only grown more intense since the downpour began that evening. After one dazzling burst, an object materialized beneath a tree and drifted ghostlike through the air, illuminating the surrounding rain with its orange glow. And as it floated, it seemed to play the sound of a *xun*. Less than twenty seconds later, it disappeared. . . .

This is no science fiction story, but my eyewitness account of a thunderstorm during the summer of 1982 in the city of Handan, Hebei province, at the southern end of Zhonghua Road, which was remote in those days. After that, you were into farmland. Over the course of the next two decades I found myself accumulating all sorts of fanciful ideas about ball lightning.

That same year, I read two books by the British writer Arthur C. Clarke, *2001* and *Rendezvous with Rama*. The translation of those two books into Chinese marked the introduction of modern western science fiction to mainland China; previously, the country's exposure to western science fiction had been limited to the work of Verne and Wells.

In these two events I was fortunate, since only about one person in a hundred claims to have seen ball lightning (this figure comes from a paper published in a domestic meteorology journal, but I suspect it is too high), while the number of people in China who have read those two books is probably fewer than one in a thousand. Those books set the foundation for my concept of science fiction and were a catalyst for the later Three-Body trilogy; however, their influence did not extend to *Ball Lightning*. When I wrote this novel in 2003, I already had a mostly complete Three-Body series, but I felt that Chinese readers would respond more readily to a novel like *Ball Lightning* at that time.

China's science fiction was born more than a century ago, at the close of the Qing Dynasty, but for most of its history it developed in relative isolation, and for a long period was entirely cut off from modern western science fiction. The field's independent development gave the work of that period a distinct style, a difference that is clearly evident from a comparison of *Ball Lightning* and the Three-Body series.

Chinese science fiction during that closed-off period was dominated by the invention story, a form that was preoccupied with the description of a futuristic technological device and speculation on its immediate positive effects, but which barely touched the invention's deeper social implications, much less the tremendous ways such technology would transform society. And so it is with *Ball Lightning*: the emergence of such a powerful technological force is bound to have huge, far-reaching effects on human society—in politics, economics, and even in culture. The book addresses none of this.

But this similarity to early-period Chinese science fiction is only skin-deep; at its heart, this is not a Chinese-style story. The ball lightning described in the book may resemble that sort of futuristic device, but the flights of fancy it gives rise to are nowhere to be found in the science fiction of that period. And while the book is set in a China that is altogether real, those little balls of lightning seem like they're trying to transcend that reality, like how a man's tie, within the confines of its narrow dimensions, has the freedom to indulge in a riot of colors and patterns unbounded by the rigid formula of a business suit.

In a way, *Ball Lightning* is a prequel to the Three-Body series, since it concludes with the first appearance of the aliens that would eventually threaten humanity and features a version of Ding Yi, who also appears in later books. At the end of the novel, when humanity detects the presence of a mysterious, omnipresent observer that causes ball lightning's quantum state to collapse, the narrator, Dr. Chen, remarks, "If you are really able to prove that a super-observer is watching our world, then human activity becomes very indiscreet. . . . You could say human society is in a quantum state, and a super-observer will force it to collapse to a state of reason again." However, society's reaction is the exact opposite of what Chen predicts, because the super-observer is far more sinister than even humanity: unlike ball lightning, which coexists with the human world, the alien super-observer will overturn human society and push Earth civilization to the brink of extinction.

Eight years after this book's first publication, during a thunderstorm in the city of Lanzhou in July 2012, a research team from Northwest Normal University conducted spectral and video observations of a ball of lightning five meters in diameter that appeared unexpectedly. The team's recording, from the initial appearance of the phenomenon until it vanished, marked the first scientific observation of ball lightning in the wild.

In fact, ball lightning is not an especially rare phenomenon, and the progress of research in recent years suggests that its mystery is close to being solved. When that day comes, one thing is certain: the scientific explanation for ball lightning will be nothing like what's described in this book. Science fiction writers may consider many angles on a subject, but they always choose to write about the least likely. Of the myriad possible predictions of the behavior of cosmic civilization, the Three-Body series selected the darkest, most disastrous one. So too with this novel, which describes what may be the most outlandish of possibilities, but also the most interesting and romantic. It is purely a creation of the imagination: curved space filled with lightning energy, an incorporeal bubble, an electron the size of a soccer ball. The world of the novel is the gray world of reality—the familiar gray sky and clouds, gray landscape and sea, gray people and life—but within that gray, mundane world something small and surreal drifts by unnoticed, like a speck of dust tumbling out of a dream, suggesting the vast mysteries of the cosmos, the possibility of a world entirely unlike our own.

One last thing: It's the seemingly unlikeliest of possibilities in science fiction stories that tend to become reality, so in the end, who knows?

M O R E

TOR

SUPERNOVA ERA

Eight light years away, a star has died, creating a supernova event that showers Earth with deadly levels of radiation. Within a year, everyone over the age of thirteen will die.

And so the countdown begins. Parents apprentice their children and try to pass on the knowledge they'll need to keep the world running.

But the last generation may not want to carry on their parents' legacy. And though they imagine a better, brighter world, they may bring about a future so dark humanity won't survive.

In those days, Earth was a planet in space.

In those days, Beijing was a city on Earth.

In the sea of lights of this city was a school, and in a classroom in that school, a class was holding a middle-school graduation party where, as in all such events, the children were talking about their aspirations.

"I want to be a general!" said Lü Gang, a skinny kid who gave the impression of power disproportionate to his size.

"Boring!" someone said. "There won't be any fighting, so all a general can do is lead troops in drills."

"I want to be a doctor," a girl named Lin Sha said in a quiet voice, to mocking laughter.

"Yeah, right. Last time we went to the countryside, even the sight of cocoons freaked you out. And you want to cut people open?"

"My mom's a doctor," she said, either as proof she wasn't frightened, or to explain her reason for wanting to be one.

Zheng Chen, their young homeroom teacher, had been staring out the window at the city lights, lost in thought, but now turned her attention back to the class.

"What about you, Xiaomeng. What do you want to do when you grow up?" she asked the girl next to her, who had also been staring out the window. The girl was plainly dressed, and her large, spirited eyes revealed a melancholy and maturity beyond her years.

"My family's not well-off. I'll only be able to go to a vocational high school," she said with a small sigh.

"What about you, Huahua?" Zheng Chen asked a good-looking boy whose large eyes were always lit up with delight, as if the world was perpetually a riot of newly exploded fireworks.

"The future's so cool I can't decide. But whatever I do, I want to be the best!"

Someone said they wanted to be an athlete, someone else a diplomat. When one girl said she wanted to be a teacher, Zheng Chen said gently, "It's not easy," and then turned back to stare out the window.

"Did you know Ms. Zheng's pregnant?" a girl whispered.

"That's right. And the school has cutback layoffs scheduled for right around the time she'll be giving birth next year, so things don't look good," said a boy.

At this, Zheng Chen laughed. "I'm not thinking about that right now. I'm wondering, what will the world be like when my kid is your age?"

"This is boring," said a small, scrawny kid. His name was Yan Jing, but everyone called him "Specs" because of the thick glasses he wore for nearsightedness. "No one knows what the future holds. It's unpredictable. Anything could happen."

"Science can make predictions," said Huahua. "Futurologists can."

Specs shook his head. "It's science that tells us that the future's unpredictable. Any predictions from those futurologists are imprecise, because the world is a chaotic system."

"I've heard about that. When a butterfly flaps its wings, there's a hurricane on the other side of the world."

"That's right," Specs said, nodding. "A chaotic system."

Huahua said, "My dream is to be that butterfly."

Specs shook his head again. "You don't understand at all. We're all butterflies, just like every butterfly. Every grain of sand and every drop of rain is a butterfly. That's why the world is unpredictable."

"You once talked about an uncertainty principle . . ."

"That's right. Microparticles can't be predicted. They only exist as a probability. So the whole world is unpredictable. And there's the theory of multiple worlds, where when you flip a coin the world splits in two, and the coin lands heads in one world and tails in the other . . ."

Zheng Chen laughed. "Specs, you yourself are proof enough. When I was your age, I'd never have imagined that one day a middle school student would know so much."

"Specs has read lots of books!" said another child, and others nodded.

"Ms. Zheng's baby is going to be even more amazing. Who knows—maybe genetic engineering will let him grow a real pair of wings!" Huahua said, and everyone laughed.

"Students," their teacher said as she stood up, "take a last look at your campus."

They left the classroom and strolled with their teacher through the grounds. Most of the lights were off, and the city lights that shone in the distance lent the campus an air of hazy calm. They passed two classroom buildings, administration, the library, and finally the row of Chinese parasol trees before reaching the athletic field. The forty-three children stood in the center surrounding their young teacher, who opened her arms to the sky, its stars dim under the lights of the city, and said, "Now, children, childhood is over."

In those days, Earth was a planet in space.

In those days, Beijing was a city on Earth.

It may seem like an insignificant story. Forty-three children leaving their peaceful school and continuing their respective life journeys.

It may seem like an ordinary night, a moment in the flow of time between the endless past and the limitless future. "One can't step twice in the same river" is nothing more than the babbling of an ancient Greek, for the river of time is the river of life, and this river flows endlessly at the same unchanging speed, an eternal flow of life and history and time.

That's what the people of this city thought. That's what the people of the plains of northern China thought. That's what the people of Asia thought. And that's what the carbon-based life-forms called humans everywhere on the planet thought. On this hemisphere, they were being lulled to sleep by the flow of time, convinced that the sacred eternal was unbreakable by any force, and they would wake up to a dawn identical to that of countless previous mornings. That faith, lurking in the depths of their consciousness, granted them the same peaceful dreams woven for untold generations.

It was an ordinary school, in a peaceful corner of a brilliant night in the city.

Forty-three thirteen-year-olds and their homeroom teacher looked up at the stars.

The winter's constellations, Taurus, Orion, and Canis Major, were already below the western horizon, and the summer's, Lyra, Hercules, and Libra, had been up for a while. Each star was like a distant eye blinking at the human world from the depths of the universe. But on this night, the cosmic gaze was somewhat different.

On this night, history as known to humanity came to an end.

ABOUT THE AUTHOR

CIXIN LIU is a prolific and popular science fiction writer in the People's Republic of China. Liu is a winner of the Hugo and Locus Awards, as well as a multiple winner of the Galaxy Award (the Chinese Hugo) and the Xing Yun Award (the Chinese Nebula). He lives with his family in Yangquan, Shanxi.

ABOUT THE TRANSLATOR

JOEL MARTINSEN (translator) is research director for a media intelligence company. His translations have appeared in *Words Without Borders* and *Pathlight*. He lives in Edinburgh.